|||| ||| ||||||||| ||| |||||||||||||||||||||||
◁ **W9-BNS-536**

A LETTER TO MY READERS

As a young and curious child, I used to rummage through several old cartons stashed away in my parents' bedroom. For the most part, the boxes were repositories for old black and white photographs of the family, including faded U.S. Army pictures of my handsome uniformed father when he was stationed at Mainz and Frankfurt, Germany. One day I dug a little deeper and came across a dagger, the hilt emblazoned with a swastika. When I questioned my father about it, several long-buried stories surfaced.

Fluent in Yiddish, his childhood language, my father communicated with concentration camp survivors—sometimes acting as a translator for his superior officers—as well as with average German citizens living around the camps. They claimed they did not know what had gone on in their city. "Meanwhile," he said, "you could smell the stink of the burning bodies two miles away."

The dagger, along with a gun and a pair of binoculars, had been the spoils of war. Beyond that, he didn't elaborate. Extracting information from Dad had always been an arduous and incomplete process, and since he died at fifty-three, I never did learn all the specifics of his time in the service. But what he did relate to me, I remember very clearly.

(cont'd)

Now, at the not-so-coincidental age of fifty-three, I present to you my novel STRAIGHT INTO DARKNESS, a work born of my passionate desire to connect to a hidden part of my father's life. Set between the two world wars in a city that nurtured the ultimate serial killer, the book is my attempt to understand the inconceivable. But it is also a personal journey. Perhaps as you read the novel, you, dear reader, might also remember a personal story about your mother or father, grandmother or grandfather. My advice to you is to write it down before it's too late.

Faye Kellerman

ACCLAIM FOR
FAYE KELLERMAN'S NOVELS

"Kellerman is terrific."
  —*Newsday*

"One of the finest sisters in crime."
  —*Los Angeles Times*

"A master of mystery."
  —*Cleveland Plain Dealer*

"No one working in the crime genre is better."
  —*Baltimore Sun*

"Kellerman is splendid."
  —*Milwaukee Journal Sentinel*

DOUBLE HOMICIDE
(with Jonathan Kellerman)

"The Kellermans get it right."
  —*Kirkus Reviews* (starred review)

"A double whammy."
  —*New York Times*

"Well-developed characters and evocative descriptions."
  —*Entertainment Weekly*

"Fully rounded characters and an evocative sense of place . . . haunting and heartbreaking."
  —*Publishers Weekly*

"The collaborative writing style drives home gritty drama, compelling dialogue, and believable characters . . . Sure to appeal to new readers as well as established fans . . . Highly recommended."

—*Library Journal* (starred review)

STREET DREAMS

"Entertaining . . . solid . . . takes the characters' relationships to a new level."

—*Booklist*

"Dive in . . . Kellerman still has a warm and wry flair for describing Orthodox Jewish culture. And she captures the complexity of young people who have to meander awhile before finding each other."

—*People*

"Fans will find a lot to like in *Street Dreams*: fast pace, clever plotting, and a number of twists."

—*BookPage*

STONE KISS

"Bravura storytelling, vintage Kellerman."

—*Kirkus Reviews*

"Reading a good thriller is very much like taking a great vacation: half the fun is getting there. Faye Kellerman is one heck of a tour guide."

—*Detroit Free Press*

"High-voltage stuff."
—*Booklist*

"It's a credit to Kellerman's storytelling abilities that long after she reveals 'who done it' readers will be frantically flipping pages to find out just how and why."
—*People*

"Kellerman has become a real pro at setting up crime puzzles, laying on lots of real and fake clues, and keeping everyone guessing."
—*Pittsburgh Post-Gazette*

"*Stone Kiss* will hold you in your seat from beginning to end and keep you turning the pages."
—*Mansfield Journal (OH)*

"An excellent book."
—*Sullivan County Democrat*

ALSO BY **FAYE KELLERMAN**

The Ritual Bath

Sacred and Profane

The Quality of Mercy

Milk and Honey

Day of Atonement

False Prophet

Grievous Sin

Sanctuary

Justice

Prayers for the Dead

Serpent's Tooth

Moon Music

Jupiter's Bones

Stalker

The Forgotten

Stone Kiss

Street Dreams

Double Homicide (with Jonathan Kellerman)

STRAIGHT
INTO
DARKNESS

FAYE KELLERMAN

WARNER BOOKS

NEW YORK   BOSTON

If you purchase this book without a cover you should be aware that this book may have been stolen property and reported as "unsold and destroyed" to the publisher. In such case neither the author nor the publisher has received any payment for this "stripped book."

This book is a work of fiction. Names, characters, places, and incidents are the product of the author's imagination or are used fictitiously. Any resemblance to actual events, locales, or persons, living or dead, is coincidental.

Copyright © 2005 by Faye Kellerman
Excerpt from *The Garden of Eden* copyright © 2005 by Faye Kellerman. All rights reserved. No part of this book may be reproduced in any form or by any electronic or mechanical means, including information storage and retrieval systems, without permission in writing from the publisher, except by a reviewer who may quote brief passages in a review.

Warner Books
1271 Avenue of the Americas, New York, NY 10020

Printed in the United States of America

Originally published in hardcover by Warner Books
First International Paperback Edition: December 2005
First United States Paperback Edition: July 2006
10 9 8 7 6 5 4 3 2 1

ATTENTION CORPORATIONS AND ORGANIZATIONS:
Most WARNER books are available at quantity discounts with bulk purchase for educational, business, or sales promotional use. For information, please call or write:

Special Markets Department, Warner Books, Inc.
1271 Avenue of the Americas, New York, NY. 10020.
Telephone: 1-800-222-6747 Fax: 1-800-477-5925

*For Tech Sergeant David Kellerman
of blessed memory—my dear father-in-law.*

*For Corporal Oscar Marder of blessed memory—
my treasured father whose life and stories
live inside of me.*

ACKNOWLEDGMENTS

✠ *Straight into Darkness,* like many historical novels, posed inherent problems that at times seemed daunting and insurmountable. Thankfully for me, many people volunteered their time and expertise, and I remain indebted to them for their services. I took creative liberties in writing the story, so any inaccuracies are solely my invention, certainly not the fault of anyone listed below. I hope that by mentioning their names, I don't cause them undue embarrassment.

To the following people, I say thank you, thank you, thank you.

Robert Hultner is a distinguished crime writer in Germany. The information he imparted to me about Germany between the wars was invaluable. I still remember the reading of his book that took place at a German beer hall complete with orchestra and actors. It wasn't just a reading, it was drama!

Heinz Prinz, Erster Hauptkommissar of the Munich police, is now retired. He authored an enormous history of the Munich Police Department that was a major source of information for me. Over coffee at a crime festival in Munich, he offered me many unique insights and perspective into the workings of the police department.

Dr. Barbara Distel—Leiterin der Gedenkstätte Dachau—

is the director of the Dachau memorial. There is a Jewish saying that the world is based on righteous Gentiles. Certainly this is Barbara, a tireless worker in a thankless job. She didn't set off to become a hero, but that's what she is.

Rudolf Herfurtner is an award-winning writer of children's books in Germany. Generous with his time and knowledge of Bavarian history, he carted me all over the countryside as I took copious notes. He gave me a glimpse into the intricacies of Bavarian life, everything from rococo architecture to farm equipment.

Chaim Frank gave me a detailed tour and history of Jewish life in Munich. For years he has worked tirelessly to keep a Jewish presence in a land that tried so hard to eradicate it.

Ellen Presser is director of the Jewish Cultural Center of Munich. Her warmth and hospitality made my stay in Munich special. The synagogue was my home away from home, something that was emotional and familiar, something I could reach out and touch.

Deanna Frankel is a dear friend. I thank her for the Russian lesson.

Agnes Krup went way beyond the job description by agreeing to read my novel for correct German names and grammar not just once but *twice*. Many many thanks.

How many Germans who were alive during the Holocaust would dare to speak to a Jewish woman who identifies herself as such? There were two of them who did.

Maxi Besold died in 2004, but I distinctly remember her describing the tears running down her mother's face while listening to the radio reporting the election results in 1933. Meeting her was an enriching journey into a past that is being increasingly relegated to pages in a history book.

Franz Geiger is an author, playwright, and literary translator. Now in his eighties, he was a member of the World War II resistance group the White Rose. I was in awe of his memory as well as his energy. His help was invaluable, especially his descriptions of the Munich he recalled as a young boy. His hospitality and his tour of Bogenhausen added immensely to the richness of my understanding of the times.

Ulrich Moritz and Sabine Deitmer turned my working stay in Dortmund into something warm and wonderful, from the strictly kosher lunch to the stories of their new Israeli family.

Dr. Andreas Heusler, senior scholar in contemporary and Jewish history, is one of Munich's premier archivists, and I say without hesitation that I could not have written this book without his help. Dr. Heusler was a font of esoteric information: maps, streetcar lines, gas lines, the police station, the electricity lines, and phone directories. During the past two years, he has made himself available to me in person as well as by e-mail, answering my persistent nagging questions with accuracy and good humor.

My *utmost* thanks belong to one fabulous individual. Dr. Regula Venske is a scholar, crime writer, award-winning children's author, and, most important, a wonderful friend. From the beginning, she has been my eyes and ears in Germany. Fluent in English with a beautiful speaking voice, she has been *my* voice in Germany since we first appeared together to do readings five years ago. During my subsequent visits, it was Regula who arranged for me to meet all my sources and contacts for *Straight into*

Darkness, schlepping me back and forth, translating written material as well as conversation. Once in Germany, she basically took charge of my life, from scheduling events to finding Orthodox synagogues and kosher food. She was meticulous in every way and flawless in the execution of details. Over the past years, I have pestered her with countless questions and she has always been so gracious in indulging me, giving me stories and anecdotes, enriching my knowledge of Germany as well as my life.

And of course, my final thanks go to the one person who has been my truest and most constant source of support, not only through this project, but also through my entire life. Jonathan Kellerman is not only an award-winning author extraordinaire, but a supreme gentleman and the best husband and boyfriend a woman could ever want. Thanks for the last thirty-four years, babe. And like they say: to a hundred and twenty.

STRAIGHT INTO DARKNESS

PROLOGUE

New York, 2005

✠ I paint because I am still able to do so. Stiff and knobby, my fingers can bend just enough to grasp a brush and dip the boar bristles into puddles of reds: crimson, ruby, garnet, cinnabar, rose, rust, magenta, vermilion, Venetian—the list seems endless—turning my wooden palette into the full tonal spectrum. I am known as the painter of red because that is how I see the world.

Back in 1980, at the opening of one of my many New York art shows, I was asked by a waif of a child what exactly did I mean painting in all those reds. Her expression was very earnest, and I noticed her face was very pretty. Midnight eyes were hooded by long lashes, and an alabaster complexion was surrounded by chin-length, straight black hair. Her lips had been painted bright red, and I flatter myself that she did so to honor me. She must have been in her early twenties, wearing a clingy black dress with spaghetti straps that criss-crossed over a smooth, creamy back. A lovely back to complement a lovely front: full breasts that spilled out of a plunging neckline. She could have stepped out from a page of my history: I saw her as a sultry hostess in a 1920s Berlin Kabarett.

Immediately, I wanted to take her to a room and liberate one of those luscious tits, sucking on it for hours. I even thought about making love to her. Back then, it would have been possible—not easy, but possible. Now, at my advanced age, even with the advent of the little blue pills, some things are better left in the perfect world of imagination.

<u>What exactly did I mean by painting in all those reds?</u>

Many critics have pondered and analyzed my art. The consensus is that given my background—growing up in a city consumed by horrible events, disarray, and death—how could I not express my soul in the color of blood? Then there are some who liken my reds to Picasso's blues, a different interpretation if you will. No matter that the master was years older than I and had painted his teals and slates while I was still in diapers. Why let logic interfere with facile thinking? Finally, there are the mavericks who say that I paint in red because red is the color of shame.

The last point is well taken.

When one is embarrassed, one turns red. The greater the embarrassment, the deeper the infusion of color. It is the shame of my generation, of a people who accepted genocide as the most expedient way to restore the Fatherland to purity and greatness. I paint in red because the children of my homeland, the children of my generation, must carry the burden of shame and guilt for their elders' unspeakable acts. <u>This</u> is the real German shame.

Ah, but this is not the German shame <u>I</u> remember. The German shame of my childhood was the shame of having to endure the injustices heaped on us good <u>Volk</u> by the November Criminals and the hated Versailles Treaty. The degradation of being bullied by the leaders of the Weimar Republic, those good-for-nothing Prussians who looked down their noses at Bavaria and all of Süddeutschland.

I must explain.

It is simple. Germany didn't <u>really</u> lose the Great War. We "lost" because the hated fates conspired against us, the bloody Kommunisten, the licentious Americans, the impetuous, warmongering Serbs, and, most of all, the ugly, evil Jews with their hook noses and inferior bloodlines and their pernicious cabals and conspiracies to take over the world. Why should <u>we</u> take responsibility for a debacle that should have been settled internally by the Austrians, for a disaster that was not of our creation? And if, because of misinformation, you actually considered Germany a defeated country, think again. It wasn't we Bavarians who were defeated. No battles were waged on our soil, so how could the losses be attributed to us? No, you see, the responsibility and guilt do not lie with Bavaria in the south but, instead, with the hated Prussians up north and the despised Weimar Republic with its heinous rules and regulations, and the foreigners who carved up our beloved country. This is the shame that <u>I</u> remember—that inferior minds were allowed to control our land.

We Bavarians did not need Prussia and its ridiculous experiment of American democracy. Nor did we need the Soviets tutoring us about the ideals of Kommunismus. We needed the restoration of our beloved Wittelsbacher monarchy, although we knew that wasn't going to happen, not with the Prussians at the helm. So in lieu of a king, Germany would accept a dictatorial leader who would take from us the shame of defeat and lead us back to glory.

And didn't the Fatherland find the perfect Führer, the anointed one who would erase the humiliation of ignoble failure and eradicate the abasement suffered by the people of the Aryan race.

That is the shame I remember. That is the shame of my youth.

The shame of genocide came later to the Fatherland, after the Allies pointed out that the Germans might garner more sympathy if, at the very least, they felt a tiny bit disconcerted by the corpses spilling out of the gas chambers, and the bones and ashes clogging up the ovens.

So I paint in reds because I express myself in paint. Words have always been harder for me. I have tried writing, but it is not the same. Painting involves corporeal participation—the eye, the hand, the fingers, the physicality of the sweep of the brush against the blank canvas, the palette knife gouging through layers of impasto. There is no bodily participation in writing, in punching out little black letters in the same script, the same hue, the same size—all in neat little lines. No, I cannot write. Still, as I clack away at the letters on my Remington, if I were to write, I think I would have a good story to tell.

MUNICH, 1929

ONE

✠ Papa, it's them again!"

The banging on the door accompanied by the panic in Joachim's voice roused Berg to action. Flinging off the covers, he bolted from the warmth of his feather bed, scarcely registering the frigid air as his bare feet contacted the worn oak floor, running into the common room of the family's apartment. He was awake and ready for confrontation.

It was still dark, but Berg could make out the duvet draping over the sofa. Of late, his son had taken to sleeping on the couch, leaving his sister alone in the room they had once shared. Privacy issues: typical of a boy of fifteen. His body demanded attention without his sister as an audience. Joachim was tall, lean, and movie-star handsome with hound-dog blue eyes and a thick mop of hair, blond in color from his mother, but the curl came from Berg.

The room shook from hurling rocks hitting the outside stone.

"That's it!" Berg turned on the lone electric bulb that hung over the dining table and fit the crank into the window. It was a blessing that his family lived on the top floor. The hoodlums below did not have enough force to propel the rocks up to their unit. "That is *it*!"

"Axel, what are you doing?"

His wife's voice. Berg stopped and turned. Her eyes were still heavy with sleep, and her tresses stuck out at odd angles. Even though the rainstorm had passed, the air was filled with static electricity. He said, "Go back to bed, Britta. It's cold."

"If it's cold to me, it's cold to you."

"Then be a love and get me my coat."

"Axel, leave them alone. At least, they don't break anything."

"Not yet."

"You don't know who they are."

"Of course I know who they are. They are the Austrian's finest—"

"How do you know? They're not even dressed in brown."

"I know punks!" He leaned into the window crank and felt his face get hot from exertion. "They are punks."

"If they are from Hitler, it's not you they want. It's probably the Jews down below."

"Which Jews?"

"The Weinstocks on the second floor. Or the Maslanokovs."

"The Maslanokovs are Russian, not Jewish."

"Kommunisten. What's the difference?"

"I thought they were Social Democrats."

Britta dismissed him with a wave of her hand. "Same thing."

"I beg to differ. I voted Social Democrat in the last election."

"I wouldn't publicize that if you want to keep our windows intact."

Berg ignored her and gave another push on the crank. "What is it with this window? You would think we glued it to the framework."

"We did. We shut it with paste because it was letting in so much cold air."

"What? When was this?"

"About a month ago—"

"Aha!" The window sprang open, and immediately a bitter cold wind slapped Berg's face. He could almost taste the snow from the Alps. He shouted at the boys below. His displeasure just egged them on. The projectiles began to fall at a faster rate. "Shout at them for me, Britta!"

"I will not!"

"I need you to distract them. I ask little of you."

"And risk being stoned?"

"I'll do it, Papa."

Britta glared at her elder child. "So you join your father in stupidity! One moment I have a clever son. Then he grows to a certain age and becomes idiotic like all men!" She huffed and went back into the bedroom, slamming the door.

Joachim suppressed a smile. He turned to his father. "What should I do?"

"Distract them." From the closet, Berg took out his jacket, his boots, and thick woolen socks. "Yell at them, make faces at them, whatever comes to mind. Just keep them occupied."

The boy looked out the window and frowned. "There are four of them, Papa."

After pulling on his socks and boots, Berg quickly tied

up the laces. "That's good. When they scatter, my luck at catching one of them will improve." He put on his coat.

"You're going outside in your pajamas?" Joachim asked. "You will freeze."

"Ice doesn't form on a moving object." Berg kissed his son's forehead. "They seem to be losing interest. Curse at them, Joachim. Be loud and vile. That should fire them up again."

Berg slipped out the door, down the hallway, and into the nearly black stairwell. Using the wall as his guide, he jogged down four stories' worth of steps, heels clanging against the metal. The air was pure frost, making it hard to breathe. He scrunched his face in disgust as odors assaulted him: rotting garbage, fresh cat piss, and predawn cooking smells, specifically sizzling sausage. That anyone had money for breakfast meat surprised him. Berg's own breakfast—when he ate breakfast—was usually a roll with butter. Times were better, yes, but no one had any savings. The city was still reeling from the Great Inflation of five years earlier. There was little trust in the present currency or the fools in Berlin who now claimed a healthy monetary system.

As soon as Berg hit the ground floor, he threw open the outside door and pumped his legs to full speed. The boys homed in on the squeaking hinges, saw the charging figure, and took off in all directions. Berg elected to take on not the one closest to him but, rather, the biggest, the ringleader.

The boy appeared to be around Joachim's age but stockier, more muscled across the chest like a typical Bavarian. Like Berg, Joachim had the lean build of an effete English schoolboy. But also like Berg, he had strength in those sinewy arms. More than once Joachim had come home with a bloody nose and a sly smile. At the Gymnasium, he was known as a boy who could hold his own.

Berg lengthened his stride, having an advantage over his quarry because he was already running while the teenagers were warming up. But the punk managed to elude immediate capture. The kid turned right, then left, then right, then left, in an effort to shake Berg off, but all it did was slow them both down. Finally, the boy realized he could pick up speed if he ran in a straight line, and was able to pull ahead by several meters. He appeared to be heading northwest toward the Isar, a debatable strategy because it limited his options. Once there, he'd either have to run alongside the river or cut across one of the bridges. Although Berg wasn't the fastest runner, he had endurance. He decided the best plan was to keep up a steady gait and increase his speed later, after the kid had tired from the wind, wet, and cold.

Dawn was imminent but there was no glory in the skies, just a mass of pewter clouds wafting through charcoal globs of sooty smoke. The little light that did break through only served to make the city more depressing; it revealed lines of row houses with thatched roofs and locked shutters instead of the newer glass windows. Interspersed among the residential buildings were the infamous cigarette rooms, but it was too early even for the prostitutes. Heart banging against his chest, Berg flew by several fleabag hotels that housed jobless men curled up in blankets, sleeping behind the display windows. When the kid hit the levee, he abruptly turned left and scrambled down the knoll until he was at the riverbank. He continued north.

Berg kept apace, his body in rhythm to his run.

Last night's rainstorm had turned the ground into a treacherous slush of mud, debris, and lumpy tree roots, all working in tandem to trip him up. The churning river was deafening, especially in contrast to the empty streets. Lungs burning, Berg continued his chase, each step spraying mud against his pajama bottoms and the hem of his coat. Working hard to keep his balance, he choked back icy spray from the roiling water as the river danced over rocks and collided with huge boulders. A sticky, gelid mist chilled his face. His nose and ears had turned numb. His fingers had become stiff and lost feeling, but internally he was warm from running, sweat accumulating under his armpits and around his neck.

His body in sync with metronome of his feet: thump, thump, thump, thump.

Within minutes, he passed the new German Museum of Science and Technology, Munich's proof to the rest of the country that it was a forward-thinking city. The sky was turning light gray. Soon the streets would fill up with bicycles, pushcarts, motor scooters, buses, streetcars, and the ever-growing population of privately owned automobiles.

It would be easier for the punk to lose him in traffic, so Berg lengthened his stride. The kid turned his head and looked over his shoulder. The action slowed him down, allowing Berg to narrow the gap between them. Now he was on the punk's tail . . . just a little more momentum.

A final sprint, legs extended to the maximum, then Berg reached out and grabbed the punk's coat, trying not to trip over his own feet as they both pitched forward. The teen tried to get away by slipping his coat off, but Berg was ready. He grasped the scruff of the boy's neck with his long, dexterous fingers, yanking him backward. Then he gave the kid a solid kick behind the knees. The teen buckled and slipped, then fell facedown in the mud. Berg jerked him back up to his feet and slammed him into the wire fence that lined the river.

"Heil Hitler!" the punk groaned out as he dropped to his knees.

"Your devotion is touching." Berg was breathing hard but remained in control. He pulled the kid's arms behind his back, took out a pair of handcuffs from his coat, and locked the boy's hands together. Once again, he snapped him to his feet. "Perhaps he can visit you in prison. It is a place he knows well from firsthand experience."

"Your days are numbered. There are more of us than you."

"Yes, yes. Still, you are in handcuffs and I am not." Berg pushed him up the hill and onto the street. Without speaking, they walked a couple of minutes until they reached Ludwigs Bridge. Berg pushed him left. "This way."

Berg was surprised. The kid offered nothing in the way of physical resistance. He had some girth but was soft in the arms. Short, too. He had a pink face but any face would be pink in such cold weather. Piggish blue eyes. To Berg, they all were pigs. Underneath his worn coat, the boy wore a beige work shirt, the rough fabric probably woven from nettles, thick woolen pants, and boots with more holes than leather.

Abruptly, the young Nazi broke into song. "O Germany, high in honor . . ."

Berg tightened his grip. "Quiet! People are still sleeping."

The teen changed the song but not the volume. *"Deutschland, Deutschland über alles."*

Berg kneed him in the back. "I said, Quiet!"

"You object to Germany's great national anthem?"

"Not the anthem, only your voice."

Weighing several options, Berg decided on the main police station on Ett Strasse. It was ten minutes away, and Berg felt more comfortable holding the kid in his own territory. A push forward, and the two trudged through the fog and the cold on the cobblestones, trying to avoid the numerous puddles. Berg could hear the city begin to stir: the occasional clopping of hooves, the squeaking of wooden wheel axles on wagons, the purr of motor vehicles, the clanging of streetcars. Heavy objects—most likely crates of food being unloaded and delivered—were falling to the ground at Viktualienmarkt, only blocks away. Berg decided to bypass the market in order to avoid unwanted attention, specifically from the punk's compatriots who seemed to be everywhere these days. "What's your name, *Junge?*"

"I don't have to answer your questions."

"You will eventually."

"No, you are wrong. One day, you will have to answer *my* questions."

"That day has not come, *Junge.* What is your name?"

The kid shrugged. "Lothar."

"Lothar what?"

"Lothar Felb."

"Lothar, why do you throw rocks at our building? It houses many of your own."

"But it also has many degenerates—Jews, Kommunisten, Independent Socialists, Social Democrats, Bavarian Workers, German Democrats, Liberal burghers, German Socialists—"

"That's a lot of people, *Junge*—everyone in the city other than Nazis."

"Exactly." The kid stopped walking and turned his head. "Do whatever you must. But we both know, Inspektor, that I will find a sympathetic ear with the police. Especially when they see you dressed so comically."

Suddenly Berg realized he was still in his pajamas. Embarrassed and angry, he backhanded the teen across the left side of his face. "You underestimate me, *Junge*." Before the kid could respond, Berg backhanded the right side. "Don't talk anymore. You're irritating."

The kid opened his mouth, but no sound came out. They plodded the rest of the way in silence. Berg shivered. He was chilled, wet, and very troubled. There was more truth than lie in the young Brownshirt's words.

TWO

✠ Built on land once owned by an Augustine cloister, the Central Police Station on Ett Strasse was a Gothic labyrinth of multistoried stone structures encircling an open central courtyard, the faces of the buildings overlaid with a checkerboard pattern of windows. A steel-rimmed pebbled lot provided an area to park official police vehicles—scooters, cars, and motorized wagons. The gate to the car lot was flanked by two monumental stone pilasters supporting muscled, snarling lions—the symbol of Bavaria. Horses were stabled in the back of the complex, fewer in number now that motorbikes were rapidly replacing them.

The primary entrance to the station house was reached by walking up stone steps sandwiched between square pilasters festooned with friezes. The main doors were imposing and heavy. Inside, the ground floor held a narrow, high-ceilinged anteroom where a uniformed officer with a sign-in sheet sat behind a desk. Included in his duties was the dispensing of detailed directions to the various interior offices. But he also gave out forms. Bavaria, like all of Germany, had many, many forms, the most important being the registry of addresses. Any German resettling from one city to another was required to report the move and his new address to the proper authorities. The Fatherland wanted to know where its citizens were at all times. It not only made for an orderly society, but also greatly simplified the process of conscription, now rendered illegal by the Versailles Treaty. There were also the requisite forms for citizens to lodge official crime reports and complaints.

The layouts of the building's floors were nearly identical: a series of interconnecting whitewashed hallways punctuated by many doorways. The pine floors, discolored and scuffed from constant use, creaked under heavy foot traffic. By the time Berg had accompanied his charge up the staircase to the fourth floor, it was close to seven in the morning. It was nearly eight when he finished with the processing and paperwork and disposing of the youth. Several of his colleagues were now at work.

Because Berg and these men were part of the newly established *Mordkommission*—the Homicide Unit—and often dealt with complex crimes, they shared a premium office with high ceilings, crown moldings, and floor-to-ceiling paned windows that allowed in steely light and lots of draft. Old-fashioned gas sconces were still used to augment the newly installed but rather weak yellow-tinged electrical room lighting that flickered with each uptake of wind. The radiator was diligently hissing out steam, but still the place was frigid.

Rubbing his hands together, Berg felt eyes were upon him, specifically those of Georg Müller, who had looked up from the communal worktable that he shared with Berg and Ulrich Storf. Müller had just turned forty, a man of medium height and dense physique—thick limbs, barrel chest, wide neck. His face was round and ruddy, topped by a helmet of chestnut-colored hair. His pewter eyes, hooded under lazy, drooping lids, belied a quick mind, though he was a little lax in his report writing . . . skimpy with detail. Georg just couldn't be bothered with the usual preciseness that was the mark of the German Zeitgeist. Still, he was a good worker and an amiable fellow, and Berg considered him a friend. Right now, he was staring at Berg's pajamas, his lips barely resisting a smile. *"Grüss Gott, Axel."*

"Guten Morgen." Berg blew warm breath on his hands, regarding his co-workers attired neatly in appropriate dress. The basic Munich police uniform consisted of dark waistcoat with buttons hidden under a front pleat, a detachable round collar, and matching dark trousers. Georg's police cap—the newer style without the heavy metal spire—sat neatly beside his paperwork. "I'm going home to change. I stopped by so no one would think I'm shirking my duties."

"May I ask why you're half-naked?"

"I am not naked—neither half nor whole."

"But neither are you in clothing."

It was Ulrich Storf who had piped up. Still in his twenties, he had recently been promoted to this division. Although it was unfair to assume favoritism, Berg felt that the man had been advanced either because he was a relative of some higher-up or because he was in the right party and knew the right people. A tall man, he was quite thin but still had a double chin. His shiny face with its rosy cheeks smacked of youth and impertinence, yet there was definite intelligence in his eyes. "If it's a costume you're seeking, I remind you that it's past *Fasching.*"

"With all the Brownshirt clowns who clog up Königsplatz, I'd say this city is one continuous carnival."

"If you feel that every day is *Fasching,* then at lea.
a good Bavarian and put on your lederhosen."

"I am *not* Bavarian."

Müller tossed him off with a wave. "*Ach,* you Prussians have no sense of humor."

Berg retorted calmly, "I am *not* Prussian."

"He is worse than Prussian." Müller winked at Storf.
"He is Danish!"

"Ah . . ." Ulrich grinned back. "So when he grows up,
we will let him be German."

"Many Danes would bristle at such an invitation," Berg
answered. An angry gust of wind rattled the windows.
The walls were damp and smelled of mold. "No, my
Kameraden, though many Bavarians would dispute it, I
fear that I am as German as the rest of you."

"So he's even worse than Danish," Storf whispered to
Müller sotto voce. "He is a Kommunist!"

Berg smiled. "I think I will see you all later."

Storf said, "Button up your coat, Axel. It wouldn't be
nice to scare the good people who ride the streetcar."

"I think I will go by foot," Berg said. "It's not so far."

Müller said, "Still, you are not dressed for the weather,
Axel. I'll boil some water for tea. It will warm up the innards. Not just for you, but for all of us. The radiator lacks
energy this morning. Would you like it with or without
schnapps?"

"Whatever you bring, Georg, I will be glad to drink."

Berg took his place at the table and closed his eyes, trying not to think about the piles of paperwork in front of
him. Once again, general crime was on the rise after a dip
in '24, that anomaly due to the more stable but devalued
mark. Still, things were not as bad as in '23 when inflation

had been lethal. This year, crimes against property were down, as was juvenile crime. Berg had a theory about the decline; he believed that once the government lifted the ban on the NSDAP, the delinquents redirected their anti-social proclivities into being good little Nazis. So maybe Hitler was good for something after all.

Unemployment was up. Of the seven hundred thousand people who resided in Munich and its environs, over forty thousand were out of work. Troubling, yes, but even the current joblessness with its ebbs and flows wasn't as worrisome as the alarming trend of deaths from traffic accidents. Automobiles had increasingly become the transportation of choice for the rich, their cars choking the streets with din and noxious smoke. Nothing but menaces, the motorized vehicles, pushing out the competition with their size and weight, honking at bicycles and knocking over wagons and, too often, people. Cars should be confined to government use only.

"Sleeping on the job, Axel?"

Berg snapped open his eyes and sprang to his feet, recognizing the voice of his superior.

"It is convenient since you're already dressed for bed." Hauptkommissar Martin Volker held up his left hand. The fingers on his right hand were locked around sheaves of paper. "No need to explain. As a matter of fact, I prefer that you not explain, that you don't even talk until I've asked you several questions about this trivial matter."

The trivial matter was Lothar Felb. Someone had cleaned him up; his face was scrubbed raw and pink, although his hair retained bits of this morning's mud bath. He was standing to Volker's left, a distinctive smirk across his lips.

The Kommissar's pale blue eyes were unreadable. He was dressed in an exquisitely tailored dark suit, silk tie, and starched white-collared shirt, the gold chain of his pocket watch dipping from his vest pocket to the pocket of his trousers. White-haired and tall, Volker was aristocratically handsome. It was rumored that he had independent money. If so, why he was working in Munich's police department—even as head of the *Kriminalpolizei*—was anyone's guess.

The expression on the punk's face told Berg that he had gotten up early for nothing.

"You are the one who arrested this boy, Axel?"

"I brought him in, yes."

"What for?"

"For disturbing the peace, vandalism, wanton destruction of property, resisting arrest, and running from a police officer."

Lothar said, "I didn't know you were a police officer—"

"Quiet!" Volker snapped.

"His acts are described in detail in the papers, sir," Berg stated. "If you read the file, it's all there."

"I did read the file, Inspektor."

Berg swallowed hard. "Of course."

Volker showed him the paperwork. "Correct me if I'm wrong, Berg, but I don't recall any mention of his actually attacking you."

"Herr Kommissar, he's been throwing rocks at my building for at least a week."

"Broken anything?"

"Not yet."

"Let me ask you this, Inspektor. Did he attack you directly? Punch you? Slap you? Hit you? Kick you?"

Berg licked his lips. "No, sir."

"Did he threaten you in any way?"

"Not more than any others in his party, no."

"This is not a political matter but rather a criminal one."

"No, he didn't threaten me . . . not seriously anyway."

"Did he use obscenities in your presence?"

"No."

"In other words, what he is . . . is a nuisance." Volker looked at him intently. "Is that accurate?"

"A big nuisance."

"A big nuisance, then." Volker shook his head in disgust. "The boy is my nephew, my wayward sister's child. Her husband hasn't been employed in over a year. My brother-in-law is slothful and drinks heavily. The family has all but disowned her. It's very hard on my sister, it's hard on my nephews—there are six of them as well as three nieces."

"A fecund lady . . ." Berg muttered.

"Excuse me?" Volker replied. Berg was silent. Single-handedly, the Kommissar crumpled up the paperwork and let the sheaves fall to the floor. "I think the *Junge* has learned his lesson."

The two men locked eyes. Berg's answer was slow and spoken through clenched teeth. "I'll take you at your word, Herr Kommissar."

Volker smiled at his nephew. "Lothar, listen to me carefully. If you or your friends ever so much as pick up a stone again, let alone hurl it at any building, I will personally cut off your stones. Do you understand?"

Grinning, the boy could scarcely contain a snicker. "Yes, Uncle, I understand."

STRAIGHT INTO DARKNESS 23

"That's good." Volker turned to Berg. "Are you satisfied?"

Berg nodded. "If you are satisfied, then I am as well, sir."

"I think not." With unerring speed, Volker viciously backhanded the boy across the face twice in rapid succession. Even Berg winced when he heard the crack from Lothar's nasal septum. Blood poured out of his mouth and nose. He broke out into tears as Volker shook out his right hand. "Lothar, if you want to be a good German soldier, first learn discipline. Does someone have a handkerchief?"

A stunned Storf offered Volker his own pocket square.

"How kind of you, Ulrich." Volker wiped up Lothar's face as the boy wailed. Blood was still flowing. "Stop carrying on so! What if Ernst Röhm were to see you like this? What do you think he'd say?" Again the Kommissar shook his head. "Go wash your face, then go home. And tell your mother that if this happens again, I will not save you." He gave him a shove toward the door. "Go, go. I have pressing matters." A more insistent push. "Go!"

Clutching the white cloth to his face, the boy dashed out just as a befuddled Müller returned with two mugs of schnapps-laced tea. "What was *that* all about?"

Volker took one of the mugs. "Georg, how very thoughtful of you." To Berg, he said, "Go home and get dressed properly. You may use one of the motor scooters from the department. Go immediately to the Englischer Garten. I will meet you there." He faced Georg. "You, too, Müller. And you, Storf, as well."

"What's the problem, sir?" Berg asked.

"Not necessarily a problem at this point, more of a mystery. A woman's body has been found. If she was connected, then we'll have a problem."

"Homicide?" Berg asked.

Volker shrugged. "Perhaps a homicide, perhaps a suicide, perhaps an accident, perhaps even natural causes. The only thing we know right now is that she is dead."

THREE

Four years ago, Munich police had gone from bicycles and horse wagons to a motor pool of nine Stolle-Viktoria two-wagon *Kraftrader*, or scooters, two Viktoria-Solo, single *Kraftrader*, and one motorized BMW-Dixi-Wagen Typ 3/15 to replace the horse-drawn wagon that had been used to transport the police or round up suspects. The BMW worked so well that within a few years, concomitant with the development of the *Mordkommission*, the department ordered another one for the specific use as the *Mordwagen*—the official vehicle for investigations of homicides. As much as Berg groused about the new motorized traffic, he was grateful to be riding home in a *Kraftrad* after this morning's chase.

The city was now awake and filled with sounds from the squeaky wooden wheels of pushcarts to the constant clang of streetcars. The previously empty streets had filled with activity: heavily clad pedestrians holding their hats against the wind, bicycle riders attempting to maintain balance while dodging people, animals, and motorcars. Berg noticed a gang of school-age boys with rucksacks, whipping a cup to make it spin, a game known as *Kreisel*. There were also several bands of older boys—Social Democrats judging by their green shirts—who were passing out leaflets to pedestrians for an upcoming rally in

Theresienwiese, a large meadow used for the annual Oktoberfest. The people who took the flyers gave them a momentary glance before tossing them aside, and the discarded paper wound up wafting through the blustery air.

Despite the heavy coat, Berg shivered in the open air. His face smarted from the cold, his fingers and nose nearly numb. The good part was that the fifteen-minute walk was condensed to a four-minute ride. He pulled up alongside his apartment house and turned off the motor. He opened the door to the lobby, then, holding the gate with his shoulder, Berg managed to lug the scooter inside. He had no lock for it. He hoped no one would steal it because he wasn't about to schlep the machine up four flights of stairs. Halfway up the steps, he met Joachim and Monika on their way to school. Joachim was holding Monika's rucksack as well as her hand.

"Guten Morgen." Berg planted a kiss on his towheaded children.

"Grüss Gott, Papa." Joachim asked, "Is everything okay?"

"Everything is fine."

"And the boy—?"

"It's been taken care of."

"What has been taken care of?" asked Monika.

Joachim said, "The boys who throw rocks at our building."

"I don't like them." There was fear and moisture in Monika's eight-year-old eyes. It broke Berg's heart that she had to live in such tumultuous times. "They scare me. Sometimes they follow me home from school."

"If they do it again, you tell me."

Monika's expression was grave. Then she suddenly brightened. "We're going on a field trip today."

"How nice. Where to?"

"To see a real live camel. And a *Niggerlippen*!"

Berg wrinkled his nose. "A *what*?"

"A camel and a *Niggerlippen*," Monika answered.

"There is a display of an African village at the exhibition hall," Joachim explained. "In one of the stands, they have a *Niggerlippen* in a loincloth."

Berg took this in. "An African man . . . in a loincloth . . . on display."

Monika nodded with excitement.

"What does he do?" Berg asked. "Does he just stand there being . . . African?"

His children shrugged. Monika said, "Maybe he sings *Swingjugend*."

Joachim's jeweled eyes became mischievous. "Maybe he will bring a woman to do a fan dance like Josephine Baker."

"Somehow I doubt that, since the real fan dancer wasn't allowed entrance into Munich."

"What's a fan dance?" Monika asked.

"Never you mind." Then, to his son, "And don't say anything, either. It's bad enough I sneak into the clubs to listen to American Negro music. If your mother hears talk about Josephine Baker, she will surely kick me out." Berg tousled Joachim's hair. "Well, go on. No sense being late. You might miss that one-of-a-kind field trip."

They smiled and continued down the steps. Berg waited until they were at the ground level before proceeding upward. After taking off his muddy boots, he walked through his front door. It was warm; someone must have turned up the radiator. He could smell coffee from the percolator. His stomach rumbled.

Britta was still in her bathrobe, sitting at the kitchen table, her fingers clasped around a red can of Onko Kaffee from Bremen. She brushed blond strands from her gray eyes and held up the tin.

"We're out."

Berg poured two mugs from the percolator and added a teaspoon of milk and sugar to each. "That's the second time in a month."

"It's my one weakness. I can check the black market. It will be cheaper than the stores."

"Suit yourself."

Britta plucked a cigarette from a red-and-white Schimmelpennick tin and lit up. Berg brought the mugs to the kitchen table and raised his eyebrows. "I thought you said coffee was your one weakness."

She took a drag and blew smoke in his face, then smiled. "I guess I have several weaknesses."

She offered him a cigarette. Instead, he took hers and inhaled deeply. Then he brought the hot coffee up to his face and let the steam warm his skin. She took a piece of stale bread and dipped it in the coffee to soften it. The radio was playing more static than music—some kind of nationalistic Bavarian accordion humdrum that was all the rage. "Did you buy a paper?"

Berg gave her back the cigarette and sipped his coffee. "No. I have pressing business right now. If you want, I will pick up a copy of the *Post* on the way home."

"Then pick up a copy of the *Beobachter* to balance it."

"I will not have that trash in my house."

"Then at least buy the *Neueste Nachrichten*. Men came

to the school last week, Axel. They asked the children what newspapers were in the house."

Berg thought of the implications. "And they told them nothing?"

"Of course. They've been trained well and they're not stupid." She chewed on soggy bread. "But what if one of their friends says something? They've been up to the apartment. Children talk. You have to be practical."

"You're right. I'll buy both papers."

Britta was surprised by his acquiescence. He must have had other things on his mind. "So he is behind bars? Your punk?"

"I think he won't bother us again."

"Ah!" She shook her head and took a drag on her cigarette. "And who is he related to?"

With a pocketknife, Berg began to clean his nails. "He is Volker's nephew."

"Nudge-nudge, wink-wink. They are all disgusting!"

"Volker clobbered him across the nose." He put down the knife, held up his hands, and examined his nails. Satisfied, he folded the knife back into its frame. "I believe Volker broke it."

"Good. Maybe next time Volker will break his head."

"It's quite likely." Berg went to the closet and pulled out his uniform. "The man doesn't take guff from anyone."

"So our windows are safe until the next punk comes along." She looked around the room. "It would help if you took down those awful pictures. Anyone looking in our windows would think that Kommunisten live here."

His eyes swept over the wall, landing on Joachim's drawing—a floral still life done in pastels when the boy was just ten. Berg had been so proud of it that he had made a frame from junk wood, protecting the chalk with glass from an old window. "You object to your son's artwork? What kind of mother are you?"

"Stop it, Axel." She sighed. "You know what I mean."

What she meant were the pencil drawings by Klee the Swiss and Jawlensky the Jew. "Liking avant-garde art does not a Kommunist make."

"But it is not favored by members of the workers' parties."

Berg agreed silently as he put on a clean undershirt and poked his arms through the sleeves of his jacket. He washed his face and shaved in the kitchen sink. Then he retrieved his boots and scrubbed the mud from their soles. "Is it my fault that southern Germany is filled with philistines? Can I use this cloth to dry my shoes?"

"Why do you need to dry the shoes? They will just get wet anyway."

His slipped the knife back inside the boot. "So I won't track mud in the house."

She smiled. "That would make sense." Again, she dipped her bread in the coffee. "This is terrible. It's like eating ersatz."

"We have fresh rolls."

"I know, but I hate to waste."

Berg kissed the top of her head, then went to the icebox. He pulled out the butter and the two fresh rye rolls that she had bought yesterday morning. "Think of the long lines five years ago." He bit into one of the rolls. "I don't trust Hindenburg, nor do I trust Scharnagl." He offered the second roll and the butter to his wife. "I say we eat as if inflation is around the corner."

Britta took the roll and slathered it with butter. She nibbled on the bread, then took a big bite. She closed her eyes and chewed slowly. "You are right. This is so much better."

"Marmalade?"

"No, thank you." Another bite. "I don't trust them, either. No one does. What does that do to a country when no one has faith in its leaders?"

"I don't like to think about it." Properly dressed, Berg sat down and slipped on his boots. "It is nice to discuss politics with you, Britta, but some of us have to work. I am on a case. A body in the Englischer Garten."

Britta's mouth fell open. "Are you joking?"

"I am not."

"Murder?"

"At this point, we don't know."

"And the deceased?" She stubbed out her cigarette. "Who, Axel?"

"I don't know that either." He finished lacing up his boots and kissed her forehead. "Be careful, darling. Turbulent times we live in."

FOUR

✠ Clad in warm, dry attire, his belly calmed by a cup of coffee and a roll, Berg felt ready to take on death. Even the sky was offering penance as blue peeked out from leaden clouds. The wind, though present, had lost its bite. Crossing the Isar on Maximilian's Bridge into the western side of Munich, Berg turned his scooter to the right, down Widenmayer Strasse, a thoroughfare lined by stately Gothic buildings rich in ornamentation and architectural features. The exterior paint added color to the landscape, the bricks and stone often awash in gentle grays, soft creams, buttery yellows, terra-cotta, or burnt umber, rich earth tones more fitting in sunny Lugano than in overcast Munich. Some of the multistoried structures were divided into apartments, but some were still private residences housing the elite old money as well as the nouveau riche.

As Berg headed west onto Prinzregenten Strasse, he passed a band of black-shirted youths with red bow ties marching in step to their leader's call—Kommunisten, about twenty of them, young and callow. Stupid children playing at war with their uniforms, their speeches and flag waving, and their endless parades, doing all of their politicking from a safe distance, far away from the Soviet bloodbath. Berg never recalled any glamour in battle. All he could remember, as he hunkered down in trenches, drenched in his own piss, was terror as he dodged bullets from the Tommies and the meddlesome Yanks.

His mouth suddenly was parched. He swallowed dryly, thinking about a midmorning snack of weisswurst and Löwenbräu on tap. A puny roll and a cup of coffee were only going to carry him so far. Maybe a quick bite after this initial investigation . . .

At the southern end of the Englischer Garten, Berg pulled the scooter to the curb, turned off the engine, then dismounted. As he entered the premises on foot, he realized that Volker hadn't pinpointed the location of the crime scene. The park was over nine hundred acres, and certainly Berg could cover more ground riding through the area on the pedestrian pathways. Yet he elected to walk, dragging the *Kraftrad* at his side, because it would be unseemly to disturb the atmosphere of peace and serenity with din from the industrial world.

Designed by Friedrich Ludwig von Sckell over a hundred years earlier, this oasis of greenery reached its full splendor in summertime when the trees were canopies of leafy boughs and the shrubbery exploded with color and scent. During the warm season, the Kleinhesseloher See—a small lake next to the spacious beer garden—rippled lazily from the oars of canoes and paddleboats. But even in winter, the land was tranquil, with its streams and walkways that were perfect for a meditative stroll as one brooded on German politics.

Right now, Berg's mind wasn't focused on the fate of the Fatherland. Just past the Japanese Teahouse, in a copse of tall brush and detritus that was ringed by the bare arms of maple, birch, and chestnut trees, there was a flurry of activity, although most of it nonproductive. A

dozen policemen were milling about, smoking and talking. Off to the side, the *Mordwagen* sat on the grass, its
doors opened wide. Professor Josef Kolb was pulling out
boxes from the interior, setting up a makeshift forensic
station containing a multitude of investigation acces-
sories: bottles, vials, tweezers, magnifying glasses, saws,
chemicals, scissors, rulers, calipers, brushes, and photographic equipment set on spindly stands. Kolb was a
slight man with bug eyes and unkempt hair. He saw Berg
approach and waved to him with a gloved hand. Berg
leaned the scooter against its kickstand, but before he
could walk over to Kolb, Volker emerged from the crowd,
wearing a displeased expression. That was nothing new.
The boss lit a cigarette and cocked his head. The two
of them walked away from the activity, away from the
Mordwagen.

"Look at them! A bunch of gnats—all movement and
no purpose." Volker blew out a plume of smoke. "How
many do you think you'll need for your investigation?"

"What am I investigating?"

"A woman strangled by a stocking. A delivery boy on a
bicycle spotted her in the tangle of brush. He summoned
one of the foot patrolmen, who promptly issued him a citation for riding his bicycle on the walkway."

"No good deed goes unpunished."

"Rules are rules. Because of the early hour, he thought
he could get away with it. Cigarette?"

"Please," Berg answered. "Was the woman a prostitute?"

"I don't know." Volker blew smoke into the misty air.
"So far, the only thing I can say is she isn't dressed like

one. Her clothes are good quality. So if she is a lady of the evening, she has a generous benefactor."

"What does Professor Kolb say?"

"Professor Kolb has been playing with his accoutrements. And it doesn't take an appointment at the university to determine death by garroting. The stocking is still tightly bound around her neck." Volker huffed. "I have a department to run in a city on the brink of chaos."

"Chaos is standard business, sir."

"But garroting isn't. I'm not pleased by this turn of events. Find out who she is and what happened. How many men will you need?"

Berg looked at the crowd of officers. "None except Storf and Müller. We're capable of scanning the area for witnesses as well as evidence. Are they here? Storf and Müller?"

"They are interrogating the delivery boy."

"Very good. Is he a suspect?"

"How in bloody hell should I know? He is as good as anyone, I suppose. If he gives you an inkling of wariness, lock him up and we'll consider the homicide a closed case." Volker broke away and barked at the foot patrolmen, "All of you! Back to your posts!" He clapped his hands loudly. *"Now!"*

Rattled by Volker's ferocity, the officers scattered like ants. Berg frowned. "It might have helped if they left in some order, sir. Their shoeprints could have very well obliterated those of the culprit."

Volker turned his anger on Berg. "First of all, that is Kolb's concern and not yours. Secondly, the Professor can certainly distinguish what is a standard-issue police-shoe print and what is not!"

"I stand corrected. May I take a look at the body, sir?"

Volker stalked off, stopping abruptly at the edge of the corpse. Berg followed and stood next to him.

She was very young and very pretty despite the death pallor. An oval face framed petite features, except for large blue eyes fixed in their gaze. Copious black hair tumbled over her shoulders and framed her face as if she were modeling for a Pre-Raphaelite painter. She was trim, but lacking in chest. Her shapely smooth legs were bent at the knees, and peeked from under the hem of her evening dress. Volker was correct. Her attire was expensive. The dress was flowing and modern, made of black chiffon and of a length designed to show off ankles. A feathered fan lay ten feet from the body. Berg bent down and picked it up, running his finger across the soft plumes that had been dyed sable black. He held it up to Volker.

"I'll keep this if you don't mind."

Volker shrugged. Berg stowed the fan in his coat pocket, then took out a pad and pencil and began to note details—the position of the body, where it was found, what was around it. He looked at the ground for shoeprints, but there was nothing but mud and detritus. "Kolb will take a photograph of the body?"

"I certainly hope the equipment is for something."

"She isn't wearing a coat," Berg noted.

"And?"

"Surely she would not have gone out last night without a coat."

"Surely."

"And only one shoe." Berg exhaled. "Perhaps we have a killer who collects coats and shoes." He thought a moment. "One stocking is still on, the other of course is around her neck. Has anyone checked for undergarments?"

"A garter is holding up the lone stocking. As far as bloomers or underpants, there are none. And yes, she was violated." Volker's expression was flat. "Up close, one can smell it."

"Does she look at all familiar to you, sir?" Berg asked. "You are better acquainted with high society."

Volker answered without hesitation. "No, she does not."

"Sir?"

Berg and Volker turned toward the sound. It was Storf. His nose and cheeks were red. He rubbed his bare hands together and blew on his fingers. "An officer just reported that a call has come into the station on the 22222 emergency line. It seems a gentleman—Herr Anton Gross— has reported his wife missing."

Volker checked his pocket watch. It was heading toward nine. "And he has just discovered she's gone?"

Storf went on, reading from a notepad. "It seems that Frau Gross is usually up by eight. According to her husband, she is punctual. But yesterday she was not feeling well. Herr Gross thought she was sleeping late."

"Meaning they have separate bedrooms," Berg said. "And quite a large apartment if they can afford separate sleeping quarters."

"I was told that the family business is jewelry." Storf sneered. "I'm sure he did quite well during the Great Inflation."

As if it were the man's fault that stones held value while the Mark became worthless. But wasn't that the essence of the German mentality? It was much easier to point a finger than to internally dissect. Progressivism was synonymous with Kommunismus and anti-Order, and anything was better than disorder.

Volker threw his cigarette on the ground and crushed the glowing embers under his heel. "You have an address, Storf?"

"Right here, sir." Storf handed him a slip of paper.

Volker glanced at the information, stowed the paper in his pocket, and straightened his cravat. To Berg, he said, "Ulrich and Georg can clean up this mess. You come with me. Together, we will talk to him. Leave your scooter for the others. We'll take my car." The Kommissar pointed to his cigarette stub on the grass. "Take care of that for me, will you, Ulrich?" He started toward his car, talking over his shoulder. "No sense littering our beautiful parks, hmm?"

Storf bent down, picked up the stub, and called out, "Of course not, sir." To Berg, he whispered, "Bastard."

"Ulrich, make sure Professor Kolb takes several pictures of the body and checks thoroughly for anything that might have been left behind by the culprit, including shoeprints and clothing. And I think a woman like her would carry a compact, but I didn't notice a bag."

"Thieves?" Storf suggested.

"I don't doubt it. My first suspect would be the delivery boy. Go through his items carefully."

"Yes, Axel. You'd better go," Storf said. "The dictator needs his henchman."

"Indeed he does." Berg had to trot about a hundred feet to catch up with Volker. "And you're sure you want me with you, sir?"

"Meaning?" Volker was walking at a very fast clip.

"Perhaps the man would respond better if the questioning was done by someone of his class without interference from me."

"Ah. I see." Volker slowed his pace as he neared his black Mercedes. "A good point, Inspektor, but still I want you to come. If someone is going to offend, better you than I."

FIVE

✠ It was eminently logical that the body found was that of Frau Gross, because the address given to the police was not more than ten minutes from the park, the numbers corresponding to a four-story, apricot-colored building on Widenmayer Strasse. Perhaps the woman was coming home from a secret tryst in Schwabing and decided for discretion's sake to shortcut through the Garten. Or perhaps she was murdered in her home and dumped in one of the many thickets there because it was the closest and best place to hide the evidence. Theories sifted through Berg's mind as he and Volker headed toward the car.

Berg was even more mystified by the Kommissar's decision to drive when it would have been simpler to go by foot. It wasn't like Martin Volker to be inefficient, so there must be other considerations at play. The Mercedes belonged to Volker and not to the police, so perhaps Volker wanted to establish parity with Gross by displaying wealth.

After they had parked and walked a block to the building, a doorman escorted them to a pair of etched-brass elevator doors. The lift, which was manned by a uniformed, white-gloved operator, was painfully slow and jerked with each yank of the pulleys. Finally, it stopped on the fourth floor and the operator opened the folding doors of the wrought-iron cage. Herr Gross laid claim to the entire floor. Volker and Berg got out, and the Kommissar waited until the man had gone and the elevator needle was pointing to three before proceeding to the Grosses' door. Volker lifted the iron knocker and gave the rich reddish-brown mahogany door several loud raps. It was answered by a butler—uniformed and staid—with bland features and thinning white hair.

"Yes?"

"We are the police." Volker gave him a calling card. "I believe Herr Gross is expecting us."

"Ah, yes. One moment."

The butler was about to close the door and have them wait outside, but Volker would have none of that. He pushed his way in and, in doing so, pushed the butler aside.

"I beg your pardon, sir!" the butler said stiffly.

Volker turned his steely eyes on the servant. "We haven't got all day, man." The eyes narrowed. "Get your master."

Several silent moments ticked away. Then the butler folded. "Very well."

As he started to walk away, Volker called out. The butler turned around just quickly enough to catch Volker's coat. "You can hang it up for me, thank you."

It was all the butler could do to hold his temper, especially after Volker added in sotto voce, "Tyrolean help just isn't what it used to be."

"I wouldn't know, sir," Berg answered as if it were a legitimate statement.

Volker laughed. He took off his hat and told Berg to do the same. "Come. Let's look around."

"We haven't been officially invited in, sir."

"Nouveau riche Kosmopolit," Volker scoffed. "What does he know about protocol?"

"But . . ." It was useless. The Kommissar was already several steps ahead, his formerly immaculately polished shoes clomping against the white marble, leaving behind flecks of mud. Berg had no choice but to follow. They both stopped at the entrance to the great room and took in deep breaths of admiration. Fifteen feet high, the walnut ceiling was coffered and carved. The floor had been laid out with black and white marble tiles arranged in a diamond pattern, although much of it was covered by intricately woven Persian rugs.

Volker dared to step inside.

The decor was elegant and in the most current of fashion, the highly polished furniture modern, sleek, and pure in form. Everything in the room was of top quality, but especially impressive were an elegant rosewood bombé chest and a Macassar ebony table whose centerpiece was a Lalique vase holding fresh calla lilies. The items could have been lifted from the Decorative Arts and Industrial Expo held in Paris several years earlier, displays that featured innovative design at its finest. Mixed in with the modern furnishings were several choice pieces from the Empire period to give the setting a sense of history and balance.

There were several groupings of sofas and chairs allowing for simultaneous conversations. In a stone hearth, a fire roared behind an etched-glass screen. Burgundy velvet drapery framed six tall multipaned windows. But most of the wall space was taken up by modern artwork that most certainly would have been denounced by the

Workers Party as degenerate: canvases by artists associated with the Blaue Reiter group—Franz Marc, August Macke, and Wassily Kandinsky. There were many paintings, drawings, and sketches by the Expressionists as well: works by Egon Schiele, George Grosz, Gabriele Münter, Paul Klee, Georges Braque, and Lyonel Feininger.

"Avant-garde but still German," Volker noted. "That way no one can accuse him of being too Kosmopolit."

"Braque and Klee are Swiss," Berg said. "Schiele is Austrian; Grosz, Kandinsky, and Feininger are Jewish; plus Kandinsky was born in Russia."

"Anyone who speaks the mother tongue is either German or wishing to be German," Volker said. "Just ask Hitler."

"Have his citizenship papers come through yet?"

"Now how would I know that?" Volker said.

"You know everything, sir."

Volker raised his eyebrows. "Axel, you make me blush."

Berg walked over to one of the windows. He stared outward—a panoramic view of the Isar, of Bogenhausen and beyond. The clouds were breaking, and Berg could feel the sun's muted warmth through the glass. This, combined with the intense heat from the fireplace, made him feel swaddled in his overcoat. While deciding whether or not to remove it, he heard a throat clear and turned around.

Presumably he was looking at Herr Gross, a delicate but handsome man with pale skin and intelligent dark eyes. Spectacles rested on a slender, prominent nose. His long, bony fingers massaged one another with worry. He was thin but tall, perhaps over six feet. He nodded first to Volker, then to Berg.

"Anton Gross, here. I have arranged for tea. As it is quite warm, perhaps you will be more comfortable without your heavy overcoat. Haslinger will hang it up for you."

That was Berg's cue to take off his coat. He handed it to Haslinger, the butler. The man took the outer garment, turned on his heels, and left, his eyes still smoldering from Volker's previous superior attitude.

"Do sit." Gross perched on the edge of a stiff sofa covered in ruby satin. Volker selected one of two tapestry-upholstered side chairs, likewise sitting with a straight spine. Berg chose the chair's twin. The two policemen faced Gross, waiting for him to speak.

"I am quite alarmed. It is not like Anna to leave the house without a proper escort. These are . . . troubling times. There are many street hooligans."

"Indeed," Volker said. "It's what happens when the unemployment rate soars."

"Yes, of course. But the reason behind it doesn't change the facts. There are way too many of them . . . the hooligans. It is frightening enough for a man, let alone a young woman."

"And you're sure that no one accompanied her?" Berg asked.

"She never told me she intended to leave the house. Besides, who could have escorted her other than I?"

An unknown lover? Aloud, Berg said, "Her father or a brother, perhaps?"

Gross waved them off. "No."

Berg looked around the great room. There were many objets d'art placed on the tables and on the mantel: Tiffany vases blown from iridescent blue or gold Favril glass, decorative Galle bowls made from layers of cameo glass, a zoological garden of Daum pate-de-vert animals. Yet there wasn't a personal photograph in sight. "Would you have a picture of your wife, Herr Gross?"

"A photograph, you mean?"

"Yes, a photograph."

Again Gross massaged his hand. "I have a wedding photograph of her by my bedside. But that is quite old . . . five years."

"That will do."

"I shall fetch it for you." But before he could stand, Haslinger appeared, wheeling a cart that held a Baroque silver tea service with matching spoons and forks, porcelain plates, cups, and saucers, and a platter filled with biscuits, small cakes, and cookies.

The ritual began. Volker and Berg took one lump, Gross two. Volker and Berg each took a single piece of *Mandelbrot*—an almond biscotto—and a thin slice of poppy-seed cake. Gross selected a single petit four frosted with pink icing.

"Anything else, Herr Gross?" Haslinger asked.

"Yes," Gross answered. "Would you please bring the police Anna's wedding photograph from my bed stand."

"Certainly, Herr Gross."

The butler left; the men ate and drank in silence. Politeness dictated that Berg eat at least half of the cake. It wasn't hard because the pastry was delicious—full of butter and *Mohn* and eggs. After several minutes of eating, Berg placed his cake plate on the tea cart and balanced teacup and saucer on his knee. He took out his pad and pencil. "I thank you for the refreshments, Herr Gross. Now, if I may . . . a few questions."

The man nodded.

"When was the last time you saw your wife?"

"At eight o'clock last night." Gross sipped his tea. "I brought her up a cup of hot cocoa and several poppy-seed cookies. She wasn't feeling well."

"And if I may ask, in what way was she ill?"

Herr Gross's cheeks took on a rosy glow. "She was sick to her stomach."

"With child?" Volker said neutrally.

Gross nodded. "Five months, though you could scarcely tell by looking at her." This was said with pride. "She had a beautiful figure and was meticulous about her weight. So meticulous that the doctor thought it was unwise for her to be so careful." He smiled, showing straight teeth. "That's why I was plying her with cocoa and cookies."

Berg took a final sip, then placed his empty cup and saucer on the cart. He was glad to get rid of the china without breaking or dropping something. "And you haven't seen her since eight o'clock last night."

"No . . . We have . . . since the beginning of her condition, we have maintained . . . privacy."

"I understand," Berg said.

Haslinger was back, a silver frame in his hand. Herr Gross took the picture, gave it an idle glance, then offered it to Volker. The Kommissar's eyes betrayed nothing. He handed the photograph to Berg.

She had been so radiant in her white gown and veil. How sad was it that this woman—more like this girl—had been reduced so cruelly to lifeless flesh. Berg caught Volker's nod. Of course, the bastard wanted *him* to break the news. The day had started poorly: It wasn't getting better.

"Herr Gross . . ." Berg glanced at Haslinger, waiting for the servant to excuse himself. Finally, the butler got the hint. "Sir. There is no easy way to tell you this. We found a woman's body in the Englischer Garten this morning. This was reported to us not more than two hours ago. After looking at this photograph, I have reason to think that it is . . . was . . . your wife."

Gross's stare was a mixture of vacancy and stark confusion. After several false starts, he said, "Are you telling me that my wife is dead?"

"I . . . Yes, that is what I fear . . . after looking at this picture." He cleared his throat and looked to Volker for corroboration. None came. "Yes. It is she, yes."

"Are you sure?" Gross's eyes beseeched Berg's. "Could you be wrong?"

"I . . ." Berg blew out air. "I don't believe so, no."

Carefully, Gross stood up and placed his china on the cart. Then he paced for several moments. Abruptly, he stopped and mustered some strength. "Well, I'd like to see that for myself!"

Volker stepped in. "Of course, Herr Gross. We will take you there straightaway. But first, may we ask you a few questions? Just routine protocol, sir."

"Yes, of course." Gross's eyes were wet, his mind a thousand miles away.

"Assuming the worst, sir, do you know of anyone who'd want to harm your wife?"

"No!" Adamant. "Of course not!"

"I'm sorry, Herr Gross," Volker said. "But I had to ask."

Gross bit down on his lower lip. "May I see her now?"

"Please bear with me one more minute. You said it was

her habit to get up around eight. But you waited until nine to disturb her because she wasn't feeling well last night."

"Exactly."

"And she went to sleep around . . ."

"About eight."

Berg said, "And you heard nothing in the middle of the night to suggest that she might have gone out?"

"Nothing."

Volker said, "But it is possible that you, being in another room, did not hear her movements."

"Unlikely," Gross insisted. "I heard nothing. I have nothing else to say."

"Yes, of course," Berg replied. "But just assume for a minute that maybe you didn't hear *everything*. Can you think of any reason why she might have gone out at night without telling you, sir?"

The implication was obvious. Gross's eyes turned furious. "None whatsoever! And I don't believe that she would go out without telling me, especially in her condition! Maybe some hooligan broke in last night when I was asleep and took her."

"Ah, Herr Gross, entirely possible," Volker said. "And we will look into that. But then you must admit that it would be possible for things to happen in her part of the house without your knowing . . . provided that you were in a deep sleep."

Gross grew red with anger. "I cannot believe . . . She would never go out so *late* and on her *own*."

Berg tried to soften the shock. "I'm sure she would never do it under ordinary conditions, Herr Gross, but maybe an emergency came up and you were sleeping. Out of love and consideration for you, she ventured out on her own."

"Any idea what kind of *emergency* might draw her out?" Volker added.

"Only if it had something to do with her family, and I haven't heard— Oh, *mein Gott!* Her family!" His eyes, focused on Berg, pleaded for support. "Someone must tell them. I cannot. . . ." He squeezed his eyelids shut to prevent tears from rolling down his cheeks. He turned away and blotted his face with a white linen handkerchief.

Berg said, "I will tell them for you, Herr Gross."

The man heaved a deep sigh of grief. "Thank you. It is most appreciated."

"Of course, I will need their names and addresses."

Gross shook off his sadness and pulled a pad and pencil from his coat pocket. He was grateful to be doing something with his hands other than wringing them. "I will give them to you right now."

"And what is your wife's father's employment?" Volker asked.

"Banking." Gross finished writing and tore off the piece of paper with a flourish. He handed the information to Volker, who said nothing. But Berg detected the slight rise of his superior's eyebrow.

"The bank . . . it is family-owned, correct?" Volker asked.

"That is a personal question, Herr Kommissar."

"I don't mean to overstep my bounds, Herr Gross, but I am trying to assess the situation. I'm thinking of perhaps a kidnapping for ransom."

Gross had regained his composure, replacing shock

with anger. "You can hardly ask for ransom if there is nothing to ransom."

Berg said, "Perhaps there was supposed to be a ransom note this morning, but someone found her too soon."

Gross ignored this hypothesis. "Again, I ask you! *When* can I see her?"

"First, we would like to make her presentable for you—"

"I want to see her!" Gross raised his voice. "I want to see her now!"

His cries brought in Haslinger. "Sir, is everything all right?"

Gross turned his fierce stare onto his servant. "No! Everything is not all right. It's Anna. The police think she . . ." He turned his head away from Haslinger and faced Berg. "You tell him."

Upon hearing the news, Haslinger gasped. Gross repeated loudly his demand to see his wife's body. Haslinger tried to calm Gross down by offering him a drink of brandy. Gross slapped the snifter from Haslinger's hand and began to pace. He grew increasingly more agitated as the dreadful words were finally registering.

His wife was dead!

The situation was spiraling downward. Volker took control. He stood up and said, "Herr Gross. I will accompany you to see the body. But I must warn you. It is hard to look at if one is not used to such things."

Gross's face registered horror. "She was mutilated?"

"No, not at all," Volker assured him. "But there is always something in the face . . . sometimes haunting . . . the eyes that no longer respond. I really do suggest you wait until the shock has worn off."

Defeated, Gross fell back onto the sofa. "If you think it's best."

"I do."

"Was she . . . violated?"

"I don't know," Volker lied. "We will find out, of course."

Haslinger broke in. "I'm sorry but I must ask you to leave right now! Herr Gross cannot stand any more shock!"

Volker patted the butler's shoulder with condescension. "Of course, my good man, we understand. Our coats, please?"

Gross said, "See them to the door, Haslinger. I'll be . . . all right."

"This way," the butler said stiffly. As they walked down the hall toward the front door, Haslinger made a slight detour. A moment later, he came back and thrust their coats against their chests. Then he threw open the front door. But Volker took his time before leaving, slowly putting on his coat. "We'll just be a moment, Haslinger. We must look presentable."

Haslinger tapped his foot. Berg waited, flipping the piece of paper between his fingers. Volker smoothed the brim on his Borsalino and gave it a flick with his fingers.

"Ah, that should do it. You need not bother waiting for us, Haslinger. We can let ourselves out."

The butler didn't move.

Volker smiled and stepped out into the hallway. He and Berg didn't speak until they were outside the building. Berg took a deep breath and let it out. It had been stifling inside the apartment. Never had the cold felt so good. He put on his hat.

Volker regarded the slip of paper Gross had given him. "Kurt Haaf. So Anna was his daughter. Interesting."

Berg waited.

"The People's Bank of Southern Germany." Volker handed him the address. "It almost went out of business in '25."

"Not exactly newsworthy, sir. Many banks went out of business."

"Those banks whose presidents did not marry their daughter to rich Jews, yes, they did go out of business." Volker laughed softly and shook his head. "An arrangement right out of a cartoon from *Simplicissimus*. Knowing Kurt, I'm not surprised. He should have been a Jew the way he loves his money."

"As if Jews are the only ones who love money . . ."

Volker smiled. "I see you're ready to join the leagues of the disenfranchised."

Berg ignored him. "And we're interviewing him together, sir?"

Volker thought a moment. "The address is in Bogenhausen, not at the bank. I want you to go to the family home and see if anyone's there. I shall go back to the crime scene and see what has been accomplished. When you have located Kurt, check back with me. I shall meet you then. Done?"

"Done." Berg sighed. "Poor people. Such a pity!"

Volker regarded him with appraising eyes. "Be courteous, Berg, but do leave the sympathy to the women of their household. The police are to be respected as Munich's soldiers of safety. Let us save the maudlin outpouring for the theater, no?"

"It was a simple statement, sir, not an overwrought snit."

Volker took in his words and found them satisfactory.

SIX

✠ It was one grand home after another, not Berg's usual homicide investigation. Most of Munich's deaths were mundane: a man flattened by a runaway horse or an out-of-control motorcar, a drunken onlooker crushed at one of the town's numerous political rallies, angry men reduced to fisticuffs in beer brawls gone awry. Murders weren't beautiful young women from wealthy families.

A fast walk over the Luitpold Bridge brought Berg into Bogenhausen, a residential area of stately homes on tree-lined streets, of green parks and cobblestone walkways. Quiet and peaceful, yet the neighborhood had none of the sterility often associated with affluent districts because it housed a considerable number of artists. Thomas Mann lived here. So had Oskar Maria Graf, Hans Knappertsbusch, and Max Halbe. In the cold months, most of the foliage was bare and spindly, but spring was coming, evidenced by the greening limbs of the elms, birches, and chestnuts. A pleasant place to stroll had murder not occupied Berg's mind.

Kurt Haaf's two-story detached villa was painted yellow with windows framed by green shutters. The roof was constructed from red tiles, high and peaked, allowing room for several attic gables. There was a second-story balcony ringed by scrolled wrought iron; a fence of the same design surrounded the lot. A pricey home but some-what modest for a banker. If Volker's pronouncements were true, however—that the bank had almost failed—Haaf was most fortunate to end up with such prosperous accommodations.

Berg knocked on the door, and his rapping was an-swered by a young man in a partial state of dress. He wore long, black wool pants held up by suspenders and a white, long-sleeved shirt with cuffs but without a collar and tie. His face was lean and boyish; his lips so thin that they were almost invisible. Dark brown eyes rested behind half-glasses perched on a long nose. His entire expression was one of annoyance. He held a coffee cup in his right hand.

"Yes?"

"*Guten Tag,*" Berg said. "I am looking for Herr Kurt Haaf."

"Yes."

A pause. Berg said, "Are you Herr Haaf?"

"No, I am his son, Franz. What's this about?"

"I am sorry for the intru—"

"Yes, yes. Get on with it."

"I am Inspektor Axel Berg from the police. May I come in?"

Haaf waited a moment. "Police?"

"Yes." Berg took a step toward the threshold. *"Bitte?"*

There was a pause, then Haaf opened the door all the way. Berg followed the young man through a marble entry hall into a sizable living room that looked smaller because it was crammed with ponderously ornate furni-ture. The room did boast high ceilings with carved mold-ings and highly polished hardwood floors. But the dark brooding pieces along with the heavy drapery ate up most of the natural light coming through the windows. The ivory walls were dressed either by sepia-toned landscapes or stern-looking portraiture.

Haaf did not sit. "May I ask your business, Inspektor?"

"It is . . . personal," Berg said. "I think I will need to speak with your father."

"My father is already at work—a good Münchener burgher—the model of industry. I, on the other hand, being a resolute wastrel, have spent too many nights in the city's most roguish Kabaretts."

Berg licked his lips and said nothing.

Haaf looked around the room. "If my father were here, he'd insist we talk in this stuffy mausoleum." The man smiled. "But he isn't here, is he?" He crooked a finger. "Come this way. No reason you should interrupt my morning coffee."

The young man led Berg into a glass solarium. The room was surprisingly warm and moist, no doubt due to the dozens of potted plants emitting heat as well as the odor of moss and must. The atrium looked upon a rose garden, dormant now, but Berg could picture the palette of color that would explode in a few months' time. Seating was provided by wicker furniture with cushions upholstered in tropical flowers. A table was prepared with a coffee set, a plate of pastries, and a variety of newspapers—the *Münchener Neueste Nachrichten,* the *Münchener Post,* the *Völkischer Beobachter.* There was also a copy of the Red Dog—the satirical magazine *Simplicissimus.*

Berg's eyes jumped from one party headline to another

party headline. *So viele Meinungen haben wie Winde auf dem Dach*—as many opinions as winds on the roof.

"Do sit." Haaf lifted his mug. "Would you like a cup? Perhaps a fresh pastry from the Viktualienmarkt? The apple strudel is excellent."

Berg remained standing. "I'm not hungry nor thirsty, thank you. And I think my poor news may impact on your appetite." He closed his eyes, then opened them. "This morning the police found a woman's body in the Englischer Garten. I have reason to think that it is your sister, Anna—"

Immediately, Franz broke into spasmodic coughs, spewing out the hot liquid. The force of his hacking sent coffee sloshing over the rim of his cup and burned his hands. He cried out in pain, then placed the cup and saucer on the table. He shook out his fingers. "This is impossible!"

"I'm afraid it's—"

"Impossible!" The young man began to pace. "How can that be?"

"I was hoping that you could provide me with some clues."

"Me?" He turned livid. "Just what are you implying?"

"Nothing, Herr Haaf, other than one sibling's knowledge of the other."

"Dear Anna hasn't lived here in five years."

"And you are not close to her?"

The young Haaf sputtered out, "Of course, we're close. Oh dear, this is just . . . and you're sure it's she?"

"We think so, yes. Her husband will be making the identification later on today."

"So you're *not* sure."

"I have seen a picture. The likeness is uncanny."

"Oh, *mein Gott*! You must tell me what happened."

"We're still determining that. May I ask for your help in this matter?"

"Of course!" Haaf stopped pacing and sank into a chair. "This is terrible."

"Yes."

"Terrible, terrible, terrible!"

"Yes," Berg agreed. "I would like to ask you something. We are trying to ascertain why a lady of Anna's stature would have gone out last night without a proper escort. Can you think of any reason for such conduct?"

"What makes you think she went without Anton?"

"Because he did not accompany her last night. As a matter of fact, he insists that she went to bed last night at eight because she was feeling ill. Apparently she was with child."

"Oh, dear . . ." A sigh. "That is truly tragic. They have wanted a child for quite some time. Anton was quite insistent on producing an heir."

Berg's brow rose. "Your sister wasn't anxious for motherhood?"

"Of course, she wanted a child." Haaf started to speak, but thought better of it.

"There is more you are not saying, Herr Haaf," Berg replied. "Now is not the time for discretion. We must bring your sister's killer to justice immediately. What are your thoughts on this matter?"

Haaf shook his head.

Berg said, "Perhaps the marriage wasn't a happy one?"

"That is personal, Inspektor."

"Yes, but it may be relevant to the crime. You do want to know what happened, correct?"

"Of course." Haaf licked his lips. "What can I say? Both fathers were pleased with the union. Anton is a gentleman. His looks are certainly passable, and his manners are beyond reproach."

"But . . ."

"Anton is a fine man and provides wonderfully for my sister, but he is stiff even for the burghers in the region. He is a teetotaler. Not even a splash of beer. To say he is a conservative would be understating his political views. My sister, on the other hand . . ."

Berg waited.

"My sister is progressive . . . very modern with a keen sense of justice."

"A Social Democrat?"

"More like a—" Haaf stopped himself.

"A Kommunist?" Berg filled in.

Haaf averted his gaze. "She visited me when I was in school in Berlin. She had a fierce laugh and could drink with the best of my schoolmates. Her life . . . It is very different now—a beautiful bird in a gilded cage. If someone were to open the door, I think it might be quite possible that she would spread her wings."

"Ah . . ." Berg said. "Another gentleman in her life?"

"I'm not suggesting that that is the case. But I know she loved the theater and Anton did not. Their apartment isn't too far from Schwabing."

"And she'd go out unaccompanied to a play at night? With all that is going on?"

"Ironically, it is only under the cloak of night that one's

movements are often undetected." Haaf hung his head in sorrow. "Maybe not this time."

"And you did not see her last night?"

"Ah . . ." He shook his head. "No, I did not see her last night, Inspektor. I wish I had."

"Then I shall check the theaters. Perhaps someone remembers her. Such a lovely woman and unaccompanied, she would stand out." Berg thought a moment. "Or perhaps she wasn't unaccompanied."

Haaf said nothing.

"In either case, I have a picture of her . . . her wedding picture."

"That awful thing . . . so rigid and posed. Wait here."

Haaf left the solarium. Berg eyed the pastries, a piece of strudel with raisins and apple extruding from the flaky crust. It was all he could do not to nip off a piece of the fruit and pop it in his mouth. A moment later, Haaf returned, picture in hand.

"One of my friends experiments with photographic equipment. I think this one captured the spirit as well as the face."

Indeed it did. Shining eyes burned through an angel's face. Thick hair cascaded down a long neck, falling past bare shoulders. Since the picture had been cropped just below her neck, one could imagine her body as nude instead of clad in an off-the-shoulder blouse.

"Thank you," Berg said. "This will help."

"I want it back."

"Of course." He stowed the picture in the pocket of his coat. "Now I have the onerous task of telling your father the dreadful news."

"I will come with you."

"Are you sure?"

"I cannot allow my father to hear such awful words without being there to support him."

"Very good. How far is the bank?"

"A five-minute car ride."

"I have no car," Berg told him.

"Then we shall take mine. It is parked right outside. I shall have one of the servants crank it up."

"And if you wouldn't mind, I would like to use your telephone . . . of course, you have a telephone."

"Of course."

"I would like to call up Herr Kommissar Volker. Out of respect for your father's position in the community, Herr Volker would like to be at the bank when we break the news to Herr Haaf."

"Certainly. If you just wait here for a moment, I shall arrange everything. And please . . ." He pointed to the table. "Help yourself."

"Thank you."

Once Haaf was gone, Berg again eyed the pastries longingly. He bit his lip, then sat down, idly brushing crumbs off the tabletop. Then he picked up several granules of heavy white sugar with a moistened index finger, licking the tip with his tongue.

What's done is done.

His hand inched over to the plate filled with sweets.

Life is fragile.

He picked up a piece of strudel and allowed himself a healthy bite.

SEVEN

✠ The gleaming black BMW was given its due respect as pedestrians stepped aside to clear a path for such a fine machine. The rumbling engine cut through the air, making the ride a loud one. Progress in Munich was measured in decibel levels, though most of the noise still came from the human voice box—the constant parades of uniformed members of political parties or the drunken roars emanating from beer halls.

Regarding his town through the back window, Berg could not help but admire its beauty: the sinewy banks of the Isar, the green parks, adorned bridges, tree-lined boulevards, majestic architecture, and the ornate, double-onion–domed Frauenkirche peeking through the sky from the old city. Though factories meant jobs and money, he hoped that Munich wouldn't end up with problems like the coal belt cities spasmodic from industrial fever, all hard-edged and gray.

The People's Bank of Southern Germany was located on Leopold Strasse past the state library just north of the Ludwig-Maximilian University—an enclave of academia originally started by royalty, but now run by the state. The current rumor was that many of its professors and students belonged to the occult right-wing Thule Society and supported Hitler. When the educated got behind a dictator, there was always cause for concern. Berg couldn't dwell on politics, though. He had more-immediate concerns.

Like its neighbors, the bank building was five stories, with the tellers on the ground floor. Volker had already arrived, standing at the curb, expectant as he checked his pocket watch. The junior Haaf parked his car between a sausage cart and a gaggle of resting bicycles. The two men got out, and Berg immediately noticed that Volker had begun to wilt around the edges. His coat was wrinkled in back, the brim of his hat less than perfectly smooth, his shoes soiled with mud. Trivial imperfections but conspicuous because it was Martin Volker. Berg made quick introductions, and Volker offered condolences. Franz Haaf nodded gravely, then opened the door to the bank.

They went inside.

If customers were an indication of success, the business appeared to be prosperous. Bespectacled men in three-piece suits holding overcoats and several well-adorned, feather-hatted older women stood in four straight lines, waiting patiently to step up to the tellers. The handsomely attired employees, working with efficiency, sat behind scrollwork iron cages. The place was well appointed with white marble on the floors and fluted Doric columns holding up the beams that ran across a carved wooden ceiling. The walls were fashioned from picture-frame paneling, and hanging inside the frames were stiff portraits of bedecked, bellied burghers, past presidents of the bank, all of them displaying the esteemed Haaf escutcheon.

The young Haaf passed through the scene quickly, taking Berg and Volker behind the activity and into a web of private offices. The elder Haaf had a young private secretary with pinched features and a sour face. He looked at Franz and, in a nasal voice, immediately informed him that his father, Herr Haaf the *bank president,* was in an *important* meeting with several *important* Bavarian financiers. "Your father specifically asked not to be disturbed."

"It's an emergency, Wilhelm. Inform him that I need to speak with him now."

Wilhelm wrinkled his nose. "I was instructed not to disturb him, sir. So you may tell him yourself."

"But you're his secretary. It's your job to tell him."

"Not when he's in a meeting and he asks me not to disturb him."

"Oh, for goodness' sake," Berg said. "I'll tell him."

Haaf stopped Berg, then glared at the obstinate young man. "If you don't tell him at this moment, I will have your job."

The young man gave a snort. "I doubt that." But he got up anyway. He knocked at the door to the inner office and went inside.

Franz was furious. "Upstart!"

Volker pulled off his gloves. "Indeed. You should inform your father."

"I will when the timing is more . . . suitable." Then the young Haaf's eyes misted. "I don't know if I can tell him what happened."

"We'll do the talking, Herr Haaf." Volker's voice was without comfort.

Wilhelm had returned with the elder Haaf in tow. Kurt Haaf was tall but so thin as to be almost skeletal, his finely tailored suit hanging on his narrow shoulders, suggesting that once this man had weighed more. His face was gaunt, his eyes sunken.

"Grüss Gott." He clicked his heels together in a sharp snap. "Kurt Haaf, here. I am in the middle of a meeting. What is it that couldn't wait an hour?"

"Papa," Franz said. "Do sit down—"

"I don't want to sit! I want to get back to my business. Some of us earn money. And don't tell me it is another gambling debt, Franz! That is not my concern."

Symmetrical pink spots rose on Franz's cheeks. "It's Anna."

"Anna?" The banker made a face. "What did she do this time?"

Franz's pleading eyes traveled from his father's face to Volker, then to Berg, who regarded the senior banker. "I am Polizei Inspektor Axel Berg, Herr Haaf. This is my superior, Erster Kriminal Hauptkommissar Martin Volker—"

"Yes, yes." Haaf's eyes went to Volker's. "We have met."

"We have, Herr Haaf," Volker answered. "At the house of Polizei Kriminal Direktor Max Brummer. One of the reasons I am here personally. And also out of respect for your position in the community. I am afraid we have terrible news."

Berg felt his face tighten. Kurt Haaf's eyes darkened. "What?"

Volker nodded to Berg.

Bastard!

Berg kept his gaze somewhere over Herr Haaf's shoulder. "The police were called into the Englischer Garten early this morning. A woman's body was found. We have reason to believe that the woman . . ." He cleared his throat. "We believe that the woman was your daugh . . ."

Haaf clutched his chest and pitched forward. Volker grabbed his right arm, and Berg took his left as he told Franz to bring his father a shot of whiskey. Wilhelm, who was standing, started to speak, but only sputtered instead.

"Move!" Volker pushed the young secretary out of the way.

Slowly, Kurt Haaf was lowered into Wilhelm's chair. Franz came back with amber liquid in a shot glass. Kurt drank it down and coughed, shaking off any help. To Wilhelm, he said, "Go in there and tell them an emergency has arisen. I'll be back in five minutes . . . ten at the most. Pass out the cigars—the ones from Havana—and tell them to take a smoking break."

Franz stared at his father in disbelief. "Papa, we should send them home."

Kurt ignored his son and whispered fiercely to Wilhelm, "Go!"

The young secretary disappeared behind the closed doors. Berg chose the temporary lull to look around the secretary's wood-paneled office. His desk was small but modern, made of blond ash burl and trimmed with ebony. On the top sat piles of papers along with a lovely Egyptian-style, gold-plated desk set inlaid with dots of mother-of-pearl. A nineteenth-century grandmother clock had been pushed into the corner.

Kurt's face was now deep red; a thin layer of sweat coated his forehead. "You are sure about this?"

"Your son-in-law gave me a picture . . . your son as well." Berg looked down at his shoes. Then he made eye contact with the old man. "It's the same woman."

This time, Haaf's voice cracked. "Still, I would like to be sure. When can I make the identification?"

Volker stepped in. "Herr Haaf, we shall avail ourselves to you at this difficult time. But first, sir, we would like to make the body presentable."

Kurt nodded, then suddenly clutched his chest again.

"Mein Gott," Franz exclaimed. "I shall call Doctor Wiess."

"I don't need a doctor!" Haaf turned to Berg. "You say you found her body this morning?"

Berg nodded.

Kurt pulled out his pocket watch, flipped open the cover, then stared a moment before closing it with a snap. "So the attack . . . it was not in her house?"

Berg said, "It is always possible that she was . . . that she expired in her house and was placed in the park afterward, but that being the case, we have no suspects for the crime."

"What about Anton?" Kurt suggested. *"He* was in the house."

Franz regarded his father as if he were speaking an unfamiliar language. "Papa, you can't be serious. Anton doesn't have enough gumption to step on a fly."

"That's because he is a bug himself. A bug and a Jew—"

"Father, you were the one who approved of the match!"

"I approved of the money, not of the weasel." He let out a gush of air. "Your sister's spending habits required nothing short of a small fortune. Why not take it from the Jew?"

Franz rolled his eyes. "Forgive my father. He's not thinking too clearly."

"There is nothing wrong with my thinking," the elder

Haaf declared. This time he managed to stand up. "Their marriage was a sham. They fought all the time."

"Father! This is surely not police business."

"Don't be stupid, Franz!" Haaf had turned damp and florid. "Nothing but conflict from the day she moved into that house."

"What did they fight about?"

"What didn't they fight about? Money, religion, politics, friends, what to eat for supper. The only thing likable about Anton was his unerring sense of business. They are born with it, you know. And don't you tell me that I sound like one of Hitler's finest. I don't agree with everything he says, but not all of his rhetoric is drivel." His eyes threw daggers at Berg. "The Jew couldn't even impregnate her!"

Franz shook his head like a father indulging a petulant toddler.

"As a matter of fact, Herr Haaf," Berg said, "she was pregnant."

"Not by his seed—that I can assure you!"

"Papa!"

Berg said, "And you know that for certain, Herr Haaf? That the baby did not belong to her husband?"

Haaf snorted out an unintelligible grumble. "Not as fact, no." He grabbed his pocket handkerchief and dabbed his face. "But if it indeed wasn't his child, it could be the reason for her . . ."

"Demise." Berg provided the word.

Haaf wagged his finger in the air. "The weasel finally broke. He got angry. Another fight and this time he couldn't control himself. If you've been to the house, you know it's a stone's throw to the Garten." He poked Berg's chest as he spoke. "Take him into a locked room! Beat the confession out of him! He's weak. He'll buckle."

The young Wilhelm had come back. "The gentlemen await your return, Herr Haaf."

"I need another moment. Give me your handkerchief, Wilhelm. I need it out of necessity more than you need it as an ornament!"

The young secretary paused, but complied. The old man mopped his sopping brow. "Bring them refreshments, Wilhelm. Löwenbräu—dark. Also pretzels, mustard, and wurst. That will occupy their stomachs until I can regain my composure."

"Certainly." The young employee licked his lips. "Are you feeling better, sir?"

"Better? Hardly!" He waved the handkerchief with an air of dismissal. "Go!"

Again, Wilhelm disappeared. Haaf turned to Berg. "You will apprise me of the progress of your investigations."

"Of course, sir."

"And what about Anton?"

Berg said, "Perhaps another visit will be in order."

"You're damn right another visit is in order!"

"I will ensure it, Herr Haaf," Volker said.

"I certainly hope so, Herr Kommissar. I've given you plenty of my time. I'd like to think that I haven't wasted it." He took a deep breath and let it out. "And when may I see . . . see her?"

"This afternoon . . . maybe three hours from now." Volker thought a moment. "Say . . . two o'clock?"

The old man shook his head. "I've another appointment." He turned to his son. "Perhaps you can go make the identification in my stead, Franz."

"Of course, Papa."

The old man placed a bony hand on his son's shoulder, then dropped his head and squeezed his eyes shut. "We should both be grateful that Mother is no longer with us to witness such heartache, no?"

Franz nodded. Berg said nothing. What a terrible thing for which to be grateful.

EIGHT

✠ Once outside, Berg felt as if an enormous stone had been lifted off his shoulders. Sadness loomed even larger when confined to the indoors. He inhaled deeply, then let it out slowly, adjusting his breathing to the rhythm of the city. He gave his companions a quick glance. Haaf's expression was grave, Volker's distracted.

The Kommissar adjusted his hat. "Your father's perspective on his son-in-law was quite interesting, Herr Haaf."

"My father is being ridiculous," Haaf snapped. "Anton adored Anna; he would never hurt her."

"His adoration combined with a sudden betrayal could have been the cause of the inexplicable action."

"Nonsense!" Haaf insisted.

Volker remained unconvinced. "Even if your father was ranting to deal with the shock, I think another visit to your brother-in-law is called for." Volker turned up the collar of his coat. "I will leave that up to Inspektor Berg. In any case, I shall meet you at Ett Strasse Station at one-thirty."

Haaf was momentarily confused.

Volker said, "For the identification?"

"Ah, yes, of course. Thank you for accompanying me."

"How could I do anything less?" The Chief nodded to

Berg. "I will leave you two gentlemen now. *Auf Wiederschau'n.*"

"*Auf Wiederschau'n,*" Haaf mumbled.

Volker walked half a block, then got into his Mercedes, driving off amid clouds of black smoke.

"An extravagance for a policeman . . . to have a car, no? And such an impressive one at that." Haaf stuck his hands into his coat pockets. "He wears expensive clothing—his suit, his hat, his overcoat. How does he manage on a civil servant's salary?"

"You may ask him."

"I'm asking you."

"I don't know, Herr Haaf. He has never consulted me on financial matters."

"Your superior has style."

"The Kommissar is one of a kind."

"Said without a trace of irony," Haaf said.

"There is no irony. Simply a statement of fact."

"Hmmm." Haaf took out a cigarette tin, shoved a smoke between his lips, lit up and blew out a thick billow of gray fumes. "What next?"

Without thinking, Berg looked at the tin. English writing. Tobacco from The States was expensive.

"Oh, sorry." Haaf offered him a cigarette. "Here. I insist." Berg took it, and Haaf lit it for him. "So you will see Anton again?"

"I think yes. Did Herr Gross and your sister fight as often as your father said?"

"And you don't fight with your wife?"

"My wife is alive. Did Anna ever confide in you her dissatisfaction with her marriage?"

"It was rough for her, yes. But there was affection as

well. I witnessed the flirtatious smiles between them. Genuine smiles."

Berg sucked in smoke from his cigarette and let it out slowly. "Still I would like to hear how your brother-in-law viewed his marriage."

"I'm sure he will tell you everything was perfect, that there were no problems at all."

"Then I would know that he was lying. In a marriage, there are always problems. And then there is Anna's pregnancy. If the child was not his, it could be a motive for homicide."

"My father spoke out of anger, out of prejudice, out of crazy agitation upon hearing such horrid news. I don't believe that Anton could possibly be involved. You may interview him, of course, but I doubt if my brother-in-law will speak ill of my sister or talk about any dissatisfaction with the marriage. Not in his current state of mind, certainly."

Haaf spoke sense. Gross would probably be too distraught to say anything remotely negative about his wife. In the months ahead, she'd probably become a saint. Berg reconsidered. "I should also like to take the photograph of Anna that you have given me and show it to the theater owners in Schwabing. I'd like to find out if your sister was there last night."

"I think it would make more sense than thumping on poor Anton," Haaf said. "Would you like me to drop you off someplace?"

"Thank you, Herr Haaf, but no. A smoke along with a short walk will clear my mind."

"There is a very good bakery on Türken Strasse.

Kulms, near the Komödien Theater. Just in case you are in need of a quick bit of nourishment."

"Thank you for the recommendation," Berg said.

"I shall leave then." A slight bow. *"Auf Wiederschau'n."*

"Auf Wiederschau'n." Berg watched the young man pivot and walk away, then whispered, *"Pfueti"*—an informal Bavarian way of saying good-bye. It was a contraction of *"Behüt dich Gott"*—may God protect you. This time, *Pfueti* was exactly what Berg had wanted to say.

✠ ✠ ✠

BERG STROLLED several blocks down Leopold Strasse, then turned right onto Franz Joseph Strasse and into Schwabing, the heart and soul of the city's artistic and intellectual community. Called the Munich Montmartre, the area was still vibrant with life, although its glory days had dulled as the decade wore on. Once it wasn't unusual to see Kandinsky sipping coffee with Berthold Brecht, or Lenin engaged in a heated debate with Trotsky outside one of the many Russian tearooms, giving rise to the term Schwabing Soviet.

Once was a very long time ago.

The neighborhood abounded with sidewalk cafés flying blue and white state flags as well as banners of all colors. Plenty of men still occupied the outdoor tables, smoking and sipping hot spiked beverages to keep warm while indulging in a game of cards or a round of chess. Berg couldn't walk more than a few steps without passing a Kabarett, a tavern, a beer hall, or a restaurant featuring the newest in Italian cuisine—a current trend that had started with Osteria Bavaria.

Down the side streets were apartment houses, dignified stone structures but built for function, the simplified architecture steering away from the ponderous government buildings with their heavy Gothic facades. They were the residences of the bourgeoisie—the doctors, the lawyers, the businessmen, the Protestants, and the rich Jews. A while back, Berg had contemplated moving into Schwabing. It was close to the Englischer Garten and filled with stimulation for the children. But Britta feared that the children might be *over*stimulated, and Berg had to admit that there was some justification to Britta's concerns. More than once, he had passed window posters of skimpily clad female boxers or Josephine Baker in her infamous banana-peel skirt. Because she had not been allowed to dance in Munich, she had become an icon, taking on more importance than she was worth.

Berg pulled a notepad from his pocket and drew up a rough map of the area. Then it was just a matter of routine, going into each public establishment one by one, writing it down on his list . . . each tavern, each beer hall, each coffeehouse, and each Kabarett.

Have you seen this woman before?

Nothing but a shake of the head or the simple *"Nein, es tut mir leid"*—no, sorry: the same answers from proprietors and patrons alike, from the men and from the women. None of the street vendors recognized Anna Gross as someone they knew, nor did the corner paperboys recall her face.

Truly a lady of mystery. If she had sneaked out of her house to play night games, she had been discreet.

An hour dragged by, and still no luck. It was nearing one in the afternoon and Berg felt his empty stomach protesting. Perhaps Ulrich and Georg had come up with some meaningful clues at the crime scene. Much better to meet with them over lunch and discuss other possibilities than to continually engage in fruitless endeavors.

He decided to return to the station house.

As he walked south, he came across a small theater, not much more than a cave with a door. Outside the establishment was a bright red sign that featured a smiling comedy mask painted in gold, surrounded by an assortment of white champagne flutes tilting at all angles. The lettering was black.

Das Spielhaus: Kabarett und Komödie.

Berg read the playbill. The theater specialized in skits satirizing Kapitalismus and conservative Munich, complete with a cartoon of an overstuffed burgher, a monocle magnifying his widened eye as it peered upon flowing piles of marks. Many of Munich's theaters catered to individual tastes, each having its own special troupe. Since Anna Gross had once flirted with Kommunismus, Berg figured his stomach would be patient if he gave the assignment one last try. He banged on the locked door, and his knock was answered by an irritated male voice. A moment passed, then the bolt slid back and the door opened.

The young man was sickly thin and pasty. His eyes were washed in the palest of blue, and his short, spiky hair was so blond as to be almost white. He wore a black sweater that didn't quite reach the waistline of his black pants. Berg could see a hipbone jutting from the gap between the clothing.

Eyebrows arched upward. A heavy sigh. The man spoke. "Not again!"

"Excuse me?"

"Clearly, you are the police."

"Clearly," Berg answered.

"All of our licenses are in order. Why do you pick on us incessantly when Nazis routinely throw bricks through our windows? Surely there must be one policeman who is not a member of the NSDAP."

"I am not a member," Berg answered.

"Really? Then make yourself useful and go arrest a Nazi."

Berg narrowed his eyes. "You should watch your mouth, man. Such impertinence to authority could result in a very bad headache for you."

The young man ran his fingers through the straw on his head. "Do you demand to see our licenses?"

Berg inched toward the threshold. "Let's talk inside."

It took several moments for his eyes to adjust to the dimness because very little light was filtering through the lobby's dusty windows. Resting against one wall was a compact mirrored bar that advertised absinthe and cigarettes. A velvet-upholstered bench stood opposite the bar. Two doors punctured the back wall, one marked *Eingang,* the other *Ausgang*—entrance and exit—the doors to the theater. The wooden floor had suffered many dings from the stomp of heels and could have used a swipe from a mop. The room did have modern electric lighting, but someone had elected not to use it.

The man said, "As I stated, all our licenses are in order."

"I am not interested in your licenses. What is your name?"

"Gerhart Leit." Suspicion in the faint blue orbs. "What do you want?"

"Patience, Herr Leit, is not your strong point, is it?"

Leit said nothing, his eyes focusing on some distant spot. Berg took Anna's picture from his pocket and showed it to him. "This woman . . . do you know her?"

Slowly, Leit's eyes lowered until they rested on the photograph. Then they reacted, but only for a moment. "I don't know her."

"But you've seen her, yes?"

"I see many people."

"Yes or no. Have you seen her before?"

"I might have."

"And might you have seen her last night?"

"Why?" Leit asked. "Is she in trouble?"

Pesky fellow. Berg said, "Not anymore. She's dead."

Immediately, Leit slumped against the bar. He brought his hand over his mouth. "Oh my! *Dead?*"

"Yes."

"*Dead* as in *murdered?*"

Berg ignored the question. "She has come to your theater before?"

Leit nodded.

"Last night?"

Leit looked away. "What happened?"

"Her body was found this morning in the bushes at the Englischer Garten. Perhaps you might have a theory as to what happened."

"*Me?*" Leit was clearly shocked.

"I'm always interested in you theater types, how

you come up with your stories. How would you have written it?"

"I write satire, Herr Inspektor, not grisly drama about dead women."

"Even so, creativity is creativity. Try, Herr Leit, try."

Leit's eyes swiveled onto Berg's face. "I wouldn't know where to begin!"

"You can start with her physical description, of course. What did she look like last night? What was she wearing?"

"That's easy. I remember her because she was a pretty thing with a delightful laugh." He struggled to get more clarity. "She had on a beautiful black dress that swayed as she moved . . . modern style . . . longer in the back than the front. Black shoes . . . satin, I believe. A feathered fan."

"You recall her in detail then."

"I recall the fan, yes. She used it quite a bit last night and not as mere decoration. It was hot in here . . . lots of people. The show has been successful. We still have believers who defy this exclusionary nonsense."

Leit's description—the particularity of it—had credibility. Berg took his notepad. "And her coat?"

"I didn't see it. But of course, she wouldn't be wearing her overcoat while inside."

"Did she drink anything?"

"Drink?"

Berg pointed to the bar.

"Beyond beer, I don't recall. Her companion had absinthe."

"Ah." Berg nodded. "A companion. Tell me about him."

"He was tall . . . sophisticated . . . smooth like a Berliner. You know, well dressed and seemingly suave. The Putzi Hanfstaengl type."

"Was it the art dealer?"

Leit let out a small laugh. "As if a Nazi would dare to step foot in this place other than to vandalize it. Why on earth would he come here?"

"Maybe to pick up the latest piano tune?"

"More likely to spy for the Austrian, if anything at all. I don't think it was him."

"You seem unsure."

"It was a mere glance, Inspektor. He could have been a thousand different men."

Berg took out his pad. "If you could describe him, perhaps I could sketch him." He drew an oval. "We can start with the basic face. Was his longer or shorter?"

"Longer."

Berg extended the oval. "Light eyes . . . blue?"

"Yes, I believe so."

"Big, small, close-set, far apart?"

"I don't know. Draw something and I will change it."

Berg drew standard eyes, a standard nose, and a standard mouth. By the time he was done, he had a picture of a mustachioed man with a long face, deep-set eyes, an aquiline nose, and thin lips. He looked vaguely familiar, but one often draws from the inner mind. One interesting thing that came out: Leit remembered that the man wore a monocle and a top hat.

The Kabarett owner stared at the sketch. "The drawing does look a little like Hanfstaengl, but Putzi wasn't the man. I'm sure of that. The man I saw wasn't as tall and his brow and chin were less pronounced."

"One of his brothers perhaps?"

Leit shrugged.

Berg said, "How did she and her companion interact?"

"They weren't fighting, if that's what you mean. On the contrary, when they left, I saw her arm linked in his. But of course, I didn't follow them out of the theater. Why would I?"

"They looked happy together?"

"Very happy, Inspektor. Being a sentimentalist, I might even say they looked as if they were in love."

NINE

✠ It was a variation on the words of the famous American president Abraham Lincoln: God must love stupid people because He certainly made a lot of them. Touching his forehead lightly, Volker tried to remain calm and self-possessed. After all, Polizei Kriminal Direktor Max Brummer and Polizei Kriminal Kommandant Stefan Roddewig were his superiors in rank. Yet the more they talked, the harder it was to maintain his composure.

He took another sip of his beer and licked foam from his lips.

Hans und Franz: two dunces almost identical in their small-minded thinking. Brummer was the stupider of the two, a staunch follower of the Socialist German Workers Party, a good friend of Hitler and utterly without charm. He was rabidly anti-foreigner, anti-Semitic, and anti–modern aesthetics, calling the works of such geniuses as Klee, Picasso, Dix, Grosz, Kandinsky, Feininger, and Marc degenerate rubbish. It was this last deficit—Brummer's utter lack of taste—that was truly unforgivable.

Thick in the jowls as well as the shoulders, with a head of white, unruly cowlicks, he had just turned sixty. His conservative politics stemmed not from the ideals of the Nazis but from the loyal Royalists, those antiquated beings who nursed futile hopes that one day the Wittelsbacher would restore Bavaria to its former—albeit illusory— eminence. No matter that there hadn't been a king in over a decade. No matter that Munich had not only survived, but also thrived. Some were slow to catch on.

The Direktor had come up through the ranks of the department, attaining the coveted position due to favoritism. His war record was not particularly heroic, but he had served under the right leaders. He was not very clever, but past events had shown that he could be very brutal.

Kommandant Stefan Roddewig was more of a cipher. Over six feet with long arms and big hands, the Kommandant was born up north, but moved to Munich early in his adult life. The only remnant of his youth elsewhere was a slight but distinct accent that gave his Bavarian German a little charm. Other than that, he had melded into the population so adroitly that he had become a typical *Bierbauch* Bavarian with his flabby stomach and his thinning hairline. Whatever was left on his head was colored dishwater brown. It was hard to believe that the man was still in his thirties: He had the cunning of a seasoned politician.

Roddewig had risen through the ranks of the Munich Police Department with unprecedented speed, leaving a wake of gossip, including rumors that money had bought certain positions. The Kommandant had stifled the scuttlebutt by purging the department of his enemies. At that time—in the wake of Kurt Eisner's assassination and Hitler's failed putsch—Volker had been one of Stefan Roddewig's staunchest supporters, sensing the need for law and order. Soon afterward, it became clear that the Kommandant was enamored of his position and his power. Now, the two barely tolerated each other and Volker wondered how long that would last.

It was almost one in the afternoon, and the beer hall was crowded and noisy, each workers' union, each political party, each *Verein* claiming its regular table—its *Stammtisch*—with a banner or flag inscribed with the club's official insignia. The tables' occupants often became boisterous in their proclamations of predominance. Sometimes the competition got ugly. Volker eyed each patron, mentally sorting wheat from chaff: who would help and who would hinder, who to watch and who to ignore.

His brain sparked from auditory stimuli. Max was talking.

". . . don't need is more panic and lawlessness, Martin," cried Brummer. "Things are too unstable as it is."

Volker focused his eyes on the stout man. "The case is six hours old, Direktor."

"Even so, you know how these things feed the public's anxiety."

"No one even knows about it except for a few select individuals."

"Martin . . ." Roddewig sighed. "It won't take long for the papers to pick up on this. Then, it's chaos."

"I'm not talking to anyone, Stefan." Volker tightened his fists, then slowly released his clutched fingers. Being angry wouldn't help at all. He looked his boss squarely in the eye. "I assume everyone else is being equally discreet."

The Kommandant took out his cigarette case and hid a smile behind the process of lighting up. "Surely you know better than anyone, Martin, that there are spies everywhere."

Volker took out his own cigarette case, and tried to hide his annoyance at the bastard. "But if we remain circumspect, Stefan, I don't foresee mass hysteria. Besides, we are making progress—"

"What kind of progress?" demanded Brummer.

A sip of beer with an infinitely long-suffering sigh. "Steady progress. I have my best Inspektors working on it. We mustn't be rash in our assignment of guilt."

"Why not?" the Direktor called out. "The woman was a whore!"

The table next to theirs fell silent and stared at Brummer. Volker cleared his throat and dropped his voice. "That very well could be true, Herr Direktor, but we don't know that for certain." He spoke as if he were the teacher and the two men his pupils.

"Then make up a lie, Martin," Brummer said. "Imply that a secret lover murdered her because she spread her legs for someone else. Or that this lover was blackmailing her for money."

Volker said, "Meine Herren, neither story would settle well with Herr Haaf. The woman was his daughter, remember?"

Brummer downed his stein of beer, then pursed his lips. "Kurt Haaf is not as well off as he once was . . . but he still owns the bank. That is something to consider. Haaf just may be too important to scandalize."

"Then perhaps you can suggest that it was Anton Gross who did it," Roddewig put forward.

At this outrageous accusation, Volker looked at his superior with disbelief, but Brummer jumped on the suggestion. "Martin, you just told us that Herr Haaf can't stand the Jewish dog. Who'd miss him?"

"The man has a point, Martin," Stefan added. "Who cares if another rich Jew hangs?"

"It's unseemly for the police to randomly charge people with crimes," Volker said. "Why are you two so keen on closing this case in a preternaturally short period of time?"

"Because the last thing this city needs is an excuse to panic," the Direktor answered. "We've had much too much upheaval . . . things are finally quieting down."

Volker spoke soothingly. "No one is panicking."

Except you two.

"I will keep everything in order, I assure you both."

And where were either of you last night?

Brummer said, "If Haaf thinks you should concentrate your efforts on the Jewish dog husband, then I suggest you give it some thought. After all, it appears his wife was screwing another man."

"Why are you saying that?"

"Why?" The Kommandant sliced a chunk of veal sausage, speared it with a fork, dipped it in mustard, and popped it in his mouth. He spoke as he chewed. "Wasn't she drowning in semen?"

"Yes, she had had sex," Volker said, "but it could have been with her husband."

"Her husband didn't even know she was gone, Martin, yet you found her in an *evening dress* and filled with semen. If that isn't an indication of cheating, what is?"

"It could have been that she was dressed in her gown postmortem, Stefan."

"Only her husband could have done that. Maybe they had an argument and it turned into something very nasty, and he killed her. It could have been an accident, but he panicked, dressed her in a gown, and dumped her in the park. Your suggesting that she was dressed postmortem strengthens my case instead of weakening it."

"Good point, Herr Kommandant," Brummer said. "And even if Herr Gross didn't do it, he had some culpability by not controlling his wife. Since there is no love lost between Herr Haaf and Herr Gross, if we hint at the husband, it will make Herr Haaf happy and calm down the city."

Volker rolled his eyes. "You want me to charge Anton Gross for the murder of his wife based on no evidence?" He tried another angle. "Didn't Anton Gross's money help support the Munich Police Exhibition in Berlin a few years back? And Gross also helped finance the exhibition here in Munich. The Lord Mayor thanked him personally, if I recall correctly."

Brummer considered the facts that lay before him. Angering the Lord Mayor was not a good idea. "Our main concern is to keep panic out of the streets. I'm sure Stefan agrees with that as well."

"Of course," Roddewig thought out loud. "So maybe there's no need to arrest or charge him. All we have to do is implicate him. Cast suspicion and let rumors do the rest."

Volker said, "Idle gossip, Stefan?" The Kommandant shrugged. "This is all very premature. Let me work on the case a while longer before we take such drastic actions."

"And then if you do investigate and still come up empty?" asked Brummer.

"Idle gossip . . ." Volker nodded at his superiors. "With minimal effort, Herr Direktor, that can be done."

TEN

✠ In Munich, there were beer halls for tourists and beer halls for the locals. The Old City had the former establishments: Das Kellnerhaus, located in the southern area of Giesing, fell into the latter category. As soon as Berg stepped inside, he was enveloped in an intense cloud of heat, smoke, and grease. Mixing in with the odor of frying sausage and tobacco was the stink of sweat and gases pouring out from the raucous crowd of workingmen enjoying a hearty lunch. With all those bodies, it would have been noisy even without the band. Factoring in the din from the brass musicians and accordion player, the clamor was deafening. But few if any noticed the drawbacks because the place was warm, the beer was cheap, the food was good, and the atmosphere was home.

It took only a few moments for Berg's eyes to adjust from the outside glare to the interior's weak lighting. Although the shutters were open all the way, the afternoon sunlight was minimal. The decor was dark: dark wooden paneling on the walls, dark wooden floors, dark wooden ceiling planks and rafters. In Germany, the Black Forest was not just a name but a way of life.

The single room was packed with endless rows of benches and trestle tables holding people who sat shoulder to shoulder. Deft waiters in lederhosen and agile waitresses in dirndls carried multiple mugs of beer while balancing platters of food. Faces soaked with perspiration, they worked with efficiency and speed. Once Berg spotted Ulrich and Georg, he had to dodge the harried help just to walk from the door to where his colleagues were sitting. Berg managed to squeeze himself a place on the bench. The tabletop held plates of cold cuts, cheese, rye bread, and pretzels. Within seconds, a filled beer stein was plopped in front of his face.

After draining it, Berg shouted, "We can't talk business in here."

"So first we eat and then we talk," Georg Müller shouted back.

That made sense. Berg heaped cold cuts and cheese on his plate, slathered a slice of rye with butter, and proceeded to wolf the food down without even registering the taste. A few minutes later he devoured a pretzel. With his stomach satisfied, he nursed a beer until he reached his thirty-minute time limit. The heat was stifling, the racket was overwhelming, and the smells began to play havoc with his digestive juices. After paying his tab, he got up, signaling for the others to follow.

Outside it was cool and windy, but the bitter chill had lifted. A block down was a small *Platz* where a coffeehouse had set up a half-dozen tables outside. Berg pointed to an empty spot.

"How about here?"

"Then we have to order coffee," Storf groused.

Berg sat down. "I'll take care of the tab."

"Then I won't complain." Storf took a seat. "Shouldn't we go inside?"

"It's more private out here, I think." Berg looked

around. The *Platz* was across the street from a small public garden. The trees were still bare, but the flower beds had been planted with tulips. "Drink something hot if you're cold." He rubbed his hands.

Storf pointed out, "You are cold as well. We should have waited out the crowd at Das Kellnerhaus."

"That would have been impossible, Ulrich; the place is always jammed. At least here we don't have to breathe in the stenches of farts and belches."

Storf bristled. "If you want effete university intellectuals, Berg, go to a Kabarett in Berlin and sip absinthe. A Munich beer hall is strictly for real people—those who eat and belch and fart and fuck."

"Pigs eat and belch and fart and fuck."

"That could explain why we eat so much pig," Müller said, laughing.

"There is nothing wrong with taking an occasional shower," Berg said.

"Yes, that would be fine, Axel," Storf said. "Showering in freezing temperatures and catching a death of a cold. Some of us don't have indoor plumbing."

"Besides, who sweats in the winter?" Müller added.

"My nose tells me many people sweat." Berg pulled up the collar on his coat. "Putting up with a little nip is better than the stink of bodies and tobacco."

"You are too delicate for this city," Storf commented. "The Brownshirts will eat you up."

"The Brownshirts are nothing but punks."

"Why you'd want to think of yourself as Kosmopolit is beyond me." Storf shrugged. "To be associated with *those* kinds of people."

"You mean the Jews?"

"The Jews, the Kommunisten, the intellectuals. They are subversive. In this climate, Berg, it is not good to be associated with subversives."

"I am considered subversive because I don't join up with a bunch of hooligans—"

"Shhhh . . ." Müller silenced him. "Giesing is his domain."

"So why do we come here?" Berg complained. "It's dangerous, stinks of garbage and horse dung, and the Austrian has spies breathing down our necks."

"And where would you suggest we go, Axel?" Müller said. "Not all of us have married so well."

"Your runaway mind has grossly exaggerated my financial condition."

Storf said, "You have a two-bedroom apartment, you have indoor plumbing, you have electricity, and you have a building with heat. That is rich by our blood."

Berg rolled his eyes. "Let's just order." He signaled for the waitress, a bored, heavyset woman in a blue working dress. He ordered coffee for all and a plate of pastries.

But Storf would not let the discussion end. "Why do you insist on defending degenerates?"

"I do not defend degenerates; I defend intellectualism. There is nothing degenerative about being educated."

"Except that all the universities are overrun with Jews."

"They are educated."

"They are subversive." Müller grew angry. "What is your affinity for those who steal from good German citizens, Berg?"

"Ask him about a young woman, Georg, of a certain subversive persuasion," Ulrich said under his breath.

"You!" Berg pointed a finger at Storf. "That's quite enough!"

Ulrich knew he had gone too far. He held out his hands defensively. Müller's smile had turned into a wide grin. "Ah . . . at last you make sense. Little kitty is very hard to resist, no matter where it comes from. I must ask you who she is or else I threaten to go to your wife."

"That is a fart without wind, Georg," Berg answered listlessly. "I know at least two 'working' Fräulein who take money from you."

"I see we must have women in common."

"Not quite."

"Yes, that's true. Even I wouldn't lower myself to fuck a Jew."

"You might if you saw this one." Storf brushed off Berg's glaring eyes. "I am only defending you, Inspektor."

"Ah, Axel, please!" Müller said. "Don't give the impression that you're sweet on her. It is bad to fall in love with whores."

"Especially subversive Jewish ones," Storf added. "The next thing you know she'll be talking revolution."

Fortunately, the waitress returned with three cups of coffee and a tray of sweets. Berg picked up a poppy-seed cookie and took a bite, chewing slowly as he thought about how to defuse the situation. He wanted to punch them both in the face, but it was best to keep emotions hidden in these uncertain times. "I am protective of my property, including my whores." Berg forced the words out of his mouth. "Especially one so young."

Storf broke into a venal smile. "Yes, women run dry very quickly. And how old is she? Fifteen? Sixteen?"

"You're repulsive." Berg laughed it off, but in truth

Margot wasn't much older. Although she had been eighteen for at least three months, the affair had started over a year ago. Blood rose to his cheeks. He hid his embarrassment behind his coffee cup.

Müller said, "The youngest girl I ever fucked—I mean fucked as a man—was thirteen. She was a Gypsy. And she wasn't even a virgin. Gypsies fuck very young."

Ulrich said, "How was she?"

"Dark," Müller said. "Very dark. Dark all over except pink where it counted: pink and swollen and ready. I went through a stage . . . I fucked many Gypsy girls. But now . . ." His voice dropped to a whisper. "It is too dangerous. Though not as satisfying, it is safer to be content with the old German whores."

"Why not a young German whore?" Storf asked.

"A money issue."

"Not Axel's problem," Storf added.

Berg said, "And exactly how would I explain to my wife that I'm spending her money on whores?"

"I'm sure she doesn't ask for an accounting." Storf picked up a tiny cream-filled shell and popped it into his mouth. "How much does she cost you . . . your young one?"

Berg looked away. "Cigarettes, beer, an occasional trinket . . . the usual." He gave them both the heat and fury of his eyes. "May we talk about Anna Gross?"

"Murdered by strangulation," Storf began.

"Did you ever find her shoe?"

"I didn't know I was to look for it."

"We found nothing that appeared to belong to her in the area," Müller joined in. "No articles of clothing."

"No shoe, then."

"No."

"No coat?"

"No."

"A pocketbook?"

"Nothing means nothing, Berg."

"She had semen in her," Storf said. "Professor Kolb verified it with his microscope at the crime scene. What I can't explain is how this pregnant woman managed to leave the house in evening attire without her husband knowing she was gone. It seems to me that her husband must have known she was gone."

"Maybe he didn't know until she came home," Müller said. "He catches her as she sneaks in, and confronts her. Then he kills her and drags her body to the park and calls the police to cover up his crime."

"It is certainly plausible. But what about the shoe?" Berg brought up. The two men regarded the Inspektor. "Why would her husband remove her shoe? Why would he take her coat?"

"Why would anyone remove her shoe?" Storf asked.

"Because there are some perverted people who like to collect mementos of their victims."

"You read too many lurid stories from those cheap magazines."

Berg shrugged. "There is a witness who may have seen Anna last night with a man. They appeared to be intimate."

Müller sneered. "With so many wives whoring, is it any wonder that we good German men seek others for solace?"

"Can we keep the discussion on Anna Gross, *please*?" Finally having their attention, Berg spoke about his conversation with Gerhart Leit, then revealed the sketch of Anna's phantom companion. The men studied it in earnest.

Berg said, "He looks familiar, doesn't he?"

"He looks like a thousand people," Storf said.

True enough. Berg continued. "In answer to your question, Ulrich, about how she could have escaped her husband's notice . . . what about a sleeping potion in his nighttime tea or drink?"

Storf said, "Except she went to bed before he did."

"Obviously she didn't *stay* in bed," Müller said.

"A trusted servant could have slipped something in his beverage," Berg answered. "After Herr Gross fell into a deep sleep, someone could have informed Anna Gross that it was safe to go out."

"I reckon it's a possibility," Müller said.

"I will go back to the house of Herr Gross," Berg announced. "I think it will serve me better if I speak to the help. Usually it is the chambermaid who knows if her mistress has access to laudanum or some other sleeping medicine."

The trio drank coffee.

Müller said, "Are you going to show Herr Gross your little sketch?"

"He will only deny knowing the man," Berg answered. "The help is another matter. Especially the women. They are more open to police questions, no?" Berg checked his pocket watch and frowned. It was well past two o'clock. "We talk too much about trivia. Herr Gross is with Volker identifying Anna. I can't make it back before the husband."

"So go tomorrow morning," Müller said. "Your mind will be refreshed by a good night's sleep."

"But Gross will be home, planning the funeral. I need to talk to the help when he is gone."

Storf said, "You must look for an opportunity, Axel. I'm sure the Jew will have business to tidy up. Just be patient."

Müller said, "And how do you intend to get Anna's chambermaid to speak about such personal matters?"

"My dear Georg, you don't start out talking about personal matters, you segue into them only after you've sufficiently charmed the lady in question."

"And if your charm fails, Berg?"

"It is well known that many in the Munich police are not only sympathetic to the Austrian's cause but also well versed in his hooligan methods." Berg stowed the picture in his pocket. "The threat of a night in jail will be enough to loosen the tightest of lips."

ELEVEN

✠ When Berg returned to the Ett Strasse station, it was just past three. Awaiting him were two officially stamped envelopes on his desktop. If that didn't speak for German efficiency, what did?

Immediately, he took out a green folder containing a homicide file—a *Mordakte*—for Anna Gross. Also inside were eight postmortem photographs taken at the scene, all of them very clear, very focused, and very obscene. The second package was paperwork, an extensive report on the cause of Anna's death by strangulation. Also detailed were other marks and bruises on her body. Fresh indentation marks were found around her arm and wrist, made from fingertips squeezing flesh. She had tried to escape? Maybe he held her back.

The other papers were mainly lists: items found at the crime scene, names of suspects, names of potential witnesses. To all of this, Berg added his own notes, his own interviews and reports as well as the original sketch he'd drafted under Gerhart Leit's instructions. In order not to ruin the drawing by repeated exposure, Berg copied the face into his notebook, comparing the two versions, making them as close as possible. By the time the church bells chimed out the six o'clock hour, Anna Gross's homicide file had developed girth. Berg had been working for over twelve hours. He was tired and dirty and thirsty. A pint of beer would go down very smoothly.

But unlike most men after a hard day's work, he didn't head for the nearest beer hall. Nor did he take steps to go home. His decision was dictated by drives other than hunger pangs. She worked just a few blocks away from the station.

Proximity was how they had met. They had both been eating lunch in a nearby square. It had been a stunning autumn day, the sky cloudless and blue, the leaves in full color. The air had been crisp and cool at that turning point when the bite of winter started sinking its fangs into the bone marrow. She had been wrapped in a tattered wool coat with a scarf around her neck and a ski cap on her head. Her teeth were chattering. Her hands were encased in mittens, but her exposed nose had turned bright red. Had he known from the start that she was a Jewess, Berg wouldn't have bothered, but her looks were deceptive with her fair complexion and her bright blue eyes. He had offered her some hot coffee from his thermos, and they started talking.

One month later, they wound up in bed.

Margot worked in a small textile factory in the Isarvorstadt region—a swampy, low area where the banks of the Isar did little to stem the rising waters when the skies opened like faucets. It was a neighborhood of flooded streets and poverty, teeming with East European immigrants. The conditions were crowded, sanitation was poor, disease was rampant, and crime was pervasive. Still, roses grew in the most adverse of conditions.

The mill was hot and humid from the steam used to press the cloth, from the sweat of its workers: the weavers, dyers, laundresses, and pressers. The plant made many textiles, but specialized in the blue fabric that made up the typical *Arbeitsmaid-Kleid*—the farm-girl dress. It was Margot's job to press the fabric. Then she sent it down the assembly line where somebody else rolled the yards around square bolts or cardboard dowels for wholesale distribution.

It used to be that whenever Berg wanted to see her, he sent a messenger with instructions telling her when and where. In the past few months, however, he had turned bold, walking into the plant unannounced and right up to Margot's station, throwing his arms around her small waist and kissing her neck with the passion of ownership. She would scold him, of course, just as she was scolding him now.

"Not here!"

"Then come outside."

"I am working," she told him.

"It is past six."

"I know, but if I don't finish this job, he will fire me."

"How much longer?"

"Maybe ten minutes."

"I will wait," Berg said.

She smiled at him, perspiration covering her face. A hand, burned and roughened, settled gently on his forearm. "Then wait outside. Your association with me hurts both of us."

Berg regarded her pink, round wet face. Her long, curly hair was covered by a white cap. She was wearing a blue dress made out of the fabric she was pressing, a white apron tied around her waist. Her fingertips were callused. He kissed her palm, his tongue gently licking her skin. "Ten minutes, huh?"

"Yes, please."

He loved the urgency of her voice. Everything she did was urgent, as if time were running out. "Very well, then. At our usual spot?"

"Yes. Please. Go before my boss sees you."

Reluctantly, Berg left and stepped outside, into the dark made bitter by icy drizzle. The usual spot was a cigarette house—a front for prostitution. The police knew about these establishments, but since many frequented them, arrests were never made. He waited for her, tapping his foot, smoking a cigarette, biding the time of anticipation. Finally, he saw an outline coming his way. Still, he didn't recognize her until she was a few feet in front of him, the blackness was that thick.

Reacting instantly, Berg scooped her up and kissed her fiercely, driving her hand between his legs.

She pulled it away. "My God, you're forward."

"And you stink of sweat."

"So do you," she retorted. "But at least I come by my sweat honestly. What beer hall took my money this time, Axel?"

"*Your* money?"

Margot raised an eyebrow. "What did you bring me?"

He reached in his coat pocket and pulled out a tin of cigarettes.

"And?"

"And?" He frowned. "That's not enough?"

She pouted. "The cigarettes are used up, and then I have nothing to show for it. I want something I can hold in my hand."

"Something you can swap for money."

"I can swap cigarettes for money, silly man."

"How about this, then?" With flash, he pulled out the feathered fan he had pilfered from the crime scene.

Her eyes widened. "Oh my gracious!" She gasped. "It is so beautiful!" She grabbed it, fanning her neck made wet by heat and steam and now drizzle. "Does it suit me?"

"Perfectly."

She threw her arms around his neck and kissed him hard. Her smile was radiant. "Thank you very much. But now I must do something for you."

"I can't stay long, Margot."

"It doesn't take long, Axel."

He wagged a finger at her. "Naughty girl."

"And aren't you happy that I am." She hooked her arm around his and together they crossed the street and went into a dilapidated rooming house. The man at the counter was fat, florid, and bored, picking dirt out of his nails. His eyes went first to her face, then to Berg's. He held the key aloft. Berg paid the fee, the entire transaction done without a word spoken.

Their third-floor room was dank and moldy. The decor consisted of a pitcher and bowl for washing hands and a bed covered by a worn feather duvet. The bedsprings were noisy, but as she had stated, it didn't take long. Afterward, she leaped up and started to dress, pulling on her garter belt and securing it around her hips.

"I hate this," Axel said. "This dirty room, this dirty bed . . . sneaking about like a couple of thieves."

"You're married." She rolled a stocking over her leg, then looked in his eyes. "You're married, you have children, and I'm a Jewess. It is suicide for both of us to have more."

"You don't aim high enough, my dear." Berg pulled up

his trousers and buttoned his fly. "If you don't dream, you will always be at the bottom of the heap."

"Sometimes dreams turn to nightmares." She put on her other stocking and hitched it to her garter belt. Then she slipped her dress over her head. "Aren't you happy with what we have?"

"Of course I'm happy. You're so beautiful, Margot. You deserve better."

"You're enamored of youth, not of me."

"Not true! If it were just youth, you think I'd randomly take up with a Jewess?"

"I don't cost as much as the young Christian whores."

"Stop that, Margot, you are not a whore."

"Ask my mother. She will tell you differently."

Berg stared at her. "Your mother knows?"

"Of course she knows! Everyone knows. Don't be naive."

He stared at her.

She became irritated. "Axel, you can't keep coming to my workplace and not arouse suspicions." She took out a compact and started smoothing her curls. "My mother is very upset by it. She tells me that I am not a good marriage candidate. What kind of Jewish boy will tolerate a girl who has been pricked by an uncircumcised snake."

He winced at her words. "I have to go."

"So go."

But he didn't. Instead, he continued to sit on the feather bed. He placed his hand on his forehead, massaged his temples. Within minutes, she sat next to him, her lithe body still smelling of sex. "Don't be mad."

"Your mother is right." He kissed her cheek. "You should get married."

She stared at him. "Ah . . . you want to end it?"

"That's not what I said."

"So why this talk about me getting married?"

His stomach dropped. "I can't give you what you want."

She responded with anger. "Such arrogance. You don't even *know* what I want."

He didn't answer. Perhaps he had been flattering himself this past year.

"You shouldn't even be with me," Margot said coldly. "There are Brownshirts everywhere . . . especially within the ranks of the police."

He looked at her. "I'm not worried."

"You should be." She lit up two cigarettes and gave him one. "They are everywhere. It's no wonder the Nazis have so many young boys as fans. Fist first, they take whatever they want."

His face registered concern. "They bother you, Margot? Tell me who they are and I will take care of it."

She laughed cheerlessly. "Don't bother. As soon as one is gone, another will come along to take his place." She bit her lip. "Every week that passes, the Austrian gains more power. You really shouldn't come by anymore."

"Is that *your* way of saying we should end it?"

She laughed again, her chortle made throaty from cigarette smoke. Then she took his hand and placed it between her legs, still wet from their lovemaking. "No one makes me feel like you do. The very thought of you makes me sizzle. It is why I continue to put us both in danger." They kissed long and hard. Still, it was she who broke away. "I must go."

"It will pass, Margot," Berg told her. "Hitler has his followers, but the rest of the country is not like Bavaria. The rest of Germany is more . . . worldly. He will pass."

Margot's eyes flooded with tears. "I hope you're right. I fear that you're not. You shouldn't come anymore."

There was no power behind her words. They both knew that he'd be back.

TWELVE

✠ The haze rose above his lips, enveloping his nose and eyes in a nicotine fog. Inhaling deeply, then breathing out slowly, he took it all in: the outline of her swaying hips, her sinewy arms, her curls bouncing as she threw her head back in hearty laughter. Though he couldn't see that well in the darkness, he was aware of her neck—smooth, long, skin as pale as alabaster. From this distance, she looked small, but still, her silhouette suggested nothing other than luscious curves. For a moment, the two of them drew close. Seconds later, they drew apart. She returned to her drudgery, and he hurried back to hearth and home.

He took another puff of his cigarette, enjoying the sting in his throat and continuing to stare at the space once occupied by two lovers. His gloves shielded his hands from the cold, and his hat protected his head. He was utterly alone.

There was no one waiting at his flat, no solicitous wife, no sticky-fingered children, no gregarious dog. Only room after room, meticulous in style and in perfect taste, but static nonetheless. Tonight he longed for the music of raucous laughter, for passionate kisses, sweat-soaked skin, and parted legs, revealing all that was warm and wet and womanly.

It had been a taxing day. Despite his best efforts, the

afternoon papers were already screaming out the murder in their headlines. A little levity was in order to calm the nerves.

He threw his cigarette onto the ground and crushed it out with his heel. He turned up the collar of his overcoat and crossed the street, heading toward the factory.

✜ ✜ ✜

JOACHIM SOPPED UP the last bits of gravy with his brown bread, then longingly eyed his father's pork cutlet. "You're not hungry, Papa?"

There was no response.

Britta cleared her throat. "Axel, the boy is talking to you."

Berg blinked several times. He leaned over and brushed an errant curl from Joachim's forehead. "Sorry, I'm distracted."

"Yes," Britta agreed. "You haven't touched your dinner, no matter that it's the first time that we've had solid meat in two weeks. And your left hand keeps drifting from the table. How can we teach the children manners if we don't model them?"

Berg cut the meat in two pieces. "I am very aware of what you've done to acquire such fare, and I thank you, Britta. I'm just not particularly hungry." He put half of his cutlet onto Joachim's plate, then sliced off a forkful for himself, careful to keep his left hand on the tabletop as he ate.

"It's delicious." Chewing thoroughly, Berg decided it really was delicious . . . cooked to perfection. He was stupid for giving away half to his son, whose appetite had grown to gargantuan proportions. The boy ate so quickly he scarcely had time to taste. Berg was convinced the child would have been equally content wolfing down shoe leather.

Joachim finished his meat and was already staring at his sister's plate. "Leave Monika's food alone," Berg told him. "And keep your left hand on the table." He looked at his daughter. "Both of you."

"It would be criminal to waste the meat," Joachim said. "She never finishes."

"You never *let* me finish," Monika retorted. "I'm a slow eater."

"Let her be, Joachim," Berg ordered. If there were leftovers to be had, he'd eat them. In the meantime, he'd have to be content with potatoes and cabbage. Britta had seasoned the vegetables with salt, pepper, paprika, and butter. They melted in his mouth. "So what is happening in the lives of the Berg family?"

"What happened with the hooligans, Father?" Joachim asked.

The hooligans? That was this morning? It seemed like ages ago. "I told you they will not bother us again."

Joachim smiled. "You put them in jail?"

"No, they're too young." Berg winked at his son. "But we have ways to ensure their good behavior."

Again Joachim beamed. It was validating to be a hero to someone.

"The food is excellent," Berg told his wife. "You should be a professional chef."

"You seem cheery tonight," Britta said.

There was accusation in her voice. Did his pleasure show that much? "I am happy not to be working," he countered. "It was not a routine day."

Britta backed off. "Now you look hungry, Axel; I can fry you up some sausage."

"Take mine, Papa," Monika broke in. "Joachim is right. I never finish."

"That's a good girl," Berg told her. "I'll take whatever you don't want."

Monika gave him her leftovers. "We saw the camel today. And the *Niggerlippen*."

"Right," Berg said. "How was that?"

Joachim broke in. "They put on an exhibition of an African village with grass huts and stuffed wild animals in the background. They had people banging on drums, saying it was authentic African music. But the musicians weren't Africans—just people in black makeup. The camel smelled. It was pretty stupid."

"I liked the *Niggerlippen*. He was tall and purple and very full of muscles and had big white teeth." Monika spoke with enthusiasm.

"What did he do in this exhibition?"

"Mostly just sat around," Joachim said.

"He shot a bow and arrow," Monika told him. "And he could talk."

"Of course he could talk," Joachim said disdainfully. "He isn't an animal."

"He looks like an animal. He wore a grass skirt and had paint on his face and looked very wild."

"He is a famous actor in Africa," Joachim told her.

"How do you know that?" Monika asked.

"He told me. We talked. He speaks decent German."

"He speaks German?" Monika was wide-eyed.

Joachim rolled his eyes. "I drew a picture of him."

"A very good one," Britta said.

"Would you like to see it, Father?" Joachim asked.

"Yes, of course," Berg told him.

As Joachim got up from the table, it seemed to Berg that the lad grew by the hour. As thin as a reed, though; his growth was concentrated in height rather than girth. Berg regarded his daughter, who gave him a lovely, serene smile. She was small for her age and a bit on the immature side. Already, Monika's friends were preoccupied with gossip. She seemed more content to pass her time by reading and drawing.

The boy returned with a very detailed drawing. The rendering wasn't perfect—the eyes were too wide for the face, the mouth too big as well, but the expression spoke volumes. The face was fierce with intense eyes, but nonetheless sad, as evidenced by the downturned mouth.

Monika looked at the picture. "Where's the bone in his nose?"

"It wasn't a real bone," Joachim said.

"It looked real."

"It was a real bone, but it didn't really go through his nose. It was like the arrow through the head that you see on *Fasching*."

"Bone or not, the picture is excellent," Berg told him.

"Better than those awful flowers I did when I was ten," Joachim said. "Why do you insist on keeping them framed and on the wall?"

"I like the flowers. They're happy."

"I was happy when I was ten."

Berg regarded his son. "You're not happy now?"

"He's growing up, Axel," Britta broke in. "Life is not about pretty colors and flowers." She stared at the portrait over her husband's shoulder. "Look at the *Niggerlippen*.

He seems so dispirited." She picked up a pile of plates. "No doubt from living in Munich. I'm sure in Africa there isn't a shortage of meat."

Berg smiled. "Just a shortage of food in general. The famine is terrible there. Not to mention water."

"There is water in Africa," Britta said. "What about the Nile?"

"The continent is filled with barren deserts."

"And us, sitting in the breadbasket of Europe, we have plenty of cheap food?"

"The farmers do."

"A lot of good that does us here in the city." She picked up another plate. "I will clear the table, Joachim will wash, and Monika, you can dry. Afterward, if you finish your homework, we can all listen to *Liebe und Leben an der Welt*."

"What will Father do?" Joachim asked. "He dislikes radio dramas."

"Not all of them, just the bad ones," Berg said. "That's a bad one."

"Father will do whatever he wants to do," Britta responded. "Why should anything change around here?"

✠ ✠ ✠

BERG STARED as his bedside wick fluttered, burst with sudden light, then faded to black. He put his book on the floor, then stretched out in their soft feather bed. The shutters were still open, revealing a city in repose. Scattered yellow lights twinkled in the fog, but otherwise all was still. Britta was silent and motionless, but Berg knew she was awake. He shifted onto his side and brought her into his arms, her firm backside resting against his stomach. He laid his hand upon her breast covered by a flannel nightgown. When she didn't object, he removed his hand and brought it under the cloth, making contact with her bare skin.

"*Ach,* your hands are cold!" Britta complained.

"But you are warm." He worked his fingers between her legs. "Very warm."

"I am not a blanket!" She swatted his hand. "Go away!"

"Don't be nasty."

"I shouldn't be nasty? I work until I'm dead with exhaustion, and what do I get for it?"

"You get all my love."

Abruptly, Britta turned to face him. "Don't insult me."

Berg stared into her angry eyes. "And you . . . don't insult *me.*"

She searched his face for sincerity, but found nothing in his steely orbs. His eyes were locked on hers; his face still as handsome as on the day they married. He was a cheater and a liar, but what of it? He worked steadily, he didn't drink away his earnings, and he had never laid a hand on her in anger. She had the ring, the home, the children, and the security. His whores had nothing.

Slowly, she brushed her lips against those of her husband of sixteen years. She ran her hand down his chest onto his rock-solid abdomen. He hadn't gone fat like so many of his colleagues in the department. She patted his belly. "Very good."

"I'm glad you approve."

They exchanged smiles.

He helped her off with her nightgown.

It was an act filled with passion, though not a word of love was exchanged between them.

THIRTEEN

In his starched and pressed uniform, the butler was trying to maintain the decorum in keeping with his station. Nevertheless, his practiced bland expression of yesterday had turned into vinegar. It was painful for him to deal with police matters so early in the morning. "Herr Gross is indisposed."

Berg gave a hint of a smile. "I am aware of that, Haslinger. He isn't even here. That means I am here for other reasons. May I come in, please?"

"It is not my place to allow that, Herr Inspektor. I must insist that you come back another time."

The white-headed servant's obstinacy was easily surmountable. "Then you leave me no choice, Haslinger. I shall wait in the lobby in full uniform for all the neighbors to see. Don't blame me when the gossip starts."

"It has already started."

"Then it is a good idea not to add any more fodder, no?"

The butler's sour face darkened. Vanquished, he stepped aside. Berg came into the apartment. "Would you mind if I took off my coat?"

"I wouldn't be getting too comfortable, sir."

"You don't like my company, Haslinger?"

"What I like is of no consequence."

"Not to me." Berg removed his coat and offered it to the butler. "Please?"

Haslinger tapped his foot, then took the coat. "What do you want?"

"Frau Gross had a personal chambermaid. I'd like to talk to her."

"She is busy."

"Then interrupt her. She may have been one of the last people to see Frau Gross alive. After all, her mistress wasn't feeling well when she went to bed. Maybe she brought Frau Gross some tea and a biscuit to relieve her stomach."

"And why would that be important?"

"To establish a time schedule, for one thing. I wouldn't bother if it weren't important."

Haslinger hefted Berg's coat. "Wait here, Inspektor. And I do mean wait *here* and not in the great room."

The butler snorted, leaving Berg alone with his thoughts. It was unlikely that Frau Gross's chambermaid had served her anything last night. Frau Gross wasn't sick. She'd gone out. Berg had hopes that the maid might know something about the secret man. He stopped his musings when he saw Haslinger approaching. The coat was gone: a good sign that he was being allowed to stay.

"I have arranged for you to meet with Fräulein Astrid Mauer in Frau Gross's withdrawing room. She is understandably upset; therefore, please be brief." He looked at Berg's shoes and sniffed disdainfully. "May I clean those for you, sir?" He glanced at the immaculate white marble floors. "Now?"

"Too kind." Berg removed his shoes and handed them

to the butler, who took them with grave trepidation. "Thank you in advance."

Again Haslinger sniffed. "This way, Herr Inspektor."

Berg had expected the young wife's parlor to be dark and heavy and out-of-date Victorian. But of course, that wasn't the image painted of Anna by her brother. The withdrawing room was very much in keeping with the few facts he had gleaned about her—a Kabarett girl who had flirted with Kommunismus. The space was avant-garde and done up in excellent taste.

The silk wallpaper had a sage-green background with hand-painted twigs of cherry blossoms at random intervals. For seating, Frau Gross had chosen a gilt wood-frame and tapestry suite: a love seat, a chair, and an ottoman. The upholstery was a swirl of multihued oranges, greens, and golds, Japanese inspired but French executed. Between two tall mullioned windows sat a bombé palissander-veneered commode inlaid with Macassar ebony flowers and mother-of-pearl blossoms. The artwork on the walls included Cubist interpretations: a figure in gold and greens by Aleksandr Archipenko, a woodcut on Japanese paper by Walter Dexel, a mélange of objects by Pablo Picasso, and a red sphere painted on aluminum by László Moholy-Nagy.

An older woman stood next to the Dexel, teary-eyed but composed. Garbed in a black uniform with a crisp white apron, she appeared to be in her forties with a trim figure but a wrinkled face. Loose skin sat above and below her eyes, and bunched at her mouth. Her ears were quite prominent. Despite her deficits, she cut a handsome image. Her chest was ample, and with a little more rouge and a lot more lipstick and flash, she could have been a Madam.

"*Grüss Gott,*" she said quietly.

"*Guten Tag.*" Berg bowed his head. "Fräulein Mauer? Inspektor Berg here."

"It is Astrid." She tried out a weak smile. "Please sit, Inspektor. May I offer you something to drink?"

"Thank you, but no." A pause. "If you continue to stand, so will I."

They both sat. Berg chose the settee; the woman rested on the ottoman, her spine straight, her hands in her lap.

"I would like to ask you a few questions, Fräulein Mauer."

The woman waited.

"Herr Gross informed me that his wife took to bed early two nights ago."

"Yes."

"Do you know what time, Fräulein Mauer?"

"Early. No later than nine."

The woman's eyes lowered to her lap as she spoke, a sign that she was being less than honest. Berg nodded. "Nine, you say."

"Yes."

"Herr Gross said around eight."

"Then I'm sure my recollection is wrong."

"Mistaken, Fräulein Mauer, mistaken."

The woman smiled. "Mistaken, then."

"You were Frau Gross's personal maid, yes?" Berg asked.

"Yes."

"And how long have you worked for Frau Gross?"

"From the beginning of the marriage." Her eyes moistened. "I had worked for Frau Gross—the elder Frau Gross—before coming to Herr Anton's home."

"And your relationship with your patron?"

"It is . . ." A pause and a clearing of the throat. "It was very good, I think."

"Tell me your impressions of the young lady."

The chambermaid replied, "Why are you interested in my opinions? They mean nothing."

"Perhaps they mean nothing to certain people, but to me they mean much."

The woman smiled. "I was brought here by Herr Anton Gross. A lovelier man does not exist. I think he has a problem, though—his mother. She became Anna's problem as well. While I have only the utmost respect for the elder Frau Gross, she can be opinionated. That can be hard on a new bride. And when the man is put in the middle—between mother and wife—oh dear, it can be very trying."

"Mother-in-law and daughter-in-law did not get along?"

Astrid's voice dropped to a whisper. "Occasionally words were exchanged. There were problems from the start. Herr Gross is an upstanding citizen, but very conservative. Anna . . . Frau Gross was a liberal. . . ." The voice was even more hushed. "A free spirit. While Herr Gross was tolerant of her youth, Frau Gross was not."

She paused.

"I talk too much." She fidgeted. "You mustn't tell anyone this. I would lose my position for gossiping. It's just that Anna was so dear. . . ."

"Fräulein Mauer, tell me about Frau Gross's friends."

"Call me Astrid."

"Very well, Astrid. Who came to call on Frau Gross?"

"Frau Hultner . . . Frau Grün . . . they live close by."

"These women. They are your mistress's age?"

"Yes, I think. Frau Hultner maybe is a little older."

"Any other friends?"

"Many, but the names escape me right now."

"And men?"

The woman bristled. "Of course not."

Berg let the words resonate. Then he leaned over. "And you're positive of this?"

"Yes!" More fidgeting. "Yes!"

"You were close to Frau Gross, yes?"

"Of course."

"So if Anna had a secret liaison, you would have known?"

"Frau Gross was a proper wife, Inspektor. If I implied otherwise, I am deeply sorry."

"Ah, yes. And if I mistook your words, I am deeply sorry. It's just that whoever did this . . . stole her life from her. This animal should not go unpunished. You agree with this, I'm sure."

"Certainly." Astrid gazed at her lap. "I adored Frau Gross, but that doesn't mean I knew everything about her private life."

"So it is conceivable that she might have had friends that you were unaware of?"

"Of course."

Berg decided to get specific. From his jacket, he pulled out the sketch drawn by him under Gerhart Leit's guidance: pencil lines that featured a man with long, thin features and deep-set eyes. He showed the rendering to Astrid, and immediately she gasped.

"You recognize him, Astrid?" Berg asked.

It was useless for the woman to deny it. Playing very smart, she said nothing.

"Maybe he has been to the house?" Berg suggested.

Silence.

"Come, come. This was your mistress. You owe her your loyalty, even in death. *Especially* in death."

"I was always her staunchest supporter!" the woman protested. Then tears leaked from her eyes.

"Of course you were," Berg soothed. "You were no doubt the only woman in the world whom Anna could trust with her secrets. Please, Astrid. Tell me about this gentleman."

Her voice was hushed. "It was a while ago . . . two months . . . maybe even more. He called on her twice. The second time I asked Frau Gross who the gentleman was. She told me he was a politician. When I asked his party, she was very vague."

"One of Hitler's boys?"

"Good heavens, no!" Astrid cried. "Just the opposite. A Kommunist. He spoke with an ever-so-slight accent."

"Russian?"

"Maybe. They met in this very room while Herr Gross was at work . . . on a Wednesday in the afternoon . . . when Haslinger was off. They talked of politics and revolution. Frau Gross made me swear that I would not betray her secret to her husband, who was very conservative."

"Are you sure it wasn't only politics that was on their minds, Astrid?"

"Positive. I heard talking from behind the doors. A spirited discussion, not the sounds of infidelity. There was nothing improper about it."

"But you weren't there the entire time."

"No." Astrid blushed. "But there was nothing between them to suggest anything other than politics."

For the first time, Berg considered that Anna's death

might have been motivated by something other than sex. "And this man in the sketch . . . he looks like the gentleman who visited Anna?"

"Yes."

"And do you have a name for this man?"

"Frau Gross didn't introduce me."

"But surely he must have announced himself either verbally or with a calling card."

Astrid thought for a moment. "Yes . . . the first time he did bring a card."

"Did Frau Gross keep her calling cards?"

"Some." Astrid rose in one stiff movement. "Give me a moment, *bitte*."

She came back several minutes later with a stack of calling cards. As Berg flipped through them, he said, "Could you help me identify some of these names?"

"Of course." Astrid stood by his side. "He is Anna's uncle. That one is a cousin, another cousin, a friend, another cousin, an aunt, another cousin, another cousin—"

"She had quite a few male cousins who visited her," Berg remarked.

"Frau Gross was a vivacious woman." Astrid took out a handkerchief and wiped her eyes. "She charmed everyone who met her."

Berg recognized a name: Elisabeth Hultner. "This is her friend who lived nearby?"

"Yes."

A visit would be in order. "May I keep the card?"

"Of course."

Berg riffled through the stack until he came upon a name that Astrid could not identify: Robert Schick.

Fräulein Mauer stared at the spelling. "I don't remember him."

Berg said, "Perhaps this is our Russian?"

Astrid stared at the card. "Schick isn't a Russian name."

"No, it isn't. May I keep the card?"

"If you think it will help. Again, I want to remind you that all of Frau Gross's visitors were respectable people."

"And is there any reason to think that this man—Herr Schick—is anything less than a gentleman?"

"I think he must be a gentleman worthy of the highest regard. I just don't remember him." She tapped her forehead. "An old woman."

"I don't think so." Berg smiled at her and pocketed the cards. "I think you remember things very well."

They exchanged glances. She stood up. "I will see you out." She glanced at Berg's feet, and her eyes widened. A smile played on her lips.

"Haslinger was kind enough to clean my boots," Berg said. "I don't think he fancied my footprints on the clean white marble."

"Haslinger is meticulous. I will get them for you."

"Thank you."

She returned five minutes later holding footwear that Berg barely recognized. Astrid said, "Here you are. I hope the job is satisfactory."

"They have never looked so good."

Berg sat down to put them on.

Investigating rich people had its perquisites.

❖ ❖ ❖

THE WHITE-HAIRED BUTLER turned the calling card over and over. He wasn't tall, but his thinness made him look that way. "Frau Hultner has retired to her chamber."

Berg pushed. "It is important."

The servant glanced at Berg's face, then at his shoes. "One moment."

He closed the door, leaving Berg to wait in the biting cold. He bounced up and down to keep warm. He rubbed his arms. He wrapped his wool scarf around his face. At least the bastard could have invited him inside to wait like a human instead of a horse. When the valet finally came back, it felt as if he had been gone an hour. In fact, it had been just under five minutes.

"You may come in now," he told Berg.

Shivering, Berg stepped across the threshold. *"Danke."*

"This way." The butler led him into a compact, French-style withdrawing room. The pastel blue room framed oval wall panels depicting idyllic outdoor scenes of nymphs and satyrs. The ornate furniture was thin and delicate, more eighteenth than nineteenth century. A rococo writing desk sat in front of a multipaned window, and a small harpsichord was placed next to a chevalier mirror. Berg chose to sit on a pink divan, the most substantial piece of furniture available to him. His teeth were chattering uncontrollably.

"Would you like some tea, Herr Inspektor?"

"Bitte."

Ten minutes later, a chambermaid brought in steaming-hot tea. It was cold by the time Frau Hultner finally decided to make an appearance. The woman wasn't so much lovely as she was well appointed—lissome and manicured, with chestnut hair cut in a pleasing manner. She wore a forest-green suit trimmed in sable about the collar and cuffs as well as around the hem of the jacket. Her shapely legs were encased in silk stockings, black pumps on her feet. Her skin was pale, although her cheeks were rouged. Her lips had been painted as well. Her eyes were the reason Berg knew something was wrong. The blue orbs were red-rimmed.

Her voice was throaty. *"Grüss Gott."*

Immediately, he stood. "Inspektor Axel Berg here."

"Yes, I read your card. More tea?" Without waiting for a response, she rang a bell. "I apologize for keeping you waiting."

"No, Frau Hultner, it is I who must apologize for my intrusion. I wouldn't have come unless I felt it was absolutely necessary."

"It is about Frau Gross? Anna?"

Berg nodded.

"Such a horrible thing. I can't stop thinking . . ." Her eyes filled with tears. "The poor, poor dear." She shook her head. "That could have been anyone. That could have been me!"

Berg regarded her. "Why would you say that?"

The eyes zeroed in on his. "Do you know how many times I have walked through the park?"

"Many, I am sure. But do you walk alone at night?"

Elisabeth gasped. "Anna was alone when it happened?"

"Possibly. I know she wasn't with her husband or brother."

Elisabeth looked the other way.

Berg jumped in. "We think she might have gone to the theater. One of the owners remembers seeing her accompanied by a man."

"Who?" Elisabeth asked anxiously.

"That is precisely why I have intruded on your privacy. I was hoping that you could provide that answer."

Tears began to fall as Elisabeth shook her head. "I can't help you. I'm sorry."

Berg looked at her intently. "Please, Frau Hultner. I know you don't want to besmirch her memory. I know she was your friend. But I ask you to reconsider. It is a moral and legal necessity to punish the wrongdoer, even at the expense of Frau Gross's memory."

"I would tell you if I knew." She looked at him with wet eyes. "But I don't." The chambermaid came in with a fresh, steaming teapot. "Not for me, Isolde." She looked at Berg. "Can I freshen your cup?"

"*Danke.*"

Isolde poured him a new cup. Berg sipped delicately, breathing in the hot, fragrant air. "Perhaps you didn't know a name . . . but maybe you knew that there was someone new in her life?"

"No, Anna was much too private to divulge such intimacy."

"But as a woman . . . you could tell."

At last, she relented. "I suspected."

"I thought so." Berg smiled. "What made you suspicious?"

Elisabeth laughed. "She was happy."

"Ah . . . Her marriage was not a . . . peaceful one?"

Elisabeth sighed and slipped on short gloves. "It wasn't filled with bitter rancor as far as I could tell. Anna was always . . . pleasant. But she suddenly turned lighthearted. Like a young girl instead of a married woman."

"She was a young girl."

"Who was trying very hard to be mature. She took her responsibilities very seriously. That was the Anna I knew in the beginning. Then suddenly . . . it was as if a cloud lifted. Gone was the good wife, replaced by a young girl again. If that wasn't love, then I don't know what love is."

"Maybe it was because she was expecting."

"She *was*?" Again, Elisabeth gasped. "Oh, that is awful! Poor, poor Anna. Poor Anton. She never said a word." She shook her head. "I'm sorry. I can't talk about this anymore. It is too upsetting. Furthermore, I must go meet my mother. I don't want her to see me in a state. She is old and worries too much."

"One more question if I may?"

"Hurry."

"Have you ever met a gentleman named Robert Schick? He may be Russian."

She thought a moment. "No. Was that Frau Gross's friend?"

"Maybe."

"I wouldn't be surprised if he was Russian. Of late, she began to talk politics . . . to the point of being boring. I'm sorry. I really must leave."

"Thank you for your time. May I walk you to the streetcar or secure you a taxi?"

"I have an automobile, actually. Can I take you to your destination, Inspektor?"

"I am not too far from the station house."

"But it is cold outside. I am happy to take you to the station house . . . as my civic duty." Elisabeth picked up a brown leather purse, extracted a silk scarf, then snapped it shut. She covered her hair and wound the scarf around her chin. "I insist. Let's go."

Berg managed a smile though he was in quite a dilemma: to freeze in the cold or to trust a woman behind the wheel of a motorcar.

✠   ✠   ✠

"SUCCESS!" Berg announced as he walked into the *Mordkommission* room at the Ett Strasse station. Georg hadn't arrived, but Ulrich was at his desk, looking very busy. It was more like preoccupied. "Not only do I suspect that Anna Gross was having an affair, I might actually have a name to go with the anonymous face that I drew under Gerhart Leit's direction. Good news, eh?"

"Good news, yes . . ." Ulrich looked up at Berg. "But it hardly takes away the bad news. They've found another body."

"Ach, mein Gott!" Berg choked out. "You can't be serious! Where?"

"Not at the Englischer Garten but close to it. The woman was found on the banks of the Isar in a tangle of brush. Apparently, she was dressed up in an evening gown."

"Just like the first one." Berg sat down, dejected. "I'm . . ."

"Shocked?"

"That's a good word, yes."

Ulrich sat back in his chair. "I reckon it could be a coincidence."

"I hope so. Because if it isn't, I pray that this does not represent a killer's pattern."

Storf licked his lips. "That would be something, wouldn't it. A Haarmann in Munich."

Said without much emotion.

But wasn't that just like his people? They wept buckets over maudlin love songs, yet accepted death with a single shrug.

FOURTEEN

✠ The mist was always thicker by the river. Within minutes, Berg could feel the chill seep through his clothing and into his bones as wet organic material scrunched beneath his feet. Not that he could hear his footsteps. The Isar was a deafening rush of violent water tumbling over the turbines. His head pounding, Berg walked rapidly along the banks, wondering with whom or with what he was dealing.

The body had been dumped in the southern part of the city, the temporary grave just a five-minute stroll from the new German Museum of Science and Technology—a bold, massive piece of stone-and-dome architecture that occupied its own island within the Isar. The Institute had opened with a splash, paying tribute to the industrial age—past, present, and future. The police had had an exhibition within those esteemed walls entitled "The Science of Murder." The displays included modern-day fingerprinting techniques, corpse analysis, and evidence evaluation under the microscope. Yet all that up-to-date knowledge did nothing to countermand the atrocity that lay on the ground nearby.

About fifty yards ahead, Berg could see the gathering of official people, along with the *Mordwagen*. He merged into the sea of black uniforms until he found Müller.

Georg walked him over to the crime scene. Berg kneeled down and regarded the body.

She appeared to be in her thirties, her face round, her waxy skin gray in death, but most likely pink in life. Chemically lightened blond hair had been bobbed, splayed about her face similarly to Anna Gross's tresses. Her scalp was covered with a black beaded cloche framing dull blue eyes. The features were ordinary, even painted with lipstick and rouge. Her body was garbed in a sleeveless black dance dress with a drop waistline that flared at the bottom. The dress was costly, having extensive beading on the top and bottom. She resembled the pictures Berg had seen of American flappers.

Again, she wore only one silk stocking. A feather boa lay at her side. Professor Kolb knelt beside him, his bulging eyes seemingly startled by the corpse.

Berg stared at the red line running across the woman's neck. "Killed in the same manner as Anna Gross?"

"*Ja*, both strangled," Kolb told him. "But this one was more brutal. The wound suggests something sharper and thinner—twine or a piece of wire. It sliced past the neck cartilage clear to the cervical vertebrae."

Berg felt momentary nausea. "So she wasn't strangled with a stocking?"

"Not likely, no."

"Then what happened to her other stocking? She's wearing only one."

Kolb turned his bug eyes to Berg's face. "I wouldn't have the foggiest notion."

Berg called out to Müller, who came over and crouched near the body. "Has anyone removed anything from the body, Georg?"

"As far as I know, she hasn't been moved or disturbed. The policeman who answered the call was very particular."

"Interesting." Berg stood, and the others rose as well. "And how were the police alerted to the body?"

"A gentleman was walking his dog. His name is . . ." Müller took out a pad and consulted his notes. "Here it is: Anders Johannsen. He lives on Widenmayer Strasse. Not far from Anna Gross, actually." Georg put his pad away and took out two cigarettes; he lit both smokes and handed one to Berg. "Just an observation."

"Has he been questioned?" Berg took a deep drag on his cigarette. Kolb fanned away the smoke. "Is this bothering you?"

"That stuff is poison," Kolb announced.

"Nonsense." Müller took another puff. "It clears the head and allows me to think straight."

"It's made of tar," Kolb told him. "Tar belongs on city streets, not in the lungs."

Berg snuffed out the cigarette with his fingers and placed the remnants in his pocket. "Has Johannsen been questioned, Georg?"

Müller said, "I will pay him a visit."

"I think that would be wise." Berg thought a moment. "It is a puzzle. The first killer uses Anna Gross's stocking to garrote her. But with this one, it appears he used a twine or a wire." He faced Kolb. "Am I correct, Professor?"

"I would say so, yes."

"It could be two different people." Berg swallowed drily. "But *if* it is the same man and he murdered twice— Anna and now this woman—my question is this: Did he approach this woman with the express purpose of killing her?"

Kolb smiled. "You are thinking that he took such delight in slaying Anna Gross that he decided to murder again—but more efficiently?"

"Exactly. With the trumpeted headlines from yesterday's afternoon papers, there are monstrous individuals who might derive perverse pleasure from such attention. Men like Haarmann or Grossmann or Denke."

"*Lustmord.*"

Berg nodded.

"An interesting theory you propose, Herr Inspektor, that killing Anna made him want to kill again," Kolb commented with a raised finger. "Unfortunately, it is most wrong. Observing egg deposits from the flies attracted to the corpse, I would have to assume that our Fräulein here was murdered first."

Berg blinked. "She was murdered *before* Anna Gross?"

"Yes, Inspektor, at least three days ago. She is beyond rigor mortis, lividity is quite set . . . and the maggots . . ." Kolb kneeled back down. "Maggots come when the body is several days old. Come look, meine Herren."

Berg hesitated but complied. Müller had no choice but to join them. Kolb poked a long instrument into the dead woman's nostril and lifted the flesh. Out crawled a tangled ball of white worms. "Here." The instrument parted her lips. "Here as well . . ." Next came the ear canal. "Here, too."

"*Herrjemine!*" Müller stood up and coughed twice, biting back bile. "That is repulsive!"

Kolb got to his feet. "Not at all, Inspektor Müller, it is science!"

Berg stood suddenly and felt his head spin. Despite the cold, he broke out into a sweat. He wasn't used to seeing the aftermath of murder in such explicit detail. "What kind of madman would do such a thing?"

Kolb was pensive. "It is amusing, Berg. If you kill two women, you are a madman. If you kill thousands, you are a general leading your troops to valor."

"Since when have you become a cynic?" Müller wiped perspiration from his brow. He was relieved to see that Berg had the same reaction.

"Since the Nazis are now back in politics."

A voice broke into their conversation. "Hitler has many supporters amid our ranks."

"Welcome, Storf," Kolb said. "Are you counting yourself among the Austrian's latest fans?"

Storf answered, "He has his points about the degenerates—"

"Jews," Kolb interrupted.

"The Jews, the bohemians, the homosexuals, the new artists . . . all of the Kosmopoliten. They continually bring about lawlessness and disorder."

Müller said, "As opposed to the Brownshirts, who think nothing of beating old men in the street and vandalizing every beer hall in Munich."

"I don't support them, either," Storf said. "But I understand the anger."

Berg said, "Can we put aside politics long enough to study a murder? Or . . ." He raised his eyes. "Maybe we should consider politics. Anna Gross was a woman to whom politics were important. She had Kommunist leanings. Maybe someone did not approve."

Kolb said, *"Fememord?"*

"I wasn't thinking specifically of them, but why not?" Berg said.

"There is no evidence that this secret society exists," Storf pointed out.

Berg said, "Everyone knows it exists. Just ask Amalie Sandmeyer's family." The young farm girl had made an important discovery—a stash of illegal arms in an abandoned barn. Her mistake was being a good girl, reporting the cache to the police. She was murdered soon after her discovery. "At the very least, we should consider it."

Storf gave the theory some genuine reflection. "Yes, it is possible that Anna Gross was done in by fanatic nationalists. She was married to a Jew and flirted with Kommunismus. But *two* murders? Why would any secret society bring such attention to itself?"

"Storf has a point," Müller piped in. "The Brownshirts are trying to clean up their image. Why would they risk such bad publicity?"

"To make them fearsome . . . fear is a great persuader."

"Such publicity will land Hitler back in jail, Axel," Storf said.

Berg crossed his arms. "Okay, if it isn't political, it is personal. Was she raped?"

"My guess is no," Kolb stated, "but I haven't examined her that closely."

"Back to basics. Who *was* she?" When no one answered, Berg said, "Georg, I want you to talk to Herr Johannsen as soon as we're done over here."

"You think he's the culprit?"

"He lives near Anna, he reported the newest body . . . he piques my curiosity."

"I will do that right away."

"Good. Next is identification of the victim. Ulrich, that will be your task."

"If no one has reported her missing, what am I to do? Go roaming the streets of the city, randomly showing the photograph from person to person all by myself?"

"I will get you some beat policemen for help. Also, Ulrich, I will need you in another capacity." Berg took in his colleague's flaming blue eyes. "The Brownshirts know how I feel politically. You, however, are more . . . sympathetic."

Storf stiffened. "I am not sympathetic to their lawlessness. And I resent you lumping me in the same category as common hooligans."

"I'm not categorizing you, Ulrich, I'm just saying that among the three of us, you would be least conspicuous joining their *Verein*, true?"

Storf grumbled out something unintelligible.

"The next time you have a beer, just listen to their conversation. They may have an idea who this woman is, especially if she was a subversive. After the newspapers blast this latest one in their headlines, I would think everyone will be talking about it."

"And you don't think they'll be suspicious, Axel?" Storf asked. "I've never sat at their *Stammtisch* before."

"As you yourself said, we have many sympathizers in our police ranks. And your presence should give them legitimacy. They will welcome you with open arms. And even if the Nazis had nothing to do with the murders, they still might have information that would help with our police business."

No one spoke.

Berg said, "It is done, then?"

Storf nodded. "You have assigned the tasks quite nicely, Axel. What is left for you?"

"I have a picture of a man who might have been the last person to see Anna Gross alive. I also have an unknown person from one of Anna's calling cards—Robert Schick—who could be Russian. I would like to show the picture around at some of the teahouses in Soviet Munich and see if anyone identifies the picture as Schick."

"Not as difficult a task as mine," Storf complained. "I should like to switch with you."

"Very well," Berg said. "That means you must meet with Hauptkommissar Volker about this matter."

"*What?*" Storf sputtered.

"Ulrich, if I am to wait for Kolb to develop the picture of the woman to pass around, I will be late for my meeting with Volker." He checked his pocket watch. "I am expected in thirty minutes. Go now. The man will not tolerate being kept waiting."

Storf reddened, then looked away. "Volker would not like that . . . my showing up instead of you."

"Probably not. He's a very rigid man." Berg's face was impassive. "We shall switch back to our first arrangement then?"

Ulrich lifted his hands and let them fall at his sides. "If you think it wise, certainly."

Berg smiled and nodded. It was easier to face Hitler than Volker's wrath.

FIFTEEN

Volker's office was a cloud of cigarette smoke.

"This is obscene!" The Kommissar had taken off his jacket, giving his arms more freedom to swing as he paced. Hanging from his vest pocket, his gold watch fob swayed like a pendulum. On his feet were worn rubber-soled shoes, at odds with his hand-tailored, blue pin-striped suit. Viciously, he smashed a cigarette butt into a blue Murano glass ashtray only to light up moments later. "Outrageous!"

"Indeed, Herr Kommissar," Berg answered. "So, with your permission, I will put all available manpower on the case."

"How does such a thing happen under our noses, Berg? Have you come up with anything?"

"A few leads—"

Abruptly, Volker stopped pacing, his eyes focusing on Berg's face. "Tell me."

"We have a drawing of a man who may have accompanied Anna Gross on the night she died."

"A drawing?"

"Yes."

"Who is he?"

Berg paused. "He has yet to be identified, but—"

"So what good does a picture do?" Volker shot back.

"There are over half a million people in Munich, and at least fifty percent of them are male! How are you going to identify this unknown figment, eh?"

The man was irrational. Someone was breathing down his neck. Berg said, "I would like to start by talking to active party members. There may be political implications, too, sir."

"Ach, Gott im Himmel!" Volker turned to face him. "What kind of politics now?"

"Anna Gross had been meeting with a Russian gentleman. It might be political. It might be personal. Or maybe both."

Volker said, "A Kommunist?"

"Maybe. Anna's brother, Franz Haaf, did tell me that she had flirted with Kommunismus before she married."

"And you think this man, this murderer, is a Kommunist?"

"Possibly."

"And what do politics have to do with this latest corpse? Have we even identified her yet?"

"We're working on that."

"You're working on many things. It would be nice to have some answers."

Berg held his temper. "Indeed, Herr Kommissar, answers are always desirable. Georg Müller is interviewing Anders Johannsen, the man who found the body. He lives near the Grosses' apartment."

Volker's eyes narrowed. "Is that significant?"

"We don't know. No one has reported a missing woman who fits her description. I instructed Herr Professor Kolb to take some pictures of the woman's face. I plan to show them around the area as well."

"A slow process . . . and distasteful. Our good citizens might bristle at seeing such strong photographs. Can't you find another way?"

"If you can suggest something, I would be happy to comply."

Volker didn't answer.

"The woman had on evening attire," Berg told him. "She was dressed for dancing. If she frequented the Kabaretts, someone could have remembered her."

"That could take days or even weeks . . . months."

"The case is only two days old, mein Herr."

"And how long before panic takes over the city, Berg?" Volker dabbed his forehead with a white handkerchief. "We need an arrest. Go pull in some vagrant and tell the papers we have a suspect in custody."

Berg was flabbergasted. "You want me to arrest someone at random, sir?"

"No, not a random person, a vagrant . . . a drunk . . . a man without resources and family. The streets are littered with them. Treat him kindly. Give him a hot meal and a hot shower, but keep him locked up. We'll eventually let him go, but in the meantime, having someone behind bars will calm the fear bound to arise as soon as the afternoon headlines are published." Volker inhaled deeply and let it out slowly. "Yes, that will do. Go out and arrest someone."

"And you don't think that will make us look silly, sir? Arresting one man only to let him go when we find the true suspect?"

"On the contrary, it will make us look responsive and efficient. It will be cheered by the overstuffed burghers of the city. Hopefully, they will remember us when it comes to our share of the budget."

"And if we don't find the suspect right away, are we to execute this innocent man?"

Volker waved his hand in the air. "He'd most likely die a horrible death by consumption or pneumonia."

"Excuse me, Herr Kommissar? I don't believe I heard you properly."

"No, we will not execute him," Volker said flatly. "We will not do it because before the noose is tied, you will find the correct man." He sat down at his desk. "Go out and find a sacrificial lamb." Berg hesitated. Volker crushed out another cigarette butt. "What now?"

"Before I go . . ." Berg cringed. "Before I arrest our vagrant, I'd like to at least *try* to identify the mystery man in the drawing. I was planning to show the sketch to patrons of the Russian teahouses in Schwabing. The afternoon papers don't hit until three, so I have several hours before the citizens learn of another body."

Volker slowly warmed to the idea. "If you find a man worthy of arrest before the afternoon papers come out, I will be thrilled."

"So we have the same objective. All that differs is the time frame."

"What do you have in mind, Berg?"

"Before I make any arrests, I'd like to confer with Müller and with Ulrich, who is out trying to identify our mystery woman. If you'd just allow me another day or two, I think I could find out crucial things."

"I'm not interested in *things*," Volker said; "I need names!"

Berg said, "Kommissar, suppose we arrest someone

and another murder happens right away. It is going to be obvious that we messed up."

"Then we'll haul in another vagrant and say the first one had a partner. If nothing else, we'll clean up the streets."

"Sir?"

"Fine, fine. I'll give you a day." Volker shook his head. "Perhaps I can stave off the hyenas for that long."

Berg smiled. "Your superiors, sir?"

Volker did not smile back. "In rank only."

✠ ✠ ✠

THE RUSSIAN EATERIES in the northeast area of the city were small storefronts with wooden shutters and hand-painted Cyrillic lettering on the doors. As Berg walked down Kaiser Strasse, glancing at the numerous establishments, he knew his job would be made easier if the Russians wore uniforms like everyone else in Germany. Because they didn't, he had to figure out which tavern belonged to what party in order to ask the proper questions. Within this sizable ethnic group, there was lots of discord and constant infighting.

Munich, with its charm, beauty, and accessibility, had been a natural magnet for Russian expatriates. The first wave of immigration began after Gregory Gapon led a march to Winter Palace Square in Saint Petersburg that terminated in a riot known as Bloody Sunday. The ensuing demonstrations and strikes forced the Czar to establish the Duma, a somewhat democratic parliament. Though the coup was unsuccessful, its aftermath left Russia's central government disorganized and feeble. Still reeling from economic woes brought on by the Great War, Trotsky and then Lenin saw an unparalleled opportunity for seizure of central power in 1917.

The brutal murders of the Czar and his entire family sent a flood of royalist Russians across the border where they found sympathy with the Bavarian monarchy. For hundreds of years, the Wittelsbacher had reigned without dispute, levying taxes, maintaining their own armies, and building numerous castles in the Alps.

By 1918, it was all gone. The Germans had taken their lead from their Russian brethren, and Bavaria was a baby step away from joining the Soviet Union. German Social Democrat Kurt Eisner, a thin, bearded Jew, led a revolt, his party eventually forcing the Wittelsbacher into exile. Elected Prime Minister of the Bavarian republic, Eisner promised a government that would serve all citizens. A year later, Eisner's utopian dream was cut short by an assassin's bullet, which threw the region into upheaval and culminated in the Great Inflation of 1923. It was not so long ago that a wheelbarrow's worth of paper money was needed to purchase a single egg.

Russia's Kommunist postwar economy, like those of all of Europe, suffered. When Stalin usurped control, his wrath brought yet another mass exile of Russians streaming into Munich in the mid-twenties: This time it was the Bolsheviks.

Each Russian faction set up its own teahouses, taverns, chess parlors, and dance halls. The Kabaretts were identical in menu, smell, and language. The people looked the same, dressed the same, and drank the same. Once in a while, a teahouse or tavern would try to assert its identity by waving a royal flag or the hammer and sickle or even a poster of Trotsky. Within days, opposition had ripped the offending object down. Although Berg didn't come to Soviet Schwabing to talk politics, casual conversation always seemed to go in that direction.

It was lunchtime. Cooking smells wafting from the open shutters were pungent: a workingman's meal of onions, cabbage, turnips, and potatoes—and a little meat if the price was right. The evening menus were more varied, offering Russian delicacies such as blinis or gravlax cured in vodka. These tasty morsels were served along with German specialties like *Spätzle* and *Maultaschen*. Meals were washed down with locally brewed beer or vodka: The more the alcohol flowed, the rosier the atmosphere.

A chess tournament was taking place. Dozens of card tables were set out on the sidewalk, the benches occupied by men of all ages clothed in thick work shirts, patched pants, tattered jackets, and wool caps. The players sipped beer and smoked heavily, pondering the boards, then punching the timer after each completed move. The competition was due to end soon. Berg's plan was to pass around Anna's picture and the sketch of her unknown escort after the games broke up.

In the meantime, he found a small tavern that looked inviting and sat on a stool at the empty bar. He held out a finger to the barkeeper.

"Löwenbräu, *bitte*."

The German out of Berg's mouth made the barkeeper suspicious. Even so, he poured the beer from the tap until foam rushed over the glass. He gave it to Berg along with a plate of nuts and broken pieces of pretzel.

"*Danke*. Work here long?"

The tapster's eyes turned hostile with a touch of fear. "Why you ask?"

Berg showed him the sketch. "Do you know this man? I think he may be Russian."

The barkeeper gave the picture some attention. *"Nyet."* A shake of the head. "I don't know him."

"Do you know a man named Robert Schick?"

"No. Who is he, please?"

The tapster's accent was thick, but his German was decent. He'd been in the country for a while. Berg finished his pint and wiped his mouth on his sleeve. He took out Anna Gross's photograph. "What about this woman?"

A shrug. "No."

"She doesn't look familiar?"

"No."

"She was murdered yesterday. The story was in all the papers."

"I don't read German papers."

"I'm sure it was in the Russian papers as well."

"I don't read any papers."

"Her name is Anna Gross. She might go by the name of Anna Haaf."

"I know none of these people. You ask many questions. You are police?"

Berg shoved a handful of pretzel pieces into his mouth and shrugged.

The barkeeper said, "All my papers are ordered."

"I'm not interested in your papers."

"Then you are interested in what?"

"In answers. Think again. Do you know Robert Schick?"

"Nyet!" A firm shake of the head. "I don't know him. And I don't know man in drawing. Bother someone else."

Berg took several coins out of his pocket to pay, but the barkeeper stopped him. "I give you beer. You say you never ask me questions. German police in here is no good, *verstanden?"*

"Yes, I understand." Berg wrote his name and the phone number of the police station on a piece of paper. "I'll leave now." He slid the paper across the countertop to the barkeeper. "But if you find something out, you'll do your local duty and tell me. *Verstanden?"*

"Da, da . . ."

Berg stared at him.

"I tell you. I tell you. I am good man."

"I know. All your papers are ordered."

✠ ✠ ✠

BERG LEFT just as the tournament was breaking up. He took out the drawing and the photograph of Anna and began to show them to the chess players.

Nein.

Nein.

Nyet.

Nein.

Nyet.

Nyet.

Nyet.

A gnome wearing a cap asked if the man in the sketch was a Kommunist. When Berg said he might be, the man stiffened and announced *he* was a royalist.

Berg asked where he would find the Kommunisten.

The gnome replied that with any luck, he'd find them in a mass grave.

The name Robert Schick drew blank stares as well.

The only thing left to do was to visit each individual establishment. He took out his notebook and started at one end of the block.

When he entered his seventh teahouse—a tiny space of tables and chairs and the ubiquitous bronze samovar—he realized he was hungry. He waited ten minutes for an empty chair, and for the price of a mark, he had a lunch of smoked fish, a beet and celery-root salad, a roll, and all the hot, dark tea he could drink. Expensive but satisfying.

A youth of sixteen or seventeen in a vest and cap was playing music on a balalaika. Berg liked the ethnic music, but his favorite was American jazz. He was disappointed when Joachim seemed more interested in classical guitar music after they had seen Andrés Segovia in concert.

The place was thick with people and conversations, but since Russian was spoken, Berg was lost. Sipping tea, he realized that he was taking up desired space. Just as the balalaika player took a break, he got up, realizing this was an opportune moment.

He followed the youth outside.

The kid had a smooth, white face and not much in the way of a beard. His eyes were brown, and his hair was the color of rust. The musician leaned against the wall and took out a cigarette. Berg was there with a light. The young man stared at him, but took the proffered match. There was suspicion in his eyes. *"Spasibo."*

"I'm not Russian, I'm German," Berg answered. "I liked your playing."

The suspicion hardened. The teen's eyes darted from

side to side. But he nodded at the compliment, puffing on his cigarette.

Berg said, "Do you play at other cafés?"

"I play where anyone will pay me. You have café?"

"Maybe. What's your name?"

"My name?"

Berg smiled. To prevent the musician from leaving, he leaned over, arm extended with his hand against the wall, blocking his escape. "Yes, your name."

"You are not café owner," the player pronounced.

"No, I am a policeman. What's your name?"

The musician froze. Berg took the cigarette from the player's lips. "You want to stay in Munich, no?"

"My papers are good."

"I'm sure they are. Your name?"

The player tapped his toe. "Sergei."

Surely a false name but Berg didn't pursue it. "I bet you've played at many cafés, Sergei. I bet you've met many people."

The young man said nothing.

Berg showed him the sketch of the man and the picture of Anna. "Do you know either of these people?"

Sergei stared at the pencil rendition, then at the photograph. His eyes gave nothing away. "Why you ask?"

"Yes or no. Do you recognize either or both of them?"

"The woman, no." He pointed to the sketch. "Maybe I see him."

Berg tried to hide his excitement. "Maybe?"

"It's like you say. I see many people." Sergei squirmed, but had nowhere to go. Instead he reached for his cigarette still in Berg's hand. "He has name . . . this man?"

"I'm sure he does, but I don't know it. Describe him for me."

"Why I describe? You have picture."

"Short, tall—"

"Tall."

"Hair color?"

"It is brown, I think."

"Eyes?"

"I don't remember eyes. But he wore monocle like he was important man."

Berg nodded, trying not to show emotion. "Important in what way?"

"Like he was big-shot royalty." The young man spat on the ground.

"Aristocracy?"

"Maybe. But there are many here that act like important peoples."

"A *Schlawiner*?"

"Maybe he is impostor, but a good one. He is always with the ladies."

"With this woman?" Berg showed him Anna's photograph again.

"I tell you I don't know her." He flicked ashes on the ground. "She is beautiful. He knows many beautiful women."

"Do you know a man named Robert Schick?"

"He is this man?" Sergei asked.

"You tell me."

Sergei shrugged. "Robert Schick is not Russian name."

"I know that. If he was *Schlawiner,* maybe he was using more than one name." As soon as Sergei finished his cigarette, Berg offered him another. "Have you ever heard someone call him *any* name?"

"Maybe I hear someone call him Ro."

Berg lit Sergei's cigarette. "Ro? What kind of a name is that?"

"You say his name is Robert. Maybe Ro is Robert."

Berg smiled. Inadvertently, he had fed him the answer he wanted to hear. "Could Ro be a Russian name?"

"Possible. Maybe Roman, maybe Rodion, maybe Rostislav, maybe even last name like Czar . . . Romanov." A wry smile. "So maybe he is big-shot royalty. These days only God knows friend from enemy."

"But you're sure he's Russian."

"I hear him speak Russian. But where he's born . . ." The musician shrugged.

"If you see him again, you contact me." Berg gave the youth his card. "*Bitte* . . . or should I say *Potzhalusta*?"

Sergei lifted his eyebrows. "You know Russian?"

"I know 'please' and 'thank you,'" Berg answered. "My mother raised me with manners."

SIXTEEN

Anders Johannsen sat on a damask sofa. A white, fluffy thing with a gold necklace and a pink bow was curled up in his lap; at his feet was something live, large, and ominous. "It was so horrible! I knew something was amiss because Otto kept pulling at the leash, but I never expected . . ."

His iridescent blue eyes were moist and a little wild. He appeared to be in his mid-fifties, and was tall and thin. He flailed his arms as he spoke, nearly knocking the little critter off his lap. The thick, brooding beast on the floor picked up its head, pendulous maws dripping with saliva. Otto stared at nothing for a moment, then tucked his head into his bent legs and went back to sleep.

"Otto picked up the smell." As the man petted his lap-dog, white fur flew into the air like snow. He sneezed.

"Gesundheit," Müller said.

"Danke."

"This one . . ." Johannsen framed the doggy's face with his long, tapered fingers. "She went right to the spot."

The man's hair was almost as light as the little dog's white fur. He was no doubt from the north. Müller said, "Dogs have good noses."

"Very good noses," Johannsen concurred.

Squirming on a dark purple settee, Georg Müller sat opposite Johannsen, his feet tucked underneath his seat to prevent his toes from nudging the brute's ribs. His notepad in his lap, his sharpened pencil poised, he was ready to write down anything crucial to the case. But so far, all he had done was listen to an unseemly display of emotion.

Johannsen's apartment was simple but fastidiously clean: sparkling white plastered walls, polished wood floors, and big windows letting in whatever light Munich had in the late winter. Hanging on the walls were several Cubist paintings—square torsos in bright colors without arms and legs and heads—a set of primitive drawings that could have come from African caves, and another group of drawings with very few lines.

Back to business. "Did you touch anything at the scene of the crime?"

"You mean the body?" Johannsen shuddered. "Good heavens, no! Otto was licking her face . . . trying to wake her up, I think. At first, I thought she might be a drunk. But then it was obvious. I was in total shock!"

"It must have been quite upsetting."

"Very upsetting." He shuddered again. "I must say that as a citizen here, I do hold the police accountable. So forgive my presumption if I ask what is going on."

"It is . . . puzzling."

"Were the murders political in nature?"

"Why do you ask?"

"Because everything in Germany is political."

"You say Germany and not Munich, Herr Johannsen. Were you born here?"

"No. Up north."

"Hamburg?"

"Farther. Neumünster."

Müller said, "What brought you to Munich?"

Johannsen flipped his hair off his forehead. He had thin features, a protruding forehead, and a sharp nose. He looked like Beethoven's blond twin. He sighed deeply. "I came before the Great War because of what the city *used* to be—so alive and full of ideas."

"I've always found the Bavarians a conservative lot," Müller answered.

"The county of Munich yes, but the city . . . it was different. At the turn of the century, we were the true bohemians, not the silly Parisians. We *were* the Blaue Reiter."

"You are a painter, Herr Johannsen?"

"No. I talk metaphorically." He waved his hand in the air, then let it fall back down on his lapdog. "I am a collector." He pointed to the Cubist paintings. "Munich was an unrivaled artists' community. Since the Great War and the Austrian, nothing has been the same. Hitler claims to be an artist. That's a laugh. Surely you have seen Karl Valentin with Liesl Karlstadt at one time or another. His latest interpretation of modern times is quite apropos to what we're talking about."

If you say so. Müller was forever wary of those who expressed themselves so strongly. Political rivals were always setting traps. "What time do you walk your dogs, Herr Johannsen?"

"I rise and dress at six in the morning. I am out for my walk by seven. You may set your watch on my routine. You do not want to keep a hound like Otto waiting when necessity calls."

"I suppose not. So you discovered the body around . . ."

"I did not look at my watch, but I would say around fifteen minutes into my constitutional."

"Seven-fifteen."

"I would say so, yes."

"And then what did you do?"

"I found a policeman and apprised him of the situation. I could tell he wanted to question me, but instead he took my name and address and let me go home to compose myself."

"Did you see anyone suspicious coming into or going out from the area?"

"There were some people around me, *ja*? But no one I'd label as suspicious."

And even if he did see people, what did it matter? According to Herr Professor Kolb, the woman was murdered at least two days ago. Müller tapped his pencil against his notepad.

Johannsen became impatient. "I have nothing else to add." He rose from the sofa. "If you have no more questions, Herr Inspektor, I would like to get back to my work."

"Ah . . ." As Müller got up, he awakened the beast, still drooling. This time a low growl emanated from the depths of its throat. "Is he going to bite me?"

"Otto?" Johannsen placed his shod foot squarely on top of the dog's head. "He's a baby."

"A very large one then," Müller said, sidestepping around the ruffian. Then he hesitated before saying, "Your work . . . what is your work?"

"I am a composer."

"Ah . . ." Müller glanced around the living room. "But one without a piano."

"I have a separate music room. Soundproofed." A slow smile spread across Johannsen's face. "I would not like it if my neighbors complained. *Auf Wiedersehen.*"

✠ ✠ ✠

SHOWING A PICTURE of a dead woman to people at random, hoping that *someone* could identify her, was a rigged game of hit-and-miss. But sometimes even the tremendous odds stacked against you were rendered meaningless. Such was the case when Storf spotted a young, attractive woman wearing a hat over a short bob coming out of Konigen's Milliners, near Maximilian Strasse. She toddled awkwardly because she was toting two very bulky hatboxes. She wore a brown tweed suit and had on leather pumps.

Storf corralled her just as she was readjusting her packages and showed her the postmortem photograph. Expecting nothing, he was stunned when her dark eyes got very big, her red-painted lips tightened into an "O," and her throat uttered an audible gasp. Quickly, she averted her glance.

"Is that Marlena?"

Storf's heartbeat quickened. "I don't know, meine Dame, perhaps you can tell me."

"I am Fräulein Erika Schulweiss." She looked up into Storf's blue eyes. "And *you* are?"

"My apologies for not introducing myself properly. I am Inspektor Ulrich Storf. I am sorry to trouble you with such unpleasantness, but the police are desperately searching for the identity of this woman. Perhaps you can peek at the photograph one more time?"

She did. "It *looks* like Marlena."

"Marlena who?"

"Marlena Druer."

Storf glanced at the young woman. She appeared to be in her early twenties with a slim figure, but ample hips. *A lovely girl with a body meant for breeding.* He felt a tug below his waist, then looked away, knowing he was red-faced. But the woman hardly seemed to notice.

"At least I think it's Marlena." She bit her thumbnail. "It looks like Marlena."

Storf took out his notepad and pencil. "And where does Frau Druer—"

"*Fräulein* Druer."

"Ah, yes. Where does Fräulein Druer live?"

"Not here," Erika answered. "I mean, not in Munich. She lives in Berlin. She is a longtime family friend . . . a friend of my older sister actually. My sister also lives in Berlin. The two of them come out to visit our family around this time every year . . . right after *Fasching*. They have been doing this for the last six years. But this year, Henrietta—that's my sister—she wasn't feeling well. She just had her fourth baby not more than two months ago. So Marlena came by herself." She stared at Storf. "Are you writing all of this down?"

"Yes, I am trying to do that."

"I'll slow down then. I talk very rapidly. It drives my family to distraction, I'm afraid. I grew up in Spain. There are many Germans in Spain. If you think I talk quickly, you should hear the Spanish. Especially the Cubans. We had several Cubans who went to my school. My school had all kinds of people—Spanish, Cuban, German, Portuguese . . . a regular League of Nations—"

"Fräulein Schulweiss?" Storf interrupted. "I'd like to talk about Marlena Druer, please."

"Yes. Marlena." Erika put down her packages on the sidewalk, straightened her hat, and raised the veil so she could see a bit better. She glanced at the picture again. "*Ach mein Gott!* I'm sure that's Marlena. This is just dreadful! She looks so young in that photograph."

Death tended to do that, especially to the face. It smoothed out the wrinkles. Ulrich said, "How old is she?"

"She is thirty-five. The same age as my sister."

"You are much younger than your sister, then?"

"Yes, this is true. I am twenty. I come from a large family. Henrietta is the oldest and I am the youngest. Only my brother and I are left . . . at home. The rest have married and moved away. The house keeps getting emptier and emptier, but my parents refuse to move."

"Marlena was staying with your family, then?"

"No. My sister of course stayed with my family, but Marlena never did. Instead, she rented at a small pension. Marlena always insisted on her privacy, which I never could understand because she could get plenty of privacy in our house."

"When was the last time you saw her?"

"Oh dear, maybe three days ago."

"And you weren't alarmed that you hadn't heard from her in two or three days?"

"Not at all. Marlena came and went as she pleased. If she didn't come calling for several days, we just figured she had other plans. She and my sister always brought their skis. It was entirely possible that Marlena had gone skiing nearby . . . or even in Switzerland. Or even that she suddenly changed her mind and went back to Berlin. Or even Paris. That was Marlena. I think that's why my sister adored her. Henrietta was very shy and Marlena was outgoing. They're quite a pair." Again, her eyes watered. "This is terrible!"

Storf patted her back in a comforting gesture. "I am so sorry to have burdened you with this ugly matter. Perhaps we can contact someone to come with us to the mortuary to identify the body. Perhaps your father or brother may be able to do that?"

Now Erika's eyes filled with tears that ran down her cheeks. "Yes, of course." She took out a handkerchief from her purse. "You will tell them this dreadful news. I cannot do it."

"Of course, Fräulein Schulweiss. We would never allow a lovely woman such as yourself to dirty her hands with such awful doings."

Erika smiled. "That is very kind of you, Inspektor."

"Think nothing of it."

The two of them engaged eyes for a moment.

Storf picked up her packages. "Perhaps you would be so kind as to accompany me to your family's home so I may talk to the gentlemen in your house?"

Erika reddened. "My father is working. My brother as well."

"Ah . . ." Storf nodded. "So perhaps you can give me the address of your father's employment so I may speak to him right away?"

Erika didn't answer.

"These are pressing matters, Fräulein Schulweiss."

"My father is a doctor, Herr Inspektor. Today is his day for surgery."

"Then perhaps I can speak to your brother?"

"He is not home, either."

"Oh . . . that is a problem. Still, I would like to accompany you home and carry your packages. It is the least I can do after bringing you such terrible news."

"That is very kind of you, Inspektor." She gave Storf a smile. "My streetcar is not more than two blocks away. Come."

They walked without speaking. Storf wanted to question her further about Marlena Druer and her habits, but with all the noise and the pedestrians bumping into the packages, he could scarcely manage to walk without toppling over.

"I have an idea," Erika said brightly. "Why don't you wait at my house for my brother? I do think that it would be much better for police matters to be handled in the privacy of one's home."

"And when do you think your brother might return home?"

"Well, it is around three. . . ." She paused. "Perhaps in an hour. Maybe a little longer."

Again, Storf felt his heart beating against his chest. Not only was the girl very well formed, her face was pleasing as well. She was, however, completely out of his class. Still, there was no harm in taking a break. He had been on his feet for the last three hours. If nothing else, he'd get a hot cup of tea and a chance to rest. Maybe he'd even get a beer, if the family was generous. "If it's no inconvenience to your mother, I will wait at your home, then."

"It will be no inconvenience to her whatever." A slow smile spread across Erika's face. "She is out of town."

SEVENTEEN

✠ The beer hall was packed, most of the tables taken up by *Vereine,* the numerous clubs that had formed and dissolved and formed again, each one indicated by a flag with its insignia on the tabletop. *Vereine* weren't just off-shoots of the major political parties. These days, the clubs included the carpenters' union, the plumbers' union, the masons' union, the tailors' union, and, of course, the city police, although in this beer hall—Der Bierkeller—Berg couldn't see his departmental banner. After a minute of surveying the masses, he spotted some free seats at the end of a long trestle table. He and Müller sat down and ordered a couple of Löwenbräus.

Berg checked the clock and compared it to his wrist-watch—a wedding gift from his father-in-law. It had an eighteen-karat gold case and was engraved, but it ran slow. He adjusted the time to quarter past five, then wound the stem three times, putting the face to his ear to make sure it was ticking. He said, "Not like Storf to be late."

Two beer mugs were plunked in front of their faces, foam swelling over the lip of each stein.

"Maybe he's discovered something." Müller took a big gulp of brew. "Ah . . . *das tut gut.*"

"Discovered what? Has he contacted you?"

"No." Müller took another swig. "Just postulating."

"Did Professor Kolb say anything more about the deceased?"

"Just what he told you. From the insect eggs, it appears that she died around three days ago. Frankly, I think he just enjoys playing with repulsive things."

"And no one discovered her until Johannsen. What a pity."

"Yes, a pity."

"Anything else on her condition beyond being strangled?"

"It wasn't done with the stocking."

"Yes. Kolb said it was a wire or a piece of twine. I was there."

Georg popped pretzels into his mouth. "When he looked at the ligature mark under the microscope, he found a repetitive pattern etched into the skin . . . in the part where the wire didn't actually cut through the flesh. Little, lined circles—"

"A necklace chain."

"That's what he was thinking, yes."

"Did you find a necklace near her?"

"No," Müller responded. "But she was dressed in evening wear. It's logical that she had on a necklace. The culprit murdered her with it and then stole it."

"Did we find the other stocking?"

"No."

"So maybe the murderer took that as well."

"Whatever for?" Müller asked.

Berg thought a moment. "Some criminals are like that. They take things from their victims—clothing or jewelry."

"More likely, they rob for profit."

"Yes, of course. But they take insignificant things as well. I've seen a case where the murderer actually cut off pieces of his victim's hair. When asked why, he said he simply wanted a memory."

Müller shook his head. "Very strange."

"And she wasn't violated?" Berg asked.

"It appears not, but she has spent several days moldering. Herr Professor took swabs of the region. Perhaps he'll spot something under the microscope."

"So already there are differences. One was violated, and the other was not. Different implements to use as a garrote. It could be different murderers."

"Indeed." Müller took another gulp. "I'm starved. Are you eating, Axel?"

Berg was lost in thought. "But in both cases, the matching stocking is gone. That indicates the same hand, wouldn't you think?"

"What I think is I am hungry. How about a plate of cheese and cold cuts with some brown bread and butter?"

Berg stared at Müller for a moment, then slowly brought his thoughts back to the present. "Yes, that would be satisfying."

A waiter was summoned and Müller shouted the order over the din. People were laughing loudly, bellowing over one another. Not only that, the singing had begun—a cappella and off tune. The brass band had yet to set up, but in its stead was an accordionist in traditional Bavarian dress of white shirt, suspenders, and lederhosen, taking his instrument out of the case. Glasses were clinking, and momentary friendships were being formed. Beer-induced frivolity—and why not? Life was dreary and so was the weather. It was advisable to take whatever was offered.

Berg's musing made him think of Margot. He pictured her coy smile as she preened in front of a mirror, fanning her face with luxurious black feathers. He had thought about visiting her before meeting Müller, but then had quickly dismissed the notion. It was not wise to get too involved, even though being faithful made him testy.

"Where is Storf?" he groused.

"He'll be here, Axel. Relax."

Forget about her! "Anything productive come out of the interview with Anders Johannsen?"

"All business, eh?"

"Do you think I keep your company for pleasure?"

Müller smiled. "He claims to have found her around seven-fifteen in the morning."

"He is sure?"

"The old man's constitutional is like clockwork."

"He is old?"

"In his fifties, although he looks younger—except for the white hair."

"What does he look like aside from having white hair?"

"Sharp features, long nose . . . tall."

"He's tall?"

"What?" Müller was shouting over the racket.

"I asked if he's tall," Berg said, shouting back.

"I'd say about six-two."

The singing had picked up in volume and in spirit. Each *Verein* was boasting its superiority in animated melody, and when challenged by a rival club, the members flung back insults in song. The cacophony was enough to render any tune meaningless.

"The man who was with Anna Gross was tall and blond."

"Johannsen isn't blond, he's white."

"But in certain lighting white can be mistaken for blond." Berg took out his sketch. "Did he look anything like this?"

Müller regarded the sketch in earnest. "On a very basic level . . . the thinness of the face . . . the sharp nose." He looked up. "Really, Berg, this drawing could be just about anyone."

He was right. Still, Berg would not dismiss the thought that the man might have been more than just an unfortunate onlooker. "Was Johannsen nervous when you talked to him?"

"Not nervous, Axel, upset. It isn't every day that a citizen finds a decomposing corpse. Why are you suspicious of him?"

"Because some criminals love to revisit their handiwork. He could be toying with us . . . like Britain's Jack the Ripper—"

"Frau Gross was a married woman, not a prostitute."

"She was a woman who could have been carrying on an affair. And we know nothing about the other body."

"Maybe Storf knows something about that," Müller said.

"Wherever he is," Berg grumbled.

The waiter presented them with plates of food and a basket of brown bread. Conversation stopped temporarily as they ate.

Berg said, "I showed my sketch around the Russian

teahouses today. A balalaika player told me he looked like
a man known as Ro—a gentleman who presents himself
as fallen aristocracy, although his authenticity is dubi-
ous."

Müller raised an eyebrow. "So the man in your sketch
really does exist?"

"I think so, yes. Anna Gross's chambermaid also recognized the man in the sketch as someone Anna had entertained—possibly a Russian. We turned up a calling
card that she could not place. The name on the card was
Robert Schick. Ro . . . Robert. More than a coincidence,
I'd say."

"Yes, I agree." Müller looked annoyed. "Since you
have a name and a picture, why are you even considering
Anders Johannsen as the culprit?"

"Impostors take on many names."

"Johannsen lives in a nice apartment. He appears to be
a man of means. He doesn't seem like an impostor."

"Just a comment," Berg said. "Besides, I have to keep
considering that there may be more than one murderer."
Out of the corner of his eye, he saw Storf—harried and disheveled—and waved him over. Storf was weaving his
way through the crowd, bumping into elbows and knocking over beer steins, apologizing profusely for each
mishap. At last, he took the chair next to Müller.

"Sorry."

Berg looked at the clock: quarter to six. "You were tied
up with police work?"

"Yes, certainly." Storf was breathing hard. "It is hot in
here."

"Hot and loud," Berg complained. "I don't know why
we keep meeting in beer halls."

"You look thirsty, man." Müller signaled the waiter for another beer.

"Thank you, Georg," Storf replied.

"I hope your tardiness resulted in some good news?"

Storf drained half a stein. "All business, Axel?" He smiled, then took a picture out of his pocket. "This woman is our murder victim, no?"

It was the corpse in her more robust days: a pretty, dark-haired woman with round brown eyes, a wide smile, and two very charming dimples. Berg and Müller looked at him with admiration.

"Well done," Müller said.

"Where'd you get the photograph?" Berg asked.

Storf sidestepped the question. "Her name is Marlena Druer. She's from Berlin. She came down to visit family friends in Munich . . . the family Schulweiss. They haven't seen or heard from her in three or four days. They never reported her disappearance to the police because it was not unusual for her to come and go as she pleased. The family tells me she was staying at a pension—Der Blumengarten in Giesing. I haven't gone through the room. I thought we could all go together when we're done with supper."

"How did you find out about her?"

"I was lucky."

"Good job," Berg said. "Excellent, in fact."

"*Danke.*" Storf finished his beer and smacked his lips. "I needed that."

Müller poured him another round. "Drink up."

"I will." Storf sipped, then looked at Berg. "Is something wrong?"

"You have blood on you—"

"Blood? Where?"

"Something red on your neck." Berg reached over and touched him right under the jawline. He wiped it away with his thumb. "Gone."

"Nick yourself shaving?" Müller asked.

"It was lipstick." Berg laughed and raised his stein to Storf. "To a man whose dedication to his bound profession knows no professional bounds."

EIGHTEEN

✠ Volker was listening with less than half an ear. The context of the speech was hackneyed and worn, but still Hitler kept going with force and energy as if he were delivering the diatribe for the first time, his blue eyes flashing something that was not quite human. The confidence that oozed from his voice belied the nervousness in his hands as he picked up a third roll from the bread basket, working it through his fidgety fingers and turning it into dust. Immediately, one of his devoted followers appeared, a boy not more than fourteen with bad acne and a bulging Adam's apple. Whisk in hand, he brushed the bread crumbs from the tabletop into a plate. The Austrian was a meticulous man.

Osteria Bavaria was normally one of Volker's favorite restaurants, featuring the cuisine of Italy, dishes lavished with wonderful cheeses, spices, exotic vegetables like artichoke hearts, and noodles in all shapes and sizes. Tonight's special had been a superb veal parmigiana with fresh asparagus. The bistro sat in the heart of Schwabing and attracted many from the artistic community, along with Nazis who mistakenly fancied themselves as painters. On other days, Osteria Bavaria was filled with bohemians who might have thrown dinner plates at tonight's speaker. But Hitler and the National Socialist

German Workers Party had conned enough money from benefactors to rent out all the dining rooms for the party supporters. The man's lecture ranged from topic to topic—from degenerate art to degenerate Jews.

The space was appointed with traditional Bavarian furnishings made from dark walnut and carved with southern German scrollwork. Brown leather booths were lit by the amber glow of electric lighting. There were fresh flowers on each table and sketches on the wall that extolled the thrill of the hunt. Oversize tankards and painted mugs were set on shelves and fireplace mantels. A roaring blaze had been set in each of the three hearths and still the stone building let in a draft. No matter. Whoever wasn't made comfortable by the heat from crackling logs was warmed by alcohol.

Drumming his fingers against his pants leg, Volker glanced at his table companions: his immediate superiors, Direktor Max Brummer and Kommandant Stefan Roddewig, and *their* superior, assistant mayor Roderick Schlussel—a morose man in his fifties. Though Schlussel had outwardly forgiven Hitler for his 1923 misstep—a lapse in judgment that cost sixteen lives—he still did not fully trust the Nazi. Volker recognized the predicament the man was in. Schlussel and the government were forced to deal with the rising popularity of a very moody man, who shifted from charmer to lunatic within a heartbeat. Such unpredictability bore watching.

Hitler continued his ramblings for another ten minutes, then abruptly stopped. Without warning or explanation, he clicked his boot heels like a Prussian, gave a little bow, and, with legs extended at the knees, marched out the door before anyone knew he was through. Quickly, his attendants pulled napkins from their chins and followed, being caught off-guard by his sudden exit. His dinner—a plate of spaghetti with vegetables in tomato sauce—was left untouched.

After the entourage had left, Volker sat back and whispered to the ceiling, "My God, he's long-winded!"

Roddewig leaned over to Volker and whispered, "Careful . . ."

"I'm not saying his points don't have some merit," Volker backtracked. "But I am suggesting that he could be more succinct." But secretly he was relieved that Hitler spoke as long as he did. It meant that there was little time left for his superiors to discuss the two murder cases—and the lack of progress made by the police.

Schlussel sipped coffee laced with liqueur. "Yes, it is always preferable that things be done in a timely fashion."

Leave it to the politician to make the pointed comment. Schlussel was a bald man with a long face. Spectacles were perched midway on his prominent nose. Ignoring the barb, Volker reached into his pocket and offered each of his dinner companions a cigar. Within minutes, the table was engulfed in foul-smelling smoke.

Schlussel persisted. "Were you aware that Herr Hitler mentioned the murders more than once?"

Volker retorted, "Distraction is the bread and butter of politics."

"It is not a distraction, Martin, it is a reality," the assistant mayor answered. "It's on everyone's mind. We cannot have Munich engulfed in panic." Schlussel exhaled acrid fumes. "We need answers."

Slowly, Volker turned to his companions, giving each one the full heat of his eyes. They both knew that Volker, although inferior in rank, held unmentioned power by virtue of his family wealth and position. His contributions to the police were also significant. Without his keen, organized mind, many of the recent police developments, including the newly formed *Mordkommission,* would have dissolved long ago in disarray. Most important, Volker had somehow managed to accumulate dirt on notable Munich politicians. It allowed him to operate as a maverick. His power was effective but only if he wielded it with subtlety. Too much greed and he'd wind up with a bullet in his back. "And what, gentlemen, would you propose that I do?"

No one spoke. Then Roddewig signaled the waiter for another brandy by holding up his glass. "What about Anton Gross?"

Again we are back to him? Volker said, "What about him?"

"Once again, I think it would be wise if you brought him in for questioning."

"And how, Stefan, would you explain to the public Herr Gross's connection to the newest murder victim, Marlena Druer?"

His query was met with resounding silence. Schlussel sipped his coffee. The haze of cigar smoke thickened.

Max Brummer finished the last of his apple schnapps and then spoke up. "Bring in Gross, then suggest that the two murders are unrelated. That way, at least we have a suspect for one murder."

"But what if the killings *are* related?" Volker said.

"Since you don't know one way or the other, it does no harm for us to assume they're not," Schlussel said. "Perhaps these killings are the Jewish conspiracy that Herr Hitler warns about: Jews killing their German wives."

Volker tried to keep his temper. "Druer was not even *married.*"

"But from what you've told us, Martin, she was bohemian," Brummer stated. "Maybe she was murdered by her Jewish boyfriend."

"What Jewish boyfriend?" Volker said. "We are looking for a Russian, not a Jew."

"How about a Russian Jew?" Roddewig suggested. "No matter what Stalin does, the Bolshevik Party continues to be flooded with them."

"So if it is a Bolshevik Jew, let me find him," Volker said.

"You may do that on your own time," Schlussel told him. "In the meantime, it is not so hard to construct charges against Gross . . . that he, like many of his race, is infected with *Lustmord,* which compels him to swoop down on our virginal German women."

"One minute Druer is a bohemian, the next moment she is the Virgin Mary." Volker blew out a cloud of smoke and smiled. "With all due respect, gentlemen, I do believe that it would be more constructive to stop the perpetrator of the crimes than to blame it on the Jews."

"But perhaps it is the Jews."

"Fine," Volker said. "If it's the Jews, everybody will be happy. And even if it isn't the Jews, we can find ways to blame the Jews. But right now, the best thing to do is to find the murderer because what we really want is for the crimes to be stopped."

"They better be stopped," Schlussel snapped. "This is

just the kind of propaganda that Herr Hitler can use against our government. We can't afford another putsch."

"That's not going to happen. If the Austrian fails again, he'll be permanently discredited."

"Ah, but what if he doesn't fail?" Schlussel shook his head. "I think you're being a bit naive, Martin."

"So maybe we should blame the murders on Hitler's minions before he blames them on us."

"Go back to the Jews, Martin," Brummer piped in. "Arrest Gross and put him in custody. When you find the real murderer, you can let him go."

"I have no grounds on which to arrest him, Herr Direktor. We've gone through this before."

Schlussel stared at him with hatred. "I must ask you, Hauptkommissar Volker. Is your reticence a sign of sympathy for the dogs?"

Volker smiled, although the corners of his mouth barely rose. "I don't have sympathy, I don't have antipathy, I am merely trying to solve a puzzling case."

"One day you will be called on to take a stand!" Brummer preached.

"Perhaps one day, but not at this moment."

Schlussel said, "Since you insist on being impartial, I'm afraid I'm going to give you a direct order, Herr Kommissar. Tomorrow morning I want you to arrest Anton Gross for the murder of his wife. I will make sure all the papers are notified. If Anton Gross turns out to be guilty of the crime, then we were one step ahead of the dog. If he is innocent, we'll sort it out when we have a real suspect. But we need to calm down the public." He turned to Brummer. "I hold you responsible for this."

"It will be done." Brummer regarded Volker. "And of

course you have no trouble accepting these orders, Kommissar Volker?"

Volker was livid, but maintained his outwardly calm appearance. "If you order it, it will be done."

"Good man," Brummer said.

"Are we finished with our business?" Volker asked.

"In a hurry?" Schlussel asked.

"Just a bit uncomfortable," Volker said. "I am full, more than a little drunk, and the room is filled with much hot air."

Roddewig said, "I'll walk you to your car, Martin."

Volker was taken aback. "You need a lift, Stefan?"

"If you're offering, I won't say no." Roddewig turned to the table. "Gentlemen, if you'll excuse us."

Brummer said, "We're having a meeting with the Scharnagl tomorrow. Ten o'clock sharp, Stefan."

"I'll be prompt," Roddewig answered. "You know me, Max. You can set your watch by my arrival. Good evening."

As soon as they were out the door, Volker said, "You were rather quiet tonight, Stefan. I would have thought that you'd enjoy a good witch hunt."

"I don't mind blaming Jews, but that really doesn't solve the problem, does it? If the two murders are related, we have another possible Haarmann."

"It's only been two murders."

"These types . . . they never stop at two. Look what's happening in Düsseldorf. How many has the Vampire killed?"

Volker didn't answer.

"The police over there look like inept fools. That will be us unless we find him." A small smile rose to his lips.

"Hitler will make political hay with this. I don't think Herr Direktor realizes how precarious his position is right now."

"Indeed."

"In the meantime, arresting the Jew might get the public's mind off of murder long enough for your boys to find the real culprit."

"That would be nice."

"Yes, it would be nice." Stefan nodded. *"Gute Nacht, Martin."*

"You don't want a ride?"

"Right now, I'd prefer to walk. It helps me think."

✠ ✠ ✠

MARGOT'S FINGERTIPS brushed the bruise on her cheek as her eyes peered into the dull mirror of an old compact. Though the pain was gone, it had turned ugly—a jaundice-yellow inkblot in the middle of her face. She wanted to cry out in protest, but to whom could she possibly complain when the source of the indignities both external and internal was a man who had sworn an oath to protect Munich's citizens?

Brief thoughts entered her mind. She wondered why he had become so nasty of late and with so little provocation. Normally she would think it had something to do with the two murdered women, but his rage had begun weeks before. Margot suspected he was jealous.

Idiot.

They are all idiots.

Still, he had his good points. He was strong. He was handsome. More important, he was powerful. He had connections, and he had used them to help her out in the past. When those swine at work were tormenting her, all she had to do was mention it once. They hadn't bothered her since.

It was good to know someone like that, because she was a Jewess.

In the end, it was worth the intermittent outbursts and the occasional welt. Besides, what couldn't be rationalized away was hidden behind the application of makeup. With deft hands, Margot dipped the powder puff into her compact and dabbed a fresh pink cover over the hideous discoloration, smoothing out the blotches with her fingers.

Almost as good as new.

Almost was acceptable.

NINETEEN

✠ Der Blumengarten Rooming House for Women was a two-story wooden structure, one of the many broken buildings that littered the southern area of the city. Fronted by a mud-filled rut that, in drier times, passed as a lane, the place was badly in need of repair. Some shutters were missing slats, rot had settled into the steps of the porch, and paint was peeling from the wood siding. It could easily have been mistaken for a notorious "cigarette room," but the proprietor had put up an additional sign stating FOR PROPER LADIES ONLY. Most of the units had been rented to long-term residents, but two ground-floor flats were let out at weekly rates.

The lobby was little more than a front desk, and everyone—tenant as well as guest—was required to sign in and sign out. Tending the register was an English lady named Ruth Baylor, a desiccated old woman with gray hair that had been knotted into a tight bun. She was initially inattentive, but her indifference was shattered as soon as Berg, Müller, and Storf pulled out their police identifications.

Flipping through the pages of the guest book, Frau Baylor confirmed that Marlena Druer had signed out four days ago, at three-thirty in the afternoon to be exact, and as of yet, had not signed back in. Since she had paid two weeks' rent in advance, and since two weeks had not elapsed, Frau Baylor saw no reason for alarm.

"And what is this about?" she finally asked.

"We need to look in Fräulein Druer's room." Berg looked around. Why someone like Marlena Druer—a woman of supposed means—had chosen to stay in such an establishment was an interesting subject of speculation.

Consternation spread across the Englishwoman's face. "For what reason? Is she in trouble?"

"No, madam, she is not," Storf replied.

"Then why are the police here?"

Since the morning papers hadn't identified the newest body, Berg decided to lie for convenience. "We were told that she was looking for a specific item of importance. It might have been left behind in her room."

"What item is that?" Frau Baylor asked.

"That is all we're allowed to divulge, madam," Müller broke in.

Berg said, "Am I correct in assuming that no one has disturbed the room since Fräulein Druer left?"

"But of course! I run an honest establishment."

"Then you'll not mind escorting us to her room?"

Frau Baylor hesitated. It was then that her English heritage showed itself. A true German woman wouldn't have stalled when given an implied order.

"Bitte?" Berg requested.

Slowly, the woman rose from her desk and retrieved a ring of skeleton keys hanging on the wall behind her. "Come this way."

The trio followed her down a dark hallway, trampling on a wood floor that creaked under the weight of human travel. Using the weak illumination of a gas wall sconce, Frau Baylor took several tries to find the correct key. Since it was evening, the chamber was dark. Frau Baylor lit two kerosene lamps that bathed the room in a flickering orange glow. The fuel gave off a stale odor. It took several moments for Berg's eyes to adjust. When they did, he gave the room a quick look around, eyes traveling floor to ceiling. A decent amount of space, enough for a bed, a chair, and a cluttered desktop—books, papers, pamphlets, and a Remington 2 model typewriter.

The Englishwoman arched her brow, eyes affixed on the printed material strewn across the desk. As her hand inched toward one of the pamphlets, Berg blocked it with his body. "Thank you, Frau Baylor, you may leave. I know you must get back to your duties, looking after your women . . . and their guests." Berg smiled. "My men and I can conduct the rest of the search without inconveniencing you."

Frau Baylor took a step back, arms folded across her chest. "And how do I know that you will not steal anything?"

Berg conjured mock outrage. "Are you accusing the police of misbehavior?"

There was a moment of stiff silence. Without responding, Frau Baylor turned on her heels and stomped out. The men waited a few moments, then attempted to stifle spontaneous laughter.

"What a witch!" Storf said.

"Nothing that a good ramming couldn't change," Müller added.

"If you put a sack over her head, I suppose it would be possible," Storf retorted.

Berg laughed jovially, then picked up two piles of paper from the desk, handing one to Storf and the other to Müller, who asked what they were looking for.

"You'll know it when you see it." Berg took a third stack, mostly political leaflets, material that would have been passed out during Munich's numerous rallies. Sorting through the papers under poor lighting, Berg found two pamphlets that were marked up by hand with marginal notes and underlining. One was entitled *A Summons to the Kameraden*, the other *Workers of the World:* pieces of Russian propaganda that invited German workers to wake up to the call and join the great Socialist cause. "Apparently Marlena, like Anna Gross, flirted with Kommunismus."

Müller said, "Haven't these women got better things to do than to stir up trouble?"

Berg turned to Storf. "In the course of your interview with Fräulein Schulweiss, did she express any interest in Kommunismus?"

Ulrich's mouth turned sour. "We talked about Marlena, Axel, not politics. With an air of distaste, Fräulein Schulweiss described Druer as wild and bohemian. Though she was upset by Marlena's murder, I think she would be appalled if she knew her sister's friend was interested in an abomination."

Müller said, "If Marlena was a Kommunist, why would she associate with staunch conservative people like the Schulweisses?"

"They gave her respectability," Berg said. "Allowed her to penetrate circles not otherwise available to her. At least, we are detecting a pattern, no? Two bourgeois women with Kommunist leanings: A political motive for the murders is looking better."

Müller looked up from his papers. "You think it's some fanatical anti-Kommunist?"

"Perhaps."

"That's ridiculous," Storf said. "There are a lot bigger animals to hunt than these pathetic women who dress like aristocrats, fanning themselves with peacock feathers while embracing proletariat causes."

"Both women had money," Berg said. "If you want to weaken a cause, cut off its source of income." He held up the papers. "Someone has to pay for these pamphlets and for all the professional political agitators." He squinted in the murky glow of the lamps. "Let's sort the papers by date . . . if they're dated. We are looking for references to the mysterious Russian or to Robert Schick."

The men worked in silence for fifteen minutes. When the papers were properly stacked, Berg began to go through the desk drawers. One of them contained a locked steel box. Storf looked up with interest.

"Money?"

Berg rattled the container. "Perhaps." He took a pocketknife from his boot and worked the tip into the lock. It was of very poor quality and popped open without much prodding. Inside were a bundled stack of letters and a thick wad of new marks. "*Herrjemine!* This woman could have supported a lot more than a few proletarians!"

"How much?" Müller asked anxiously.

Berg exhaled as he counted out the bills. "Almost five hundred new marks. It is clear from this find that no one has been in the room since her disappearance."

"Who was it meant for?"

"Lord only knows." There was a moment of silence. Wordlessly, Berg counted out one hundred fifty marks apiece. The three men pocketed the bills.

"What are you doing with the remainder?" Müller asked.

"It will be recorded along with the rest of Marlena Druer's effects."

"Why leave so much, Axel? It makes much more sense that she would have traveled with her money, no?"

"That brings up a good point," Storf said. "Why didn't she take this much money with her?"

"Fear of robbery," Müller said. "Way too much to carry around in these dangerous times."

Storf said, "But she'd leave it here? In this dump?"

Müller answered, "No one would dream that she traveled with this much cash. And perhaps no one except the Schulweisses knew she was here."

"The better question is what had she planned to do with the money?" Berg divvied up the letters. "Let's find out a bit about her personal life, shall we?"

"And the rest of the money, Axel?" Müller persisted.

Berg said, "She was carrying around this fortune for a reason. If we find the reason but leave behind no money, it will cast suspicion on all of us. We were blessed with good fortune. Let's not spit at the fates, hmmm?"

After five minutes of sifting through Marlena's correspondence, Storf looked up. "Our luck is still with us. Here is our Schwabing Soviet." He handed Berg the letter.

My Dearest Lady—

I count the days until your arrival, my most beautiful and elegant woman. How fortunate is my luck to have made your acquaintance and so much more. There is no way for me, a man made meager by the whimsy of fate and the wickedness of hatred, to repay you for all your goodness, generosity, and support. I will do my most profound best to ensure that your goodwill is not in vain, and that in the future, Munich will be liberated from the loathsome, petty burghers who feast upon Germany's good citizens. May our days together be filled with excitement and drama and the personal connection we dream about. Until we meet, may I forever remain in your heart as well as your debt.

With true fondness and deepest gratitude and, dare I say it, love,

Robert

"Robert," Berg said out loud. "There's our link. He appears to be Marlena's paramour . . . although she wasn't the one with semen inside of her. I wonder if she was pregnant?"

"Why?"

"A motive to kill. Two women, *both* pregnant, and a man who doesn't want either of them." Berg gave the letter to Müller. "Although in the context of this letter, it appears that Fräulein Druer was more interested in politics. She appears to be financing something very big."

"Like a major rally?" Müller said. "That is not so big. Just hire a bunch of hooligans or schoolboys to pass out the leaflets. They cost next to nothing."

"Yes, hooligans cost nothing," Berg said. "Good military soldiers are more expensive."

Müller said, "She was financing a putsch?"

"And why not? It almost worked for Herr Hitler. With a little bit more planning and a lot more money, who knows what could have happened?"

"Do you think it was this Robert who was responsible for both Anna's and Marlena's deaths?"

Berg said, "It would seem pointless for Robert to murder a woman who was supporting him."

"Maybe something changed *her* mind," Storf said.

"Like what?" Müller asked.

The men thought a moment. Berg said, "If this is Robert Schick, the same one who was very well acquainted with Anna Gross, maybe Marlena was jealous of his relationship with Anna. We know that Anna was involved with someone."

Müller said, "So Marlena found out about Anna and decided to cut off her support for Robert?"

"Perhaps."

"But why would Robert *kill* Druer?"

"It was accidental," Berg said. "They fought, and things became rough. Or perhaps Marlena threatened to tell Anna's husband of her affair with Robert. Robert killed Marlena to silence her."

Müller said, "Axel, I thought you told us that the maid implied there was no affair?"

"Out of loyalty—she was covering for her mistress."

"Didn't you *just* say this was a political murder?" Storf said.

"I don't know anything for certain, Ulrich; I am entertaining possibilities."

There was a pause. Then Müller said, "I need a smoke."

The three men lit up. Within moments, the room became clouded in nicotine. Storf exhaled a puff of rancid air. "Axel, even if we assume for a moment that Robert Schick murdered Marlena Druer . . . why would he then murder Anna Gross? Remember she was killed after Marlena."

"Maybe Anna found out about Marlena's murder and threatened to go to the police. A quick romp in the hay is one thing. Hiding a murder is quite another."

"How would Anna Gross know about Marlena's death when we just discovered it?"

Berg shrugged. "Maybe Robert Schick told her."

"That is not credible," Storf said.

"Just a thought," Berg said.

"Maybe the two murders are unrelated," Storf told him.

"That is another thought." Berg held up the letter. "However, if this Robert turns out to be Robert Schick, that is more than a coincidence." He glanced at the letter. "It has no last name, but there is a return address and it's not too far from here." Berg checked his watch. It was half past six. "Shall we pay a visit?"

"It's been a long day," Müller said. "I doubt if he'll be in. Perhaps it's better if we wait until tomorrow morning."

"And let this man slip from our grasp?" Berg frowned. "I will not take that chance. If you don't want to accompany me, I'll go alone."

Storf shrugged. "I'll go with you, Axel."

"You two leave me no choice." Müller rolled his eyes. "What do we do with her belongings?"

Berg looked around. Under the bed, he found a leather valise, unlocked and empty. "Put everything in here."

"Including the money box?" Müller said. "Isn't it going to look odd to our fellow police that the lock is broken and there is still cash inside?"

"We shall tell them the truth," Axel said. "That we broke open the lock. That there is still money inside is evidence of our honesty." He looked at his colleagues. "What occurred in this room remains between the three of us. Agreed?"

Müller said, "Agreed."

"Ulrich?" Berg said.

"Of course, of course," Storf said.

"So why the long face?" Müller asked him.

"Where do I hide so much cash?"

"You don't hide it, you spend it." Müller's expression became lecherous. "That is what whores are for."

TWENTY

✠ The little man blocked the door, his wiry mustache trembling with anger at the police intrusion.

"I tell you, Herr Schick is not in his room! And I will not allow strangers rummaging through his personal effects—"

"We are not strangers, we are the police!" Storf told him.

The desk clerk wasn't much of a physical specimen. Short and stout, but more flab than muscle. Berg could have easily dealt with the obstruction with a single push. But diplomacy often worked as well as physical force. "If you are worried, you may accompany us to his room. This will assure you that we will take nothing."

The little man reddened. "I hadn't assumed for a moment that you'd take anything!"

"This little discussion is throwing off our schedule." Berg tapped his pocket watch. "You are not going to prevent us from going to his room. So get the key and let's go upstairs."

"I cannot leave my post," the little man said.

"Then give us the key." Berg became irritated. "Come, man. It's late and we have families!"

Reluctantly, the clerk handed Berg a ring of keys. "Bring it down when you're done."

"Which key is it?" Berg asked.

The little man shrugged with indifference, then pointed to the stairs. "Fifth floor."

Slowly, the men trudged up the steps. When they got to the correct room, Berg began feeding the skeleton keys into the lock. The first key didn't fit, nor did the second. Berg cursed as he worked the locks. His grumblings brought out a neighbor.

"Excuse me?" the man said. "What do you think you're doing?"

Spoken with an English accent. The man was rail thin and hadn't a single hair on his head, which was smooth and round as a baby's behind. He wore a crumpled black suit and a gray shirt that had once been white. No tie. The man had probably slept in his clothes. Berg snarled out, "Police business. Please go back to your room, sir."

"I doubt you'll have any luck even if you find the correct key."

Berg looked up from his task. "Pardon?"

"Lord Robert left yesterday . . . took all his baggage with him."

"*Lord* Robert?" Müller said. "He is aristocracy?"

The bald Englishman smiled. "That is how he introduced himself. But I have my doubts."

Storf took out a pad. "And your name is?"

"Michael Green. I'm a reporter for the *London Eagle*." He extended his hand to Berg. "And you are . . ."

"Inspektor Axel Berg of the *Mordkommission*." He shook Green's hand, then took out Gerhart Leit's sketch of the man who had been with Anna the night she died. "Are we speaking about the same man?"

Green studied the picture for just a moment. "That

very well could be him. If you give me that sketch, I'll put it in the paper for you."

"I think not," Berg answered. "You are English, sir, but not exactly."

"Good ear," Green answered. "American. Born and raised in Boston. I went to university at Oxford and never left. What do you want with Lord Robert? Oh, I forgot. You are the police. You ask the questions."

Berg's lips formed a small sneer. "I see you understand the German way. Tell us about Lord Robert."

"Why should I?" Green said.

"Because I have the power to arrest you," Berg said.

"On what grounds?" Green said.

"It doesn't matter," Berg said. "That is also the German way." He tried another key, and this time his efforts met with success. He opened the door, and switched on an electric light, staring into an immaculately made-up room devoid of any belongings. Berg swore under his breath.

Boldly, Green marched through the door and scratched his bald head. "Told you so."

Berg spoke to his men. "It does not look promising, but let's go through the drawers anyway."

Green ambled about the sterile space with his hands in his pockets. "So what do the police really think about Herr Hitler?"

"Can you kindly step out and let us do our job?" Müller said.

"Nothing *to* do." Storf slammed the closet door shut. "There is nothing here."

"I told you he left with all his baggage."

"Did he say where he was going?" Berg asked Green.

"Not to me, but why would he? I barely knew the man."

Müller said, "So tell us what you do know about Lord Robert Schick."

"Schick?" Green arched his brows. "He told me his name was Robert Hurlbutt."

Berg looked under the bed, then stood up. "The downstairs clerk knew him as Robert Schick. It appears the man has a few aliases."

The American smiled. "Robert was a puzzler."

"How so?" Berg asked.

Green thought a moment. "He spoke a serviceable English, but not the most educated English. This is not surprising. Many Englishmen with fathers in the diplomatic corps have been raised in other countries, so their English might not be as refined as that of the native born. But the accent bothered me. If you have an English father who speaks to you in English, your English shouldn't have a Continental accent."

"What country?" Müller asked.

"Maybe German, maybe Russian. Perhaps a mixture."

"How was his German?" Müller asked.

"To my foreign ear, it sounded fluent and beautiful. He spoke very poetically and used many long words. That also made me suspicious. Who was he trying to impress?"

Müller said, "Any ideas?"

"If you ask me, he's what we call an impostor in English."

"A *Hochstapler,*" Berg translated.

"Yeah, that's right. *Hochstapler*—although I don't know what his game was. I have been around the English peerage. They are all pompous asses, but with Hurlbutt, there was definitely something off."

Berg took out his notepad. "Off in what way?"

"As a reporter you have a sixth sense about these kinds of things . . . who's lying and so forth. He was smooth, but most con men are."

"Con men?"

Green gave a hint of a smile. "I have seen several well-dressed ladies come in and go out of his apartment. A curious sort would ask what they were doing there."

Berg smiled. "And did you ask?"

A pinkish tinge dotted the American's cheeks. "I'm a reporter, so of course I asked. He said his relationship with the women was strictly a professional one. And I never did get any solid evidence of impropriety. No breathless noises, at least. And let me tell you, these walls are thin. You could knock a hole through with a single blow."

"Was this lady one of his guests?" Berg showed him the picture of Marlena Druer.

"This lady looks dead."

"Yes or no."

Green sighed. "I couldn't say yes or no."

Out came Anna Gross's photograph. "How about this one?"

Again Green hedged. "I think . . . yes. But I wouldn't swear to it. I don't spend a lot of time in my room." The American paused. "She looks alive. Is she?"

"And what profession did Lord Robert profess to be engaged in?"

"You didn't answer my question."

"I know I didn't," Berg said. "Still, it would behoove you as a foreigner to answer mine."

"Tough guy, huh?" Green smiled. "*Lord* Robert never elaborated. I think it was conning women out of money."

"Any specific reason to think that?" Storf said.

"No, not really. Just . . . certain things paint a certain picture."

Berg said, "Thank you for the information, Herr Green; you have been most helpful."

The American regarded Berg, unable to ascertain if the Inspektor was putting him on. "You're welcome."

"If Lord Robert should return, I would like you to tell me immediately." He handed Green his card.

"All right," Green said. "Now how about helping me out? You said you're from the *Mordkommission.* You show me a picture of at least one dead woman. I've got to ask: What has Lord Robert got to do with the two murdered women in the papers?"

"This is Germany, Herr Green, not America. As you stated, I ask the questions; you answer." Berg stuck his notepad into his jacket. "If I have more questions, I may visit you again."

"Sure, I'm not going anywhere . . . unless I'm kicked out of the country."

"Why would you be kicked out of the country?" Storf asked.

"A lot of people in England are not too fond of your Munich *Meister,* Herr Hitler."

"He is not our *Meister,* Herr Green," Berg said.

"Not now . . ." Green pulled out a cigarette. "But the situation here, Inspektor, is a volatile one."

Berg opened the door and pointed to the hallway. After

everyone had left the room, he shut the door. "*Guten Abend,* Herr Green."

"Don't you Bavarians say . . . what is it? *Pfueti?*"

"How about 'good-bye'?" Berg said, speaking English.

Green blew out a cloud of smoke, which wafted through the cold air and traveled down the dimly lit hallway. "By the way, the Hurlbutts are a very prominent Harvard-educated family from New England. Lord Robert or whoever the heck he is may have spent some time at Harvard . . . or at least in Cambridge . . . Cambridge, Massachusetts."

"Yes, I know that Harvard is in Massachusetts, Herr Green." Berg paused. "Choosing that name Hurlbutt, sir . . . does that mean anything?"

Green shrugged. "I don't know, Inspektor. You're the police, you figure it out."

TWENTY-ONE

Trying to plead a case that held few concrete clues and very little evidence, Berg used drama and feigned excitement to further his cause. By the expression on Volker's face, it was a useless endeavor.

Berg plodded on. "We are *closing in,* Herr Kommissar. Yesterday we discovered his apartment."

"Whose apartment?"

"The suspect. He is using aliases."

Volker studied his nails, a practiced mannerism that showed he was bored. "So you do not know his true identity, much less know where he is right now."

Berg rubbed his hands together. A bitter wind rattled the ill-fitting windows and chilled the stone floors of the Ett Strasse station house. The country's coal supply was strained; the mines had been stripped almost to the center of the earth. Suppliers were asking exorbitant prices. Volker and his family grew wealthier by the hour. Not surprisingly, the Kommissar was dressed in a fine woolen three-piece suit with a silk tie. Why the man continued to work as a public servant was anyone's guess. Why the family didn't support his sister with more than subsistence handouts was a dark mystery.

"He's been using the name Robert—Robert Schick and Robert Hurlbutt. We have no listing for either man yet, but—"

"Is he English?"

"He speaks English—"

"That was not the question."

"Possibly he is a Russian who has learned English and German. We think he may have some diplomatic connections."

"That would not be good—"

"Or maybe not," Berg quickly added. "I just brought that up because it seems that the man may have spent some time in England or America."

"Accusing a diplomat of murder would be out of the question," Volker told him. "I hope you understand that."

No one should be allowed to kill without consequences. Berg would simply have to explore the diplomatic possibility without Volker's help. "Most likely, he is a bourgeois who has done some traveling."

Volker grew irritated. "I need to know if you've made significant progress beyond what you have told me."

"I think that *is* significant progress."

"Perhaps to you, but for others it is not enough."

"You are getting pressured, sir?"

"I am accountable for answers, yes. But in the end *I* make decisions." Said with ego and a hint of malevolence. Volker adjusted his tie, knotting it high on his throat, more for warmth than for vanity. "I've decided to go back to my original plan. Arrest Anton Gross for the murder of his wife, Anna. If people demand a reason why—and I suspect they won't because Gross is a Jew—tell them that Anna was making a cuckold out of her husband. Moreover, she was pregnant with another man's child. It was this last fact that sent Anton into a murderous rage."

Berg swallowed hard. It was early in the morning, and

his throat was dry. This morning's coffee was bitter, laced with cheap grain used as an extender. A little bit was tolerable, but Britta had used way too much. "And where is our proof of Anton's guilt?"

"You don't need *proof* for an arrest, Axel. It is early, Herr Gross should still be home. You may take the *Zweikraftrad* rather than go on foot."

"And what about Marlena Druer?"

"What about her?"

"Are you telling me that her murder is independent of Anna Gross?"

"Can you find something that links Anton Gross to Druer?"

"Of course not. I cannot even find a link between Anna's murder and Anton Gross. He was in bed the entire night."

"So Anton hired someone to do the nasty deed." Volker took out a cigarette and lit up using an engraved silver lighter. He took a deep inhalation, then offered the cigarette to Berg.

"*Danke*," Berg said. *The bastard!* Volker knew how expensive such cigarettes were. He was trying to bribe him into compliance with a whiff of fine tobacco.

Volker lit a fresh smoke for himself. "You will continue to investigate Druer's murder. If your suppositions about Marlena and Anna dying at the same hand turn out to be true—*and* you find a reasonable suspect—we will release Anton Gross."

"And if he is executed before I can establish my case?"

"Such is the fate of Jews, Axel. They are cursed from birth, but we Germans are civilized. We carry out the execution in a swift and painless manner. We are nothing if not efficient."

✠ ✠ ✠

"THIS IS AN OUTRAGE!" the butler cried out. "A complete and utter outrage!"

"Now, now, Haslinger." Gross reassured his servant with a pat on the shoulder from his gloved hand. "I am sure this terrible mistake will be rectified before the day is over." He glared at Berg. "It is not enough that I have lost my wife? That I am still grieving for her? You have the audacity to accuse me of being her murderer?"

Berg felt small. The best reply was none at all.

"My attorney will have your job for this recklessness. I will have your head!"

"I don't think so, Herr Gross, and I would recommend that you cooperate."

Gross put on a dark wool overcoat. "I don't understand why I must ride in that silly contraption of yours when I have a perfectly suitable car."

"Orders from Herr Kommissar Volker."

"He thinks I am going to escape?"

"It is not my duty to question his orders, only to comply with them."

"Yes, God forbid a good man like you would question!"

Berg flinched at the sarcasm. He took his charge's arm, but Gross pulled away.

"I can walk without an escort, thank you."

Haslinger, the ever-faithful butler, opened the door for his master. Quickly, he ran ahead and pushed the button for the elevator operator. There were tears in his eyes. "Do be careful, sir. Please. The climate in Munich is not at all favorable to . . ."

He stopped short.

"To Jews, you mean." Gross smiled at his servant. "Yes, I know, Haslinger. And your loyalty to my household has been a source of light in these dark times."

The butler bowed his head. "Thank you, Herr Gross."

"Be strong, Haslinger, be strong." The elevator door opened and Gross stepped inside, giving his servant a jaunty wave. To Berg, he said, "Are you coming, Inspektor?"

Wordlessly, Berg entered the lift. The quick ride down was uncomfortable: The elevator operator's eyes remained fixed on the buttons. Gross's demeanor was expressionless.

Outside, a small band of hoodlum teenagers wearing swastikas jeered as soon as they saw Gross. Berg helped Gross inside the sidecar of the *Zweikraftrad,* then glanced at the group of ruffians. The tallest of the young boys had a familiar face—long and red and pitted with acne. Lothar Felb, Volker's nephew, was in the throes of puberty, beginning to develop a layer of muscle. That was truly worrisome. Lothar taunted Gross as if his actions were without repercussions, a stupid move considering his jaw still had a lump from the whack his uncle had given him a week ago.

"Away with you now," Berg shouted. "This is a police matter. Out of my way!"

"This is a matter for the people!" Lothar shouted back. "Herr Hitler will see to it that justice is done."

Berg went up to Lothar until they were nose to nose. The lad's breath stank of onions and cheap beer. Berg spoke quietly and pointedly. "Herr Hitler can mete out justice when Herr Hitler is in power. Right now, he isn't in power. But your uncle is."

No one spoke.

Berg said, "Out of my way, lad. Don't be foolish."

Lothar didn't back down. To avoid confrontation, Berg let the kid save face. He turned around and tended to his business.

"Idiots," he whispered. But Gross heard him.

"It is idiots like you who urge them on."

"I suggest you watch who you are addressing." Berg's words rang hollow. He was getting nervous. The crowd was gaining in numbers. One of the boys picked up a small rock and hurled it at Gross, hitting him in the arm. The lawless act emboldened another to act accordingly. A bigger rock followed. Then another. Berg started the *Kraftrad* and bolted onto the street, hoping to speed away. Unfortunately, he was slowed down by roads clogged with pedestrians, bicycles, autos, wagons, taxis, and buses. The vagabonds dogged the motorcycle, running as they shouted epithets.

"*Jude! Jude!*" the boys screamed.

"*Schmutziger Jude!*"

"*Dreckiger Jude!*"

"*Übler Jude!*"

Their obscenities attracted attention. The crowd grew steadily, swarming toward the *Kraftrad* as Berg frantically tried to steer it through the congested streets. If Berg had been on a single motorcycle, he could have dodged the hooligans easily. But with this vehicle's cumbersome sidecar, it was hard to maneuver through the traffic. He began to worry about Gross's safety.

Damn Volker!

Berg was forced to stop for a streetcar. The crowd swelled.

"This has gone beyond absurd," Gross protested. "I feel threatened. I'm leaving the car this instant!"

A rock pelted Berg across the chest. "Stay where you are!"

"And get stoned? How dare you!"

"It's for your own safety!" Berg called to the crowd to disperse immediately, but his shouts were drowned out by the mob's booing. Without conscious thinking, Berg reached down for the pocketknife hidden in his boot, but before he could retrieve it, he was knocked in the chest by a rock. "Damn it!"

"Yes, I see how safe you're keeping me!" Gross ducked, barely escaping the path of a whizzing projectile. "Damn you and damn the police! I am getting out of here before these monsters kill us both!"

Gross hoisted himself out of the sidecar.

"He's getting away!" screamed one of the hoodlums.

"The *Jude* is trying to escape!" yelled another.

"I've got the bastard!" Lothar Felb cried in delight. He pulled back his fist and punched Gross in the stomach. Berg jumped off the motorcycle and vaulted onto Lothar, clipping him across the chin. Lothar reared back and elbowed Berg hard in the ribs. Berg fell to his knees. Lothar and a buddy continued to kick him until he lay on the ground, prostrate, his arms over his face, his hands over his head. Finally, the kicking stopped, but that was only because he was being trampled to death, beaten and crushed by a malodorous pile of hot human flesh.

He gasped and sputtered, his lungs begging for fresh air, his hands flaying about.

I am not going to die like this, he told himself. *Not without a fight!* Using his limbs as weapons, he kicked and grabbed and poked and yanked until his eyes made out the cool gray mist of daylight. Clawing like a caged cat, he dug his way out of the human mass, using his fingernails as rakes as he gashed through clothing and skin. Once he had surfaced, he inhaled hungrily, and as he did, a sharp pain coursed through his lungs and chest. His nose was bleeding and so was his lip. As he ran his tongue across his teeth, he thanked God that he could feel his incisors still firmly rooted in his mouth. In the distance, Berg could hear the welcome sound of official horns blowing.

Out of the corner of his eye, he saw what he hoped was the police wagon. He was feeling woozy, barely able to stand on his feet. Abruptly, he felt an arm on his jacket. He pivoted around, and a tingling shiver went down his spine.

Face-to-face, staring into calm blue eyes. Black hair, a long face, and a swatch of black mustache hiding a thin upper lip. "I would never sanction an attack on our good German police," Hitler said to Berg. "Never!"

"Just as you would never sanction a putsch!"

Hitler's brows narrowed, his nostrils flaring in indignation.

"You sanction nothing but lawlessness." Berg was suddenly aware that his speech was slurred.

A smile formed on Hitler's lips. "I sanction whatever is necessary to get rid of the enemies of our Fatherland. Make sure you are not counted among them."

"I hold you responsible for this!" Berg barked. He coughed sputum veined with blood.

Hitler's upper lip twitched. He turned to one of the youths and nodded.

Without warning, Berg was grabbed by his coat collar and pulled upward. Before he could react, a granite-hard object thwacked his cheekbone. Immediately, he went light-headed, as his vision turned to pinpoints of light. His stomach turned into a pit of acid as bile wormed up through his esophagus. When his eyesight cleared, Berg realized he was looking at the world in blurred duplicate.

But even through his compromised vision, he could make out the remnants of what was once Anton Gross, now a bloodied mass of flesh and pulp, unrecognizable as a living being. One of the Jew's eyes dangled from its socket on the white twine of a nerve. The man's nose had been crushed so hard, his face was now concave.

That was the last image that burned in Berg's brain before he blacked out.

TWENTY-TWO

✠   In and out of a drug-induced stupor; mercifully, the pain lasted only for brief interludes. It took several days for Berg to wake up, for the medication to wear off sufficiently until he knew he was in a bad way. Head throbbing, his mouth caked with dust, each pulse of his heart sending waves of agony through his jaw. He blinked several times, then tried to swallow. When no saliva materialized to soothe his throat, he hacked drily, his temples pounding with each cough. He knew he wasn't dead, but he felt as if he were.

"Papa is up!" Monika shrieked. "Papa is up."

"Hush!" Britta scolded, then softened her tone of voice. "This is a hospital, dolly."

"Here, Papa." Joachim brought a wet rag to his father's mouth, moistening his lips, and wiping his face with filial love. With great effort, Berg hoisted his body upward until he was in a semireclined position. Monika smoothed his sheets as Britta propped up his head with soft pillows.

"You want water, Axel?"

The answer was yes, but Berg couldn't move his head. He blinked because that was all he could do, and even that seemed Herculean.

A needle in his arm was attached to an IV. That meant

he was in a hospital ward. The muscles of his neck creaked as he slowly turned his head.

Ten beds on each side, and all of them were occupied. Above the headboards hung wooden crucifixes; nuns in black habits and nurses in starched white uniforms scurried about—a life-size chessboard. As the grogginess lifted from his brain, he became aware of sounds . . . moans . . . groans . . . the soft sighs of weeping. Whispers crackled through the air like radio static. He freed his hand from under the sheets and pointed to the water glass.

Britta held the cup to his lips. "Sip slowly."

As if to sip any other way was an option. Feeling the cool liquid course down his parched throat, he nodded for more.

Again, Britta offered the glass, but this time his thirst was greedy. Trying to make up for forty-eight hours of breathing hot, stale air.

"Slowly, Axel," Britta told him.

Within a minute, he had finished the entire glass.

"Good man," he heard Müller say.

Georg was here?

"More water," Berg said. His voice was tinny. It reverberated in the hollows of his skull.

Britta held her hand to her face and tears leaked out. "It's good to hear your voice, Axel."

"Water."

"Let me ask the nurse—"

"Damn the nurse," Berg responded. "More water."

"Das ist gut," Storf told him. "He's recovering quickly."

Georg and Ulrich were *both* here. For them to have come . . . had he been that close to the other side?

Joachim poured water from a pitcher into the empty glass, then brought it to his father's lips. Berg managed to take the vessel out of his son's hands and into his own grip. "I'm fine," he stated.

His announcement was met with laughter from everyone except Britta. "You are not fine, Axel. You were beaten up, and you must stay in bed if you hope to recover."

"Horseshit!" Berg insisted. "How long have I been here?"

"Talk slowly, Axel," Storf told him. "Your jaw and lips are twice their size. It's hard to understand your words."

"How . . . ?" Another swallow. "How long . . . have I been . . . here . . . in a hospital?"

"You came in Monday morning; it's now Wednesday," Storf told him.

"What some people won't do to sleep late in the morning," Müller said.

Berg felt his lips break into a lopsided smile. His hand traced the topography of his jawline, his fingertips delicately moving over an enormous swelling. There were no bandages around the area. Though very tender and sore, his mouth had mobility. "It isn't broken . . . my jaw?"

Monika stood at his bedside and plopped a kiss on top of his head. "You have a giant bump, Papa. The size of an egg. I didn't know a bone could grow a bump so big."

"It's not broken, Papa," Joachim told him. "Just bruised. Very badly bruised."

"It's all purple and red and icky," Monika told him.

Joachim pushed blond hair out of his pale blue eyes. "The doctor was amazed, Papa. None of your bones are broken. He said you must have bones like lead."

"He has a brain like lead," Britta whispered. But he heard her. He offered her his hand and she took it. Again the tears escaped her eyes, trailing down her cheeks.

"Come, come," he told her. *Gott in Himmel,* how he hurt. "I'm tough. You're not going to get rid of me that easily. What's going on?"

Storf said, "If you rest properly, the doctor thinks that you'll be up and about in a week."

"A *week?*"

"Maybe a little sooner," Müller said.

"Maybe a little longer . . ." Britta turned her head.

Footsteps. Berg homed in on the source of the sound.

Volker.

"Our patient has awakened."

Fuck you, Berg thought. But he must have spoken out loud—and clearly, too. Volker bristled. "Britta, dear, can you take the children out for a spot of air."

Britta didn't move. As Volker repeated his request, she told him that she had heard him the first time. She looked down at her hand, her fingers laced with her husband's.

"Can't it wait, Herr Kommissar?"

"I need to speak with your husband, Britta."

Without the *dear.* Volker was angry. *Fuck him.* But this time, Berg managed to keep his words in his head.

With reluctance, Britta let go of her husband's hand and took Monika's small, soft hand. "I'll be back in five minutes, Axel."

As soon as his family was out of earshot, Volker said, "I'll assume the profanities were due to your delirious state. How do you feel, Axel?"

"I'll recover," he said softly. "What . . . what happened to Anton Gross?"

Müller blew out a gust of air; Volker played with the knot in his tie. "He died . . . trying to escape arrest."

Berg sat up, his eyes filled with fury. "That's a lie!"

Volker ignored his outburst. "He was trying to escape justice, and you were beaten up by him as you tried to restrain him. A true hero you are, Axel, risking your life for the honor of your profession. Deserving of a citation. I have talked to the Lord Mayor in regard to this—"

"This is pure shit!" Berg interrupted.

"Don't excite yourself, Axel." Volker smiled. "And don't waste your breath talking. No one can understand a word you say."

"It was your nephew who . . ." Berg suddenly felt a bomb of pain detonating in his head. For a brief moment, he was back in the trenches. He couldn't complete his sentence.

"Did you say something about Lothar?" Volker shook his head and clucked his tongue. "Quite a troublemaker. You needn't fret about him, Axel. He will be dealt with. You need to summon all your energy into recovery. I'll try to drop by tonight . . . after the rally." Volker took out his pocket watch. "Quarter to nine." He flipped the cover on his watch. "Are you gentlemen coming? It would not look good to our citizens for their officers to arrive late for duty."

"Five minutes, Kommissar," Müller said.

"No longer than that, Georg. You know how I frown on tardiness."

"We'll be there, Kommissar," Storf said.

"Good man, Ulrich, good man." Volker turned and left.

"Motherfucker!" Berg said. "It's all bullshit!"

"Axel, you must understand," Storf said. "There was a riot. People were hurt. Not only you."

"Badly?"

"None as badly as you were," Müller said. "But there were some bruises and broken bones."

Storf said, "They blame it on the Jew."

"It wasn't the Jew!" Berg said. "It was Hitler's gang . . . thugs and hoodlums." Lord, how his head hurt—but he couldn't let go. "They were there from the very beginning, throwing rocks at Gross . . . at me, too. Absolutely no regard for the law!"

"The Nazis say the Jew was trying to escape—"

"Lies!"

"It is in the official police report," Storf said. "It is over and done, Axel. There is no sense protesting because you cannot change it."

Berg leaned back on his pillow. It was all a nightmare—the pain that racked his body, the humiliation of being beaten by thugs, Gross's horrifying death. "I hurt" was all that he could say.

"Then you must sleep," Müller said.

Storf tapped Berg gently on the shoulder. "Heal up, Inspektor. All is not lost. We're still working on Marlena Druer's murder. Come back soon. We need your help—not to mention the extra duty we must work with you gone."

Extra duty? Like tinder against a flint, Berg's brain began to spark. "What rally was Volker talking about?"

"Herr Hitler is holding another gathering at Das Kellnerhaus this evening," Storf said. "Big crowds are expected. Emotions will be high."

"The department fears another '23 putsch," Müller

said. "The Nazis are taking their politics to the streets. Volker has assured Mayor Scharnagl and Polizeipräsident Mantel that he will keep things under control. If another riot breaks out, he can wave his job good-bye."

Berg sat up. "And it's tonight?"

"Yes, Axel, tonight," Storf said. "Don't worry. This time the police will not be caught with their pants down."

A political rally by a hot-tempered maniac, and he was in a hospital. He was trapped, confined, and caged, a mere spectator of life. Berg broke into a cold sweat. "My wife will be back any moment." He grabbed Müller's hand. "I'll get rid of her by lunchtime. Then you need to come back here. In a bag, bring in two pillows, and under them hide a long coat, a scarf, and a hat. If anyone asks you what you are carrying, simply say extra pillows for me."

The men appeared stupefied. Perhaps they couldn't understand him. Berg said, "I want you . . . to bring in—"

"We understood you," Storf said.

"Good. Then there is no problem—"

"Axel, you need to rest," Müller said.

"Don't argue with me, Georg. I don't need rest. What I need is you two helping to get me out of here!"

Georg sighed. "Axel, it's—"

"I'm giving you an order. You have no authority to countermand me."

"Volker does," Storf said.

"Volker does not need to know about this any more than he needs to know about the contents of Marlena Druer's strongbox."

Storf's eyes darkened. The binds of sin were stronger than the bonds of duty. Berg sank into his pillows. "You've got to help me. I *order* it."

Müller shrugged. "An order is an order. I will do it. Take care of yourself."

He and Storf hadn't gone more than a couple of feet when they heard Berg strain his vocal cords. His words were: *"And bring a cane!"*

✠ ✠ ✠

BERG INSISTED that Britta go home to care for the children. They had been living at his side for two days and needed to eat properly and rest. Having rid his family from the hospital, his next tactic involved having Storf accompany him to the bathroom while Georg stuffed the pillows under his bedsheets. It was agony to walk and, just for a moment, Berg doubted his sanity. But as in every action, it was always the first step that was the hardest. Once he found his balance, he was able to move at an acceptable pace for the old man he was dressed up to be.

The cane really helped.

Storf was supporting him on his left. "This is lunacy."

"No," Berg countered, "this is stupidity. Hitler is lunacy." He was barely audible behind the scarf wrapped around his mouth.

Georg was at his right. "Careful . . ." A pause. "Exactly what do you hope to accomplish with this breakout? You're not in any position to go anywhere except to a bed."

In silence, Berg slowly shuffled down the stark white hallways until they reached the elevator. The doors parted; the operator gave them barely a glance. They rode down in silence. As soon as he stepped out of the hospital doors, Berg felt an exhilarating surge of newfound freedom—the sights, the sounds, the smells of life. Even Munich's dowdy skies seemed bright and hopeful. "Take me to your apartment, Müller. I'll rest there until the rally tonight."

"And who do you think your wife will run to when she finds out that you're gone?"

"Tell her you know nothing about my whereabouts."

"I'm not a good liar."

On the contrary, Müller was an excellent liar. Berg had learned how to handle a mistress from him. Never admit to anything.

"Then I'll check into a *Wirtshaus*. That way you really won't know where I am. I'll find my own way to the beer hall."

"This isn't a good idea," Müller told him. "You don't show up, we worry that you're lying on a street run over by a wagon."

"Such is life," Berg said. "Nothing is certain."

TWENTY-THREE

✠ The Brownshirts had chosen a spacious beer hall for their circus and filled it to capacity. Das Kellnerhaus was packed and ripe with body odor, but better to sniff at the smells of life than to fill the nostrils with the reek of hospital decay. There was not a chair to be had even if Berg had belonged to one of the *Vereine,* the clubs and unions that laid claim to most of the tables. He was sweating profusely under his coat and scarf but there was nowhere to stow them. The coatracks were sagging under the weight of wool, and many a jacket and bowler lay in a puddle of cloth on the floor. Besides, he didn't dare remove his scarf. He'd scare anyone who looked at his face.

The first time he had regarded himself in the mirror, he'd almost passed out. His face could have been a model for a Cubist painting. Although he couldn't change the asymmetry of his bones—only nature's healing would do that—he could, with deft use of powder and rouge, smooth out the blotches. His artistry had its practical applications.

Berg inched his way to the back of the establishment, sharing the rear wall with the coppers who lined the drinking hall. The police were all business, nightsticks in hand, hard eyes scanning the room for signs of disorder. The powers in Munich weren't taking any chances. The police had been given instructions to quell any social disturbance, no matter how seemingly insignificant.

The singing had started: rival unions declaring their superiority in verse. The metalworkers, waving their table flag, went first. A stocky, florid-complexioned man with thick arms held aloft a stein of beer. His voice was nasal, and his speech was slurred. He was more than a little drunk. He wore traditional Bavarian garb except that his lederhosen were long.

The civil service worker sits in his cell,
Stamping his papers and inking his well.
Enslaved by papers, the whistles, and his bell,
He makes our lives a wreck.

But metaler's arms are forged in steel;
The work is honest, tough but real.
At day's end, he deserves his hot meal,
Having produced much more than dreck.

The hall broke into hoots and wails of laughter, the clinking of flagons, the yells of *"Auf ihre Gesundheit."* Berg looked at a red-faced *Staatsbeamter,* a civil servant, sneering and snorting and ready for the challenge. He was a short, slight man with a thin mustache, a bald head, and spectacles perched on the tip of his nose.

A man who forges metal and steel
Using andirons and air pumps,
Works by dint of muscle and zeal
And has arms the size of log stumps.

Working and slaving all day and night
To earn his family its bread,
He must be strong in body and might
For no brain has he in his head.

More hoots, more laughter, and so it went for about an hour, each union getting increasingly raucous, the police poised to strike when the inevitable drunken fistfights broke out. But tonight the rivalry was broken up before the tempers flared, interrupted by the entrance of the *Schutzstaffel*—Hitler's minions known familiarly as the SS in their brown shirts bedecked with metals and stars, their knee-high boots, and military caps. Pushing their way into a room crammed with people, shoving bodies to the sidelines to make room for the *Kampfbund*—the elite from the NSDAP.

They came in one by one led by Hitler's favorite, the round, pudding-faced Ernst Röhm. They were all there: the thin-lipped Hermann Göring, Rudolf Hess, Heinrich Himmler, and Putzi Hanfstaengl, a head taller than his compatriots. In the shadows another man marched in with the *Kampfbund*—a new face but easily recognizable. Berg's eyes widened in surprise but of course, the logic was there: Kurt Haaf—Anna Gross's father—showing his solidarity with the Nazis by wearing a black-and-red swastika armband that clashed with his elegant blue silk suit. The troops pressed their way to the front while an out-of-tune brass band played *Deutschland über alles*. Men leaped to their feet, their right arms stretched out from the shoulder.

Sieg Heil!
Sieg Heil!
Sieg Heil!

Berg was repulsed. Little men playing at war, dressed in their properly starched uniforms and their handsome leather boots. War was not so beautiful in actuality, the attire ruined by bullet holes and blood spatter of flying limbs from a grenade blast.

The noise grew deafening when Hitler entered, walking erect, his eyes forward and without expression. The Austrian had emerged armed with the sympathies of the people and an unstoppable ambition. He spoke the workingman's language of simplicity. There were rights and wrongs. The Germans were right and all others were wrong. All others were the devil. And the Jews were the worst devils of all. And so it went. Because it was easier to dismiss the success of the Jews than it was to explain the failure of the Germans.

On and on. He screamed. He yelled. He stabbed his fist into the air for punctuation. He crumbled pumpernickel rolls in his hands as he opined, letting the brown crumbs fall upon his shoes. One of his little boys crawled on all fours and periodically dusted his boots as Hitler spoke without interruption.

His demagoguery was all-encompassing and he stoked the crowd. He brought Kurt Haaf to the stage and, with tears in his eyes, Haaf spoke of his daughter, the beautiful German maiden raped and murdered by the horned, split-tailed, pitchforked Jew: the most evil type of Jew, the one masquerading as a good German citizen. He spoke about all that was vile in the city—the Jews, of course, along with the other Kosmopoliten—the depraved artists, actors, writers, and homosexuals. He segued into the Kommunisten, especially the Jewish Kommunisten, but all Kommunisten were bad. He spoke about the conniving

Gypsies, the heinous Weimar government, the lawlessness in his own beloved Munich, even though he was Austrian.

A lowly Austrian.

Maybe that was the problem.

He ranted about the thieves, rapists, and murderers of the pure, German virgins on pure German soil. His oration was met with applause and approval. He was preaching to the converted. The pitch grew more hateful and more strident. A red-faced man with veins throbbing in his neck. Spittle spewing from his mouth. Eyes flashing lightning bolts as he shouted words of redemption for the German people while articulating axioms of hate. The police rocked on their feet, some of them uncomfortable with the exuberant zeal of the throng. But Berg felt an equal number were caught up in the rhetoric.

With each remark, the mob got increasingly restless, itching for windows to break and heads to bust.

Finally, Berg saw Volker get up from his chair and approach the dais. Although the Kommissar was a man of incomparable arrogance, could he possibly think that he could stifle Hitler in his moment of glory? Berg felt his heartbeat slam into his rib cage. It would have been wise to leave the scene before it erupted, but curiosity overcame him.

What would Volker say?

As usual, the Kommissar was dressed in finery—a three-piece suit with a white shirt and broad red ascot. His collar and cuffs were starched to rigidity, diamonds winking at his wrists. His face was shaved smooth and red, his blue eyes as equally intense as those of Hitler.

What would Volker say?

At first, Hitler didn't notice the interloper. And when he did, his eyes shot out from his face, bubbles of spit brewing in his mouth and leaking over his lower lip.

His expression was a frieze of horror and indignation: *Who dares to interrupt me?*

What would Volker say?

"Herr Hitler," Volker said. "Interesting as your comments may be, closing time approaches. Soon it will be necessary to disperse and I'd advise you strongly to give instruction to all your good people to behave themselves."

Hitler swept an arm over the crowd.

"You come up here . . . and interrupt me . . . to tell me *this*!"

No one spoke.

"It is not up to *me* to tell the good people of Munich how to behave!" Hitler screamed. "It is up to their *conscience* for that! They have bigger things to consider than petty laws instilled by weak men who seek to sell a birthright that is legally ours!"

The crowd broke into roars of jubilation.

Sieg Heil.

"*You will not stop the movement!*"

Sieg Heil!

"*You will not stop the will of the people!*"

Sieg Heil!

A man of lesser ego would have backed down, but Volker was no such man. Still, he had a brain in his head. There looked to be hundreds of bodies stuffed into the beer hall, twice as many spilling out onto the streets. Volker had about one hundred police officers at his disposal. The odds weren't good and Volker, though a betting man, wouldn't play with marked cards.

It was time for appeasement.

"Herr Hitler," Volker spoke in his most soothing voice. "You command such well-deserved respect. You must tell your followers that the law is supreme above all, that a civilization cannot exist without law and order."

"Not when the law is *evil!*"

"We are all listening, Herr Hitler. Do not necessitate a war of German against German. Do not force us to do something that would be injurious to all, including yourself."

"If you mean prison, I am not afraid of imprisonment!"

The crowd cheered with delight.

Sieg Heil!

Sieg Heil!

Of course, the man wasn't afraid of imprisonment. Not the way he had been imprisoned, his followers visiting him as often as he pleased. It had been eighteen months of free room and board.

"You are not afraid of anything, Herr Hitler," Volker said mildly. "Everyone knows that. Your bravery and fortitude are beyond reproach. All I'm asking is for you to use your talents and ensure that this gathering of our fine people ends quietly and peacefully. We do not want any other good citizens of Munich to end up in a hospital."

"The Jews don't belong in hospitals!" Hitler screamed. "They belong in graveyards!"

Another thunderous clamor erupted.

Sieg Heil!

Volker managed to remain outwardly calm—except for his overworked jaw bulging out of his cheek. "Unfortunately, Herr Hitler, it is hard to tell Jew from non-Jew. And unless you choose to paint a Star of David on their foreheads, it will continue to be hard to tell Jew from non-Jew. God forbid one of our good citizens is mistaken for a Jew and is beaten up as a result."

"It is the price one pays for ridding the city of its vermin."

"Interesting," Volker said. "Perhaps you can drop by the police station tomorrow and we can further discuss the issue. In the meantime, it is late. I'm asking you personally, as a favor to the police and as a favor to Munich, to tell your followers—who are many—to disperse quietly and in an orderly fashion. Do not stress the police force beyond its limits."

Hitler regarded Volker with a mixture of curiosity and disgust. Slowly, he looked around the room. Many unarmed followers; fewer police, but they held billy clubs. Tomorrow would be another day. With this minor concession, perhaps he could build even more support among the police. To have a respected man like Volker on one's side could be very, very good.

The demagogue faced his audience. "We have met today to buttress ourselves against a slowly invading and pervasive evil—the *bloodsucking Jews,* the *lawless Gypsies,* the *debased Kommunisten,* the *libertine homosexuals,* the *corrupted artists and writers* who seek insidiously to erode our morals into chaos and depravity! Yet, out of respect for you"—in a magnanimous gesture, he swept his arm across the crowd—"the citizens of our beautiful and fair city, and out of respect for the police"—he pointed to the back wall—"who continually deal with the vermin that pollute our city, I ask all of you to disperse quietly and peacefully. So that we may come together again and again . . ."

His voice grew in volume: "And again and again and again until the sewer rats of our Munich have been eradicated."

Louder still: *"We will not be stopped, we will not be placated, we will not rest a minute until our Fatherland is once again in pure German hands!"*

He clicked his heels and headed for the door, the crowd parting for him as if he were Moses splitting the Red Sea. Berg was repulsed by Hitler but furious with his immediate superior. Though walking was painful, he fought his way through the throng of flesh until he was face-to-face with Volker. On seeing Berg, the Kommissar raised an eyebrow.

"Do my eyes deceive or is that the hidden face of Axel Berg?"

Berg could barely contain his voice. "How could you talk to him like that!"

"We are still among our citizens, Herr Inspektor. It is impolitic to speak without discretion."

"Everything said in this room tonight is fabrication at best. Actually, it is nothing but pure horseshit!"

Volker's eyes narrowed. "I realize that you have suffered a tremendous blow to the head. But the next time you use obscenities in my presence, you will use them in prison."

"I don't belong in prison. Hitler belongs in prison. Your *nephew* belongs in prison!"

"Yes, I suppose I must deal with Lothar. We can't have a hooligan beating up the police. It makes us all look bad." He put his arm around Berg, who shook it off. Volker smiled. "I know you love the mountains, Axel. It's a perfect time for a holiday in the Alps, courtesy of the department. There is still a good snow base for skiing."

Berg snarled, "Do I look like I'm able to ski, Herr Kommissar?"

"Then perhaps you can take a stroll and visit your special young friend while she is still allowed to reside here. The political climate is not good for her. You can never tell what might happen."

No words could accurately describe the look of shock that registered on Berg's face. That made Volker smile even harder.

"She preens with a certain fan that looks similar to one found at a recent crime scene. It makes me wonder what else might have been *pilfered* behind my back." Berg swallowed hard and waited for Volker to continue. "Or perhaps I was mistaken."

Berg opened and closed his mouth, his emotions reeling from stunned silence to cold fury. He would have loved to deck his superior on the spot, loved to quit his job in outrage and indignation. But he had neither the physical prowess nor the moral high ground to do either with impunity. "Perhaps you were mistaken."

Such puny cowardice. He hated himself for the lie.

"Yes, I will concede that is a possibility," Volker said. "So you see, Axel, I'm not the only one involved in appeasement. In any case, Hitler is very strong. She is Jewish. I suggest you take advantage of your pretty, young whore while she still walks with two legs."

Berg started to speak, but stopped himself. What would be the point of playing martyr, of losing his job and security, of putting his wife and children in danger for some misguided sense of honesty—or worse, for the sake of that girl . . . that . . . that *whore*?

There!

He said it!

Margot was nothing but a whore.

Berg managed to smile. "You're filled with good suggestions tonight, Kommissar."

"Glad to be of service, Inspektor."

Berg turned and limped away.

Volker shook his head. Poor Axel. Or rather poor little Margot. What a beating she'd get tonight. Ah well, such is the life of a cheap Jewess who sells her body.

Lighting a cigarette, he watched his citizens file out of the beer hall in an orderly fashion. But his appeasement wouldn't hold a man like Hitler forever. The monster had an insatiable thirst for power that couldn't be slaked.

He exhaled a rich plume of smoke. He was tired and wondered why he kept such a senseless job that paid him nothing compared to the family business. Perhaps it was because he, like Hitler, thrived on excitement, and nowhere was there more excitement than in Munich. It was a powder keg among powder kegs, and he was *so close* to controlling it all.

Now he had angered his lead Inspektor in the *Mordkommission*. This wasn't a good thing. Because despite the convenience of scapegoating Gross—the man had been tried, convicted, sentenced, and executed all in the space of an hour—Volker knew that there still was a murderer loose.

TWENTY-FOUR

✠ At this time of night, she wouldn't be at the factory. She'd either be *whoring* with someone else, or she'd be at home with her parents, pretending to be a good girl. Since Berg had no idea where she lived, he decided to drop by the cigarette house, knowing full well that he might barge in on something.

The bitch!

The whore!

Fucking Jews!

Go back to Poland!

Go back to Russia!

As if he hadn't really known what was going on all along: *He* was the stupid one.

Berg flipped up the collar on his overcoat and wrapped his scarf around his neck and jaw. The walk was slow and painful. The tenement house was crosstown over the Ludwigs Bridge near Gärtnerplatz in the Isarvorstadt region. The area was a nesting ground for insects and vermin and disease. As he limped his way over the Isar, heading southwest to the ghetto, he had unwanted time to think. But instead of cooling off, his anger became only hotter.

The bitch!

He should go home ... to those who cared about him ... to his wife and children. But what awaited him at home? Britta would be furious at his escape. He had yet to talk to her face-to-face. She would deride him and yell at him and claim it came from love and devotion.

And maybe it did. Britta was his wife of sixteen years. It should be Britta who held his interest, not some money-hungry harlot.

The bitch would get hers, Berg swore. Tonight, she'd get *hers*.

All around him were Brownshirts pouring out of the Kellnerhaus, marching in the streets, singing off-key, drunken ballads of treacle and sentimental love for a Fatherland that never existed. They weren't the majority party in Munich, but they were the most vociferous. Instead of walking in a precision military step, the youth-driven gangs staggered, bumping in one another, reeling in the streets. Some groups were attempting to pass out leaflets, but more paper ended up on the ground than in the hands of the few passersby. In the background, Berg heard the sizzling crackle of glass being broken: another Jewish store being vandalized and looted. But that was not his concern right now. Besides, what could he do in his condition?

More singing punctuated by obscenities, raucous laughter, and retching: hooligans paying for the drinking and indulgences by throwing up in the streets. Berg couldn't make out the slurred words, but he knew the song. Who in Munich didn't know it?

Durch Krieg und Schrecken aus der Welt verbannt
Kam wieder ich in mein geliebtes Land.
(Banished from the world by war and terror,
I came again into my beloved country.)

Ah, the Bavarians and their maudlin tripe. The Germany that Berg knew was a warrior country of agitation and aggression, a bellicose nation that constantly sought to enlarge its borders, here on the Continent as well as across the seas. Even before the Great War, the Kaiser had nearly waged war with Roosevelt and The States over some silly little islands in the Caribbean, thousands of miles away from the Fatherland. Not that aggression was a bad thing. There was pride in conquest. But there was also shame in defeat.

Nach München, in die schöne Isarstadt,
Die mich so hoch geehrt seit alters hat.
(To Munich, into the beautiful Isarstadt,
Which has honored me so highly from time
immemorial.)

Aryan mawkishness was a weird combination of Nordic mythology and barbaric brutality. They had their dreams and they had their scapegoats. But there was some logic to their delusions. The Berliner Kosmopoliten, palling around with the arty bohemians, in their flashy dress with their flashy drink, smoking from a cigarette holder. Gulping beer in the drinking halls wasn't good enough. It had to be absinthe in the nightclubs. The Prussians constantly mocking Bavaria . . . their dress, their food, and their broad accents.

Fuck them all.
Fuck the Jews.
Fuck Margot.
He was more than a little drunk himself.
Go home, Axel.

If he couldn't find her, he'd go home.

But what would he say to her if he did find her?

The drunken singing receded as he walked farther south. The mist had settled in, turning the city into silhouettes and shadows. He trudged deeper into the night, into quarters on the edge of extinction. In hidden corners, the tenements teemed with beady-eyed jackals and rats. Berg was constantly looking over his shoulder. Either it was the Nazis smashing glass or the vermin picking your pocket.

There was truth to the laments in the beer halls. Once Munich had been a safe and beautiful city of artists and intellectuals, the southern jewel of the Alps. Berg tried to think back. When did it all start, this seize, this paranoia? The Great War put Germany into deep debt with its reparations. The despised Weimar in Berlin levying steep taxes in all of Germany, but especially in resource-rich Bavaria. Then there was the ousting of the Wittelsbacher, followed by the assassination of Kurt Eisner. And no one could deny the economic hardships, the rampant inflation six years ago. But things were better now. Why should crime be so commonplace, enmity so accepted? The beatings, the looting of Jewish stores, the military parades and their messages of hate or revenge. And now it was the brutal murder of two women. When would it stop?

Berg suddenly realized he was in front of the cigarette house. The street was gloomy and deserted. He took a deep breath and went inside. The clerk was the same fat and florid man who worked in the daylight hours. He was reading a true-crime magazine. On the cover was a voluptuous, busty blonde with her hands on her cheeks as she let out a silent scream. His eyes barely lifted above the page.

"Herr Inspektor." He went back to his reading.

"Is she . . ."

A simple nod, eyes still on the magazine.

"Alone?" Berg asked.

The fat man looked up and graced Berg with a base smile. "I don't keep track, Herr Inspektor."

It was too late to turn back without looking ridiculous . . . without the silent ridicule that was bound to follow him if he turned tail. He made the arduous climb up the stairs and knocked on the door.

A quiet knock, not the knock of a madman. Berg was proud of his control.

Her voice was muffled. *Wer ist da?*

"Polizei," he said quite officially. He was hoping to scare off anyone who might be with her. Instead, the door opened immediately and smiling eyes greeted him.

"What a nice surpri—" Margot's voice faltered when she saw his face. "What happened to you?"

Berg slammed the door shut. "I see you don't bother to read the papers." He stared at the rumpled bed, anger rising in his face. He began to pace—slow, small steps back and forth.

"Why should I?" She stared at his limping. "News is so depressing. What happened, Axel?"

"You're a stranger in this city," Berg said harshly. "You'd do well to keep up with current events."

"I know who I am and I know what you think of me."

"Not what *I* think of you," Berg whispered. "But I am not Munich."

"You didn't answer my question, Axel," Margot shot back. "Who beat you?"

He whirled around on her and grabbed her chin. "I

should ask you that. Ask what happened to you? How did you get the bruises on your face?" He let go of her with a shove. "I treat you like a queen and this is how you repay me? By fucking other men who whack you like a punching bag?"

Tears leaked from her eyes, rutting tracks into her freshly applied rouge. "And how am I supposed to support myself on the trinkets you give me? Is my family to starve because I am paid nothing at the factory? Am I to be condemned because German men have an infinite appetite for slender young girls?"

"You could have asked me first!" Berg snarled out.

Margot's voice cracked. "And deny your wife and children by taking marks out of your paycheck for a Jew?" She shook her head. "I don't think so, Axel."

Again Berg felt sheepish and low. "How much do you need?"

"More than a married workingman can provide. My relatives are being slaughtered either by pogroms in Russia or by starvation. My need for money is infinite. But I am not the one who's complaining." She touched his face. "What *happened* to you?"

He pulled away but couldn't face her accusing eyes. Quietly, he spoke. "There was a riot two days ago."

"I heard."

"Then you also should have heard that a policeman was beaten so badly he was taken to the hospital."

"That was *you*?" Margot was aghast. "Volker sent *you* into the trenches?"

"Volker sent me to pick up the Jew. Hitler's boys did the rest."

"Bastard!" Margot spoke under her breath. "I wouldn't be surprised if he sent the boys after you."

Berg whirled around and stared at her. "*What* did you say?"

Margot averted her glance. "Nothing."

Slowly, Berg sat down on the bed. It smelled of sweat and sex. He was burning with jealousy, but her words supplanted his anger. "Margot . . . tell me what you meant by your whispered words."

She sat next to him. "That Volker is a bastard. I'm sure you know that already."

"Why did you say that he sent the boys after me?"

"I don't know that he did—"

"Is *Volker* after me?"

Margot licked her lips and was silent. Berg's survival instincts kicked in. A minute ago, he had been ready to choke her, picturing his strong hands around that white, delicate neck. Instead, he stroked her arm gently and tried to contain his anxiety. He spoke soothingly.

"Tell me, darling. What does the Kommissar say to you?"

"He will know if I've talked to you." She regarded him with wet eyes. "He grills me constantly."

"About me?"

She nodded.

"Only me . . . or others you service?"

Her anger turned hot. "Don't you understand? He has *money*. He has *power*—power to use against you as well as me."

Berg's eyes narrowed. "What does he ask about me?"

"Who are your friends! What are your political affiliations! What do you do in your off-hours."

"And how do you answer him?"

"I say that we don't talk much. That is the truth, no? But still I must tell him something. He knows you spend more time here than is necessary just to get the job done."

"And what do you tell him?"

"I tell him the truth." Again, she touched his face. This time Berg didn't pull away. "I tell him that you are a lonely and mysterious man. That you talk little about your family and nothing about work. That I have no idea what you do in your free hours and what friends you keep."

Berg looked around the tiny room. The blinds on the window were closed. He got up and peeked through the slats. The streets were empty. "Volker sent me here tonight. I wonder why."

"What do you mean?"

"I was at the Nazi rally tonight. I was angry with Volker because instead of repudiating Hitler, the bastard appeased him. And when I called him on it, he told me to go visit my little whore. Which accomplished two things: telling me that he has been with you and that he knows where I am." He let out a bitter laugh. "Why do I feel he is setting me up? That as soon as I walk out those doors, I am going to be attacked again."

Margot swallowed hard. Again, he deftly parted the slats. This time he saw three of them—Hitler's boys in their silly uniforms, loitering in the darkened lane.

"There are hoodlums out there. Perhaps Volker is trying to kill me."

"That's absurd, Axel. You are his most important Inspektor. He tells me that all the time. He tells me to keep you happy."

"Maybe it's to keep me off-guard."

"Off-guard about what?"

The answer was obvious. Berg let the slats go. "To keep me off-guard . . . because perhaps . . . he is the killer!"

"What are you talking about?"

"He speaks English; he could speak Russian as well. He certainly is urbane. He is tall. *He* killed those two women. And he knows I am getting close. So he sends his nephew to do his dirty work!" He leaned against the wall, his back stiffening in pain. "*Mein Gott*, how could I be so stupid!"

"Axel, if Volker had wanted you dead, you'd be dead!"

"I was beaten nearly to death, Margot. Volker is now choosing to finish the job." He looked at her with desperate eyes. "Is there a way to leave this dump without passing through the front door?"

"There is a fire escape—"

"He probably has his boys out there as well."

"Axel, you're not making sense!"

His eyes bored into hers. "Margot, what if they come here . . . inside this room?"

"But the door is locked—"

"You don't think three big boys could break it down with a simple push?"

Margot blurted out, "There's a trapdoor under the bed. The girls use them in case of raids."

"Show me!"

The shrill sound of a police whistle broke through their conversation. Berg could hear the rapid clops of shoes hitting the pavement. Margot got up and looked out the window. "The police are chasing the hooligans down the street. Come and see for yourself."

Berg peered through the slats. In the muted glow of the streetlights he caught sight of two uniformed men running after Hitler's youthful followers.

"Don't I have enough to worry about without you frightening me?" Margot scolded him. "Volker is many things, but he is not illogical. Why would he kill his number-one man? The beating has affected your brain. You need a holiday."

Volker had told him the same thing. Were the two of them in cahoots with each other? Idiotic to be that nervous, but something was rotten.

What had Volker said to him about Margot this evening? Something about her not being welcome in the city much longer. Was Volker trying to warn him that his association with the Jewess would put him in danger, or was the Kommissar trying to get rid of him so he could have her to himself?

And his comment about pilfering . . . Had Volker known that he had stolen money from Marlena Druer's strongbox? Had the Kommissar known because *he* had killed her? Yet, Volker looked nothing like the man in the sketch. But what did that mean? Ulrich had said it right: The sketch could be any one of a thousand men.

Berg's body was racked with pain. He needed time to sort it out. He hated to admit it, but Volker was right. Margot was right. Britta was right.

He needed a holiday.

TWENTY-FIVE

✠ Britta had always loved the mountains, whether it was skiing on the slopes, biking through one of the picturesque hamlets, exploring old castles, or hiking on a sinuous upland trail in crisp alpine air. Her smile was immediate, as soon as she stepped off the train onto the platform in Garmisch, her eyes looking skyward at the magnificent granite ridges that kissed the crystalline heavens. Spring had laid a soft verdant canopy over the hills, the pines spiraling upward, trees abloom with fragrant perfume, crocuses and daffodils poking green noses out of the patches of residual snow.

Sipping hot spiced cider, Berg tried to quell his anxiety as he watched his family skiing on Zugspitze. He tried to leave his work behind as they hiked through glorious woods with his son holding his arm. They slowly traversed overgrown pathways and secret trails or walked through the old Roman city of Partenkirchen. They chose to stay at a small rooming house on the outskirts of town. In the morning, the kitchen served fresh rolls and butter, ham and cheese, and poppy-seed cakes, as well as hot coffee and tea. Dinner was shredded pork and dumplings or homemade sausages and sauerkraut. At night, the family slept in feather beds on feather pillows, and dreams were often as sweet as the air they breathed. Honey-coated reveries . . . except for the nightmare.

The lone nightmare.

Dark and brooding . . . Berg chased by shadows and specters, formless and infinite. There was only one direction: an endless road with no escape. No choice except to go forward, to run until the stinging of his lungs and the cramping in his belly gave way to buckled knees. Just as he was falling, he woke up out of breath, sweat covering his face despite the mountain chill that had permeated the windows. Britta asked what was wrong, but Berg couldn't answer. He finally coaxed his wife back to sleep, but he lay awake, his vigilance marked by heightened distrust.

Yet, despite his anger at Volker, Margot, Hitler, and all of Munich, despite his suspicions and anxieties, Berg had come to realize that the holiday was indeed curative. It provided the necessary cement for his fractured marriage and a balm for his troubled children, who often viewed him with confusion and a small dose of fear. On the train ride home, Britta and Monika slept, lulled by the clacking of locomotive wheels against metal track. But Joachim stayed awake, occupied by his sketchbook, his hand moving quickly and precisely even when the train jostled them as it made turns through the mountains. Berg peered down at his son's latest creation, done in swift, thick charcoal strokes that captured the blurred landscape from the railcar window.

Berg unwrapped a sandwich of cold pork and onions on pumpernickel bread covered with butter. He offered half to his son, but Joachim refused with a shake of his head.

"I'm not hungry." The boy displayed blackened fingers. "I first need to wash my hands."

"Nonsense." Berg wrapped half of the sandwich in paper. "You need food for muscle growth. You must eat."

Dutifully, Joachim took the sandwich. "I'll eat when I'm done."

"An interesting statement," Berg said. "How do you know when you're done?"

Joachim's eyes slowly moved to his father's face. "How do you know when *you're* done?"

Berg stroked his chin. The lump had receded to a small, firm knot. "I believe I am done when I have nothing more to add. The work may not be exactly what I want. But adding new material will not help. So I surrender to my imperfections, curse my inability to translate to the brush what is in my head, and say, 'I quit.'"

Joachim nodded.

"That is the frustrating part," Berg added. "To see it so clearly in my brain but lack the skills to put it down on canvas."

Again, Joachim nodded. He continued to sketch even as they spoke. Berg wondered what was on his son's mind—a beautiful boy in his budding adolescence. He could truly be a lady-killer except that his personality was too kind to break hearts.

"You didn't answer my question, son. How do you know when you're done?"

Joachim's brow furrowed as he took his thumb and rubbed it against the charcoal, smudging trees and mountains to create the illusion of motion. "I used to know when I was done with a drawing because I felt happy."

"Like your flower painting hanging in the common room."

"Exactly." Joachim regarded his father. "But lately, I feel less and less content with my work. I think it is because I'm getting older. Things that satisfy you as a child are no longer acceptable when you are competing in an adult world."

Berg had no response. Sadness overwhelmed him. Why should his little boy feel so burdened? Maybe it was because Berg never set a very good example. "Eat your sandwich, Joachim."

The boy shrugged as he placed the cover of the pad over his latest endeavor. He picked up the sandwich nestled in paper and took a bite.

Lunch took ten minutes. Father and son ate in silence.

✠ ✠ ✠

THE SMELL of a shoulder roast sizzling in the Dutch oven, stewing in beer, apples, and cabbage: the smell of Sunday dinner. A trickle of hot air came in through the radiator, although the pipes clanged as if they were filled by volcanic eruption. Luckily, the heat from the stove provided additional warmth. Britta's hair was sprinkled with white flour she used to make her special Sabbath concoction—pear cake with walnuts. A sense of normalcy had infused Berg's life. He was married, he had children, he had a job, he was a good German citizen. Thoughts of Margot's firm body, her throaty laughter, and her moist womanhood brought distant tingles that subsided as fast as they developed.

If Volker wanted her, he could have her.

Still, she was lovely.

Britta called them to the table. She had just plattered the roast when the noises started—the *pling, pling, pling* of rocks hitting the side of the building. Berg leaped up and went to the closet, pulling down his hunting rifle.

"That's it!"

"Axel, don't be stupid!" Britta shouted.

"No more!" Berg threw open the window. It was Lothar. The little thug was alone this time. Imagine that! He had the gall and the gumption to torment Berg without his usual band of punks. Berg drew back the spring loader and aimed between the punk's eyes. *"Move and you're a dead boy!"*

"Axel, are you out of your mind?" Britta shrieked.

"Papa, stop," pleaded Joachim as he yanked at his father's arm. "Please stop!"

Words screamed from down below carried through the open window. "Don't shoot, don't shoot, don't shoot!"

The begging gave Berg pause. But he kept the crosshairs aimed at the kid's face. He could afford to be bold: The rifle wasn't loaded. "You have one minute to explain yourself!"

"I'm not Lothar, I'm not Lothar." The boy was out of breath, panting and gasping. As if he had run crosstown before coming here to torment. "I am Lothar's younger brother, Friedrich."

"I don't care who you are," Berg shouted back. "If you move a muscle, I will shoot you."

"Please don't shoot me." Tears in the boy's voice. "I didn't know how to get into the building. I tried the front door, but it is locked. There is no doorman. I needed to get your attention. I was sent here to fetch you for my uncle.

If I go back and you don't come with me, Uncle will beat me."

"Uncle?" Berg swallowed. "You mean Volker?"

"Yes, yes, Uncle Martin. He needs to see you immediately!"

Berg steadied the gun on Friedrich's face. "How do I know you are not tricking me? That as soon as I come down to the street, you and your brother and all your hooligan friends won't beat me up?"

Friedrich hung his head. "Lothar is dead."

Berg's hand started shaking. "Dead?"

"This past week. He was trampled underneath a runaway horse. It was a terrible accident. I swear this is all the truth." The boy was sobbing. "Please don't shoot me!"

Slowly, Berg lowered the eyepiece of the rifle from his vision. "Go tell your uncle I will be there in thirty minutes. Physical limitations caused by my last thrashing make it hard for me to bike. I must walk and that takes time." Berg drew the gun inside the window. "Go on, you little twit, off with you!"

The boy paused, then took off like a lightning bolt.

Britta said, "What about a streetcar?"

Berg sat down at the table and laid a napkin on his lap. "I want to eat first. Fortify my belly for what has to be bad news."

Dinner was an awkward, silent affair. Afterward, Joachim helped his father walk down four flights of stairs. Berg waved and began to limp his way to the streetcar.

Trampled by a horse.

Volker had taken care of the problem.

It was a forte of his.

TWENTY-SIX

✠ Because it was Sunday, the police station was quiet, and the office of the *Mordkommission* extraordinarily so. Very few Inspektoren worked weekends. The few crimes that were committed revolved around drunken fistfights at beer halls rather than premeditated felonies, minor things that could easily be handled by uniformed policemen. So Volker must have been particularly upset to disturb Berg during the traditional Sabbath dinner.

Not only had the Kommissar called him, but also he had summoned two *Mordkommission* Inspektoren. Rudolf Kalmer was standing against the wall and clicked his heels when Berg entered. Sixty and as thin as asparagus, Kalmer had been a soldier in the Kaiser's army and was disciplined and duty-bound. He was also resentful that he had not been included in Berg's personal triad. Heinrich Messersmit was also nearing sixty. A gray-haired man with sloping shoulders and seven children, he was putting in the hours until his youngest daughter married. He had a small lakeside cabin in the mountains near Austria and was there more than here.

The Kommissar was dapper but looked anything but calm, as evidenced by a clenched jaw. He pointed to the chair across from his desk. Berg sat and looked around the well-appointed office. What was particularly notewor-

STRAIGHT INTO DARKNESS 235

thy was Volker's desktop. It held an electric lamp, a calendar, an ornate inkwell and several pens, a letter opener, a letter hook, and a pen wiper. But it was clear of paperwork except for a lone file, which the Kommissar pushed across the leather surface until it was within Berg's reach.

"Read."

It was a *Kriminalakte,* a crime folder, dated eight days ago when Berg had been in the middle of his two-week holiday. Inspektoren Kalmer and Messersmit had been assigned to this case, that of a missing woman. She was a thirty-six-year-old Jewish immigrant named Regina Gottlieb. Terrible but not wholly unusual. Immigrants frequently fought among one another, with fists, with knives, sometimes even with contraband guns. Unemployment was high. Men without work had nothing better to do than beat their women. Sometimes they beat them to death, deeply burying the evidence of their misdeeds.

Berg scanned the pages. Her husband had reported her missing the night before the date on the file. He told the police that Regina had gone out to see her employer and hadn't returned. Her husband claimed that this was very worrisome. "What exactly am I looking for? Is her husband a suspect in her disappearance?"

"We questioned him," Kalmer said defensively. "Nothing points in that direction."

"Are there any other missing Jewesses besides this woman?" Berg queried.

"Why do you ask?" Kalmer questioned.

"It's a logical question, Rudolf. Of late, the Jews have been victimized."

"No one else is missing," Messersmit answered, "but several Jews have been murdered."

"Nothing unusual," Kalmer added. "A couple of old Jew shop owners. One was taken from his store and beaten to death. The other one was found in the street, also beaten to death. Also, a religious *Jude* was stabbed in the neck. He survived, but was unable to identify his assailants. They attacked him from behind."

"Hitler's boys are suspected," Messersmit said.

"Suspected but not arrested," Berg responded.

"Until we can match a specific type of blood for each specific individual, we are at a severe disadvantage in our attempts to find the correct culprit," Volker said.

"They're our cases, Axel," Kalmer stated. "We'll get to the bottom of it."

"Progress is slow," Messersmit said flatly. "The Nazis won't talk to us, but neither will the Jews. If they don't help themselves, what can the police do?"

Berg didn't answer, feeling a knot inside his stomach. Surely they could do better.

"Actually Heinrich is being modest." Volker laid a hand on Messersmit's shoulder. "The case was moving forward. There were a few boys who seemed logical as suspects. Then, my poor nephew met a terrible fate. I decided that it would not have been polite form to question Lothar's friends at his funeral."

Berg said, "But perhaps we can question them now?"

Kalmer glared at him. "Perhaps *Heinrich and I* can question them now."

"Unfortunately, Axel, we have other things to think about." Volker produced another folder. This one was a *Mordakte*—a homicide file dated four days ago. He handed it to Berg.

With trepidation, Berg leafed through the file. The deceased had been a young white woman dressed in evening wear. He looked up and locked eyes with Volker. "*Another* one?"

"Read on."

Professor Kolb had listed the cause of death as massive hemorrhage. Then Berg's eyes widened. "Her corpse was found in the Englischer Garten?"

The room's silence answered his question. Again, Berg controlled his temper. "Why wasn't I informed immediately?"

"Because the woman turned out to be Regina Gottlieb and she is our case!" Kalmer stated.

"Her death is obviously related to the others," Berg stated.

"You mean related to Marlena Druer," Volker said. "Anna Gross was murdered by her husband."

Don't insult my intelligence. Berg said, "I should have been told about this immediately!"

"The point is, Axel, you're being told about it now." Volker narrowed his eyes. "That is why you are here instead of at home enjoying your family dinner. I'd like you to look into this case and see if this murder is indeed related to the murder of Marlena Druer. It will take the burden off Kalmer and Messersmit so they can proceed with murdered Jews."

Both men's expressions were as puckered as prunes, but neither argued with Volker. The Kommissar was ripping the most intriguing case from their hands. Berg realized the sensitivity of the situation. It was time for humility.

"If that is what you want, sir, I'd appreciate cooperation from Rudolf and Heinrich." Berg turned to his colleagues. "Any help that you can give me would be welcome. May I ask a few questions?"

"Go on," Volker said.

"Did you recognize the victim as Regina Gottlieb?"

"Not at all," Messersmit said. "We had no picture of her to work from."

"So who identified the victim as Regina Gottlieb? The husband?"

Messersmit shook his head no. "We passed a postmortem picture around the area. The Schoennacht family lives very close to where the body was found. It was Frau Julia Schoennacht who identified Regina Gottlieb as her former seamstress."

"Which explains why we didn't associate this body with Regina Gottlieb, the immigrant Jew," Kalmer said. "She wasn't dressed like an immigrant Jew. She was attired in beautiful clothing. Not the kind of dress a poor Jewess would wear."

"But now that we know she's a seamstress, it all makes sense. She could make her own clothing."

"Was she wearing expensive fabric?" Berg asked.

Kalmer frowned. "How would we know anything about women's fabric?"

"Surely you can tell silk from wool," Berg said.

"We didn't take her as a Jewess," Kalmer said stiffly. "Besides, she didn't look at all Jewish. Black hair . . . blue eyes . . . very pale skin."

"Everyone's skin is pale in death."

"You are hilarious, Berg. Perhaps you should be onstage with Karl Valentin. Your leanings are no doubt similar."

"Let's avoid making this a personal issue, Rudolf," Volker chided.

Kalmer said, "I'm just saying that she didn't look like a Polish peasant Jew."

"Even with her head bashed in, you could tell she was beautiful once," Messersmit said.

Berg's ears perked up. He spoke softly, more to himself than anyone else. "The others died of strangulation." He regarded his colleagues. "But this one died of a head wound. Is that what you're telling me?"

His question remained unanswered, interrupted by the arrival of Herr Professor Kolb. He was wearing a lab coat over his suit. His curly gray hair was unruly, and spectacles had slid down on his nose. Leaning on his cane, he took out his pocket watch and squinted. "Good afternoon, meine Herren. I trust I haven't kept you waiting."

Volker regarded the wall clock. It was close to four in the afternoon. "Right on time."

"Yet you have started without me."

"Axel arrived quicker than I thought," Volker said. "His recovery has been nothing short of miraculous."

"A supernatural feat that rivals the Shroud of Turin," Berg said flatly. To Kolb, he said, "You have found something of interest in this woman's death, Herr Professor?"

Kolb laughed. "Why else would I be here?"

"We were just getting into your area of expertise," Messersmit spoke up. "About the latest victim's head wounds, Herr Professor."

Kolb began pacing the floor, thumping loudly with his cane. Since there wasn't much area to pace, he was more or less turning in circles. He pointed a finger at Berg. "Frau Gottlieb was struck in the back of her head. But . . . she also had ligature marks around her throat. Frau Gottlieb was beaten and strangled."

"Lovely," Berg said. "Which came first?"

"An interesting question," Kolb stated. "I have tried to put myself in the murderer's mind. If I had been him, perhaps I would have tried strangulation first, hmmm?" His eyes became animated. "More personal . . . eye to eye."

"Why would he make killing a personal thing?" Messersmit asked.

"These 'repetitive killers' as I call them—they often make it personal. But that's for another discussion. Let us get back to the scene of the crime."

"Let us indeed," Volker put in.

Kolb nodded. "Suppose that as she was strangled, she put up a fight. Not a light, fragile flower, this one. Two of her fingernails were broken off. The others had skin underneath. She clawed like a tiger."

Berg said, "We should check her husband for scratch marks."

"A good idea, Inspektor; she got that skin from someone's arms and face." Kolb ran his knobby fingers through his wild gray hair. "I think at some point, she might have been strong enough to pull away. But then, if I were the murderer . . . thinking swiftly, I would not want her to get away. I would not want her to scream. I would grab her full and flowing skirt."

He gestured his motions.

"Then I would take my cane—"

"You found a cane?" Berg asked.

"No, I did not. I am assuming some kind of walking stick because the mark in her skull came from a round, hard object. Of course, other implements could have made that mark. But what could have made that mark *and* have been easily carried?" He shook a finger in the air. "It must have been a cane."

Berg nodded. A handsome walking cane would fit with the killer's image of an aristocrat.

"As she's escaping from my grip," Kolb said, "I grab her clothing. Then all I'd have to do is perform a quick rap behind the head—" He held up his cane and mimicked the motion. "Then, after she fell from the blow, I could finish her off by strangulation. The skirt of her dress was ripped from behind. There's nothing else that explains the evidence quite so succinctly."

Berg gave the supposition some thought. "Was the victim wearing stockings?"

"Alas, her finery was superficial only," Kolb said. "Beneath the lace and silk of the dress were very practical woolen undergarments."

"Any of the pieces missing?"

"Again, a good question, Inspektor. I would expect some article of clothing to be missing." Kolb looked at Messersmit and then at Kalmer.

"We could find only one shoe," Kalmer answered. "How did you know?"

Berg turned to Kolb. "In your professional opinion, Herr Professor, does it look like the victim was slain in the same fashion as Druer and Gross?"

"Anna Gross was murdered by her husband," Volker stated without affect. "So amend your question, Berg. Could Gottlieb's death be likened to Druer's death?"

"Her death is not only similar to Druer's, but almost identical to it," Kolb responded with enthusiasm. "Marlena had very distinct ligature marks around her neck—"

"The chain!" Berg broke in. "Both Marlena and

Regina were strangled by a necklace. You could see the pattern in their skin."

"That is correct, Inspektor!" Kolb smiled. "That is very much correct!"

"We didn't find a necklace on Regina Gottlieb," Messersmit remarked.

"Perhaps her husband took it after he killed her." Kalmer smiled. "You know Jews and their gold."

Kolb's face went red with embarrassment. Very dark red. Berg had never thought of Kolb as being Jewish, but his profound blushing made him wonder.

"I don't think so, Kalmer," Berg said.

"But you don't know that for certain, do you, Axel?"

"Why are you assuming it was her husband?"

"Why are you assuming it wasn't? What is it to you anyway? Do you really care what the animals do to each other?"

Messersmit spoke up, interrupting the heated exchange. "Someone should speak to Herr Gottlieb again. He told us that his wife was going to the Schoennachts' to collect wages. Frau Schoennacht was quite insistent that Frau Gottlieb never came to her house that evening and that she didn't owe the Jewess anything."

"Maybe Frau Gottlieb wanted to borrow money and didn't want her husband to know," Kalmer said. "They love money almost as much as they love gold."

Again Kolb turned pink. "And we Germans don't love money?"

"Not like the Jews."

"I recall a great deal of rioting during the Great Inflation."

"We had to eat!" Kalmer insisted.

"It wasn't the Jews who hiked up the prices," Kolb said; "it was the farmers who were anything but Jewish."

"Can we *please* stick to the topic?" Volker interjected.

The room was quiet. Finally Berg said, "Where do the Schoennachts live?"

"On Widenmayer Strasse."

The association clicked in Berg's brain. Anna Gross had lived on Widenmayer.

"It isn't necessary to pay Frau Schoennacht a visit, Axel," Kalmer said. "We talked to her at length. She knows nothing. She was horrified."

"I am sure you are right, Rudolf." Berg smiled with closed lips. "Still, I would like to speak to her."

Messersmit frowned. "Whatever for, Berg? You don't trust our skills as Inspektoren?"

"I'm sure that isn't the situation," Volker broke in. "Berg is a mysterious one and has his own ways. Being the head of the *Mordkommission,* perhaps he is more intuitive about these grisly matters than we are. Let us indulge him in this matter. The hour grows late. How about if we keep this quiet, a possible link between Gottlieb and the other murdered woman, Druer, *ja*?"

"Kommissar, even if this murder makes its way into the papers, who will care about a Jewess?" Kalmer said.

"A good observation, Rudolf," Volker agreed. "If the connection is discovered, we can always link it to the recent outbursts in the streets. We have just calmed the good people of Munich. There is no need to alarm the city now that order has been restored."

Berg said, "Especially since we so conveniently ascribe Anna's murder to her dead husband. It would not look good for us to backtrack."

Volker's eyes darkened with anger. He turned to Messersmit and Kalmer. "I thank you for your time, meine Herren. You may go now."

The two baffled inspectors did not react right away, but no one spoke until they were out the door. Then Volker lashed out, his anger a gush of whispered fury. "I defend you in front of those two and this is how you repay me?" Volker clenched his fists. "I was hoping a holiday would temper your cynicism. I see I was wrong. Another snide comment and I will fire you for insubordination. Are we clear about this?"

"Quite," Berg answered.

"Then you may go." A pause. "Now!"

Berg looked down at his feet. If he wanted to get to the bottom of these murders, he'd have to be more conciliatory. "Herr Kommissar! I apologize for my outburst!"

Volker stared at him, sizing up his sincerity. Decided it was real . . . more from fear than from wrongdoing. He nodded acceptance.

"If it's all right with you, sir, since Professor Kolb is here, I'd like to talk to him . . . to go over the autopsy report."

Volker thought a moment. "That's acceptable."

"We can talk at my desk then," Axel said. "That way I can take notes."

Volker said, "You two can talk here . . . in my office."

Berg said, "Sir, I wouldn't want to keep you here any longer than necessary."

"You're not. I have no appointments and if you two are discussing the case, I'd like to hear what you have to say."

Berg couldn't help himself. "Why do I feel that you don't trust me entirely?"

"It's not a feeling, it is reality. I have many reasons for not trusting you, Berg. Starting with your insolence."

"So why give me Frau Gottlieb's *Mordakte*?"

"Because you are the most competent of my men to do the task. Because I need you to catch this phantom before he kills again. We both know another murder would send the city into chaos. Can we get on with the case, Inspektor? Can you let go of your petty tantrums for one moment in order to do a greater good for your city and its citizens?"

"I will if you will."

In a flash, Volker whacked Berg across the face with an open palm. The room fell into dark silence, Volker daring Berg to respond. But the suddenness of the Kommissar's attack had stunned Berg into paralysis.

When he recovered, Berg spit at him.

Not *on* him, *at* him. And not exactly *at* him but next to Volker's shoes.

Still, the message was clear. Berg knew this was a line drawn in the sand, his own fury rendering him blind to the consequences of his behavior.

The seconds ticked on.

Finally, Volker smiled contemptuously. "Throat problem, Axel? You should really see a doctor for that."

Berg didn't answer. And that was that. They had reached another cold, distrustful truce: like the truce between Berlin and Munich . . . between Berlin and the Yanks. A truce that begged to be rewritten and ultimately broken.

Kolb cleared his throat. Both of the men turned to the sound. They had forgotten that the professor was still there.

Volker turned to him. "You have something to say, Herr Professor?"

"Whenever both of you are ready."

"Ready, Inspektor?" Volker asked.

Berg nodded, slowly withdrawing his hand from his cheek. It was still hot and sore, but not nearly as sore as his pride. The murderous rage had passed . . . for both of them. The consolation prize was that, for the time being, Berg's job was safe.

TWENTY-SEVEN

✠ What Volker wanted to do was fire the bastard. But it would be a mistake to give in to impulse. For one thing, who would he have to blame if these irritating murders remained unsolved? No, cooler heads would prevail. When this phantom killer was discovered, then he'd take care of Axel. Without looking up, he said, "Now what was it you wanted to say, Herr Professor, but not in front of Messersmit and Kalmer?"

"Very good, Herr Kommissar!" The Professor pounded the floor with his cane for emphasis. "You have deduced my true mission. May I ask now if you are familiar with the Psychological Wednesday Circle—the group later known as the Vienna Psychoanalytical Society?"

Volker frowned. "I know nothing about psychoanalysis. Nor do I follow anything associated with that swarthy Austrian Jewish Doktor."

"Ah, but you should, Herr Kommissar. His theories have much to say about the subconscious, the inner workings of the mind. I'm quite sure Professor Freud would have much to postulate about our fiend."

"Such as?" Berg said.

"This is a man who takes sexual pleasure from raping women, *ja*?"

"I think that's evident." Volker snickered.

"More importantly, Kommissar, he takes even greater sexual satisfaction from killing them. He is imbued with *Lustmord*."

Volker's look was skeptical. "Why not a man killing the primary witness against him? If the woman is dead, she can't accuse him of rape. Furthermore, Marlena Druer was not assaulted. And lastly, we don't know for certain that Anna Gross was raped. The sex could have been a consensual act. No, I don't think you are correct at all."

"Herr Kommissar, none of them consented to being strangled. And Regina Gottlieb fought off whoever assailed her. And even if no rape had been involved, it just makes my point stronger. Sex wasn't enough satisfaction for him. The fiend *had* to murder. Furthermore, he collected objects from his victims—a silk stocking, a shoe, a boot. This is clearly someone who experienced trauma during the anal stage of development, as evidenced by the man's inability to give up anything he has produced. This is definitely the result of poor mothering. If you couple a rejecting mother with a traumatizing event, the results are devastating."

Before Volker could object, Berg broke in. "What kind of traumatizing event?"

"The first thing that comes to mind is battle in the Great War."

"We all were soldiers," Volker said. "Killing in battle does not a murderer make."

"Exactly what I am saying, Kommissar." Kolb held up a finger. "Most of us can discern the difference between killing in war and killing in general. Another possibility is that the man did not participate in the Great War either because he was too young or because he was infirm, making him feel inadequate as a man. But even these deficiencies would not have made him a murderous fiend. It took the combination of trauma and a bad mother to make this man a killer. *Ja,* no doubt this man hates his mother because of what she did to him."

There was a long silence. Finally, Volker said, "Are you serious, Herr Professor?"

"Indeed, I am dead serious." Kolb laughed at his own joke. "Perhaps this man's mother was overly seductive. Perhaps she was cold and rejecting. Whatever the trauma was, we have, meine Herren, a perfect, living example of *destrudo.* He is not killing randomly. He is killing young women. Every time this monster kills a woman, in his head he is killing his mother."

Berg integrated Kolb's words into his brain; he found them very distasteful. "Why all the substitutions, Herr Professor? Why not simply kill his mother?"

"Inspektor, you have just touched upon the fiend's psychological conundrum. He doesn't murder his mother because his desire to kill her is hidden deep in his subconscious. He is not even aware of it. Instead, he murders other women, taking out his hatred on them."

"And he doesn't feel guilty about killing these women?"

Kolb shrugged. "Perhaps, but even if he does, it can't be helped. He has an obsession to kill."

"Honestly, Herr Professor," Volker scoffed, "couldn't you say that the man murdered these women in order to rape them . . . or . . . or rob them? The women he murdered were rich."

"Regina Gottlieb was not rich."

"But she appeared rich," Volker said. "Perhaps he thought she was wearing expensive jewelry."

"She didn't own any jewelry," Kolb said. "She was a peasant."

"He couldn't tell from a glance," Berg countered.

"Gentlemen, this is a man who has murdered three times. He will not stop at three because he has a compulsion to kill. The irony is that this compulsion will never be satisfied because the woman he wants to murder, he cannot."

Kolb gathered his thoughts further. "Witness the fact that he takes things from the scene of the crime. Holding the purloined object in his hand, the fiend tries to relive the satisfaction of his latest conquest. But after a while, the item fails to evoke the joy he feels when he murders. So he kills again. He will not stop at three, Kommissar, I can tell you that much."

"Twice," Volker said. "Anna Gross was murdered by her husband."

"Herr Kommissar," Berg said, "with all due respect, it might be helpful in the privacy of this room to drop the charade. Anna Gross was *strangled,* sir. And in all three cases one shoe or a single stocking was taken. So unless Anton Gross came back from the grave to steal Regina Gottlieb's shoe, we must assume that all the cases are related."

"Two women, three women . . ." Kolb rolled his cane back and forth in the palms of his hands. "There could be ten others that we don't know about. At the root of it all, this man clearly hates his mother."

"All men hate their mothers, Herr Professor," Volker said. "She is supposed to be the ultimate virgin, yet she screwed your father, making her the ultimate whore. But civilized men don't go around murdering their mothers, even soldiers with blood on their hands—which happens to be most of us."

"People have different ways of integrating the war experience," Kolb said, "especially if they have a predilection for a certain kind of expression, if you will. Artists such as Otto Dix paint their war experiences, writers write about them, composers create discordant symphonies . . . and those sick individuals with damaged upbringings, those who are inclined toward the darker side, they express their experiences by doing what they have to do . . . which is to murder."

Volker said, "I can't believe that you are comparing murder with a painting or a composition."

Berg remembered Gross and Druer, how odd it was that their hair had been combed outward as if framing their faces. Murder as art? He said nothing.

"I'm not comparing it, Kommissar, I'm just remarking that those with a particular slant express the horrors of a bitter life or of war in their own specific ways. If he had murderous impulses because of his mother to begin with, war may have brought them out."

Berg said, "Just look how similar Otto Dix's war paintings are to his *Lustmord* series of rape and sexual murder."

"If I hated my mother that much, I would just kill her," said Volker. "Freud and his theories are pure rubbish. What would you expect from a Jew and an Austrian?"

"It isn't only the Jew who talks about the subconscious, Kommissar," Kolb said. "Carl Jung isn't Jewish. As a matter of fact, he has no love whatsoever for Jews.

Yet his theories also are predicated on subconscious motivations of the *destrudo*."

Berg said, "What exactly is this *destrudo* you refer to?"

Kolb smiled. "Freud postulated that every individual has a life force, conscious or otherwise, that motivates him or her to act in a prescribed way. This life force he called the libido. But then, after the tremendous havoc of the Great War, Freud was left with a paradox: how to incorporate into his theories the terrible death and destruction he had lived through. He was left to conclude that, in counterpoint to the life force or libido, everyone must also harbor a death force called the *destrudo*. And in some individuals, it doesn't take a war to unleash this death force. Just look at the NSDAP. Everything about civilized life seems to unleash the *destrudo* in Hitler's men."

"How does this theory help us solve our crimes?" Berg asked.

"A very good question, Herr Inspektor. Let us analyze what we know. This fiend has murdered, but not in a random way. Two of the three women were rich. The latest, Frau Gottlieb, appeared to be rich because of her fine dress. Since the fiend hates his mother and is murdering rich women instead of his mother, one might postulate that his mother is rich."

"So you're saying he's a man of means?" Volker said.

"Possibly. Or it could be just the opposite." Kolb shook his cane in the air. "He could have come from an impoverished background. He could have hated all women of means, and that's why he's killing them."

"In which case he wouldn't be killing his mother," Volker said. "She would be poor like him. If he hated her, he would be killing poor women. So you have contradicted yourself."

"Not so, Herr Kommissar Volker, he still could be killing his mother and resentful of rich women at the same time. Whatever his background, rich or poor, this man clearly thinks himself a gentleman or, at least, is masquerading as one. The man who called upon Anna Gross, the flowery letter to Marlena Druer . . . everything points to a man of refined tastes."

"We knew that from day one," Volker said. "The man who accompanied Anna Gross into the theater was either a real gentleman or a *Hochstapler*. We know that we're not dealing with some thug in the NSDAP."

"The NSDAP has some wealthy supporters," Berg said. "Some of their leaders are doctors, military men . . . some come from money."

Volker said, "Are you implying that one of the NSDAP leaders is a murdering fiend?"

Berg said, "I'm just pointing out a fact."

"Which brings us to another potential motive," Kolb said. "Anna Gross had once flirted with Kommunismus. The letter to Marlena Druer from a man named Robert suggested that the two of them were on some kind of political mission. So let's refine our parameters. We have to consider that this might be a man who justifies his violence in political terms even though the subconscious motivation is hatred of his mother."

"He is sounding like the Austrian," Berg said.

Volker leveled his eyes at his chief Inspektor. "A word to the wise, Axel. You should watch your words, especially around the station house where NSDAP has many followers."

Berg was unperturbed. "I'm just saying that fanatics have often used politics to justify murder. Look at *Fememord*. A stupid farm girl who had the audacity to *obey* the law and report a hidden stash of illegal guns. For her efforts, she was murdered."

"Axel, we'll never truly know why Amalie Sandmeyer was murdered. Furthermore, we seem to have digressed from one ridiculous conversation to another."

"Yet, Kommissar, you cannot deny that there are senseless murders committed by fanatics," Kolb said. "Sometimes by fanatics who are even gentlemen."

"Count Anton Arco-Valley," Berg said.

"Exactly!" Kolb said in triumph.

"We have no indication that Arco-Valley hated his mother," Volker said flatly. "Only that he hated Kurt Eisner."

"Yes, that is true," Kolb said. "But we do know that he was a rabid anti-Semite, which is why he killed a Jew. You murder what you hate unless what you hate you cannot murder because of societal taboos. Yes, yes, I would say that most definitely we are looking for a man with fanatical political convictions who hates his mother."

"He is sounding more and more like Hitler," Berg taunted Volker. "And before you quiet me, sir, I ask you to look at the facts. The Austrian is political. He is also a bastard, and that is definitely a good reason to resent your mother. Lastly, the Austrian fancies himself an artist."

"That is absurd," Volker said. "It is one thing to strike at your political enemies, but quite another to murder helpless women."

"Regina Gottlieb was Jewish, Anna Gross was married

to a Jew, and Hitler is a rabid anti-Semite." Berg shrugged. "The leap is not a big one."

Volker was seething. "We are not, in any way whatever, going to implicate Herr Hitler in these murders, do you *understand* that!"

"I'm not saying you should, Herr Kommissar," Kolb answered flatly. "We are just having an intellectual discussion that hopefully will aid you in catching this monster. This monster will not stop killing—*especially* since Anton Gross was assumed to be the murderer of his wife. The killer thinks he got away with it! He's probably *laughing* at the police right now; at their stupidity and incompetence in arresting the wrong man."

"I hardly think *that* is the case." Enraged, Volker clenched his teeth.

"On the other hand," Kolb said, "it could be that he is angry that no one has given him credit for his murders. Maybe he's like his predecessor in London, Jack the Ripper. I fear that our fiend is a compulsive murderer. Furthermore, he wants attention for his evil deeds and will not stop until he has this attention."

Berg said, "So until we catch him, there will be more murders."

No one spoke for a moment, leaving the statement unanswered. But of course, everyone knew the answer. Why bother with the obvious?

TWENTY-EIGHT

✠ Refusing transportation, Berg limped home through a dense fog that had settled on the streets, pinpricks of drizzle tickling his nose and eyelashes. The heavy mist made him feel invisible yet strong, as if he were moving through the ether of heaven. As he huddled in the warmth of his thick woolen overcoat, he thought about three young murdered women whose commonality centered on beautiful attire. Tomorrow he would interview Frau Julia Schoennacht, the woman who had identified Regina Gottlieb, although he harbored little hope of attaining relevant information. The wealthy regarded servants as nothing more than conveniences like electricity or a car . . . or the police. Hired help was there to be used when necessary, then safely stowed away and out of sight at all other times. Even if Frau Schoennacht talked, it was highly unlikely that she knew anything about Regina other than the fact that she could sew.

As he struggled up the four flights of steps to his flat, Berg broke into a sweat. His apartment was dimly lit, one lone bulb flickering over the dining table. The rest of his home was shrouded in darkness. Joachim bolted up when his father walked in.

"Papa!" He ran to Berg, pulling up loose pajama bottoms that fell from thin boyish hips. He helped his father off with his coat. "Can I make you some tea?"

"Tea sounds good." Berg wiped his face with a handkerchief. "Everyone else is sleeping?"

Joachim nodded, then went to the stove and placed the kettle on the burner, stoking the dormant fire underneath.

Casually, Berg checked the hod: down to the halfway mark. The coal situation was still shaky. Perhaps he could do without hot tea. Sensing his father's concern, Joachim said, "The water's warm, Papa. It won't take long."

"That's good." Berg went over to the table and sat down, rubbing his eyes, then looking down. His son had been drawing with leftover coal bits, broad strokes in black on discarded newspaper. The execution was impeccable; the subject matter was disturbing.

A group of hoodlum boys wearing Nazi armbands beating up an old man who was obviously meant to be Jewish—the hooked nose, the bulging eyes, the prominent forehead, and the satanic grin. The drawing was all the more disturbing because although the Jew was a cartoon, the boys were sketched with realism. So was the blood dripping from the Jew's mouth.

Joachim brought over two cups of tea but only one lump of sugar. Britta must be rationing provisions. Berg gave his son the sugar.

"No, Papa, it's for you."

"I insist," Berg said. "I'm not in the mood for a sweet drink anyway."

The boy studied his father but took the lump, dissolving it in the dusky water and stirring it with a small silver spoon.

"What made you draw this?" Berg picked up the sketch.

"Do you like it?" Joachim asked anxiously.

"Should I like it?"

The boy didn't answer.

"Your skill is undeniable. But why this?"

"I don't know, Papa. I guess I draw what I see. What stays in my head."

"You saw some kids beating up an old man?" Joachim didn't answer. "They should be reported to the police. These boys are hoodlums."

Joachim looked at his father. A new expression in his eyes: a hint of defiance. "If they were arrested, there would be others to take their places."

"And that justifies such cruelty?"

"I don't justify it, Papa. I was not one of those who did the beating. I merely record what I see."

Berg sipped his tea, curbing the anger welling up in his breast. "And when did this take place?"

"Every day scenes like this take place," Joachim answered. "And it takes place everywhere. They should just leave."

"Who? The Jews?"

"Yes, the Jews. It would make life simple for them and for us."

"You think that would be the answer to Germany's woes?"

The boy looked his father in the eyes. Again with defiance, a little stronger this time: "If I was not wanted in a place, I would not stay. It would not be good for me."

"And where should they go?" Berg asked.

"Back to where they came from," Joachim said.

"And where is that?"

"I don't know . . . Palestine, I suppose. Let them be a problem for the Turks or the British."

"But many were born here. Many have parents and grandparents who were born here."

"It still doesn't mean they are German. And many of them were not born here. They take away jobs from our people, Papa. They take up places in the universities. They own the banks and cheat people. They open shops and charge outrageous sums of money for simple provisions."

"I see. . . ." Berg nodded. "Does this extend to your science teacher, Professor Gelb, and your art teacher, Frau Sonnenschein? Should they leave as well?"

Joachim knit his brow, troubled by this information. He liked his teachers, so he didn't answer. Instead, he said, "I know you do not approve of Herr Hitler. You think he is a thug, and maybe he is. Still, if we don't stand up for ourselves, who will stand up for us?"

"And who is trying to keep us down, Joachim?"

The boy was silent.

"As painful as it is to admit," Berg said, "the fault cannot lie exclusively with the Jews. Nor does it lie with the foreigners, the Gypsies, the Kommunisten, or even with the inept rulers in Berlin. At some point, we—and by we, I mean the German people—must take responsibility for our own messes. We were driven to war by our ambitions, Joachim. We are fierce warriors, and we have always been compelled to conquer. This is not a bad quality . . . that we go to war for the pride of our Fatherland. But we must accept when our ambition oversteps our abilities. I was there, son. I wore a uniform and marched shoulder to shoulder with my countrymen on foreign soil, where over a million of our men are buried in mass graves because the enemy refused to let us bring the bodies home for proper burial. We went to war . . . and we lost. And that, my dear son, is not the fault of the Jews."

Joachim looked away.

"It is a national tragedy that we have been shamed, yes. That we have a puppet government that bleeds us dry, and that we have to pay enormous sums of money to countries we detest. But isn't it equally a national tragedy that we have yet to realize that we brought such shame upon ourselves?"

Again, the boy didn't respond.

"And the biggest national tragedy is that we will probably go to war again." Berg finished his tea, then held up the picture. "These boys are nothing but cowards, picking on old men. Stay away from them and stay away from Hitler." He stood and kissed the top of his son's head, a mop of flaxen locks. "Turn off the light and dampen the coals before you go to sleep."

The boy nodded. "Papa, how can you shun the next leader of our country?"

Berg stared at his son. "You think he will be chancellor?"

"Yes, I do, Papa. I do think he will be chancellor."

"Then that would be yet another national tragedy."

✠ ✠ ✠

IN A RARE DISPLAY of civic optimism, the sun decided to shine. It was a beautiful morning to go walking, and there wasn't a better area to stroll than Bogenhausen with its parks, flower gardens, and cafés. It was primarily a residential area; the houses were newer, roomy, and detached, sitting on their own private lots. Since Paris was still the rage, many of the homes were built with modern Art Decorative motifs gracing the exteriors. Sometimes the architecture worked, and sometimes the houses wound up looking like stucco wedding cakes. Still, the air was pleasant and the streets hummed with activity, the cable cars snaking through the area, clanging their music against a blue sky tufted with clouds.

On Prinzregenten Strasse, Berg passed the newly constructed Brown House, Hitler's edifice and the official offices of the NSDAP. Conceived by the famous architect Paul Ludwig Troost, the building sat on one of the most beautiful streets in the neighborhood. In all honesty, the structure did have some style, but the color was insipid—not dark enough to be espresso and too dark to be mocha. The result was a hue as dull and lifeless as a turd, an indication of what lay inside.

The Schoennachts lived in an apricot-colored two-story home trimmed with multipaned windows framed by green shutters. Peaked gables jutted out of the red tiled roof, and privacy was provided by a hedge of trimmed Italian cypress trees that encircled a good-sized lot. A stone walkway led to a carved walnut door more suitable for Gothic architecture than this simple country house, but old traditions died hard—true also of politicians who extolled a past glory that never was.

A maidservant answered Berg's knock. She was young and pudgy with dark hair plaited into two braids. Her thick Austrian accent was almost indecipherable. After Berg explained who he was, he could barely understand her response. But her affect suggested that whatever he wanted, the answer was no.

Berg peeked around her shoulders, trying to see inside. From what he could ascertain, the interior was light, bright, and filled with modern furniture. "Actually, Fräulein, this isn't a request. I must talk to the lady of the house."

"That is not possible."

"It is an urgent matter, Fräulein." He gave the servant girl his calling card. "It concerns a murder."

At the mention of murder, the young girl gasped and shut the door. Berg could hear running footsteps fading away. He sighed and knocked on the door once again. This time a tall, peevish-looking gentleman answered, twirling the calling card in his hand. He wore a smoking jacket, slacks, and leather slippers, and an ascot was tied around his neck.

"I suppose telling you to go away would do no good."

His accent was that of an educated Bavarian even though his look exemplified Prussian. He was tall with a sharp nose and as bald as an egg. Deep blue eyes were set behind rimless spectacles.

"No, sir, it will not do you any good whatsoever." Berg glanced over his shoulder. "Perhaps it would be better if we could speak inside, out of sight of your neighbors."

"They can't see over the shrubbery," the tall man answered. "Nevertheless, there's no point in being rude, seeing as this conversation is bound to take place one way or the other. You may come in."

The door swung open. Berg stepped into a vestibule steeped in light: such a rarity for Munich in the early spring. The floor was white marble tiles with diamond-shaped black inserts at the corners, but most of it was covered by a silken Oriental rug woven in jeweled colors—deep blues, royal golds, and rich reds. Directly ahead was the great room with floor-to-ceiling windows that showcased spring trees abloom with white and pink flowers. The furniture was beautifully appointed and beautifully crafted—a symphony of exotic woods and stunning marquetry. The fireplace screen was the most magnificent ironwork that Berg had ever seen.

"Edgar Brandt," the man said. "This way."

Berg followed the man into a gentleman's parlor, not at all typical of Germany, let alone Bavaria. The walls were papered in concentric designs of orange and green, the furniture sleek, thin, and tall, echoing the skyscrapers heralded by this modern age. Furniture that was much more suited to New York where actual skyscrapers existed. The rug that covered the dark wood planks was a swirling whirlpool of muted green eddies. The artwork—oils, sketches, drawings, and prints by Kandinsky, Klee, Picasso, Channel, Fencer, and Matisse—was as modern and as fine as that found in any gallery in Paris. Berg couldn't help but be momentarily distracted by such wealth and taste.

"You approve, Herr Inspektor?"

The tone was slightly mocking. Berg turned around. "In my opinion, you have a wonderful eye." His own eye settled on an Otto Dix oil. Like the artist's war series, the *Lustmord* paintings were graphic and violent. This particular piece, done in Cubist primary colors, featured a mad, murderous fiend in a top hat, snickering over a floating naked woman with truncated limbs. How he wished Professor Kolb were here. "However, there are some who might consider such outlandish works to be violent and degenerate."

The man's laugh was snide. "Then those in the know will have to educate them."

Berg didn't comment, his face remaining bland. The man offered Berg a seat in an enormously large, rosewood-framed, black leather chair. It was one of a matched set. "Rolf Schoennacht." He clicked his heels by way of introduction. "I'm guessing that this nasty business has something to do with the murder of my wife's ex-seamstress."

"Then you'd be guessing correctly." The man was still standing. Berg had to crane his neck to look at him as he spoke. "I am familiar with your name, but I don't know from where."

"I often write for the *Völkischer Beobachter.*"

"Ah, yes. The *Völkischer Beobachter.*"

"You are familiar with the paper?"

"I read everything. I try to keep an open mind."

"A fine quality, Inspektor." Finally, Schoennacht sat down in the matching chair and propped up his long legs on a zebra-skin ottoman. "It is merely an amusement, my writing. It doesn't require a great deal of time. And anything I write is at least literate . . . which is more than I can say for most of the current trash that is printed." He shook his head. "If Hitler is to get anywhere, he must do better in the propaganda department."

Berg nodded. "Interesting. I would not have guessed that you were a supporter of Herr Hitler, certainly not with this art."

"I certainly don't agree with Herr Hitler's taste in art. Nor do I like the thugs and hoodlums that give the Nazis a bad name, but I do like what he has to say about honor and loyalty. And I think he has some fine ideas about how to improve such virtues."

"While I would love to address what virtues you speak of, I unfortunately must address this *nasty business* of murder."

"Regina Gottlieb." Schoennacht almost spit out the name.

"You did not like her?"

"I do not like any Jew. And I was particularly peeved at my wife for using her, a Jewess, when there are so many good German women out of work. I insisted that Julia fire her and hire one of our own."

"You did not know she was a Jew when she started working for your wife?"

"No, of course not. She didn't look particularly . . . I didn't think my wife would be that stupid. So there you have it. Never underestimate the stupidity of women."

Berg looked out the window at what appeared to be an orchard of fruit trees covered with blossoms. Then he fixed his eyes on Schoennacht. Several faint scratches at the base of his jawline extended downward until they were hidden by his ascot. "What happened to your face?"

"Excuse me?"

"The scratches?"

His fingers flew to his face. "*Ach,* that's what you get for using a dull razor."

Schoennacht's face betrayed nothing. Berg said, "May I ask where you were on the night of the murder?"

The tall man smiled. "And what is the purpose of that question? Do you think I'd risk the law to kill a sewer rat? Not that I think there should be a law against killing sewer rats."

"I respectfully ask that you answer the question."

"I was home."

"All night?"

"Yes, all night. Anything else?"

"Yes, Herr Schoennacht, there is more. Please indulge me. You were home all night. Is there anyone who can vouch for your whereabouts that night?"

"My wife, of course." His look was hard. "My valet."

"I would like to speak to both of them."

"I have no problem with your speaking to Helmut, but you'll have to come back later. He is very busy right now, packing three weeks' worth of clothing for my upcoming business trip to Paris and New York. It is quite the ordeal."

"And what kind of business demands such travel, if I may be so bold as to ask?"

Schoennacht smiled. "I am an art dealer."

"Ah. Now your collection makes sense. You have clients in The States?"

"I have many clients all over the world." He stood. "Now, if you'll excuse me."

Berg didn't budge from his seat. "When may I talk to him . . . your valet?"

"I am scheduled to leave this evening. Come back tomorrow afternoon."

"Very good," Berg said. "And your wife?"

Schoennacht shook his head. "I will not have you upsetting my wife. Her constitution is delicate, and she has been near hysteria after finding out about Regina's murder. She hadn't spoken to the Jewess since she fired her. There is no sense risking her health for your satisfaction."

"I understand your concerns, sir. I can be very sensitive, I assure you."

Schoennacht puckered his lips in distaste. "You may not be with her while I'm not at home. Come back in three weeks when I return from my business trip."

"That, I'm afraid, will not work. Exigency makes it necessary for me to speak with her before you leave. That would mean today. And since I'm here already, now would seem like a good time."

"And if I refuse to let you speak to her?"

"I don't see why you'd want to do that, Herr Schoennacht. It reflects poorly on you, refusing to cooperate with public servants."

"That is true. You are very much a public *servant*!"

Berg didn't respond.

"Very well." Again Schoennacht's fingers caressed his scratches. "I will speak with my wife and let you know if an interview is feasible."

"Thank you, sir. The sooner I ask my questions, the sooner I can leave you alone to attend to your business."

"Yes, that would be a very good thing," Schoennacht pronounced.

✠ ✠ ✠

AN HOUR PASSED without word from Schoennacht. Berg didn't care. During that time, he was offered hot tea and a platter of cakes. Refusing would have been impolite. Then, embarrassingly enough, he found that he was hungry, and it took effort not to finish off the entire tray. He had made himself very comfortable in this big chair with big armrests of wood. Too comfortable. He had to fight to stay awake. Finally, the mistress of the house came in, accompanied, of course, by her husband.

Julia Schoennacht was a beautiful woman with hair

piled adroitly atop her head in a style reminiscent of Victorian England . . . a snub at the modern cuts of today. Her chignon was formal and elaborate, and Berg decided it must be a hairpiece, but a good match to her ash-blond locks. Her eyes were the palest blue, her nose was delicate and thin, and her creamy skin was as smooth as alabaster. She wore a long-sleeved, simple dress, maroon in color with the hemline of the flared skirt dipping just below the knee. Her calves were shapely, her wrists and hands fragile with the long, graceful fingers of a pianist. Berg stood up, and she answered him with a nod.

Rolf said, "*Madame* Schoennacht has consented to answer a few questions. Please be brief as she's not feeling well."

"Do sit, madam," Berg said.

She did, then folded her hands in her lap and waited. Schoennacht took the other chair, leaving Berg to stand. To stand was fine with him.

"I would like to know when was the last time you saw Regina Gottlieb," Berg began.

The hands tightened, blanching the knuckles. "It was quite a while ago."

Her voice was light and sweet and tinged with a French accent. Her words, however, were a bald lie. He could tell by her manner and the fact that she averted her eyes from his face. Furthermore, Professor Kolb had told him more than once to look at the pupils when people spoke. The pupils of liars often dilate. For a moment, hers had widened, turning her eyes dark and mysterious. Professor Kolb had also told Berg that dilated pupils indicated sexual interest. In this regard, Berg knew he was flattering himself. He smiled inwardly.

Schoennacht piped in, "So there you have it. She hasn't seen the Jewess in a long time. I don't know what more she can tell you."

Berg looked at Julia. "Madam, women seem to have an intuitive nature about other women. Might it be possible to ask you for your impressions of Frau Gottlieb?"

Schoennacht said, "This is all nonsense."

Berg shot back, "It might be, Herr Schoennacht, but please let me be the judge. And as this might involve some personal things about Frau Gottlieb, I would like to talk with your wife privately. Not long . . . maybe ten minutes at the most."

"I will not allow that."

Julia sighed. "It's all right, Rolf." She smiled at him ever so *sweetly*. "I won't melt, my darling."

Schoennacht pinkened. "I'm just thinking of your welfare."

"I know, Rolf, you always think of me first." She looked squarely into his eyes—a hardness that Berg hadn't noticed until now. "Ten minutes."

"Certainly." Berg waited for Rolf Schoennacht to leave. He was slow in moving and more than a little irked by his wife's boldness. Still, he hoisted himself out of the big black leather chair with the rosewood frame and closed the parlor door without slamming it. Berg started to talk, but Julia held up her hand to silence him.

"The last time I saw Regina was almost a month ago. The woman was hardworking, honest, and very good. You'd be surprised at how many lazy people there are these days even with jobs being so hard to find. But Rolf insisted that I let her go. I wasn't pleased."

She began to wring her hands.

"And I would have acquiesced except I really did need a blue gown. And I just couldn't find anyone as talented . . . not among these German women." A look of distaste. "I am from Paris so I am more discerning than the average Bavarian *Dame*. I know I am certainly more tolerant than those around me. I don't care one way or the other about Jews. They don't bother me as long as they work well and are honest. Rolf is more forthright in his opinion of Jews as an inferior race. He really didn't want anything to do with them even if it meant shoddy work that cost more money."

She let her hands drop into her lap.

"What I am going to tell you has to be kept a secret, Inspektor. Do we understand each other?"

"Absolutely." Berg added encouragement. "Please, I am very trustworthy."

She smiled angelically. "Inspektor, men are *never* trustworthy!"

Berg lowered his eyes. "What is it you want to tell me, Madame Schoennacht?"

"As I have stated, I really did need this blue gown. *Le Comte* Boucher is to hold a weekend gala in his château in the Alps, and it was imperative that I have the finest that money could buy. Not for me, but for Rolf. The count is one of Rolf's biggest clients."

There was the French accent again. Biggest came out as *beeg*est.

"I wasn't going to go looking like a ragamuffin. The night of her murder, Regina was coming here to show me a sample of her work. But she failed to keep the appointment. I was very peeved. Rolf was out, and I needed to sneak her in."

A pause.

"Except now I realize why she didn't keep the appointment." Her eyes watered for a moment. "This is just terrible!"

"So you didn't see her that night."

"No, I didn't." Again, she started wringing her hands. "And I don't know why she or her family would say that I owed her wages. I hadn't ordered anything. If she made a dress in anticipation of my buying it, that wasn't my doing. I'm not required to pay for it. They should not be hounding me, especially because I had been most generous with Regina."

Not to be outdone by Professor Kolb's fascination with Freud, Berg jumped in with his own conclusions. "You are constantly kneading your hands, madam, as if you are washing them. Is anything wrong?"

"Yes, there is something wrong! A woman who worked for me was murdered."

"And that makes you nervous?"

Julia dropped her voice to a whisper. "Regina was wearing an evening dress. Not that I had ordered it, but the woman did know my taste. Perhaps she came to show me a finished product. She knew I was sneaking her in."

"Ah . . . and you think it is possible that someone mistook her for you?"

"I would not like to think about it, but maybe I should think about it."

"And who would want to harm you?"

"My husband is a man of loud opinions. The city is rife with subversive Kosmopoliten—Jews, Kommunisten, Gypsies, homosexuals, and licentious Negro dancers who wear nothing but fans. Who knows what these perverts are thinking?"

So much for the tolerant Frenchwoman. Berg wished his city had such diversity. "This is Munich, madam, not Berlin. I see many more Brownshirts than perverts."

"That is true." Julia sighed. "I wish they'd all just go away."

Berg steered the conversation back to the topic. "You say your husband was out that evening?"

"He was at one of his clubs."

"Which one?"

She shrugged.

"Herr Schoennacht told me he was with you."

Julia looked up in surprise. "Well, yes, he was with me after he came home from the club."

What the man had actually told him is that he had been with his wife the entire night. So many bald lies. Berg said, "And what time would that have been?"

He could see the look in Julia's eye—an expression that was hesitant to say the wrong thing. She hedged. "Not late, but I'm not quite sure I remember the exact time. Herr Schoennacht could tell you better than I."

"Perhaps his valet might remember?"

"Helmut? Maybe. When Herr Schoennacht comes back late, Helmut isn't always here to do his evening toilet. No matter . . ." A wave of the hand. "I am sure that Herr Schoennacht is capable of removing his clothes all by himself."

Said with a tint of anger. What was lurking behind the loyal-wife facade?

The door opened and Rolf Schoennacht strutted in. His

eyes went from Julia's face to Berg, then back to Julia. "Are you all right, my darling?"

She clasped her hands tightly. "Actually, I do feel a bit light-headed."

Rolf said, "You'll have to leave now. My wife is quite shaken, and all these questions are quite injurious to her fragile health."

This time, Julia nodded emphatically. Her cheeks had become a shade paler. Her husband helped her up and took her arm. His voice was low and angry. "This wasn't helpful, Inspektor."

"I apologize for the intrusion, Herr Schoennacht."

"You damn well should apologize."

"Rolf, there is no need for profanities."

"I'm sorry, my love." He glared at Berg. "You must go. The help will show you out."

"I can find my own way, sir."

"I'm sure that is true. After all, you are a servant." He smiled. "Public servant, private servant. You're all the *same* small-minded mentality."

TWENTY-NINE

✠ It was a simple lunch of wurst and cabbage, but everything was tastier when enjoyed under the sun. White plumes of clouds rolled through aqua skies, and the wind was fresh and crisp. Since it was before eleven, Berg had decided on weisswurst, and the pale sausage went down as smooth as butter. He had chosen a local beer, Kochelbräu, the label featuring the famous Bavarian martyr Schmied von Kochel, who led a peasant revolt against Austria in the 1700s. The brew was served ice-cold and with a good head.

Squinting as he looked up at a partially masked sun, his eyes bleached from the intense rays, Berg returned his focus to the faces of his colleagues. Georg was happily munching away; Ulrich wasn't hungry but elected to sip beer and stare at the parade of humanity that passed by the open-air café.

"Schoennacht lied about being in his house all night," Berg started off. "His wife claims he was at a club for part of the evening. He certainly had enough time to murder Regina Gottlieb and scrub up before he went home. He also has a few scratches on his face."

Storf looked up. "Recent?"

"Pale, but I could see them."

"How did he explain them?"

"Shaving nicks."

"It could be that," Müller said.

Berg said, "Or it could be wounds that Regina Gottlieb inflicted on him while defending herself."

"But why would he murder her?"

"He despised Jews. And Regina claimed that Frau Schoennacht owed her money. Maybe he didn't want to pay."

Storf crossed his legs and regarded Berg. "I doubt that a man like Rolf Schoennacht would risk his position in the community to kill a lowly Jewess."

Berg would not give up. "But then why lie about being in all night, especially since he knew the truth was bound to come out? All he had to say was that he was at the club, and we'd verify it. Then he'd automatically be eliminated as a suspect."

Müller said, "Maybe it just seemed simpler to lie."

Storf shrugged. "Or perhaps he wasn't at any *club,* Axel. What if he was at a Nazi meeting or with his mistress and he didn't want you poking around into his personal business. Even clever men like Schoennacht do foolish things when they feel cornered."

"At least we have a motive for Schoennacht wanting her dead. And we also have the scratches as possible evidence." Berg sighed. "Which is more than we have with the other two women . . . although Anna was married to a Jew." He perked up. "There's the Jewishness in common."

"So why not murder Anton Gross, who is a Jew?" Storf said. "Why murder his wife?"

"It could be that Schoennacht hates women," Berg said. "Professor Kolb thinks that our fiend has an unresolved relationship with his mother that causes him to take out his anger on women."

Storf said, "Axel, we cannot arrest a man based on some lunatic theories promulgated by a disturbed Jewish madman who is Austrian at that. We are members of the *Mordkommission,* not head doctors. Let's keep to the facts."

"You're in a mood today." Berg smiled. "Last night's date did not go well?"

Storf muttered, "If the fiend hated women, it is not so hard to understand why."

Berg signaled the *Kellner* for another beer and pointed to Storf. "We've all had those thoughts, but very few of us act upon them."

A minute later the waiter brought Storf another pint. Ulrich sat back in his chair. "What are the facts?"

Berg wiped foam from his mouth with the back of his hand. "Let us start at the beginning. We had the murder of a woman who was last seen with a mystery man. Gerhart Leit identified Anna Gross in a picture and remembered seeing her with a gentleman at his Kabarett. I drew a sketch of the mystery man under Leit's guidance. Gross's maid identified the man in the sketch as a mysterious Russian who had visited Anna. And in her personal effects we found a card from an unidentified man named Robert Schick. And that was as far as we got with Anna because her husband was arrested for her murder, then beaten to death on the streets before we could do anything. Has anyone anything to add?"

Storf and Müller were silent.

"Murder two: Marlena Druer. Her body was found near the location of Anna Gross's body. She seemed to have been murdered by the same hand because both of them were strangled with a chain. Marlena was described as a wealthy, eccentric, independent woman. We went through her personal belongings and found not only a great deal of cash, but also a letter from a man named Robert. No surname, but an address. We went to that address—a flophouse—and we found an American reporter named Michael Green, who identified the mystery man in my sketch as an Englishman named Robert Hurlbutt."

Storf scoffed. "Who can trust an American?"

"A good point, Ulrich, except that the use of the Christian name Robert gives a consistency to the entire tale. So far, everything points to a man named Robert. Even the Russian lute player who identified the mystery man as a Russian masking as an aristocrat remembered someone calling him Ro—a name close to Robert."

"A Russian aristocrat named Robert?" Storf smiled. "That's a new one."

"The man is a *Hochstapler.* Impostors use aliases for a reason. Sometimes they are chosen because they sound like the person's actual name."

"Then it is a stupid alias," Müller said.

"Not so, Georg. If you use an alias, you have to remember it."

Storf added, "Or he could be assuming the identity of someone he admires."

Berg nodded in agreement. "From Ro to Robert Schick to Robert Hurlbutt. The American told us that Hurlbutt is a famous name at Harvard University. So maybe our impostor also wants to be an American."

"God knows why," Storf snarled. "They are brash and ill-mannered."

"They won the war." Berg was going over his words in his mind. "So far he may be Russian, German, English aristocracy—or pretending to be English aristocracy—or an American."

"Ro for Robert," Storf said suddenly. "Ro for Rolf."

Berg looked at him. How could he have been so *dense*?

"I don't have the sketch in front of me," Storf said, "but you're the artist. Does he look like the man in the sketch?"

Berg thought about it. He wanted so badly to say yes, but caution held him back. "Not exactly . . . but perhaps, if he was wearing a disguise. For instance, Schoennacht is bald. Now if he were wearing a wig . . ."

Storf said, "What does Herr Schoennacht do again?"

"He's an art dealer, currently on his way to visit clients in Paris and The States."

"So he must speak English."

Again Berg knocked his head for his stupidity. At least, Storf was thinking. "I would assume so."

"Did you detect any accent in his German?"

"Not really, but I wasn't listening for one, either. To me, he was clearly Bavarian." His brain was buzzing with ideas. "Look at Putzi Hanfstaengl—German father, American mother, American wife."

Müller said, "Also an art dealer. I wonder if the two are related?"

"I don't know if they're related, but they must know each other. The art world is very small." Berg looked up at the sky. The sun was getting stronger, beating down on his neck. He removed his coat and laid it across his lap. "Gerhart Leit said an interesting thing when I interviewed him . . . that our mystery man was very tall, the Putzi Hanfstaengl type."

Ulrich smiled. "So you are suggesting that Hanfstaengl is our murderer."

"He speaks fluent German and English." Berg laughed. "Stranger things have happened. I wonder if . . . How would I set up an interview without arousing suspicion?"

"Berg, you can't be serious!" Müller was appalled. "He is a big supporter of the police. I will not be a party to this!"

"Fine, Georg, I'll do it on my own."

"You would do well to find evidence first. At least with Schoennacht, you have a scratched face."

"Schoennacht . . ." Storf said. "Is his wife German?"

"French."

"His parents?"

"I don't know." Berg shrugged. "The American Green mentioned something interesting—that Robert Hurlbutt's father could have been in the diplomatic corps. We should find out who in Bavaria has been in the diplomatic corps, especially those assigned to Russia and to English-speaking countries."

"And ask them what, Berg?" Storf said. "Have you been murdering any women lately?"

"We're not interested in them, but in their sons."

"And that makes them more accessible?" Müller said.

"Do either of you have any ideas to put forth, or is your sole job making my ideas look ridiculous?"

"Then how about this?" Storf said. "Gross and Druer were libertine women. What if they both met the wrong man at one of their Kommunist meetings? Some kind of German Jack the Ripper who likes killing whores. If you like picking on Hitler's inner circle, pick also on the Kosmopoliten who partake in questionable activities."

"He has a point, Axel," Müller said.

"Regina Gottlieb wasn't a wealthy Kosmopolit. She was a poor Jewish seamstress."

Storf stifled a smile and looked into his beer. "You know as well as I do, Axel, that there are quite a few Jewish whores out there."

Instantly, Berg felt himself turn hot and angry. "There is no indication that Regina Gottlieb was a whore."

"How do you know that? Have you investigated her habits?"

Berg was silent and fuming, but Storf was right. The life of Regina Gottlieb needed to be investigated, since most murder victims were killed by people they knew. "I will investigate Regina Gottlieb. Still, I see some merit in this son-of-a-diplomat theory. We need to proceed cautiously, though. Right now, all I want to do is compile a list. Once we have names, we'll narrow down our search."

Storf said, "And how will we get these diplomats to speak to us?"

"If it comes to that, we'll have to convince them about the gravity of the situation—three murdered women, after all." *So much to do and so many questions.* Berg said, "I was on holiday when Gottlieb was murdered. Where in the Englischer Garten was her body found?"

Müller said, "Very near the shrubbery where we found Anna Gross."

"Who found the body?"

Müller chided him with a smile. "You really should read the file, Axel."

Georg was right, but his self-righteous tone annoyed Berg. "I skimmed it in the Kommissar's office." He stared at Müller. "Is there something particular I should know?"

"Regina Gottlieb's body was discovered by Anders Johannsen while on his early morning walk with his dogs."

"The same man who found Marlena Druer?" Berg sat up in his seat. "Why wasn't I told?"

"Because I thought you read the file."

Berg could barely contain his rage. "And neither one of you thought that he was worth looking into again?"

"Relax, Axel, Messersmit interviewed the man while you were gone," Müller said. "He was as frightened as a mouse, telling Heinrich that it was positively the last time he was going to walk his dear poochy poos in that awful park."

THIRTY

From the outside, it appeared as if no one was home in the apartment. The drapes were drawn tightly across the windows that fronted the street. Still, Berg made the four-story climb up the stairs, intending to slip his calling card into the door. On impulse, he knocked and was answered by ferocious barking on the other side. He waited several moments, and then the deep barking died down, replaced by high-pitched yips.

He heard footsteps, then a shaky voice on the other side asked who it was.

Over the yipping, Berg answered, "Police. I'm looking for Herr Anders Johannsen."

The door opened but just a crack. "What do you want?"

"Herr Johannsen?"

"Yes. I already talked to the police. Twice. Go away."

"Please, Herr Johannsen, just a few minutes of your time."

The door closed, leaving Berg in the hallway, feeling stupid and small. He had limped up forty-four steps for nothing. But then he heard something rattle. Was it the chain lock on the front door or the clatter of the dogs' collars as they steadied themselves to attack?

Slowly the door creaked open, revealing a withered

man in a bathrobe. He was tall and one of the palest men Berg had ever seen. White translucent skin like an onion, with sunken dark blue eyes that quickly blackened with the introduction of light. He was holding a muff of fur, white except for brown eyes peeking through. In the background, Berg could hear a low, menacing growl.

"Inspektor Axel Berg of Munich's *Mordkommission*. May I come in, Herr Johannsen?"

There was a long pause, then the pale man stepped aside. Now it was Berg's turn to hesitate.

"And you have another dog, mein Herr?"

"Otto. Yes."

"He is restrained?"

"He won't hurt you unless I tell him to do so. He's very well trained."

Little comfort, but Berg would have to take his chances. "I may come in now?"

"Yes, yes. Come in."

Berg followed the pale man into a somber front room, and though Otto was nowhere in sight, the growling could be distinctly heard. Johannsen pointed to a dark velvet settee, then parted the thick drapes. Dusty sunlight instantly shot through the room.

The old man squinted as he looked out the window. "I see we actually have blue in the sky today."

"It is a beautiful day to go walking."

"Thank you, but no. I've taken too many walks, it seems."

Berg sat down on the deep purple settee. He took in a small, fastidious apartment. The artwork on the walls was of high quality—full of life and color—but Berg's eyes were immediately drawn to the Otto Dix war painting, similar to the *Lustmord* series, but the bodies were all men. "You have interesting taste in art."

The tall man turned around and glared at him. "Are you being facetious?"

The vehemence took Berg aback. "Not at all. I am especially taken with the Matisse dancing girls. Such kinetics in so few lines. And the Dix—such . . . power!"

Johannsen's eyes went from Berg's face to the drawing. "I am surprised that you would like such pieces. The other two men I spoke with were barbarians."

"The other two men being . . ."

The pale man waved in the air. "Those awful policemen. Inspektor Müller was just an oaf, but Messersmit was positively bestial. That man actually implied that I had something to do with the horrible murders of those two women." Johannsen was flushed. "When in doubt, blame the victim."

"It must have been very upsetting for you . . . to discover a second body."

"It was upsetting to discover the first body. The second one was dreadful!" He paced back and forth in the small room, holding his lapdog in one hand and flapping his other hand as he spoke. "Maybe you're used to such gruesome events, but I assure you that I am not!"

A deep moan was coming from another room.

"Poor Otto," Johannsen said. "He's not used to seeing me so apoplectic. I must let him out or he will show his displeasure in destructive ways." The man whispered, "He chews on the piano legs! He knows it drives me crazy."

Before Berg could protest, the tall man was out of the

room. Moments later he was dragging in a beast by a chain.

Actually, the beast was dragging him: a monster dog gray and thick, with tremendous maws, jowls dripping down excess flesh far past the animal's mandible. Foam and spittle escaped from its lips. Dense, defined muscles rippled with each step. It must have weighed nearly one hundred kilos. Immediately, it charged toward Berg, shoving its fearsome face into his lap, sniffing and drooling over his shirt. Normally Berg liked dogs, but this brute was so huge, it would give any animal lover pause. Berg didn't move, waiting for the idiot Johannsen to call off the beast. Seconds passed before anyone spoke.

"Ah, Otto likes you," Johannsen said with a smile. "His tail is wagging."

Suddenly a rough tongue washed Berg's face. "Perhaps you can convince Otto to settle down so we can talk, Herr Johannsen."

The tall man jerked on the chain, and the dog retreated into a sitting position. *"Platz."* Another jerk on the chain. *"Platz,* Otto. Down." Finally the beast flopped down on the wooden floor, his head nudged against Berg's boot. "He's just one big baby, you know. I've never been threatened but I wonder what he would do if I were really attacked."

"And you worry about being attacked?" Berg asked.

"Of course, I worry. Despite the city's assurances, the streets are crawling with thugs looking for targets to beat up."

"The disorder is exaggerated, limited to a few areas and a few of a specific ethnic persuasion."

"Nonsense. After the Jews and the Gypsies, he will go

after others—the Kommunisten, the liberals, and the free-thinking professors of our universities—what he calls the degenerates." Johannsen's voice had become loud and shrill. "He will not be satisfied until every citizen of Germany is in brown uniform, goose-stepping into Russia. I know how men like him think. I was in the army—the reserves. I was in Belgium. I am no stranger to the German love of order. But these animals . . . it goes beyond . . ." He pointed to his Matisse. "Such brilliance will be reduced to relics of a past progressive time."

His rant against Hitler left him limp. He plunked down into a chair and wiped sweat from his brow with a handkerchief he pulled out of his robe pocket. The little fluffy dog nestled in her master's lap, but Otto lifted his head in concern. Johannsen absently patted his head.

"I don't know . . . maybe I'm just too old for this city."

"Maybe it is a reaction to discovering two murdered women."

Johannsen nodded vigorously. "*Herrjemine,* that was ghastly! I mean one was bad enough, but two?"

"Terrible," Berg sympathized. "This may be a hard question for you to answer, Herr Johannsen, but can you recall any similarities between the first body you discovered and the second?"

"I cannot help you, Inspektor. All I really remember was running with Otto and Misty until I came upon a policeman."

"So you really can't recall how the bodies were lying or—"

"Nothing at all . . . well, not much, anyway."

"Go on."

"Just that both poor souls were wearing expensive

clothing. The first one had on a flapper dress festooned with beading. This recent one wore a deep blue taffeta overlaid with silk lace. Lovely material."

Telling Berg nothing he didn't already know. What did he expect? Still, there was something about Johannsen that bothered Berg. The man was out of place, out of step with Munich, yet here he was, finding two dead women.

When in doubt, blame the victim.

Kolb had once told him that men of that persuasion had conflicted relationships with women, hating them deep down. But from experience, Berg knew that most murdered women were killed by men they had been intimate with—a husband or a boyfriend—not a homosexual. What was it about this man and his apartment that was bothering him? He needed more time with the tall man to figure out what was gnawing at him.

Again, Berg looked at the paintings. "Are you an art dealer, Herr Johannsen?"

"I dabble in it. I used to consider myself a composer. Once Germans had an interest in modern musical scales—Arnold Schoenberg, Alban Berg . . . Webern." A sigh. "Now . . ." He shook his head sadly. "I am reduced to writing inane Kabarett songs. Drinking songs. Ho, ho, ho, ho . . . hee, hee, hee, hee." He rolled his eyes. "At least, there is still some money in it."

"From whom do you buy your art?"

"Here and there." The old man shrugged. "If I like the piece and I can get a good price, I snap it up. If someone sees it and wants to buy it for a good price, I am more than willing to sell."

"Have you ever purchased any works from Ernest Hanfstaengl?"

"That Nazi! I wouldn't give him the time of day, let alone my money."

"Maybe from Rolf Schoennacht?"

"He's just as bad. Besides, both of them—Hanfstaengl and Schoennacht—do most of their business in The States. Only the obscenely wealthy industrialists in America can afford such outrageous prices."

"Have you met either man?"

"We've been introduced." Stated very casually. "I remember meeting Hanfstaengl at a gallery opening in the Paris Autumn Salon. I saw Schoennacht once with Ambrose Vollard. Sometimes we frequent the same auctions. But do I *know* them?" He shook his head. "Not at all."

"I just have a few more questions, Herr Johannsen. I hope they won't trouble you too much."

"I'm sure they will." He bristled. "What?"

"When you discovered the body of Marlena Druer—"

"It's so awful!" Johannsen said. "Putting a name on the body."

"She had a name, yes." Berg looked solemn. "You told Inspektor Müller that you were out for your walk at around seven in the morning."

"Seven, seven-thirty. Right after daybreak. I used to find walking along the banks of the Isar a thing of quietude and beauty. Oftentimes, melodies would come into my brain, beautiful songs of a country that once was—all that was progressive and modern. Such a pity!"

"And the day you found the second body . . . what time did you leave for your walk?"

"I believe I told that awful man Messersmit that I left just before daybreak. Otto really needed to get outside, as he's been having some stomach problems. I've been walking in the Englischer Garten lately because I've been too nervous to walk along the Isar. Which is crazy because the first woman was found in the Englischer Garten. But at least, it has pathways and open space.

"So then this happens! Now, I'm too nervous to walk anywhere. I'm like an old crazy person, housebound . . . sitting in the dark. A living model of what this city has become—from the light of all that was new and fresh heading straight into darkness."

Johannsen rubbed his arms and shivered.

"Perhaps I would be better off moving out of Munich. I wasn't born in this city. I came here because I thought it had something unique to offer."

"You're from the north."

"Lübeck," Johannsen said. "My father was a handsome Danish seaman who fell deeply in love with my mother, who was a beautiful and creative German woman. They were terrible for each other . . . my mother and father. Eventually she got tired of waiting for her staid husband to return. One day she packed all of our belongings and moved us to Paris where she studied art. Fine for her, but horrible for me. We lived in squalor. A year later, she died from cholera. I was sent back to my father, who was still at sea most of the time and had no intention of settling down for his snot-nosed son. That's what he called me: a snot nose."

Berg nodded, thinking about Joachim . . . Monika . . . how his children's welfare had become even more important to him as they grew older.

"Finally, I convinced the old man that at fourteen, I was quite capable of living on my own. Anything was better than living with my paternal grandmother, who was very Lutheran and quite awful—punitive, stodgy, strict. It was no wonder my father chose a life at sea."

"You had quite a childhood."

"It was worse than some, better than others. At least with my father, I had enough money for food and clothing. Plus, I had this natural gift for music. A teacher at the Gymnasium convinced me to apply for advanced lessons in music. A year later, I was studying piano at the conservatory."

"What brought you to Munich? Bavaria was always very traditional."

"Yes, Munich is a progressive island in a sea of conservatism. Years ago, the city was all beauty and grace, filled with laughter and the latest modern ideas. Now . . ."

He sighed.

"I have thought many times about moving back to Paris, but my French is so rusty . . . and it brings back terrible memories. Besides, we all know that Parisians have no use for Germans. Holland and Belgium are too cold, and I don't speak Dutch or Walloon. Austria is like Munich, only worse."

"How is your English?"

Slowly, Johannsen smiled. "It's serviceable. Enough to get by. But if the French have no use for the Germans, what would that say about the English?"

"There is always Switzerland."

"When was the last time you've heard of a modern Swiss composer or a modern Swiss artist?"

"Paul Klee."

"He's basically French." Johannsen stroked his lapdog but addressed the big one: "What do you think about moving to Switzerland, Otto?"

At the sound of his name, the dog raised his head. And then with complete clarity Berg suddenly saw what was bothering him. The big dog was wearing a metal chain, heavy and ponderous, that was securely attached to his leather leash. The lapdog, however, was wearing more of a necklace than a chain. Lightweight and braided, if placed around a woman's neck and pulled tightly, it would leave an imprint that was eerily similar to the impressions found on Regina Gottlieb's throat. And if drawn even tighter, it could have sliced through the neck of Marlena Druer.

✠　✠　✠

VOLKER SHOVED THE FLYER in Berg's face. "Another rally, this one scheduled for tomorrow afternoon—three o'clock at Königsplatz. The topic is the inability of the police to keep our city safe. Not only are Hitler and other NSDAP faithful slated to speak, but also members of the BWP. Even the death of a lowly Jewess is raising alarms." He spun around and poked Berg's chest. "What are you going to do about it?"

"What would you *like* me to do, sir? Arrest another innocent person?"

"If you have to, yes. Arrest Gottlieb's husband. No one will care if another Jew dies. In fact, it may appease the restlessness in the streets."

"Maybe as a temporary measure, like Anton Gross. But we both know that another innocent man will die and, in the end, we will still be no closer to solving these killings."

"How do you know he is innocent? Have you investigated him?"

"I will as soon as I leave this office."

"You're not going anywhere!" Volker ordered. "Sit down!"

Berg sat. Volker was bright red in the face, and veins bulged from his neck as he spoke. "We are sending our men in full force. There will not be another putsch in Munich, do you understand what I'm saying?"

"Whatever your orders are, Herr Kommissar, I will follow them."

Volker seemed momentarily mollified. "You don't have a damn notion of what pressure I am under. Orders from everyone—from Roddewig, from Brummer, from Mantel, and from Schlussel, who is nothing but a mouthpiece for the Lord Mayor. They demand results!"

"More like they want someone to hang."

"They want answers, Axel!"

"I am doing all I can, Herr Kommissar. Just when I think I have a lead to follow, a new body appears and confounds everything."

Volker paced around the small room. "How does he move so quickly and so brazenly?"

He was speaking rhetorically, but a thought suddenly came to Berg. "Maybe our fiend has help."

"What kind of help?"

"One is the lookout and holds the victim down while the other rapes her. Then they switch."

Volker digested that. "*Herrjemine,* what do we have? Two murderers?"

Berg shrugged.

"Hitler's boys?"

"Ordinarily, I'd say yes, but in that case, there would be evidence of a struggle in all of the victims. The only one who seems to have put up a fight is Regina Gottlieb. The first two—Gross and Druer—I suspect they both knew the murderer . . . or murderers."

"And the only thing you have so far is a Russian mystery man named Robert Schick?"

"Who, I think, is also posing as Lord Robert Hurlbutt. I believe that this man is responsible for the deaths of Druer and Gross. Regina Gottlieb is another story. She was neither rich nor politically inclined. She worked for Rolf Schoennacht's wife in secret. He hates Jews, and he might have been resentful that he owed money to Regina Gottlieb."

"You think Rolf Schoennacht killed a woman because he didn't want to pay a simple debt?"

"Maybe his anti-Semitism allowed him to believe that since she was a Jewess, he owed her nothing."

"So why would he rape her?"

"What better way to show contempt for a woman whom he considers a degenerate bitch."

"That's absurd. If you subscribe to Hitler's doctrine, you know that sex with Jews is forbidden."

Berg thought a moment. "Here's another idea. The first two ladies thought of themselves as progressive and cultured. Rolf Schoennacht is an art dealer who deals in modern painting. So does Anders Johannsen for that matter."

"Who?"

"Anders Johannsen, the man who found the bodies of Regina Gottlieb and Marlena Druer. They don't live far from each other, Schoennacht and Johannsen, and they don't live far from where the bodies were dumped."

"Are these two men friends?"

"Not according to Johannsen. On the surface, they are

very different. One is a homosexual progressive who was born in Lübeck; the other is an old-time Bavarian conservative and a fan of Hitler. They have some things in common, though, starting with a passion for modern art. Actually, they both have Otto Dix paintings . . . others as well, but because of his violent subject matter, Dix sticks in my mind. They're also around the same age, and they are both tall. A tall man was seen with Anna Gross on the night she died."

"Do either of these men look like the sketch that Gerhart Leit drew?"

"Not exactly. And the two men don't look alike. But if they were disguised and it was dark . . ."

"And why would these two men be killing women?"

"Perhaps one dislikes women because he is a homosexual, the other because the murdered women were liberal and Jewish and he feels they're trash anyway."

"And what do you offer as evidence?"

"Nothing. I'm just attempting to find a common link. "

"Berg, how would they ever meet? They don't socialize in the same circles."

"They met through their art, sir. At galleries, at auction houses, in Paris. Johannsen said as much." Berg licked his lips. "Granted, it's a very weak link. Still, I would like to find out more about Schoennacht and Johannsen."

"As long as you're discreet. I don't care about Adolf Johannsen—"

"Anders."

"Whatever his name is. He's a nothing, a little old fairy. But I know that Rolf Schoennacht has some connections in the city. I'm sure that he counts Roderick Schlussel as a personal friend."

"I will be very careful," Berg said. "I would like to interview Regina Gottlieb's husband, please. Before it gets too dark."

Volker waved him away. "Go."

Berg got up from the chair, keeping his thoughts about the dog chain to himself. It would have been all the evidence that Volker needed for an arrest. The mobs would take care of the conviction just as they had with Anton Gross. A Jew and a homosexual: perfect fodder for Hitler. The last thing Berg wanted was another lynching.

THIRTY-ONE

✠ Hallo, Axel!" Storf called out.

There was no response. Berg either hadn't heard him or was purposely ignoring him. Storf dashed over and caught Berg just as he stepped outside the Ett Strasse station house. "*Grüss Gott*, Berg, where's the fire?"

Berg continued at a fast clip, his gait made irregular by his sore hip. "No fire, but I'd like to make it to Gärtnerplatz and back before dark." He looked up. "And while the weather permits. I have an interview to do—Volker wants me to talk to Gottlieb."

Without warning Berg's knees buckled as pain shot down his right leg. Storf grabbed his arm, preventing him from falling on his face.

"Are you all right, man?"

"Yes, yes . . ." His voice sounded shaky even to his ears.

"Sit down—"

"I'm fine!" Berg wanted to shake off the help, but didn't have the energy. He'd been pushing his compromised body until it finally had reached its limits. His face felt as hot as sizzling grease. "Really, I'm okay."

Storf steadied Berg back on his feet. "Axel, let's get a beer."

"I don't want a beer," Berg shot back. "I want to do this

interview. Then I want to go home." He took another step forward and cried out in agony. "*Herrjemine!* I'm going to *kill* those *fucking* bastards for what they did to me."

Around them, stunned passersby swiftly walked away, heads down, eyes on their feet, assuming that Berg was crazy or drunk or both. Finally, he composed himself. "Really, I'm fine, Ulrich."

"Then keep me company while I get a beer, Herr Inspektor." Berg was in too much pain to argue. Storf saw an open-air café across the street. Gingerly, he walked Berg to an empty table, depositing him in a seat. "Don't move! I'll be right back."

As soon as Storf disappeared inside, Berg tried to stand, but pain forced him to sink back into his chair. He cursed like a seaman as waitresses wearing traditional dirndls averted their eyes. Finally Storf returned with a couple of pints. Berg took a sip from a frosted mug and felt immediate relief. Chastened, he muttered, "Thanks."

"You shouldn't be walking so much."

"I can't ride my bicycle. How am I to go from one place to another?"

"There are buses, streetcars, and cabs. And you can always borrow a *Kraftrad*. The bigger issue, Axel, is that you're working too hard."

"I just took two weeks of holiday, and look what happened while I was gone."

"You couldn't have prevented the murder even if you had been here."

"How do you know? Maybe I would have caught the bastard and Regina Gottlieb would be alive today."

"And maybe not."

"Well, we'll never know." Berg took another sip, then a

gulp. "I'll survive my injuries, but as long as this bastard is out there, other women may not be so lucky. I need to reach Gottlieb before dark."

"Another day won't make a difference, Axel."

"That is where you're wrong. It was a direct order from Volker."

"Why? What does he care about an old Jew?"

"He'd like me to arrest him for the murder of his wife."

Storf sat up. "Did he do it?"

"I think not, but the Jew's guilt or innocence makes no difference to the Kommissar. All he wants is an arrest."

Storf was silent for a moment. Then he said, "It's not going to work forever . . . blaming these murders on the Jews."

Even Storf understood the very basics. Berg pulled out the flyer for the rally tomorrow afternoon. "Look at this."

Storf skimmed the announcement. "Another rally. So what?"

"Volker finds it worrisome. He fears another putsch from the Austrian."

"This is not '23: There are no breadlines. The economy is not sparkling, but it is not so depressed, eh? If the Austrian is elected chancellor, it will not be by force but by the will of the people."

"God forbid."

"We'll just have to see what God forbids." Storf took a long swig of his cold beer. "Go home. I'll talk to the Jew."

"I don't trust you. Neither will the Jew."

Storf laughed. "And you think he will trust you more than me? Axel, you are naive. You, me, all Germans . . . to the Jews, we are the enemy. And to us Germans, the Jew is the enemy."

"Bitte!" Berg was disgusted. He looked deep into his stein as if it held some magical solution to Germany's ills. In a way, it did. What couldn't be cured with a pint of beer? "Right now, I'm not open to the wisdom of a bastard Austrian."

"I speak what everyone here thinks." Storf leaned over and lowered his voice. "You can't make deals with these people. They are not like you and me. They are a different species."

Berg studied Storf's eyes. He failed to see the burning passion of hatred, none of Hitler's rage at the devil race. What rested there was nothing more than mild annoyance, akin to having one's pet piss in the house. Storf was irritated because he was the police, therefore responsible for cleaning up the city's messes. And many blamed the mess on the Jews.

Berg finished off his pint. "That was a good idea, Ulrich. Fortification. I feel better now—well enough to interview Gottlieb."

"You cannot walk by yourself."

"I will take it slowly."

"Sit a moment. I have some information for you."

"Regarding?"

"Diplomats."

Berg pulled a pocketknife from his boot and flipped the blade open. He began to clean his nails. "Go on."

Storf smiled. "You have given me an almost impossible task. In Munich there are far too many former ambassadors, envoys, attachés, emissaries, and the like to investigate every single one. But since we are narrowing our search to people who are fluent in English and Russian as well as German, I began there. I started with those who speak Russian because there is only one Russia, while there are many countries that have English and German as their primary languages. I was lucky. There was a former diplomat—a minor diplomat actually—who lived in Munich while serving as an attaché to Russia when the Romanovs were in power. He was also married to an American woman. I thought that sounded promising."

"Very."

This time, enthusiasm burned in Storf's eyes. "The man is dead now, but he had a son." He paused for dramatic effect. "The attaché's name was Dirk Schick—"

"Good heavens!" Berg shouted aloud. "And the son is Robert?"

"Rupert—"

"Son of a bitch! The man really does exist!"

"It appears that way."

"What else?"

Storf's face fell. "I thought that was quite a lot for three hours of shuffling paper. Do you know how many layers of bureaucracy I had to go through just to find out about Schick?"

"You did well, Storf," Berg said immediately. "Far better than I could have done. How did you get those vile civil servants to cooperate?" He smiled. "Charming a few *Staatsbeamte*?"

"It will take more than my charm, Axel." He sighed. "There are many, many records we have yet to go through. It could take months."

"At least we know that Robert or rather Rupert Schick is not a product of our imagination." Berg replaced his knife in his boot and checked his pocket watch. "I must go, Ulrich."

"Then I will walk with you." He stood up and helped Berg to his feet.

"This is entirely unnecessary."

"Yes, yes." Storf lit two cigarettes and gave one to Berg.

"Are you sure?" Berg asked, holding the smoke.

"I have more than my monthly ration of tobacco. Please."

Berg inhaled deeply, feeling the warmth fill his nostrils and lungs. The two men walked in silence. It was slow going, but at least Berg could move without doubling over. As they got closer to Gottlieb's apartment, the streets narrowed, the crowds thickened, and the smells intensified from a mixture of sweet and savory aromas from vendors' carts to the unmistakable stench of urine and garbage. During the rains, the lowland area of the Isarvorstadt swelled with groundwater from the river, bringing with it sewage and disease. Many of the blocks had only recently been lifted off quarantine.

But this afternoon even poverty couldn't disguise the crisp blue skies and the gentle perfumed winds blowing from the crystalline Alps. People were out in numbers. Bicycle riders cut a path through the throng of souls, dodging horses, old-fashioned pushcarts, and children who darted into traffic with no concern for their safety. All around were buildings ripe with decay and rot, barely holding up their weight. Most of the ground floors were tiny shops with windows fogged with dirt. The stores were packed with merchandise—everything from clothing to books. Noise came from everywhere: the shouts and squeals of children's games of *Kreisel* and stickball, and conversations held in many languages: German,

Polish, French, Czech, and occasionally Yiddish—the language of the poor Jewish immigrants. They passed by two musicians who stood on a stoop, one of them pushing the bellows of his accordion, the other languidly bowing his violin, the result being a plaintive rendition of "*Es liegt in der Luft.*"

Berg said, "Rupert Schick . . . how old would he be?"

"I suppose he'd be in his forties."

"Around Rolf Schoennacht's age?"

Storf slowed to a halt. "Schoennacht looks a bit older . . . but maybe he could be in his forties."

Around them, people sneaked furtive glances, then scurried away. The two men clearly didn't belong here. Berg finished his cigarette and crushed the butt beneath his boot. He espied a group of young thugs in brown shirts weaving through the street, singing a raspy, drunken version of the "*Horst Wessel Lied,*" marching and tripping at the same time. They had lots of space to move in because people kept their distance. The thugs stood out because there were no other uniforms in the area. He glanced at Storf. "There's trouble."

"They're not doing anything illegal. You cannot arrest people for what they may do in the future." Storf gave him a glance, then continued walking. "You barely survived one beating, Inspektor. Let's not tempt the fates."

Sticking his hands in his pockets, Berg resumed his pace, limping along, trying to ignore the pain. "Schoennacht and Schick," he said out loud. "We don't know anything about Rupert Schick, but Rolf Schoennacht exists. Let's find out who his parents are." Berg winced as he stepped too hard on his left foot.

Storf slowed down. "Are you all right?"

Berg didn't answer. "You say that Dirk Schick was married to an American?"

"A woman named Della Weiss. Ordinarily, I would have thought that she was German, but a carbon copy of her visa was attached to her papers. She was born in Boston."

"Was her family German?"

"With a name like Weiss, I would think yes, but I know nothing about her. And frankly, there is little on Dirk Schick as well. It took me hours just to look through all the diplomats. Schick wasn't a career diplomat, that much I can tell you. He lived in Munich about ten years."

"What was his business other than being a part-time diplomat?"

"I'm not sure." Storf stopped for a moment. "But stapled to his visa were quite a few government papers for permission to bring Russian antiques into Germany."

Berg was taken aback. "The man was an *art dealer*?"

"Maybe. He had purchased a fair number of relics and icons . . . a few illuminated manuscripts. There are carbons of all his transactions. He bought expensive pieces—the man obviously had money."

"Did he sell anything he brought in?"

Storf shrugged ignorance. "I didn't get a chance to pull up a business license. Next time."

"Did he do a lot of traveling?" Berg asked.

"He had a lot of visa stamps. But you'd expect that from someone in the diplomatic corps."

"Did he travel to America?"

"Ah, the English Lord Robert Hurlbutt. No, Dirk didn't travel to America from the stamps that I saw. There was no indication that he ever left Europe."

"But Dirk had an American wife," Berg said. "Our mystery man Robert or Rupert could have learned English from his mother."

"I reckon so, although I'm not going to find that out by looking at old records."

They started walking, ambling through the commotion for a minute or so without speaking. Finally, Berg said, "Let's assume for a moment that Schoennacht and Schick are the same person: What was there about Dirk Schick that would embarrass his son?"

"Nothing that I found out."

"Yet he uses the name Robert Schick when it suits him." Ideas tumbled in Berg's brain. "Schoennacht is leaving for Paris tonight. We should keep a watch on him."

"You are in no shape to watch anyone."

"Then help me by doing it yourself . . . but you can't tell Volker."

Storf raised his eyebrows. "You're asking me to watch a man surreptitiously—and without extra pay?"

"Volker thinks Schoennacht is too well connected to be molested by the police. There's a killer on the loose, Ulrich. If you don't do it, I will."

Storf frowned. "I'll talk to Georg. We'll do what we can."

"You're a good man, Ulrich, thank you." Berg looked at the address in his hand. "We are almost at Gottlieb's. I'll handle it from here."

"How will you get home, Axel?"

"I'll find a cab."

"Good. Don't even think about walking." Storf paused. "One more thing . . . just to add to the confusion. Once I found out that Dirk Schick was bringing in antiques, you piqued my curiosity about Hanfstaengl, since they are both involved in art."

"So is Anders Johannsen."

"Who?"

"The man who found the bodies of Marlena Druer and Regina Gottlieb."

"The fairy with the two dogs? I thought Müller told us that he was a composer or musician."

"He dabbles in art dealing. Degenerate art, as the Austrian would call it. They all do . . . a conspiracy of art critics." Berg massaged his temples. "What were you going to tell me about Hanfstaengl?"

"Nothing extensive, Axel, but I did find out that he went to university in America."

Berg stared at him. "Harvard?"

"Harvard." Storf crushed out his cigarette and smiled wanly. "Knowing the gregarious piano player, I'm sure he was quite the fraternity man."

THIRTY-TWO

✠ The Gottlieb family lived in a third-floor walk-up, the stairwell reeking of sweat, urine, and rot. As it was barely tolerable in cool weather like today, Lord only knew how rank it got in the summer. The floorboards were scuffed and black with age. There were several areas where the planks were cracked or missing altogether, requiring care with each step. When Berg reached the correct floor, he entered a morose foyer lit by a single yellow bulb. One dingy window at the end of the hall let in the last bits of afternoon sun. The sounds of squalling children and muffled conversations seeped through thin walls, along with the static of a radio. Since it was close to dinnertime, there were the smells and sounds of cooking—something frying in grease, the steady chopping of a knife against a cutting board, the clank, clank, clank of a metal spoon within a metal bowl. After locating the correct flat, he placed his ear at the door and listened. He could make out a deep male voice talking in clipped, precise tones.

Berg knocked.

Immediately, the voice stopped. Then he heard the rapid patter of footsteps followed by a slamming door.

"Wer ist da?"

"Polizei."

There was no response. Berg knocked again. "Hallo, hallo." Another knock. "I need to speak with you, Herr Gottlieb. It shouldn't take long."

Slowly, the door opened. The man who stood at the threshold was ashen, a face etched in fear from the curve of his brow to the terror in his brown eyes. He was of medium height, very thin, and bespectacled with a nose more Roman than Jewish. Coffee-colored hair was clipped short with a wisp falling over his forehead. A brush of black whiskers lined the upper lip of his twitching mouth. He wore black pants, a white shirt, and a dark gray vest. His shoes, though old, had been recently shined. He motioned Berg inside, then shut and chained the door.

"Guten Abend." He held himself tightly as if this action would quell his shaking. "What is it that you want?"

"Just a few moments of your time, Herr Gottlieb." Berg looked over the man's shoulder. The house was in disarray. Cabinets were open, items strewn all over the floor. Three boxes and two large valises rested on a beaten-up dining table. "Going somewhere?" Defying the bounds of human credulity, the man's color turned even grayer. "May I ask what your plans are, Herr Gottlieb?"

Gottlieb breathed in and out, trying to get the words out. He clasped his hands, but still the tremor was visible. "I've been through a terrible trauma . . . my children . . . and me." His eyes watered. "I am taking my daughters, and we are visiting relatives in Hungary."

"It looks like you're planning a long visit."

No response.

"You must report to the authorities if you are moving to another city."

The man looked away, his eyes scanning the disarray.

"I am not moving." He licked his lips and started to speak, but thought better of it.

"It does not look favorable, Herr Gottlieb, deciding to pay an extended call on relatives."

The man said nothing.

"Most people would say that a man who would leave so soon after his wife's death has something to hide."

Gottlieb's lower lip began to quiver. "I have nothing to hide, Inspektor. I loved my wife. I am . . ." Tears pooled in his eyes. "I would give my life to have her back."

"Talk to me, then. Help us catch the man who did this to your wife."

He looked down and shook his head. "But I know nothing."

"You may know more than you think."

Again, Gottlieb shook his head. "I will stay, Herr Inspektor. I will stay here and do whatever you want me to do." His voice rose a notch. "But please, I beg of you, let my children go. There is nothing left for them here except horrible memories, suspicion, hatred, and danger."

He started to pant. "I have some money. Not much to make you rich, but enough to help you through these uncertain times. Let me make arrangements for the girls. Let them go!" He couldn't stop shaking. "Please!"

"Papa?" a tiny voice asked. "Is everything all right, Papa?"

Berg turned around. Facing him were two angelic little girls, both with deep blue eyes, one with blond curls and the other with straight black braids. They had smooth alabaster complexions with a tint of pink on each cheek. They smiled shyly at Berg, showing white teeth and dimples. Gottlieb quickly tended to them.

"Everything is fine, everything is fine. This man is a nice policeman trying to help us." Profusely sweating, Gottlieb pulled a handkerchief out of his pants pocket and wiped his face. "I will be with you very soon." He ushered them into a room. "Just stay here and wait until Papa is finished."

Without speaking, Gottlieb went over to a trunk and pushed it out of the way. He got down on his knees and pried open a loose slat of wood, producing a locked box similar to the one found in Marlena Druer's room. He took out a key, opened the box, and showed Berg what was inside.

"This is all the money I have saved. All of it. Have pity on me because of my daughters. Take some, but I beg you to leave enough for my daughters' transportation out of this place until they can settle in Hungary." In his eyes was a combination of pathos and ferocity. "Please let them go."

Berg looked at his face, then inside the box. There was cash, and lots of it. More than he could have saved in twenty years on decent wages as a policeman. How do they do it? These *poor Jews,* how do they have so much money?

Gottlieb seemed to read his mind. "I have worked all my life. My wife worked all her life. Six days a week, twenty hours a day, only on the Sabbath we rest. All this money is honest, I swear."

"I believe you." Berg rocked on his feet, taking weight off his sore hip.

"Take . . ." He shoved the box toward Berg. "I insist."

"Why do you want to go elsewhere, Herr Gottlieb?"

Gently, he pushed the box back to the distraught man. "If it is the political climate, I believe things will get better."

Gottlieb dropped his voice to a whisper. "I have lived in Munich all my life. I fought in the war; I fought for this land. But now . . . it is a different city. It is not safe for my kind anymore. The Austrian has made his feelings known."

"There is more to Munich than Hitler."

"But you don't see what I see. You don't live where I live, Inspektor. Every day I see gangs of his men. Young, filthy, drunken boys. They terrorize old men. They push them, then laugh when they fall. They grab their canes and hit them. I see them harass women, grab them and pinch them—they would do worse if no one were around. And this is all in the open, Inspektor, in the daylight. Unashamed. No, it is worse than unashamed: They are proud of what they do. They commit robberies, they smash windows with rocks, they scare the children. I was able to tolerate it when my wife was here. She was a solid woman who could raise children in these hard times." Tears spilled over and fell onto his cheeks. "But she isn't here now. I cannot allow my daughters to grow up in this way . . . living in fear."

Sweat dripped down his face.

"If another woman is murdered, they will blame it on the Jews. They will blame it specifically on me. They will say I wanted revenge, I wanted retaliation, I wanted *blood*. Yes, I want all those things. I want them so badly that I tremble when I think about it. Yet it is against my nature to hurt anyone. Certainly, I could never kill anyone. But will that matter to them? The thugs will break into my apartment. They will kill me. And my daughters . . . I can't bear to think what will happen to them." Again, he offered Berg money. "I will help you, but you must help me."

Berg looked at the metal box, then at Gottlieb's pale face, at the feral look in his eyes. Once, Berg might have thought Gottlieb insane, but the events of the past weeks had given him pause. If thugs could beat up a police officer with impunity, what would they do to this unfortunate Jew?

"Arrange for your children to leave," Berg said. "But you, Herr Gottlieb, you must stay. If you try to leave, you will be arrested and charged with the murder of your wife. I assure you that there are those high up in the government who do not care about your guilt or innocence, only about results. Do not make a fool out of me if I grant your wish for your children."

Gottlieb blinked back tears. "Thank you. I know you have your orders, but I can tell that you are a good man."

"Yes, yes—"

"No, I can tell." He paused, then retrieved a handful of bills from the box and offered them again to Berg. "Here. Please."

Berg ignored the outstretched hand. "You do not seem surprised that it is possible for you to be charged with murder."

"I know what happened to the other Jew, Anton Gross. He also had no reason to murder his wife. And he was a rich man. If a rich man could not save himself, what chance would I have?"

Berg laid his hand on the Jew's back. "Herr Gottlieb, I know you've lost your wife, and I know you are afraid. But I think you know more than you are saying. Now is the time. Please! If you know what happened to your wife, you must tell me. Was she murdered by these hoodlum gangs? Is that why you're afraid? Do you fear retribution?"

"Yes, of course, I fear retribution, but honestly, Herr Inspektor, I don't know what happened. That is the truth."

"But you have suspicions, no?"

Gottlieb looked around as if someone was hiding in his closet.

"Or maybe it wasn't the gangs. Perhaps it was as simple as a wage dispute?" Dread passed through Gottlieb's wet eyes. Berg knew he had hit upon something. "I know that Herr Schoennacht does not like Jews."

"He is an evil man," Gottlieb whispered. "Regina would see Madame Schoennacht only when her husband wasn't around. I begged Regina to stop working for this woman. Her husband is a big supporter of the Nazis. He hates Jews the way the Austrian does. But Madame was paying her considerable wages. Finally I put my foot down, and Regina agreed. She told me this visit would certainly be the last time because . . ."

"Go on," Berg urged. "Why was it the last time?"

"Regina told me . . ." He was panting heavily. "Once she saw him just as she was leaving Madame Schoennacht's apartment. He was staring at her in a very odd way . . . with hate, yes, but hate she could deal with. We deal with hate on a daily basis. No, this was something else." His skin grew very red as rage passed through his veins. "He was looking at her in a way that a man shouldn't look at a married woman. . . . My wife was very beautiful, Inspektor."

"I understand what you're saying," Berg told him.

"She didn't want to go back, but Madame owed her money. I told her to forget about the debt, but Regina would have none of that. Then I told her I would collect the money, but she insisted that she collect it. She was afraid that if Herr Schoennacht saw me trying to collect the money . . . that he would harm me." Again, his eyes moistened. He looked away, abashed by tears. "And now she's *dead*!"

The man broke into strangled sobs, his shoulders heaving as tiny gasps escaped from his throat. There was nothing Berg could do to comfort this man for his terrible loss. He looked at the ceiling as he spoke.

"Your wife was a beautiful woman and a remarkable seamstress. The gown your wife made for Madame Schoennacht was stunning, Herr Gottlieb. I should say that your wife looked stunning in it. Such a beautiful blue ball gown."

Puzzled, Gottlieb faced Berg. "What do you mean?"

"The murderer must have snatched your wife on her way to the Schoennachts' house. Because when we found your wife, Herr Gottlieb, she was wearing Madame Schoennacht's blue gown."

Gottlieb shook his head vehemently. "Why would my wife . . . a simple woman . . . be wearing a ball gown?"

"I was told that she was delivering it to Madame Schoennacht."

"Impossible. Regina made that gown for Madame Schoennacht at least a month ago. She no longer had it in her possession. It was the money from the sewing of that very dress that she was trying to collect."

Suddenly, the absurdity hit Berg. Why was she wearing a *gown*? It was his turn to be silent. He tried to speak, but there was a catch in his throat. Finally he found his voice. "Madame Schoennacht claimed that Frau Gottlieb had arrived wearing the gown to model it for her."

Gottlieb was taken aback. "That is simply not true. As I told you, she delivered it a month ago. And she would certainly never wear it anywhere. What if she got it dirty or what if she tore it? No, Inspektor, Regina went over there simply to collect her wages." His eyes darkened to a smoky gray; his brow furrowed with rage. "The murderous bastard! Both of them! It was easier for them to kill her—and dress her body in the cursed gown—than it was for them to pay her!"

That seemed to be a plausible explanation. Berg said, "Can you think of any reason at all why your wife would be wearing Madame Schoennacht's blue ball gown?"

"None." He shook his head, then turned his attention to Berg. "Why are you asking *me*? Why don't you ask *them*?"

"I intend to do just that, Herr Gottlieb. But if they did murder her—and I'm not saying they did—they are not going to admit that the gown was in their possession a month ago. Might your wife have had any receipt of purchase or any kind of note written by Madame Schoennacht that was dated prior to your wife's death?"

"I don't know. I have to look. It will take me a while because . . ." He looked around. "Things are in quite a state of upheaval. *Bitte,* Inspektor. Let me take care of my daughters, and then I will look through my wife's business papers, I promise you."

"This is a serious crime, Herr. The sooner we have evidence to reinforce what you claim—a bill of sale, for instance—the sooner we can solve her murder."

"My wife is dead, Herr Inspektor, but my daughters are still alive. It will take me time to find the bill of sale. I'm begging you . . . allow me to take care of my children, then I promise I will be at your service completely."

Berg said, "Schoennacht is leaving the city tonight. It would be preferable to have this bill of sale before he goes. You can understand my concerns."

"Sir, if it were anybody other than my daughters, I'd help you right away. Please, Inspektor, I beg you. Give me a day to get them out of the city before the rally."

Once again, Gottlieb offered him money. This time, Berg took it.

THIRTY-THREE

After a long day, Berg decided to walk home, hoping that a leisurely constitutional might clear his head. His chosen route was through the Viktualienmarkt, and even though most of the stalls had shut down for the evening, there still were signs of life. Water had been poured over the cement, icing up in some of the colder spots, but the superficial cleansing failed to eliminate the smells. The winds picked up a pungent combination of butchered meat, leftover fish, and overripe vegetables. At this time of year when cooler temperatures prevailed, the place was pleasant even with the strong odors. In the summertime, however, the heat and humidity brought on not only rapid decay of perishables but also insects—flies and gnats— making it mandatory to do one's marketing early in the day.

Berg found a bakery on the verge of closing and took advantage of the unsold stock, buying a half-dozen kaiser rolls at a reduced price. He ate one as he hobbled across the old city of Munich, careful of his step on the cobble-stone walkways, serenaded by the deep oompah, oompah of the tuba inside the Hofbräuhaus.

It took him over forty minutes to get home, and by the time he had climbed to his fourth-floor flat, dinner was nearly over. Britta said that they had waited as long as they could.

"Don't worry about it." Berg set the rolls in a basket and brought them to the table. "Just a little butter and jam and tea will do. I'm not hungry tonight."

Britta sized up her husband, deciding his fatigue came from work rather than infidelity. Still, she glanced at her children and ordered, "Go to your room." Berg looked at his wife quizzically. She kneaded her hands. "I must talk to your father for a moment."

"But I'm not done eating," Monika complained.

"It won't take long. Go!"

When they hesitated, Berg added, "Listen to your mother."

Reluctantly, the children left the table, dragging their feet across the floor, clearly displeased by the exclusion. Britta waited until she heard the bedroom door slam shut. "Is it your desire to make me a widow and your children orphans?"

"I'm fine."

"You look terrible," she whispered fiercely. "If you don't take some time off to recuperate, I'm taking the children to my parents'. I can't control what you do, but I don't have to watch you destroy yourself. You move through the house like a ghost. It frightens the children."

She was right. Lord, how his body ached, but what choice did he have? He kept his voice low. "I've already taken time off, Britta. More time than I'm entitled to."

"I don't care, Axel. We will do without a week's salary. You need to heal."

"These aren't normal circumstances. There is a big rally tomorrow in Königsplatz. The Nazis are joining forces with the BWP. A killer is running loose in Munich. Volker demands results."

"So let him get them himself. The bastard! He wasn't beaten to a bloody pulp." She threw a dishrag on the table, stomped into the kitchen, and began running steamy water into the sink.

Berg sighed aloud, knowing how angry she must be to swear. He rose from the chair and walked over to his wife. Her hair had been tied back, and her face was pink from the wet heat. She wore a long white apron over a simple blue working dress. Her figure was still youthful, with a firm rear end and curvaceous hips. He looped his arms around her waist and kissed the back of her neck as she scrubbed a pot.

"Get away!"

"Stop being mean."

She dropped the pot in a pool of hot, soapy water and turned around. "I'm sick of this place, Axel. I'm sick of this town, and most of all, I'm sick of your job!"

"You've been very patient, Britta. We'll catch this man soon. Then it will be better."

"It will never be better as long as you insist on staying in the *Mordkommission*! What was wrong with the regular hours of a policeman?"

"It's mind-numbing, Britta. Spending your days directing traffic and your nights arresting drunks. Now, at least, I use my brain . . . such as it is."

Despite her anger, Britta smiled. "Your brain works perfectly . . . too well, in fact. There is a problem with being too curious . . . poking your nose into other people's business. It creates resentment."

"No one wants to hurt me. I'm too insignificant."

"I don't believe that for a moment." Britta sighed. "I know you don't want to hear this, but Papa *is* getting older, Axel. He could use someone smart."

Alfons Neugebauer, Berg's father-in-law, owned a sizable printing shop just north of Berlin. Thirty years of hard labor had brought him good money along with permanently blackened hands and lungs filled with poison. "We've been through this before, my darling." He shook his head. "It isn't possible."

"Why are you so stubborn?"

"I can't work with your father."

"Can't or won't?" Her mouth was tight with defiance, her eyes calling for an answer.

He pulled away. "Britta, even if I could work with Papa, I *cannot* work with your brothers." He didn't add: *. . . because they are lazy and resentful and my industriousness makes them look bad in their father's eyes.* But she understood the implicit message anyway. She softened her tone. "Papa adores you, Axel. You are more his son than my brothers are. He could help you set something up in Munich."

"And spend the rest of my days printing flyers announcing upcoming rallies? I would die of boredom."

"And your solution is to work yourself to death?"

Having no satisfactory answer, he said, "I swear to you . . . after this is over I will look for other work."

"That's what you said last time."

"I did look for work, Britta. The economy is bad. Jobs are scarce! Not to mention that I am thirty-seven and not trained for anything else. What do you want me to do?"

"I've already told you what *I* want. It's obvious that what *I* want doesn't matter. It's obvious that you're more interested in *excitement* than in your own health and the welfare of your family—"

"That is not fair."

"It may not be fair, but it's true." Britta shoved a sponge into his hand. "You can clean up. I'm tired!"

Once again, she stomped off. He jumped when he heard the bedroom door slam. He waited without moving for what seemed like an eternity, hearing nothing but the movement of the grandfather clock . . . a steady tick, tick, tick, tick. Their tiny closet of a kitchen was hot and sticky from the steamy water, and perspiration rolled down Berg's face. With nothing else to say or do, he began to clear the dishes. A minute later Joachim appeared. Wordlessly, he began to help.

"Save your sister's plate," Berg said. "She wasn't done with her dinner."

"Is everything all right, Papa?"

"Are you still drawing pictures of bleeding Jews? I'm sure there will be plenty after tomorrow night's rally." Joachim winced at his father's harsh tone. Berg blew out air. He took a deep breath, then kissed the top of his son's head. "I'm a little irritable tonight."

"Why do you and Mama fight so much?"

Because that's what married people do! "We're both tired, Joachim. We work hard. It makes us grumpy."

"Why do you have to work so hard? Is it because of the woman-killer?"

Berg was unsure how to respond. "You have read about it in the papers?"

"You don't need to read the papers. Everyone is talking about it. It scares Mama."

Berg gathered up an armful of dishes as he tried to muster up a confident tone. "The police will catch him, son." He lowered the plates into the sink. "He won't get away."

"Herr Hitler says it's the Jews who are murdering the women."

"Herr Hitler has a stick up his ass."

Joachim smiled. "That is true, but there still might be merit to what he says."

"You mustn't believe *anything* the Nazis say. They are grandstanders and liars. And what they don't lie about, they distort. Hitler is a very disturbed man."

"Maybe it was because he was shot in the war."

"And I suppose he blames that on the Jews as well?"

Joachim hesitated. "He says that there were traitors among the troops."

Berg stared at his son. "Since when do you know so much about Hitler?"

The boy looked away. "We have guest lecturers at school."

"Ah yes," Berg said. "The ones who ask you which newspapers your parents read."

"We have lecturers from the Social Democrats as well."

"And what do you tell the Nazis when they ask you which papers your parents read?"

"I tell them we read everything . . . that my father has an open mind."

Berg nodded. "That is a fine answer, I think. And how do the Nazis respond?"

"That sometimes a mind can be so open that the brains fall out."

Despite himself, Berg laughed. "Yes, they would say that."

Joachim remained serious. "It disturbs me . . . that the Nazis mock anyone who disagrees with them. Sometimes I speak up." He paused. "But sometimes I don't."

Such a huge burden for such a young boy. What times we live in! Berg smiled kindly. "Part of being clever, Joachim, is knowing when to hold one's tongue."

"But being clever isn't the same as doing the right thing."

"We all make compromises, son."

"You don't."

"Of course I make compromises. It's easier for me to lecture you about morality than to follow my own advice."

"I don't believe that for a moment."

He spoke with such admiration that Berg felt his eyes go moist. "Thank you, Joachim. I will remember your faith in me the next time my integrity is on the line." He picked up the sponge and lowered his voice as he lied: "And don't worry at all about this madman. We are very close to arresting him. But you mustn't tell anyone because it's a secret."

"Papa, he must know you are after him." Berg shrugged. The boy said, "How do you know that he won't hurt you before you arrest him?"

"Because . . ." Berg was momentarily stunned by the question. "Because that's not the way it works."

"Why not?"

"Because . . ." He attacked a dirty plate, hoping to rinse away the anger. "Just because."

"That isn't a very good answer."

"You'll just have to trust me, Joachim." He handed his son a dish towel. "I'll wash. You dry."

✠   ✠   ✠

SOMEHOW HE MANAGED to make love. It amazed him. Not his physical prowess, that despite his pain and his injuries he could achieve an erection and orgasm—but that Britta always came to him willingly despite her anger.

They never had the problems men typically complain about. Britta was agreeable in bed, warm and enthusiastic—a far better lover than Margot. He strayed not because he lacked desire for his wife. He strayed because of the bitterness of her harsh speech. He strayed because of her disapproving eyes. He strayed because his wife's flexibility was morally superior to his rigid stubbornness. He strayed because sex with Margot held no demands.

Not that it mattered much why he strayed, just that he did and that infidelity made him feel small. Then he rationalized: All men did it. Maybe he strayed because it was in man's nature to cheat, lie, and deceive—then to beg for forgiveness in the cold reality of the morning light.

Still, she came to him with a hungry mouth and a supple body.

Even if Britta made love to him out of spite, she seemed to enjoy it. And she always was in a better mood when the sun came up, when dusty beams filtered through their drapes. After the kids went off to school, they usually had a quiet breakfast together—rolls, butter, jam, and fresh coffee. They read the papers and ate. No small talk, but that was fine. Silence was preferable to rancorous words.

✠ ✠ ✠

FOR THE MUNICH POLICE, much of the morning was taken up by meetings, headed by RR Frank of Abteilung VI. The main topic was *Versammlungswesen*—crowd control—

for the upcoming rally, specifically, how the department should manage the marchers, deploy personnel, and conduct traffic coming in and out of Königsplatz.

Berg sat at attention, along with the other esteemed members of the police departments, in a dim room lit only by weak electrical lighting and gray skies. There was RR Peter Biedermann from Abteilung III, which dealt with general security. His area of expertise was the black market, the biggest problem recently being illegal guns. There was Manfred Koppl from Abteilung IV, the Special Security Police, and Wilhelm Raetz from Abteilung VI, the Special Political Police. There were several men whom Berg didn't recognize, but that didn't matter. There was no social interaction; the meeting was all business—cold and tense.

Volker had mapped out the roadblocks, police checkpoints, and emergency routes. Providing that people behaved in an orderly fashion, the rally would come and go and the biggest problem would be the litter from all the leaflets. In the unlikely event of a Nazi-led insurgence, the police would be prepared.

The formal meeting was followed by discussion—an endless barrage of questions and stock answers. Berg felt his thoughts drift off.

Why did Julia Schoennacht state that Regina Gottlieb was bringing her the gown when Regina's husband insisted that Schoennacht had purchased the gown a month ago? Was Julia so shameless that she'd wear something without paying for it? Had a sudden turn in the family's finances meant that she couldn't pay for it? Or did Rolf refuse to pay for a gown made by a Jewess and insist that Regina take it back?

Ro as in Rolf.

Maybe Regina refused to take back the dress. An argument ensued, and Regina was killed accidentally. Then Rolf dressed her in the gown and dumped her in the park to show that the gown was not in his wife's possession.

Berg wondered about the gown's fit. Was it better suited to Regina or to Julia? Assuming a specific motive—Rolf had killed Gottlieb because he didn't want to pay her—would that imply that the murder of Regina Gottlieb was independent of the murders of Anna Gross and Marlena Druer?

Yet all three had been strangled.

What did the three women have in common? Two of the three could have been Kommunisten. There was no indication that Regina was a Kommunist except that many Jews were Kommunisten. And it was clear that Rolf Schoennacht hated Kommunisten and Jews. It wasn't hard for Berg to imagine Rolf's big hands tightening a chain around the necks of all three women.

Was "hatred" of another's *politics* enough to push a sane person to actually kill? Count Arco-Valley hated Jews, and he hated Kommunisten. His fanatic rage bubbled over into lunacy, culminating in the assassination of Kurt Eisner, who was both a Jew and a Kommunist.

But at that time Munich had been languishing in a terrible postwar flux. The war had been lost, lives had been demolished, the monarchy had been overthrown, and Russia was eagerly waiting to invade Bavaria and claim it as part of the Soviet Union. In Arco-Valley's demented mind, Kurt Eisner represented all that was wrong with chaotic Munich. Eisner's assassination had momentarily quashed any hopes of Red rule in Munich.

Would the murders of these three disparate women change the city politically?

Assuredly the killings had given the Nazis plenty of fodder to feed a frenzied crowd. Hitler had been linking the murders to the "degenerates." It was a certainty that the Austrian would do it again tonight. No matter that Regina Gottlieb was herself Jewish: Facts never bothered Hitler. When cornered, Hitler simply lied.

Did the Austrian have his own personal assassin to carry out his dirty work? Was Schoennacht this decade's Count Arco-Valley? Perhaps Anna Gross and Marlena Druer were providing money to Kommunisten and this was Schoennacht's way of stopping them.

But then, why would he murder Regina Gottlieb even if she was a secret subversive? Schoennacht was bound to know that he and his wife would be questioned in Gottlieb's death. Why bring on such unwanted attention? If Schoennacht was guilty, did he honestly think he would get away with it?

Too many gaps in this theory. He simply needed more information.

Berg had assigned Müller and Storf the task of watching Schoennacht's movements from his house to the train station. After the art dealer had left the city, they were supposed to interview his valet. Whether they were successful or not, Berg didn't know. He'd been tied up with meetings all morning, dealing with the drudgery of endless discussion on crowd control. For three hours, the groups had been talking about pedestrian routes and marching lines and traffic patterns and police checkpoints. And how to man police checkpoints.

It was all important, Berg knew. Without it, the rally could degenerate into chaos. But there was a killer on the loose. In a country where order reigned supreme, catching a murderer would just have to wait.

THIRTY-FOUR

✠   The tower of sauerkraut obliterated the hot pastrami underneath. As Müller brought a forkful to his mouth, the pickled cabbage dropped back onto the plate. He chewed with enthusiasm, then said, "I am taking Karen to the country this weekend." He licked his upper lip. "She has had enough of the city."

Berg said, "After the rally, everyone will have had enough of the city."

"And are we prepared?" Storf asked.

"If talk translates into action, we will have no problems." Berg sipped his beer. "The assignments will be handed out at two-thirty. The Oberbürgermeister wants everyone in clean uniforms and in their respective positions by three. The rally is set to start at four."

Storf said, "What are the positions?"

"The *Versammlungswesen* want the crowd in a half-circle with one main aisle cut down the middle. The Nazis will go first. Hitler and his SS will use that aisle to make their entrance. Then there will be two access aisles forty-five degrees from the main aisle. Police will be stationed on the aisles, a man every few meters. The tightest security will be near their stage . . . the *Kradstaffel* will be on the periphery. There will also be a line of policemen behind Hitler making sure no one sneaks up from the back."

"And your position, Axel?"

"I am part of the *Kradstaffel*. My injuries prevent me from standing too long."

"And what about Storf and me?" Müller asked.

"You two are assigned center stage." As they groaned, Berg held up his hands. "Volker's decision, not mine. As long as you two are up there, use your eyes and ears. Maybe you'll hear something that has to do with our murders. Keep a close watch on Hitler's inner circle. Last time he had a rally, Kurt Haaf showed up. I'm wondering who the new faces will be this time."

"It won't be Schoennacht, that much I can tell you," Storf said. "He left his house yesterday evening and went directly to the station for an overnight train to Paris."

Müller said, "As soon as he was gone, we went back to his house in hopes of talking to Madame Schoennacht about the dress."

"Unfortunately, Madame was indisposed. However, we did not leave empty-handed." Storf rifled through some notes. "*Ach, ja.* Helmut Dittmar. He is Schoennacht's personal valet."

"He didn't accompany Schoennacht?"

"Apparently not," Müller said. "He refused to talk to us any further, claiming he was too busy, but we persisted. If all goes as planned, he will be at the Chinese Tower at twelve-thirty." Müller looked at his watch. "We've got a half hour."

"Good job, men," Berg said. "I'm amazed that he agreed to talk to the police."

"It took a little prodding," Müller said through a mouthful of food.

"Not too much," Storf said. "As a valet, Helmut isn't used to questioning authority."

✠ ✠ ✠

BECAUSE THE ENGLISCHER Garten had been the site where two murdered women were found—with a third discovered not too far away—the lovely green oasis was almost devoid of people. When Berg remarked upon it, Müller shrugged.

"Better than it was two weeks ago," Storf said. "Then it was as silent as the graveyard it was."

Berg rubbed his arms and checked the time, noting that Helmut Dittmar was three minutes late. He and Müller stood in the shadow of the Chinese Tower, a five-story pagoda that hovered over the park's beer garden. In the warm summer months the area was an idyllic place where Müncheners relaxed and socialized. Berg supposed that the architecture was meant to lend a bit of the exotic to the Bavarian capital. But now, under a forbidding leaden sky, with the grass dead and the trees bare, it resembled a skeletal wedding cake. The beer garden wouldn't be open for months, and rows of green tables and chairs stood empty and forlorn.

"Where is he?"

"He'll come, he'll come." Müller took out a tin of cigarettes, lit one for Berg, then one for himself. "Ah . . . there he is."

Müller indicated a short-limbed, rotund man in a black overcoat. He was approaching rapidly; from a distance, he looked like a bouncing ball. As he got closer, his stride lengthened, his short legs barely extending from the hemline of his topcoat. Under a black hat was a round face that was bland and colorless except for a bushy brown mustache that obliterated his top lip, and a bright pink nose. When the valet was in earshot, Storf made the introductions. "Inspektor, this is Helmut Dittmar, Herr Schoennacht's personal valet."

"Grüss Gott," Dittmar said, clicking his heels.

Berg put the valet's age at around forty-five, judging by the flecks of gray in the mustache and the yellowing of his teeth. "Inspektor Axel Berg, here. I thank you for taking the time to meet with us."

Storf said, "Herr Berg is the Chief Inspektor of the *Mordkommission.*"

"Mordkommission?" Dittmar's face registered shock. "What is this about?"

"It is traditional for the police to ask the questions, Herr Dittmar." Berg smiled, trying to appear less official. "And we just have a few of them." He took out a tin. "Cigarette?"

The valet shook his head briskly.

"I am sorry to bother you with this trivia, but I'd like to clear up a few irksome details." Berg took another inhalation of tobacco. He let it out slowly. "Before he left, Herr Schoennacht suggested that we speak with you."

"Speak with *me*?"

"Since you are aware of his habits, no doubt."

Storf added, "Herr Schoennacht goes to his club regularly, does he not?"

A simple enough question, one that Dittmar felt comfortable answering. "He goes to several clubs."

"Ah, maybe that will explain the confusion," Berg said. "What are his clubs?"

"I know that Herr Schoennacht belongs to the Knights of the Foreign Wars."

"And how often does he go to that *Verein*?"

"I believe they meet once a month."

"Where?"

"I believe the gentlemen meet at the members' residences."

"You are not certain?" Müller asked.

"Herr Schoennacht does not share this information with me." Dittmar bristled. "As long as I've been in Herr Schoennacht's employ, he has not held a meeting. But every time the club meets, I instruct the cab to take Herr Schoennacht to a different residence."

Müller smoked deeply, inhaling so strongly that his cheeks folded inward. "Exactly how long have you been in Herr Schoennacht's employ?"

"Just over two years."

"And before Herr Schoennacht, you were also a personal valet?"

"All my life," Dittmar stated. "Before Herr Schoennacht, I worked for Emmanuel Bosch for sixteen years." He licked his lips. "Maybe I will have a cigarette, *bitte*."

"Of course." Berg lit a smoke and gave it to the valet. "Tell me about Herr Bosch."

"There is not much to say. He was a fine man—hardworking, orderly, honest. We developed a close relationship. He treated me very well, Herr Inspektor. Even from the grave, he took care of me. He was a fellow club member with Herr Schoennacht, who hired me into his house as his personal valet shortly after Herr Bosch's death."

"I see," Berg said. Smoking appeared to relax the man.

"And do you also enjoy such benevolence with your current employer?"

"I have no complaints." Dittmar's face tightened. "None at all."

Obviously a lie, but Berg let it go. "And to what clubs did your past employer belong?"

"His favorite was the Saviors of the Royal Crest of Bavaria."

"And does Herr Schoennacht belong to the Saviors as well?" Müller asked.

"Herr Schoennacht belongs to many clubs. He goes out alone almost every night."

Müller raised his eyebrow. "And this does not bother Madame Schoennacht?"

"They often socialize . . . almost every Friday night. They have hosted quite a few dinner parties since I've been under their roof." Dittmar smoked the cigarette until there was simply nothing more to smoke. He ground the remaining embers under his heel. "In all honesty, Inspektor, I don't think Madame Schoennacht is interested in his affairs. Herr Schoennacht once confided that much of the socializing at his clubs revolves around his business. I'm sure that endless talk about business would bore her."

Berg thought otherwise. Certainly her comely face and her charming demeanor would be assets. And hadn't she told him that she wanted the dress from Regina because a count was hosting a three-day gala in the mountains and she needed something special to wear that would impress royalty? If Herr Schoennacht socialized at night without his wife, he didn't want her around for reasons other than business. He remembered a comment that Julia had made with a searing smile.

Men are never trustworthy.

And there was also Gottlieb claiming that Schoennacht had eyed his wife. Taken individually, the facts weren't much. Together they were a circumstantial indictment.

"You did not accompany Herr Schoennacht on his latest business trip—why?"

"Herr Schoennacht believed it was wise for me to stay in residence to help Madame Schoennacht."

"But surely there are other servants for that," Müller said. "A valet stays with his master."

Again, Dittmar bristled. "My position is to obey, not to question."

Berg asked, "Have you ever accompanied Herr Schoennacht on his business trips?"

Dittmar pinkened, indicating to Berg that he hadn't been invited—a solid slap in the face. The valet attempted to hide his embarrassment. "You said a few questions, Inspektor Berg. This is a lot more than just a few questions."

Berg agreed. "And I'm sorry to monopolize your time, but these queries really must be answered. How old is Herr Schoennacht?"

"That is a personal question, Herr Inspektor. Surely you don't expect me to answer that."

"From his hair loss and the wattles on his neck, I'd say he was in his fifties."

Dittmar's face solidified like setting wax. "He has yet to reach fifty."

"And he and Madame have no children?" Müller asked.

"That is also a personal question."

"On the contrary," Berg said. "I am not asking about

the circumstances. All I want to know is if they have children . . . together."

"They have no children."

"She is much younger than he," Berg said to Müller. "I'd say it was a second marriage. So perhaps Schoennacht has children from a first marriage."

Dittmar cleared his throat and kneaded his hands. "Am I excused?"

"Can you tell me which club Herr Schoennacht went to on the night of Regina Gottlieb's murder?"

"I don't know."

"But you just said that you were the one who told the cab where to take your master."

"Well, I don't remember. It was a while ago."

"Try, Herr Dittmar," Storf said. "We wouldn't ask unless it was important." Berg handed the valet a new cigarette.

The valet took a puff of the fresh cigarette and sighed deeply. "Do you recall the day?"

"Tuesday," Berg said.

"Maybe the Mystics of the North." Dittmar smoked greedily. "Yes, I think that was it."

Berg wrote it down. "And where do the Mystics meet?"

"Usually at Osteria Bavaria."

"Hitler's favorite restaurant," Müller said. "Is Herr Hitler a member of the Mystics?"

"I don't know," Dittmar said. "But I think not."

"Why?" Berg asked.

"Just . . . perhaps I speak out of turn. I really know nothing about Herr Schoennacht's clubs."

"You're doing your employer and the police a great

service," Berg said. "Just a few more questions. Do you remember what time Herr Schoennacht left his residence?"

"I can't recall the exact time. It was two weeks ago."

"Approximately, Herr Dittmar," Berg said. "Seven . . . eight?"

"It was before dinner, which was unusual. Not that he was going to a restaurant for dinner, but Herr Schoennacht almost always dines with Madame."

"A devoted husband," Müller said.

"She insists upon it," Dittmar let slip. Then he blushed.

"Good for her," Berg stated. "What time did he return from his nighttime activities?"

"Again, I don't recall exactly," Dittmar said. "Usually, he returns around eleven. Sometimes later. If it's after twelve, Herr Schoennacht has instructed me not to wait for him to do his toilet."

"That is considerate of him," Müller said.

Berg said, "On the night of Regina Gottlieb's murder, did Herr Schoennacht arrive home after twelve?"

It was as if a spark had just fired in Dittmar's brain. This wasn't just a simple fact-finding meeting: The valet finally realized that the police suspected his employer of Regina's murder. His face turned red, and he clenched his teeth so hard that his jaw muscles bulged. "Everything that I have told you . . . it is subject to my poor memory." He threw his cigarette on the ground and crushed it angrily. "I must be going. Madame depends on me when her husband is away."

"Thank you for your time," Berg said.

Dittmar picked up the butt and looked around for an ash can. "I want to make one thing very clear, Herr

Inspektor. I am very content in my position with the Schoennachts. I want to say that emphatically."

"I understand." Berg smiled.

Dittmar answered with a strained smile. "I really don't think you do, Herr Inspektor. I am no longer disposed to answer your questions." He clicked his heels, then turned and marched down the path, a soldier in the army of obedience.

✠ ✠ ✠

IT TOOK A FEW MOMENTS for Berg to formulate his thoughts. The skies had darkened, the afternoon turning colder by the hour. He turned up his coat collar and rubbed his gloved hands. "I don't think Dittmar is fond of his employer." He faced his men. "It is probably why he agreed to speak with us in the first place. A good valet would have shown us the door and locked it behind us."

"Dittmar may not be fond of him, but he certainly doesn't want to help us arrest Schoennacht," Müller said. "The valet became officious once he realized where we were going with the questioning."

Storf said, "If his boss is jailed for murder, Dittmar is out of a job and without references. It's amazing he spoke to us at all."

"One thing is clear. Schoennacht's a liar and a stupid one at that. He should have squared away his story with his valet before he left the country." Berg tightened his scarf around his neck. He had gone out without a hat, and the chill had penetrated through his helmet of curls and cut into his scalp. "It shows that their communication is very poor. From what Dittmar told us, Schoennacht had plenty of time to kill Regina."

"Or," Müller said, "Schoennacht could have been with his Mystics of the North at Osteria Bavaria the entire evening."

"The story is easy enough to verify." Berg checked his watch, looking west at the sinking sun. "Right now, we don't have time. Volker wants us back in an hour. Let's try to talk with the staff at the restaurant tomorrow night."

"Are you suggesting dinner?" Storf said. "Who will pay?"

Müller pulled out an empty pants pocket.

Berg shook his head. "How about an after-dinner drink, then?"

"If Hitler doesn't monopolize the place, that sounds fine. Can you walk, Axel, or should we take a cab?"

"Walking is good for me, especially when it's cold. Otherwise I freeze up." After a minute, Berg said, "What do you think about Schoennacht's clubs? The weird one . . . the Mystics of the North? Have either of you heard of it?"

Storf said, "Sounds like another secret Aryan society like the Thule."

Berg said, "I don't know why the Germans insist on romanticizing Norse culture. When is the last time Norway did something important?"

Müller said, "They have beautiful women."

"Some of them are. Some are as big as lumberjacks."

"What do you have against Norway?" Storf asked.

"Nothing. It's just that Denmark is superior to the rest of Scandinavia. Why not idolize the Danes?"

"Present company included?"

"If you must."

Müller said, "And didn't you say, Berg, that the

Swedes think the Danes speak as if they have razor blades in their throats?"

"That's the *German* influence."

Storf said, "Tell me, Axel. When was the last time Denmark did anything important?"

Berg stopped walking. "The Danes would do a lot better if other countries stopped invading them."

"That's because Denmark is weak and insubstantial."

"No, that's because Germany has a lust to dominate."

Storf snorted. "If you hate Germany so much, why don't you go back to Denmark?"

Before he retorted, Berg thought about the words hurled at him. He was surprised by his answer. "Actually, Ulrich, I would not want to live in Denmark. It's too cold, it's too dark in the wintertime, it's very small and isolated, and the cuisine is not to my taste. I may have been born in Denmark, and I may have some Danish attitudes, but I am decidedly German. I live in Munich, and no doubt I will die in this city unless our future rulers decide to drag us into war again."

"I'll be too old by then." Müller looked at Berg. "So will you."

"Thank God for that." Berg tightened his scarf. "I can think of no worse curse than to be buried in an anonymous grave on foreign soil."

THIRTY-FIVE

✠ It wasn't so much the cold as the stiffness. Berg was warm enough under his long uniform coat, with his hands gloved and his feet encased in woolen socks and thick boots, but his limbs and digits felt as rigid as steel. The *Föhn* was blowing from the Alps, a malevolent cold wind that swelled the sinuses and dried the throat. Several times his police cap was nearly lifted from his head. Yet the chill and the damp did little to discourage the crowd.

The stage for the speakers had been set on the Propyläen—the gateway of western Munich—a massive structure of Doric architecture built under the reign of Ludwig I. Constructed of limestone block, with its symmetrical columns and pillars and friezes, the monument to a former king could have found a comfortable home in sunny Athens rather than drizzly Munich. In front of the monolith was an immense expanse of green lawn. At the moment it seemed that every square meter of Königsplatz—every blade of grass—was covered by a congealed mass of dark-garbed humanity. Berg saw people from all walks of life, but in the main, the crowd was brimming with the everyday Münchener taking time off to hear a lunatic rant. Far more ominous than the ordinary citizens were the growing clusters of Brownshirts, especially around the podium. So far things were orderly.

Still, it was worrisome with so many people in so concentrated a space.

The cacophony of hundreds of conversations blended into one loud hum. In the background, Berg could make out the clanging of streetcars and an occasional blaring automobile horn. Adding color and spice to the human density were the uniformed opposition groups standing on the periphery. To Berg's left were fifty or so black-shirted men sporting the Kommunist accoutrements of red bow ties and red caps, conferring with one another, whispering trade secrets. The Social Democrats in their green shirts and black pants had stationed themselves to his right. It would be chore enough trying to control Hitler's hoodlums, but a confrontation between parties would surely throw everything into disorder.

As the hour grew nearer to the rally's start time, there were visible signs of tension among the ranks, the policemen rocking from foot to foot, nightsticks in hand, eyes nervously scanning for trouble. The sight of so many officials represented an imposing display of authority. No one was spared from an appearance. Not only did Volker have his assignment, but so also did Direktor Max Brummer and Kommandant Stefan Roddewig, no doubt under direct orders from Scharnagl, Mantel, and Schlussel. The paramilitary bureaucrats were stationed near the podium, although none of them were dressed in police uniform.

Being limited physically, Berg had the good fortune and the convenience of his *Kraftrad*, providing him with a quick way to disperse crowds and break up melees. He leaned against it protectively.

Suddenly a low bellow emanated from the crowd, a moan that strengthened and gathered until it coalesced into a dull-pitched roar. Berg looked over his shoulder. The Nazis were coming, marching four across in perfect step from Luisen Strasse toward the square. They wore brown uniforms with jackets cinched at the waist, knee-high boots, and matching brown police caps. They held square black banners, with the NSDAP *Hakenkreuz* emblazoned in a white circle in the middle. Above the swastika was the word *Deutschland,* and below it the word *Erwache*—awake!

And awake the people did. The crowd began to cheer in full force. In response to the cheering, the opposition parties began to chant. Their volume was minimal in comparison, but Berg could hear the protests because he was stationed nearby.

Kein Hitler! Kein Krieg!

(No Hitler! No war!)

Dieser Führer wird führen . . . in den Krieg uns führen!

(This leader will lead . . . lead us to war!)

As the Brownshirts neared the square, the adoration grew deafening. The formation tramped their way up to the center aisle of the square, then stopped. Still marching in place, they split apart down the middle, two men stepping in time on each side, forming an entrance pathway for their leader.

Two bodyguards came first, looking staid and official.

They were followed by the crazy Austrian himself, dressed in his self-styled brown uniform and knee-high boots. His black hair was slicked down and his eyes stared straight ahead, mustache twitching over his upper lip. The Austrian was slightly above average height, but he deliberately chose to be flanked by bodyguards who were half a head shorter than he was. It served the purpose of not only making Hitler look tall, but also allowing his worshipful fans to see him.

The stomps and cheers were so clamorous that the vibrations could be felt under one's feet. There wasn't a beer hall in Munich big enough to contain a crowd this size.

Behind Hitler were the supporters and officers of the NSDAP—Röhm, Himmler, Hanfstaengl, Göring, and about half a dozen civilian faces. The only one Berg recognized by name was Kurt Haaf—Anna Gross's father. The others appeared to have been plucked from the growing pack of Hitler's well-to-do bourgeois Münchener supporters, most of them looking familiar to Berg. He recognized an outspoken manufacturer who had been at other rallies. There was also that third-rate thespian who had often railed against Jews and homosexuals taking over the theater. The man was not only a poor actor, but also a dullard when not fed prewritten lines. A third gentleman reminded Berg of Rolf Schoennacht—around the same age and with the same haughty demeanor. Berg half expected to see Schoennacht, but according to his men, the art dealer was out of town. A final pair of bodyguards brought up the rear. Then the Nazi soldiers closed ranks and marched behind their leaders.

Time was of the essence. The afternoon sun was sinking, the gray light diminishing as the minutes passed. The Austrian was known for being long-winded. If the rally did not start soon, Herr Hitler would be shouting his rhetoric in darkness. The BWP, which was slated to follow Hitler, would be reduced to an afterthought.

The cheering grew to thunder as the speakers formed a

line across the stage, legs apart, hands behind their back, chin up, and eyes on the people. Hitler was in the middle, staring at his audience with a stony expression, his body stiff as bronze as he basked in his moment of glory. But it was Volker who took the first step to address the audience. Megaphone in hand, the Kommissar got out a few words but could barely be heard over the crashing noise. Hitler held out his hand to silence the crowd. Instead, the gesture had the opposite effect, stoking the audience to a frenzy.

Nervously, Berg looked around. The number of Brownshirts had increased, and most of them seemed very young and more than a little tipsy. To calm himself, he took out his pocketknife from his boot. Removing his gloves and stowing them in his coat pocket, he began to clean his nails. It felt good to flex his fingers, but it felt even better to hold a knife.

Volker tried again. This time Berg could hear him but still couldn't make out his words. As the crowd quieted, the protesters became more vocal.

Kein Hitler! Kein Krieg!
Kein Hitler! Kein Krieg!

The people in the back began to hurl insults at the protesters. The protesters, encouraged by the insults, chanted with greater volume. Volker heard them as well.

"The gentlemen in the back!" he screamed into the bullhorn. "If you insist on disrupting this peaceful rally, you will be arrested at once!"

The crowd's cheers drowned out the chanting, but only momentarily. When the noise died down, the protests were once again loud enough to hear.

"I will give you to the count of ten to stop!" Volker insisted.

The protests grew louder; the jeering grew louder. The atmosphere was becoming increasingly more tense. This time, Himmler stepped forward. A rodent of a man with a thin face, he had a weak chin, downturned mouth, and a mustache over his upper lip that resembled the whiskers of a rat. Spectacles hid narrow, hooded eyes. He made a grab for the megaphone. From his distance, Berg couldn't gauge Volker's exact reaction, but there was a brief tussle over the horn. Then, to Berg's great surprise and cheers from the crowd, Volker handed over the instrument to Himmler. It was obvious that the head of Hitler's SS had more support among the *Volk* than Volker did.

Himmler said, "I pity the police back there!" A pause. "It must stink because of all the putrid gas coming from the degenerates."

A huge roar of laughter.

"Someone should call the fire squad to extinguish the noxious fumes."

More laughter and scattered applause.

Himmler shouted, "We will have order and respect for authority! A nation cannot be run without respect for order and authority!" He put down the bullhorn, looked around, his spectacles reflecting the enrapt horde, then picked up the megaphone and brought it to his lips. "But how can you have respect for authority that undermines the people it supposedly represents!"

An outcry of approval.

"I don't mean the police, of course!" A sly and evil smile. "I am referring to the weak-willed traitors who sit in Berlin!"

More noise. Berg could barely hear Himmler once he resumed his speech.

". . . hated Weimar, which is nothing more than a puppet of Western Europe and the United States of America!"

Thunderclaps of cheers.

". . . government ruled not by the people it governs, but by wanton degenerates—the Kosmopoliten and inferior races who seek to rape and destroy the perfected Kultur of the true Aryan! How can any true German, any true Aryan, have respect for those turncoats!"

The clamor was deafening. The chants grew louder. Berg's head began to hurt. His legs were stiff and it was painful to stand. More cheers . . . more jeers.

Kein Hitler! Kein Krieg!
Kein Hitler! Kein Krieg!

"We will not submit!" Himmler shouted to the audience's delight. "We will never submit to the thieves and the perverts that befoul our Fatherland! We will root out and destroy the unclean and the mongrels that terrorize and infect our city and our country!"

A deep vibration shook the ground, the reverberating roar of endorsement. From his distance, Berg couldn't decipher the minute subtleties of the Austrian's facial expression, but it was evident that Hitler was unhappy at being upstaged by his lieutenant. The demagogue's face was distorted by a stubborn tic.

The demonstrators intensified their rhetoric. The Social Democrats insisted that Hitler was what was wrong with Germany, that the interloping Austrian would lead Germany into a doomed war in which many more Germans would die pointlessly. The Kommunisten were more direct: They accused the Nazis of being not only fomenters of evil and hate but also assassins and destroyers of the civilized world.

Berg could find nothing to disagree with, but he kept his opinions to himself, his eyes scanning the crowd for trouble—a useless endeavor. Trouble was everywhere and everyone.

One of the Kommunist bohemians—a thin redheaded youth wearing spectacles and sporting a beard—grabbed his own bullhorn and screamed into it, calling Hitler a liar, a peddler of hate, and a bastard.

This was more than the Austrian could stand. Seizing the megaphone from Himmler, Hitler stepped in front of his lieutenant and took center stage, his face so twisted as to appear misshapen, a horrifying three-dimensional representation of an Otto Dix *Lustmord* painting.

Berg's mind traveled back to Professor Kolb's psychological interpretations of *Lustmord.* Could *any* man under extraordinary circumstances be transformed into a cold-blooded murderer, or was this bloodthirsty drive unique to the Teutonic culture with its preoccupation with Ideal Man and the life/death paradigm? Were these very issues—Germany's exaggerated sense of maleness and duty and willingness to die for the Fatherland—what propelled the country time and time again into war? Were the Brownshirt punks so very different from soldiers who blew people up and bombed villages with mustard gas? For Berg as a soldier, there had been no thrill of conquest, even in victory. Not so with other soldiers, many of whom were clearly aroused by battle, so that rape was a common consequence of combat.

Berg studied Hitler. At this distance, his facial expression suggested murderous rage, but in a different situation Hitler could have been in the throes of sexual passion. Certainly his mien was suggestive of sexual *destrudo.*

Perhaps in Hitler, as in other warped men, sex and murder were intertwined.

What if Hitler was the Munich killer? It wasn't the first time Berg had entertained that notion, especially considering the women who had been slain—a Jew and Kommunisten. Maybe one day the Austrian would join the ranks of the most famous and infamous German killers: Fritz Haarmann, the Hannover Slicer; Wilhelm Grossmann, the Silesian Bluebeard; Karl Denke, the mass murderer of Münster; and most recently the "unknown" Vampire of Düsseldorf.

Berg smiled at his overactive imagination. What would Volker do if his Inspektor seriously made a case for Hitler as the Munich killer? *That* would no doubt leave Munich *zitternd vor Spannung*—trembling with excitement.

Electricity was everywhere, not just confined to the streetcars, to the lampposts, and to the newly installed wires that swayed in the wind from apartment house to apartment house. It crackled through the air, flashing forth with the power of violence and conflict.

The demagogue bellowed into the bullhorn, spittle leaking from the corners of his mouth. "It is vermin like you who pollute our beloved Fatherland. It is vermin like you, you filthy Jewdog, that will be rooted out and destroyed!"

The response was overpowering. In a flash, Berg saw all that was modern and progressive crash down, smothered in an avalanche of cheers.

The redheaded Kommunist refused to back down, as possessed with his own political agenda as the Austrian was with his. "Hitler and his punks do not scare us!" he yelled into his megaphone. "We will not rest until Hitler and his hateful, war-loving followers are erased from the political arena of Munich!"

Hitler shot back, "And we will not rest until the degenerates, the bohemians, the Kosmopoliten, the filthy Jewdogs are erased from all of Germany and from the world!"

"Let us take care of him, *unser* Führer!" The taunt was coming from the swells of teenage Brownshirts.

Volker suddenly emerged from the crowded stage. He brought his own bullhorn to his lips and declared with authority, "There will be no violence at this rally!"

He was unceremoniously booed.

The Kommissar pressed on. "Unless there is immediate order, this rally will be dissolved and the police will disperse the crowds."

The booing intensified.

Abruptly, a stone was thrown at the bureaucrats on stage. It missed Volker and Kommandant Roddewig but clipped Kriminal Direktor Max Brummer on the shoulder. Then another rock was hurled toward the stage. Before a scuffle could break out, a distraught *Hausfrau* captured the crowd's attention. She was screaming and beating her breast as she tore down the center aisle, her hair flying wildly behind her. Her cheeks were streaked with tears and her face frozen in terror.

But her words were despairingly clear.

"Another murder! Another murder!" she cried in anguish. "They lie *dead* in the Englischer Garten! My poor sister! My poor niece! She was just a child. . . ." Disconsolate sobs. "Just a little child!"

THIRTY-SIX

✠ The ensuing disarray was as deadly as random gunfire, creating panic that swelled and stretched in all directions. To his credit, the Kommissar was quick to respond, trying to take center stage to disperse the crowd in an orderly fashion, but the Austrian would have none of it. He pushed Volker aside and addressed the people, stoking the frenzied fire.

"Again the degenerates have stricken our women, and this time the lowly filth have stooped to the most heinous of despicable perversions by attacking a child! When will the police finally realize what they are dealing with and rid the city of these vermin?" Hitler shrieked. He pointed an accusing finger at Brummer, Roddewig, and Volker. "You know when the police will make Munich safe for our citizens, my friends? When we citizens demand that the police department clean up the degenerates in its own ranks!"

Supportive whoops and bellows rose from the audience. Berg shook his head in dismay. Why alienate such important allies? Hitler had no better boosters than Brummer and Roddewig, and even at a distance, Berg could see that they were furious.

Hitler's screed continued. "When will we erase the filthy dog Jews from our city? When will we take back our banks from the rotten, evil inferior races and place them in the hands of trustworthy individuals such as our dear Kurt Haaf, who has already lost his daughter to a Jewdog!" The Austrian's screams pierced the air, his face as red as a radish. "We must prohibit and prevent the Jews from breeding their filth into our pure Aryan women. We cannot afford to let the Jews bring us to despair and ruin. And if the police cannot or will not rectify the 'Jewish situation,' the good people of Munich will!"

Deafening applause drowned out any attempts by the police to respond to the indictment.

"It is the Jews who are murdering our women!" Hitler proclaimed. "It is the Jews who have been behind every evil deed from time immemorial! They have infiltrated the great Aryan race, and no rest and order will come until their inferior race is completely eradicated!"

"Get the Jews!" were the cries from a group of Brownshirts.

"Yes, we must get the Jews!" Hitler insisted. "And we must rid our good cities of other foul beasts that prey upon our citizens, like the Kommunisten who support the evil deeds of the Jews!"

Declarations of "Get the Kommunisten" were joined with the cries of "Get the Jews" until they became a singsong mantra.

Get the Jews, get the Kommunisten.

Get the Jews, get the Kommunisten.

Under these dark circumstances, Kriminal Direktor Max Brummer dared to take the stage. "There will be no rioting in this city! This rally is officially over—" But his officious manner further riled the crowd.

Hoots and jeers suffocated the rest of the Direktor's speech. The shouting continued.

Get the Jews! Get the Kommunisten!
Get the Jews! Get the Kommunisten!

Berg turned to the nearby group of Kommunisten. Because of tension and fear, they had lost about half their original number. Speaking to the redheaded youth who seemed to be the leader, Berg said, "I suggest you leave at once! There are many more of them than of you."

The youth paled, nervously adjusting his red bow tie. Still, he maintained bravado. "And this is how the great police department of Munich protects its citizens?"

"Right now, this is all I have to protect you with." Berg held up his pocketknife. "For heaven's sake, use some common sense. The assassination of Eisner occurred not so long ago. Get out of here!"

It took a few moments for the gravity to sink in, but then the youth addressed his followers. "Let's go!" He turned on his heels and ran. Seeing their leader take flight, the remaining stragglers rushed off as well.

Berg looked at the stage, at Hitler, who was comforting the anguished woman who had just lost her sister and her niece to the elusive Munich monster. The Austrian stretched out his right hand and gave his oath to reform the city or die trying to do it. The crowd responded by mimicking his arm gesture.

The Brownshirts droned on.

Get the Jews! Get the Kommunisten!
Get the Jews! Get the Kommunisten!

Volker had had enough. He picked up the bullhorn.

"The rally is over! Go home now or face immediate arrest!"

Get the Jews! Get the Jews!

"You must start clearing the square now!"

Get the Kommunisten! Get the Kommunisten!

"You must do this now and in an orderly fashion!"

Get the Jews! Get the Kommunisten!

"Anyone loitering in the square will be arrested!"

The Kommunisten have fled! Get the Jews! Get the Jews!

And in a single tick of time, the threats finally erupted into action. Stones were hurled at the uniformed policemen who surrounded the stage. The initial assault was followed by a barrage of more projectiles—rocks, stones, pebbles, rotten food, and beer bottles. Within a flash, a series of whistles were blown—the official signal to move in and suppress the insurrection.

The police responded, pushing Hitler and his cohorts off the stage. The police were on the attack, grabbing any Brownshirt that dared to confront them, punching them mercilessly, kicking the punks to the ground, and only when they were fully prostrate did the police attempt to handcuff them. This decisive action caused the crowd to rise up in volleys of protest, physical as well as vocal.

The hostile response caused the police to act even more aggressively.

That led to more projectiles flung at the uniforms.

The crowd moved as a single unit, a dark, ominous cloud rushing forward. The horde began to charge the police, demanding their rights as citizens of Munich, accusing the Munich constables of being supporters of the enemy. Haphazard skirmishes were converging too quickly into a full-fledged riot. Keeping beat to the warfare was the constant chant.

Get the Jews!
Get the Jews!

Berg was at a crossroads. Although his physical energy was much improved, he was still suffering the effects of his severe beating of less than three weeks ago. As much as he wanted to help out his *Kameraden,* as much as he wanted to fight fist to fist with the punks and the hooligans who confronted the city with disobedience, he knew that physically he was useless.

Get the Jews!
Get the Jews!

His mind was racing. It was 1923 again. The stage was thick with Brownshirts, and police were going at one another in a collage of black and brown. Although he couldn't make out any individual, he knew that Müller and Storf were up there.

For a moment of insanity, he thought about charging down the center aisle, jumping onstage, and helping them out. These were his fellow officers, his fellow Inspektors and his friends. But his options were cut short when a throng in an unbridled delirium surged toward him like a tidal wave. Arms were flailing and fists striking whatever and whoever got in the way.

What to do!

It was the murder of a woman that had led to Berg's beating. He knew that these newest murders would lead to more beatings, specifically beatings of Jews. As in '23, the Nazis would use these latest tragedies and the subsequent upheaval as excuses to riot and loot, to beat and murder Jews.

Horrible images ripped through Berg's brain—war recollections—spurting blood and seared flesh, bombs going off and bodies blown apart, the ground steeped in human remains. Hideous enough on foreign soil, he'd be damned if he allowed it to happen on his own home ground.

The first Jewish house they'd ransack would be Regina Gottlieb's. Even though the woman had been brutally murdered, the Nazis would find a way to blame her murder—as well as the most recent murders—on her husband.

The drama unfolded before his eyes. A group of Brownshirts broke free from the crowd and formed a double line. Fists in the air, they marched and chanted:

Death to the Jews!
Death to the Jews!

They moved southeast toward Isarvorstadt. Still weak in his legs, Berg knew there was no way he could keep up with them on foot. Fortunately, he was one of the few officers assigned to a *Kraftrad*. Stowing his knife in his boot, he turned on the ignition and forged through the crowd, zooming ahead. With any luck, he could reach Herr Gottlieb before the Brownshirts.

Passing the parade of high-stepping Nazis, hoping that his mind was clear enough to remember where Gottlieb lived. Racing through the streets, scaring pedestrians and motorists. His ears rang from the angry shouts and pandemonium left in his wake. Still, he could make out the constant dirge:

Death to the Jews!
Death to the Jews!

Berg cut through the old city of Munich, riding on the streetcar tracks, past the stores and the cafés, past the tobacconist and the milliner, past the majestic government buildings and Marienplatz and the china shop that had serviced the Bavarian kings. When he got to the Viktualienmarkt, he slowed, half walking his *Kraftrad* and half riding along the cobblestone walkways, casting off purveyors' curses and the enraged epithets thrown at him by shoppers. He bore down on the motor scooter until he came to Gärtnerplatz. A quick left, then a right.

The sun had dropped below the horizon. Darkness would fall within twenty minutes. Anarchy would reign: the queen of the night. Under the veil of darkness were phantoms of terror preying upon those unlucky souls who were without resources to defend themselves. Berg looked up at the dusky sky. *Just let it stay light enough to find Gottlieb.*

Another right, another left, then another left.

No time to lose. The area should have looked familiar, but all he saw were tenements—one crumbling building after another. Terrified people dashing through the streets trying to get home. Dark-skinned Eastern Europeans— Jews, Poles, Czechs, Gypsies, Romanians—all of them buzzing with frenetic activity, boarding up windows and doors.

They knew what was coming. Though still far away, the noise and singing could be heard and grew steadily louder.

Another left turn.

The block looked vaguely familiar. Yes, he thought. This was it. He slowed as he peered at the wretched structures. Was it this one or that one? The one in the middle of the street . . . or that one across the street? He settled on one of the apartment houses, hoping he was correct, dragging his *Kraftrad* up the stoop, then through the front door into the apartment house. The foyer was barely big enough to contain the bike. He took a moment to look around. Yes, he was sure this was the right building. He recognized the torn-up floor, the same rotted staircase. He didn't want to leave the *Kraftrad* downstairs for fear of it being stolen, but he didn't have the energy to carry it up the stairs. Furthermore, Berg doubted that the steps could hold the machine's weight. He left it in the foyer, blocking the stairwell, then hurried up the steps and banged on Gottlieb's door.

"Axel Berg here. *Kommen Sie schnell, schnell!*" More banging. "If you don't come out, others will break down the—"

The door flew open. The man's complexion was ashen, as if mercury instead of blood ran through his veins. He tried to speak, but no words came out. He was trembling violently.

"You must come with me now!" Berg said.

"I must pack a few things."

"No time."

"My money. I need *money*!"

Berg conceded the point. "Quickly. I will be downstairs with the motor scooter." He raced down the steps as fast as his limp would let him. Sweating with exertion, exhaustion, and fear, he dragged the *Kraftrad* outside and turned on the motor. Gottlieb appeared two minutes later.

"Into the cart!" Berg ordered him. As soon as the Jew was seated, Berg tore away from the decrepit building.

The big question was what to do with him. Berg wouldn't dare hide the Jew in his own apartment. For one thing, he couldn't get the man across town safely. But neither would he endanger his family and his career by being labeled a Jew sympathizer.

Ah, but those two little girls . . . their angelic faces. How they plucked at his heartstrings and stirred his compassion. They were motherless. How could he do nothing if nothing meant they'd be orphans?

The chanting grew louder and louder.

Death to the Jews!

Death to the Jews!

The question now was *what* to do! As a temporary measure, he thought about arresting him just to keep him safe. But then surely the police would steal his money and probably beat him as well. Moreover, the Brownshirts might take over the police station as they had done in '23. Then the man would be as good as dead.

His mind was awhirl, shuffling through a dwindling list of options. Berg could think of only one place to bring him. It wasn't a terribly good solution, but it was the only one he had.

THIRTY-SEVEN

✠ By the time the *Kraftrad* reached the cigarette house, the first group of Brownshirts were filtering into the streets, waving sticks and beer bottles, their chanting and drunken singing drowning out any ambient noise. There wasn't a police officer to be found.

Berg remained concerned about the welfare of Müller and Storf, as they had been stationed in the center of the rioting. It had been a long time since either of them had been on the streets. He remembered the helpless feeling of being outnumbered, the relentless punches and kicks; a limp and constant pain still plagued him. Surviving the trenches and mustard gas only to be beaten by blood-thirsty hoodlums, residents of the city that Berg had sworn to protect—punks with no jobs, no skills, and small brains occupied only with hate.

Braking the *Kraftrad* in front of the broken-down structure, tires splashing mud and muck onto his boots, he brought the machine to a halt. The blue wash that had once colored the strips of siding was almost nonexistent, and the wood framework had splintered and rotted. The shutters were drawn tightly over the windows. Stagnant rainwater had pooled in front of the entrance and formed a dirty, rank moat around the entire building. Each puff of wind brought up another putrid stench. Berg wrinkled his nose in disgust. His hip throbbed dully. He was uncomfortable, but if the pain stayed at this level, he could live with it.

He retrieved the pocketknife from his boot and told Gottlieb to get out of the sidecar. "Help me drag the scooter into the vestibule."

Gottlieb grabbed the cart as Berg hefted the motorcycle. Together, they carried the machine up the rotted stairs of the stoop. "What now?" the Jew asked.

"Don't talk," Berg barked out.

Gottlieb glanced with darting eyes at the streets swarming with Brownshirts. Berg tried the door, but it was locked. He banged on the wood, announcing that he was police and ordering that the door be opened immediately.

There was no response.

"*Herrjemine,* what next?" He looked at Gottlieb. "We'll have to break it down."

"Whatever you say."

Berg counted to three, then both men rushed the door, right shoulders serving as battering rams. Pain shot through Berg's torso when his body was met with resistance. So be it—he'd nurse his wounds later.

"Again. *Eins, Zwei*—"

The door swung open. The fat desk attendant staring at them through small, hooded eyes, his pocked face covered with sweat. *"Sind Sie verrückt?"*

Are you crazy?

"Help us get this thing inside now! If you don't, I'll tell the boys outside that you harbor Jewish whores."

"And don't you think they know that already?" the attendant said. "Why do you think the place is locked?"

He tried to close the door on them, but Berg was too

quick, slamming his body against the portal so hard that the wood cracked. Once inside, Berg butted his head into his opponent's stomach, causing the fat man to double over in pain. Berg pushed the attendant against the wall, grabbed a shock of his hair, and lifted his face, sticking the point of his knife into the layers of fat underneath his chin. Red liquid trickled down Berg's arm. Still leaning hard on the man and speaking just inches away from his face.

"If you move, I will cut your throat. *Verstanden?*"

The fat man whispered a hoarse yes. From the corner of his eye, Berg noticed that Gottlieb had not been idle. While he was dealing with the proprietor, the Jew had managed to drag the motorbike inside and bolt the splintered door. The Jew was panting.

Berg was breathing hard as well. "None of us wants this place to be raided by the police or vandalized by thugs, correct?"

In lieu of a nod, the fat man lifted his eyes. Had he moved, the knife would have glided through his fat as if it were warm butter.

Berg eased up the pressure. "Is she upstairs?"

Again the fat man croaked out a yes.

"Ah, very good!" Berg turned his head, his eyes sizing up the room while never leaving the attendant or the point of his knife. He spotted a door that was slightly ajar. "What's inside that room?"

"Broom closet."

"That'll do. Put your hands up."

The fat man hesitated. Berg kneed him hard in the stomach. When he doubled over in pain, Berg turned him around, pushed him face-first against the wall, then yanked his arms around his back. The clerk was so overweight that his hands did not touch. From the jacket of his uniform, Berg took out a pair of handcuffs and linked the proprietor's hands together. Yanking him upright, he marched the man into the closet. Before Berg locked the door, he said, "You'll be safer in here anyway."

Berg bolted the front door, his mind jumping from issue to issue. "Help me put my *Kraftrad* behind the counter. If the Nazis break in and see it, they will know that a policeman is here."

"Isn't that good?" Gottlieb asked.

"I told you not to talk." Berg was nervous and angry. "Right now the police are the enemy. Not as bad as the Jews, though. They'll attack you before me. Let's move."

Together, they lifted the motorcycle and stowed it behind the counter so it wasn't visible.

"Upstairs," Berg ordered. It was a three-flight climb, then Berg knocked at the familiar door. "Open up, Margot!" Another bang. "Open this minute!" A sliver of light came through the doorway. Again, Berg pushed his way in, knocking Margot's shoulder and causing her to stumble backward. "Sorry."

Her eyes were wide with fear. Even terrified, she was beautiful, incredibly delicious in fright and weakness—a lithe angelic body and a face so pale she was otherworldly. She wore a heavy blue sweater over her blue work dress. Solid shoes encased her feet. She was shaking so hard, she had to clasp her hands to keep her balance.

"We heard the shouting from work, Axel. The others tried to make it home, but I didn't want to take the chance. How bad is it?"

"Bad."

"Another putsch?"

"Another murder—"

Margot gasped.

"Two murders, one just a young girl. Hitler is using the slayings to whip the people into a frenzy."

"And where are the police?"

"We are badly outnumbered. We'll have to wait it out until morning, when people should be restored to their senses."

"Until morning?" Margot was shaking. "Night has just fallen." She looked around, her eyes landing on Gottlieb. "Who is this man?"

"A Jew. You have to hide him—"

"Are you insane? I came here to hide myself."

"If you don't, he will die."

"Better him than me."

"He has two young daughters. If he dies, they are orphans."

"And how old do I look?"

Indeed, she looked much younger than her eighteen years. Berg said, "Let him hide under the trapdoor, and you hide under the bed. If they break into the room looking for whores, I'll flash my badge and send them away."

"I am not stupid, Axel. I remember '23. I remember how effective the police were."

Her nettled barbs tore straight into his gut. Still, he postured. "We are more prepared now, my love." He lowered his voice. "Listen to me, Margot. Hide under the bed. I will protect you."

"Why should I listen to you?" she shot back. "You're a cheat and a liar. I know what will happen if they see you here. Both of us will die. First they will kill you. Then they will find me under the bed and rape and kill me."

Outside the words of hate grew louder.

Margot shook with revulsion. Abruptly, she moved aside the end table and lifted the trapdoor. She looked at Gottlieb. "Get inside." When the Jew paused, she said, "Go before I change my mind. Pray for all of us."

Berg pushed Gottlieb forward. "Stay inside until morning, then get out of the country. Don't get caught, and don't ever come back!"

Gottlieb wiped his wet eyes. "I won't forget this."

"Yes, you will, but it doesn't matter. Take care of your daughters. Go!"

Carefully, the Jew lowered himself beneath the floor. When he had cleared the opening, Margot shut the door tightly and put the end table back over it. She glanced out the window. "They're coming in!" Her face was white with dread. "You have children, Axel. Hide under the bed—"

"Absolutely not!"

"If you don't, I will betray the Jew." Margot was breathing quickly. "Then it will all be for nothing."

"Bist du verrückt?" Berg laughed. "You wouldn't do that!"

"Try me!" Her eyes were adamant. "If God is with me, all that will happen is I'll get raped!"

A loud crash echoed through the interior of the cigarette house, the din causing both of them to jump, the clomp of footsteps as the thugs climbed the stairs. Doors opened and slammed shut. The sudden screams of the Jewish whores hiding within.

"Under the bed!" Margot yelled. *"Now!"*

Still Berg waited.

"Do it!" she commanded. "And don't come out no matter what you hear. You have a choice, Axel. Choose life!"

Knife in hand, Berg dropped to the floor and squeezed between the rough wooden planks of the underside of the bed, settling himself on his back just as he heard the door break open.

Margot screamed as the mattress suddenly sagged, dipping so low that it nearly touched Berg's stomach. Hellish screams mixed with low, drunken laughter. The stink of beer and rye permeated the small room. Berg could hear the awful sounds of flesh slapping skin and loud, hard blows mixed with softer screams.

More drunken laughter. More sharp slaps.

Words penetrating his skull . . .

Jew bitch.

Over and over and over as the bed bounced up and down.

Up and down, up and down amid Margot's pleas to stop, her moans that begged for mercy.

You like it, don't you . . . disgusting Jew bitch.

Another crack.

More sounds—grunts and snorts and squawks mixed with weeping.

Berg pressed his fingers to his ears, praying that he could muffle the sounds—the horrible and pitiful groans. He closed his eyes. Still, he could sense the motion of the bed.

Up and down, up and down, up and down.

The ghastly sounds of a man reaching climax—more grunts and snorts and squawks.

Berg's blood began to boil.

Think of your children. Don't be stupid. She will survive.

Another hard crack! He startled upward, his feet hitting the frame of the bed, but no one above appeared to feel it.

Margot's screams had subsided to simpering moans.

Again the bed started to move.

He opened his eyes, but all he could see was hot white stars.

His body temperature rising!

His head pounding!

Up and down, up and down.

He closed his eyes and again tried to plug his ears, but the racket was too loud to be silenced by two fingertips. He broke into a rich, ripe sweat. It stank but what difference did that make? The entire room reeked from male violence and discharge. As the perspiration evaporated from his skin, he felt clammy . . . buried alive.

Up and down, up and down.

Grunting and groaning. Snorting . . . oinking like a pig.

Think of your family! Think of your children! She's not worth dying for!

Up and down, up and down, up and down.

He could no longer hear Margot. There were no more screams, no sobs, no moans. Her silence was all the more devastating: a life snuffed out as her soul died.

Up and down, up and down.

Think of your children, Axel!

Up and down, up and down.

Grunt, grunt, snort, snort.

Clenched jaw, clenched fist. The fingers of his right hand grasping something hard.

His knife!

Up and down.

Think of your children.

Rational thoughts could no longer penetrate his delirious mind. It was as if someone else had directed his actions. Without conscious intent, he had freed himself and was standing upright, witnessing with his own startled blue eyes the terror in full color.

Boys really. Not much older than Joachim but they had gone too far for their youth to save them. The three of them were stunned by Berg's appearance. Without a hint of warning, a vengeful poltergeist had materialized.

Berg grabbed the one closest to him by his flaxen hair and yanked his head back until the bony rings of his neck were neatly exposed. With a quick, strong, and deft hand, Berg slit the boy's throat ear-to-ear with surgical precision, then pushed him away. Since the blade was sharp, the incision was deep and smooth. The boy grabbed his throat as he staggered about, gurgling out protests, his hands drenched in his own blood. Then he dropped to the floor.

The next one was a skinny punk with acne, curly black hair, and horror-struck blue eyes. Berg pulled him off of Margot, espying a glimpse of his puny, semi-erect penis. He jammed the knife into the depression of the punk's neck just below the Adam's apple, then twisted the blade until he could feel the vertebrae separate from each other. Immediately, the kid's head fell backward as if he were looking up at the sky, blood squirting out like a red fountain, his neck hissing like a radiator as air leaked from his lungs. He dropped down at the side of the bed, his head slamming against the floor and detaching from the body, rolling a meter until it hit the wall.

By the time Berg looked around for the third boy, the punk had run out the door.

It took about five minutes for the first boy to stop shaking from his mortal throes. Berg simply watched his handiwork as they expired. There was nothing poetic in their demise, nothing glorious or noble. Berg was back in the trenches of the Great War. First, he was shooting or throwing grenades at the enemy. Then the enemy was shooting or throwing grenades at him. Bursts of gunfire, bullets flying past him. The mortally wounded, crying out for help. Stabbing them with his bayonet to put them out of their misery . . .

Twenty million people had died—and for what?

These two boys . . . just two more messy and protracted deaths.

Berg stood welded to his spot, his chest heaving in and out, his body sodden from sweat. He closed his eyes and let the blade drop from his hand. When he opened his eyes, he saw Margot, her face purple and puffy from where she had been punched. Her lower lip was split, her left eye swollen shut. The night wasn't over yet, but it was over for him.

He had chosen his course.

He looked out the window at the Brownshirts: staggering, reeling, retching, hurling stones, and waving sticks.

A loud boom was followed by the crackle of smashing glass.

The uproar continued.

Death to the Jews! Death to the Jews!

Once he had been guardedly optimistic about the future of the Fatherland. Once . . .

He walked over to Margot and held out his hand, and she took it. Slowly, he lifted her into a sitting position on the mattress. Her face was bloody and wet. Using her still-functional eye, she groped in the faint light for her clothing. Her dress had been torn, but her sweater was in one piece. Berg wrapped it around her shoulders. He looked into the Jewess's good eye and saw vengeance and anger, nothing in the way of defeat.

"*Danke,*" she whispered.

"*Bitte,*" he whispered back. He exhaled forcefully and, with great effort, willed himself to stand. The room was awash in red, glistening and sticky. It was an abattoir, rife with the smell of slaughtered meat. An errant scream shot through the hallway. Berg shuddered.

Abruptly, something shrill stabbed through the droning mantra outside. The distinct and welcome sound of a police whistle, more than one actually. Berg got up and peered through the window.

Pandemonium reigned outside as the Brownshirt marchers broke rank and fled in all directions. Down the lane, two motor wagons filled with officers had stopped next to the curb, and policemen spilled into the dark streets, waving batons and nightsticks.

Inside the cigarette house, panicked yells filtered through the doors.

"*Polizei! Polizei! Raus hier!*"

The whistles grew louder . . . nearer.

Margot choked out, "You have to get out of here!"

"*Nein.*" Berg shook his head. "I will not leave you here to be blamed for my deeds."

"It will ruin you."

"They attacked me." A shrug. "They provided me with reason to kill them."

The door to the room flung open. Berg was staring at the wrong end of a gun barrel, face-to-face with death.

It wasn't the first time. With God's help, it wouldn't be the last.

THIRTY-EIGHT

✠ Well, well, well." A tongue clucked. "You've made quite a mess of things!"

With the barrel of a P.08 Artillery Luger aimed between his eyes, Berg thought it best not to respond. Military firearms had been outlawed for years in Munich, stockpiles of weapons having been destroyed en masse over a decade ago. Yet it was well known that many men had hidden their old weapons: Luger handguns, bayonets—Berg had even seen MG 13 Dummy light machine guns stowed away in closets. This certainly wasn't done out of sentimentality but out of fear of what the future might hold. So far Munich was surviving, one step ahead of the anarchists because guns were hard to come by. History had shown that an armed Germany was a Germany at war.

"Do I even want to know how this happened?"

Berg could barely detect the words. The cigarette house echoed with hellish screams, barked orders, and piercing whistles. Several rounds of fisticuffs were taking place right outside the door.

"I . . ." Berg swallowed hard and raised his voice to be heard over the chaos. "I was attacked."

"I don't see any marks on you, Inspektor." Volker nodded in Margot's direction. "On her, there are many marks.

But on you?" A shrug. "Nothing." Slowly, the gun was lowered until the four-inch barrel was pointed at the floor. "And the question is not whether you were attacked or not, Axel. The question is what were you doing here in the first place."

"Probably the same thing that you're doing here." With the gun out of his face, Berg became bolder.

"That's not much of an answer."

"The best I could come up with under the circumstances." Berg wiped his sweaty, bloody hands on the pants of his uniform. "*Look* at her, Volker!" His eyes traveled over his handiwork . . . two dead youths. "Look at what I was faced with . . . as a police officer . . . as a man. Then you tell me what I should have done."

There was a long silence.

"I really don't know," Volker answered. "But this is clearly *over*doing whatever it was that you were supposed to do."

"It's too late for hindsight," Berg whispered.

"There you are right." Volker threw Margot his handkerchief. "Patch yourself up, my dear. You have to get out of here."

Margot got up from the bed and poured water from a pitcher into the washing bowl. She dipped the kerchief into the water and meticulously began to wipe off the filth and blood from her face. As she rinsed the handkerchief, the clear water turned rosy pink.

"I thought you had more sense, Axel," Volker said. "However, it's too late for a reprimand. You're buried in deep shit."

That he was . . . up to his neck. Berg awaited his sentencing.

Volker's lips compressed into a sour pout. "All right. If you can get out of this without anyone else knowing, I'll say nothing. If you're caught, I'll personally feed you to the dogs. Do we understand one another?"

"Perfectly."

"What were you thinking?" Volker was baffled. "With all that was going on in Königsplatz . . . coming to a Jewish whorehouse?"

"I don't know what I was thinking, sir."

"I suppose that if you do get caught, you can blame it on her." Volker looked at Margot and shook his head. "You'll have to leave the city, my dear. Leave and never come back. If you do return, I'll have you arrested and executed." He pointed to the bodies. "Two murders, my dear. If the good people of Germany don't hang you first, the crowd will tear you limb from limb."

Margot shuddered as tears ran down her cheeks. "I don't have any papers."

Volker reached into his rucksack and pulled out a sealed envelope. "Inside is everything you should need, including enough marks for travel money." He stared at her. "I hope you have other clothes."

"A few."

"Then get on with it."

Margot removed a pillow from its case, exposing a small bedroll. She untied a knot and sorted through her wardrobe—two skirts, two blouses, a pair of long underwear, and a sweater. Quickly, she changed under the scrutiny of two sets of male eyes. When she was done, she stowed what was left into a neat bundle.

Volker put his hand on the doorknob. "Well done. Wait for me downstairs; I'll take you to the train. It's not safe for a woman to walk the streets alone in these uncertain times."

"Can I say good-bye to my parents?"

"No, you cannot. I'll see you downstairs in fifteen minutes. If you try to escape, I will send out my men to hunt you down."

"Thank you, sir," Margot said modestly.

"You're welcome." Volker opened the door. "Go."

Immediately, she left. Volker slammed the door shut and leaned against it. "Anyone see you come in here besides that sack of lard downstairs?"

"You found him?"

"There weren't many places he could be. Answer the question, Berg."

"I don't think so, no."

"Very good. Leave by the fire escape. Go home and don't go out again tonight. I am loath to say this but I can't afford to lose you. There is still a murderer loose. Once this Austrian nuisance blows over, I expect you to find this monster." Volker flicked lint off of his suit. "It seems you are the last man standing for this job."

Berg's heartbeat quickened. "Why? What happened to Storf and Müller?"

"With God's help, they will recover—"

"How bad?"

"Müller has a broken leg."

There was silence. Berg sat down on the edge of the bed, sidestepping the dead youth at his feet. "And Ulrich?"

"He took quite a beating from the bastards. He was taken to the hospital."

Berg bolted up. "I must see him!"

Volker grabbed him by his shirt. "No, Axel, you must not. Didn't you hear me? Go home. The police are winning but the battle is far from over. If the streets are quiet in the morning, I will see you tomorrow at nine."

Berg didn't answer.

"At nine. Am I clear?"

"Very."

Once again, Volker appraised the situation. "If I were an Inspektor and came upon this scene, I might assume that there was a quarrel over whores." He smiled. "Women are the death of our species." The Kommissar bent down and retrieved Berg's knife. "I believe you'll be wanting this." Berg took it and slid it into his boot. Volker pointed to the fire escape. "Your wife is waiting."

"What did Himmler say to you, sir?"

"Pardon?"

"At the rally, sir. You handed him the megaphone. You weren't happy about it but you did it anyway. What did he say to you?"

"He told me that I should cooperate with him because . . ." Volker's grin was hard and bitter. ". . . Because one day he'd be giving *me* orders, and he'd remember his friends as well as his enemies."

"The man has a vision . . . even if it runs to the delusional."

"The man is a little shit!"

"Yet you acquiesced."

Volker flushed—from embarrassment at his weakness as well as from anger. "One hundred thousand people attended that rally, Axel. I am not stupid—and I am not worried. One day that little turd will get his." He pointed to the window and the fire escape beyond. "Go now, Inspektor."

"In a moment. A few moments, actually. I need to catch my breath."

Volker frowned. "Don't wait too long. Britta will worry."

"She's used to that."

Volker waited for Berg to move. When he didn't, the Kommissar slowly opened the door and left. As soon as Berg was alone, he leaned on the door, trying to slow down his breathing. When he had assured himself that Volker would not be returning, he pulled aside the end table and liberated Gottlieb.

Berg said, "Change of plans. You must leave while the city is still under siege. Once the Oberbürgermeister imposes martial law, the streets will be quiet and you'll be more likely to be noticed. Also, if you try to leave then, you will be arrested."

"I've done nothing."

"That's irrelevant. Do you wish to live or die?" Berg eyed him up and down. "You are about my size. Trade clothes with me." As Gottlieb stared at him, he said, "I am thinking of you, Jew. It will be easier for you to travel dressed as a policeman."

Biting his lip, the Jew suspected otherwise, but removed his clothing, stripping down to his long underwear. Berg greedily scooped up the discarded three-piece brown woolen suit. The Jew's clothes were finely crafted from good fabric—to be expected because the man was a tailor. Yet it was irritating that this immigrant Jew should dress much more handsomely than he, a hardworking cop.

It felt good to be garbed in such well-made apparel. The wool was warm but not itchy. Berg now had a new suit to show for his nobility. But there was more than just blatant theft behind the switching. Volker would be expecting him to climb down the fire escape. Berg had never fully trusted the Kommissar, and now he was especially wary. Volker's order could be a trap. If that were so, better Gottlieb dead than he.

Opening the window, Berg peeked outside, listening to the sounds of rioting that carried through the night air. Things seemed quieter, but the hours ahead were still dangerous, an overloaded mountain of fresh snow just waiting to avalanche with the least little bit of agitation.

"It's time, Herr Gottlieb. Go."

"You're not coming with me?"

"If we are seen together, we both will die. This is where we part ways."

"I will not forget you."

"If you do or don't, it is of no consequence. Take care of your daughters. I have children of my own." Berg turned to him. "God be with you."

Carefully, Gottlieb climbed out the window and lowered himself onto a rickety iron landing. Berg watched him tiptoe down a flight of teetering steps, then quickly lost sight of him. He shut the window and leaned against the wall.

He was panting. Waiting and thinking.

If Gottlieb was murdered, would he even know?

And if the Jew was murdered and Volker then discovered that he had killed the wrong man, would he come up here to correct the mistake?

Thinking and waiting.

Through the front entrance or through the side window onto the fire escape?

Turmoil was still roiling through the tenement. No matter. It was time.

He straightened his collar, brushed off his vest, and opened the door to the hallway. He came in through the front; he'd leave the same way, with his head erect and his eyes staring straight ahead. He'd leave not as a scared rabbit but as a *man*. He stepped outside the room.

Walk calmly.

Down the first flight of steps. A policeman emerged from one of the whores' rooms, buttoning up his fly. He looked up, saw Berg, and reddened. Berg walked by as if he hadn't noticed the man.

You are in control.

Down the second flight. Noises grew in volume. Berg could make out people in the streets—running, screaming, chanting. There was a police whistle, the rumble of motorcars, the clop of horses' hooves. Distant sounds as well.

Keep going.

One more flight to the reception area.

Five steps, four . . .

He paused. His pathway was blocked.

Sprawled across the last two steps was the fat attendant, eyes wide-open, mouth agape, lying in a pool of his own blood. A knife protruded from his neck.

In his death, he had company.

Margot lay just a few meters away, three ragged holes in her chest. The visa papers that Volker had given her were scattered over the floor, soaked with blood and excrement. Her clothing had spilled from her bedroll, a skirt and a blouse strewn across the wet, stained floor.

At first glance, it appeared that there could have been an altercation between them. The explanation would be simple: The fat man wanted something from the whore, and the whore had refused. In fact, Berg knew that the attendant had always had an eye for her.

But Berg also knew an authentic crime scene. Margot was a short woman and not particularly strong. Even stung with fear, she would never have had the muscle power to shove a knife so deeply into the fat man's throat. Even if the man had bent down, the angle of the attack would have been different, the hilt of the knife pointing down with the blade pointing up. This stabbing had been accomplished by someone tall and strong. The shots had been fired by a man who knew how to use a revolver.

There was nothing that could be done.

It was over.

Again Berg took a minute to catch his breath. Then, dry-eyed, he ambled out of the cigarette house, wiping the soles of his boots several times against the ground. Britta worked hard to keep a clean house. No sense tracking in bloody shoeprints.

THIRTY-NINE

✠ Walking into the state hospital at Ludwig-Maximilian University, Berg was limping, but no one seemed to notice or care. The hospital was rife with activity and since he was ambulatory and not in need of immediate attention, he was rightfully ignored. Moaning emanated from every corner, crevice, and wall, with patients overflowing from the waiting rooms into the hallways. Those who had sustained broken bones were lucky enough to have snagged gurneys to rest on. The remaining populace seemed less in need of urgent care, having come in for cuts and lacerations, bruises and contusions, and lots of swollen faces and black eyes from anonymous punches. When chairs weren't available, the people made do by sprawling on the floor.

Nurses were running an obstacle course around the bodies, holding paperwork, shouting out names, rushing about while trying to figure out who needed them most. When Berg tapped one of them on the shoulder, the harried young woman in a white uniform with a starched white hat jumped back in surprise. She looked no more than twenty with smooth skin and amber eyes. Berg saw Margot in them, but then he blinked and the image was gone. Her expression was stern and sour. She looked up from her clipboard, her eyes giving him a two-second evaluation. Quickly, they concluded that he was a nuisance case.

"You need to check in with the clerk before you can be seen."

A shriek cut through the corridor, followed by a curse.

"I am a policeman." Berg fished around in his coat pocket and showed the young nurse his credentials. Her face said that she was not impressed. After tonight's riots, it would probably be a while before the police were impressive again. "I am here to locate—"

"Go check in with the clerk. Rules are rules." She called out a name, checked it off her list, and gave Berg a view of her back.

After a bit of hunting, Berg concluded that Storf's name hadn't been entered into the system. Either Ulrich hadn't been brought here or it meant something that Berg chose not to think about.

Georg Müller *had* been admitted, although it took Berg over an hour to find him. His good colleague lay in a ward of twenty men—ten on each side, each with a single curtain for privacy. Müller's curtain was open, his left leg wrapped in white gauze and slightly elevated. He wore a white hospital gown, and all that pale cotton just served to emphasize his red and puffy face. Georg had taken a few nasty jabs to his right cheek, but no doubt he had returned those jabs with some nasty hooks of his own.

His wife, Karen, was standing at his side, wringing her pudgy hands, the layers of fat rolling over one another as if she were kneading bread dough. Her eyes were red-rimmed and moist. Obviously Müller's vision was still intact. He broke into a smile when he saw his colleague.

"Good to see you, man." Berg grinned and placed a hand on Müller's shoulder. "I was concerned about you."

"Likewise." Müller's nose wrinkled, and Berg knew right away that his friend smelled blood. Although he had washed his hands and arms at least four times, Berg hadn't had time to wash his hair. Müller was a professional policeman, using not only sight and sound but all of his senses for detection. "And you are all right, Axel?"

"I'm grateful to be walking." Berg sighed. "Hello, Karen. You're taking good care of him, I see."

"Better than the police."

"That is for certain."

"How is it going out there?" Müller inquired.

"I rode here on my *Kraftrad* from Gärtnerplatz. Things are settling down . . . I think."

"Thank God. Over a hundred thousand people at the rally, Axel. That is almost a fifth of the city. We were badly outnumbered . . . especially near the stage. I do think that if Hitler had known he would attract such a turnout, he would have tried another putsch."

"Then it's good that he didn't know."

"I reckon the thought of another jail sentence acted as a deterrent," Karen added.

Müller said, "By morning all will be under control, I think."

"For how long?" Karen blurted out. "Why must we deal with this constant unrest? Why does Munich seem to attract misfits?"

"It must be the *Föhn*," Berg said.

"That's not funny!" Karen scrunched up her doughy face.

"He already has a nagging wife, Karen, he doesn't

need two," Müller scolded. When tears formed in her eyes, he softened his tone. "Now, now, my dearest. You know that I'm a bit testy. Please don't make a scene."

She held back her tears. "It's today's youth! No respect for authority!"

"Not all youth, Karen," Berg answered. "Not your children, and not mine, either. These boys are just thugs . . . stupid teenagers—all aggression, no brain."

"They should have been sent to war instead of the tenderhearted like Georg. It's people like them that got us into war in the first place. It is probably people like them that will get us into another war."

"The devil, Karen, I hope not." Müller turned to Berg and said, "She is a staunch Social Democrat."

"Hear, hear!" Berg smiled.

"A minority of one in my apartment house." She shook her head in disgust.

Berg patted her hand. "Why don't you take a break, Karen? Go get something to eat. I'll take good care of him until you get back."

"A fine idea," Müller concurred.

"You're trying to get rid of me."

"I have some business to discuss," Berg explained. "It might be a bit strong for your ears."

"Business?" Karen was aghast. "Can't you see what those animals did to him? Can't you let him be for one night?"

"I'm fine," Müller insisted. "A little mental stimulation will take my mind off the pain. Go refresh yourself, my dearest. You'll feel better."

It took another few minutes of cajoling, before Karen acquiesced. Berg waited until she was gone, then drew the curtain around the bed. It provided only the illusion of privacy—a layer of thin cloth was not enough to shut out the whimperings and the plaints—but it was enough of a barrier to make them both feel comfortable.

"What happened to Ulrich?" Berg whispered.

Müller sighed deeply. "He was stabbed. Under his arm, I think."

"Dear God!"

"He underwent surgery. He has lost a lot of blood."

"And he is out of surgery now?"

"Yes, he's suffering from a collapsed lung."

"The devil!" Berg swore. "I'd like to tear those thugs limb from limb."

"Ulrich should recover if infection doesn't ravage his body."

"What about that brand-new medicine that has been effective against cholera? Pyo . . . pyo . . ." Berg tapped his foot. "Pyocyanase . . . something like that."

Müller shrugged. "I'm sure the doctors are doing everything they can."

"Of course. I will try to see him tomorrow."

"A good idea . . . when you do not smell so ripe. What slaughterhouse have you come from, my friend?" When Berg didn't answer, Georg didn't press it. "Go home, Axel. I'm sure Britta is frantic with worry."

"I already spoke to her. Our neighbor has a telephone. She knows I am safe." Dark clouds formed in Berg's brain. He shooed them away. "She will survive tonight . . . far better than the city. If it isn't the Austrian, it's this ghastly murderer who has debased himself even further by including children now."

"Maybe he's taking a lesson from Haarmann or the Vampire of Düsseldorf."

"I don't think the devil needs any lessons." Berg balled his fingers into a fist. "I cannot go home until I've learned more about these horrible murders. I have not seen the crime scene, and I should see it tonight. There is only one of us left. If I wait until morning, critical evidence might be lost."

"I reckon they've already sent the bodies to the pathology lab, Axel. Besides, it's pitch-black. You won't be able to see a thing."

"There are some gaslights in the park. I have a kerosene lamp."

Müller rolled his eyes.

"At the very least, I should visit the family."

"It's quite late, Axel. Besides, the Austrian might be there."

"To hell with Hitler. As far as I know, he doesn't run the city."

Müller shrugged, then winced in pain. "You can't go over there, Axel. Not the way you smell. You're not even in uniform."

Müller was right. He couldn't go anywhere in an official capacity until he was properly dressed. "I'll get a fresh uniform at the precinct."

"And you've cleared this late-night visit with Volker?"

Berg equivocated. "If Volker's there, I'll let him know of my plans. If not, I'll leave a note."

"Be careful, Axel. The situation is still very tense, and it's hard to know friend from foe." Müller's thoughts traveled elsewhere. "This latest crisis can't last forever. This tug of war for power, this pulling and joggling . . . eventually the rope will simply snap!"

✠   ✠   ✠

THE KOMMISSAR was last on Berg's list of people that he wanted to see. But the Fates thought otherwise, and Berg almost knocked down Volker as he dashed into the Ett Strasse station.

"I will infer from your civilian clothes that you are on your way home." Volker started to walk away. "It is good that you are finally learning to obey orders."

Berg refused to be intimidated. "We have to talk."

Volker spoke over his shoulder. "No, we need to get the city under control."

"The murders, Inspektor."

Volker stopped abruptly. "What do you mean?"

Berg knew that Volker was thinking of Margot. "A mother and daughter found dead in the park, sir."

"Ah . . . yes, of course." Volker resumed walking. "Later."

"I just came from the hospital, Herr Kommissar. Müller is indisposed, and Ulrich is suffering from a collapsed lung. I'm the only one who has worked this murder case from the start."

"And you've done a lousy job on it, haven't you?"

Volker opened his office door. Berg was not to be deterred and barged inside, shutting the door behind him. "I have leads, Herr Volker. I must *do something* before more women die."

Volker sat down at his desk and looked amused. "The tortured hero. My, you play the martyr well."

Berg said, "I owe it to my colleagues and the city to solve this case. And I will do it. I will make sure that whoever is behind these terrible events ends up in a very dark and scary place."

"Hear, hear, old man! Perhaps you'd like to start a party and lead a rally yourself."

"I would have more to say than that Austrian imbecile."

"No doubt!" Volker stifled a smile. "Go home."

"No, I'm not going home. I'm going to change into a fresh uniform, and then I am going out to visit the crime scene."

"Now?"

"Yes, now."

"It's as dark as sin outside. You'll see nothing."

"Then I'll go examine the bodies or visit the family."

A dumbfounded chuckle. "Axel, the city is a mess."

"I can manage alone."

Again Volker smiled. "Judging from tonight, I'm quite sure you can."

Berg took a deep breath. "So then, I have your permission."

Volker stared at him, at Berg's intense eyes piercing his brain as well as his soul. "I can't stop you, can I?"

Berg gave a sigh of relief, but then became wary. Was this another trap set up by Volker? *Was* there ever a trap? His fears were driving him more than a little mad. "I'd like Herr Professor Kolb to come along with me."

Volker laughed out loud in disbelief. "With the city in shambles, you want to drag out a cripple?"

"If he is willing. His scientific expertise along with his insights will help me immeasurably."

"He has Jewish blood in his veins, Axel. He will be a target for the punks. How is he to defend himself? By beating them off with his cane?"

"If he is anxious, I will not insist, but I think he will take the risk. I'll ride him to the scene in a *Zweikraftrad*. He can sit in the passenger seat."

"Very well, Axel, go ahead."

Berg was leery of Volker's uncharacteristic acquiescence. His thoughts drifted back to Margot, and to the person responsible for her death. Berg knew damn well why she had been slain. The poor girl had seen a Munich policeman murder two boys. She could no longer be trusted. Berg had to wonder if he'd be next.

"Thank you, sir. I will change into a uniform right now."

"Yes, yes. Just go. You're annoying me." As Berg was about to close the door behind him, he heard Volker cluck his tongue and whisper, "It's your funeral."

FORTY

✠ Kolb said, "I don't understand why I wasn't immediately called in to examine the death scene."

Berg took a deep breath and told himself to be patient. "The city has been in turmoil since the rally, Herr Professor. Maybe the police couldn't reach you."

"More likely, *someone* didn't want me touching a young German *Mädchen* because of my Jewish blood."

It was not like Kolb to show irritation. "The Austrian wouldn't know your religion, Herr Professor."

Kolb touched his nose. "All he'd have to do is take one look at me." The old man was aware of what Hitler was capable of fomenting. He appeared nervous.

Berg tried to be soothing. "I can't tell you how chaotic everything was after the murders were announced."

"It's a pity," Kolb said. "I'm sure everything's cleaned up by now. It would have been much more helpful if I could have examined the crime scene before it was trampled on!"

"So shall we skip the park now and go back at daylight?"

"Yes, I think so. Let's go on to the pathology lab. I'd like to see the bodies before they are autopsied. Might as well salvage what we can!"

"Whatever you think, Herr Professor."

Kolb took in a deep breath and let it out. "I am churlish tonight."

"We are all quick-tempered." Berg blinked several times, hoping to blot out murderous images: a knife, *his* knife, penetrating skin. He couldn't rid his mind of foul thoughts . . . of a murdered mother and child . . . those too-real nightmares . . . the knife slicing through the soft tendons of their windpipes. Blood squirting outward and hitting him in the face.

They were only children. Evil children, but still just children.

The magnitude had yet to sink in. Right now, he had to concentrate on external monsters, not the one within. He had to remain focused if he were to root out a killer. Later would be the time for recriminations.

He pulled out the choke of the *Kraftrad,* turning the handle several times to get enough fuel into the motor. "Are you settled properly?"

"Yes, go ahead."

Kolb lived northwest of Schwabing in a third-floor one-room apartment on the outskirts of the city: a newer building where the electricity was wired inside the structure. The Professor often worked in poor light; maybe that was why his spectacles were so thick.

Now Berg was dragging him out of a comfortable bed to ask for his help. Slowly, he guided the *Kraftrad* into the street. "They live close to you . . . in Schwabing. That is, they did . . . the victims."

"But they were murdered in the Englischer Garten?"

"I don't know where they were murdered. The bodies were found in the Englischer Garten."

"Ah yes," Kolb said. "Have you any thoughts on this monster . . . this enemy of ours?"

"I have thought of nothing but him! Who the devil he is, where he comes from, his employment, what drives his deviance."

"And?"

"I have come up with very little. The clues that I have point to different people with different names, different occupations, and different nationalities."

"Pardon?" Kolb strained over the rumblings of the motorbike. "I can barely hear you."

Berg made a series of quick turns until he was on Ludwig Strasse, then pulled over next to the walkway and turned off the motor. The tree-lined street—a main north–south thoroughfare—was deserted and dark, electric streetlights turned off by order of the Oberbürgermeister. Even the ubiquitous clanking of the streetcars had been stifled for the night. In the last two hours, a curfew had been imposed on the city. Any unauthorized person on the roads would be arrested immediately.

The stillness was eerie, but somewhat nostalgic, bringing back images of Berg's youth. On rare moments like this, he could almost touch his childhood, a time before there were motorcars and electricity everywhere, before modern invention intervened with the natural order of things. When he was a young child, he had often pretended to be sleeping, when in reality he lay in bed for hours just thinking. With his feather duvet wrapped tightly around his body, his nose cold from the frosted air, he had been careful not to move lest he wake up his two younger brothers sleeping beside him in their shared bed.

Back then, if he listened carefully, he could hear the

whinnies emanating from the horse stables. The beasts had once ruled the city, pulling the police wagons, the streetcars, and the cabs. Now only the market vendors used the beasts to pull their wagons, and not even they so much anymore because the old horses clogged traffic, the motorists beeping and swearing at them, scaring the poor animals until they reared in protest. It wasn't that the motorcar was a bad thing; it was the motorcar operator who felt as if he owned the roadways.

So long ago it was, before a war had torn the world apart, before the city was rent by politics and its legions of armies. The Kommunist against the royalist. The Social Democrats against the German Workers Party. The Bavarian Workers against the German Democratic Party. And everyone against Hitler—or so they claimed, even though the Austrian's support seemed to keep growing.

It was all too much to fathom.

"I didn't say anything that profound." Berg turned off the scooter and bundled his scarf tightly around his neck. The air was wet and biting. "Nothing you haven't thought of yourself." He repeated what he had said about the killer while Kolb nodded agreement.

"And even the victims, Herr Professor. They are not all alike. The first was a bourgeois woman who lived in a six-room apartment on Widenmayer Strasse. She was married, expecting a child. The second woman was a visitor to the city, a Kommunist—or at least she flirted with Kommunismus—whose home was in Berlin. She was staying in a rented room in Giesing. Our third victim was an immigrant Jewess seamstress who lived near Gärtnerplatz. Now we have these two new murders—a working-class woman and her daughter who lived just east of Schwabing.

"There is no consistency in any aspect—either with the type of woman, the wealth of the family, religion of the women, the geographical location of their homes, and even the time of day they were killed. The last two appeared to be slain in daylight, the first three under the cloak of darkness. It is maddening!"

"Interesting." Kolb stroked his beard. "From my point of view, they're very similar. All were young women, and so far all were strangled. The bodies were discovered in the Englischer Garten except in the case of Marlena Druer. But even she was found less than a kilometer away."

"I suppose it does depend how the case is regarded," Berg replied. "Still, finding bodies in the Englischer Garten or along the Isar doesn't exactly point to anything specific. The park is three hundred and seventy-five hectares of copses, woods, brush, and glades. I can't think of a better place to dump a corpse."

"That is true," Kolb said.

"Shall we proceed to the lab?"

"Before we do, what do you know about these latest victims?"

"Nothing at the moment. I certainly don't know how they were murdered if that's what you're asking."

"Do you know anything personal about them?"

"The woman was widowed. Her husband died four years ago from a leg infection—an old war wound, I think."

"Was the murdered little girl the woman's only child?"

"There is a surviving son."

Kolb said, "And now he is an orphan."

Berg slumped under the invisible weight pressing on his shoulders. Once again, he started the choke and guided the motorbike back onto the boulevard. He shouted, "The aunt's name is Renate Dehmel—a married woman with two children of her own."

"And the victim?"

"Edith Mayrhofer. She was forty. The little girl, Johanna, was six or seven."

"The surviving boy?"

"Ralph . . . ten. Aunt Renate was watching him because she has a son the same age. Edith had decided to take little Johanna for a walk . . . to take advantage of today's sunshine. When they were late to pick up Ralph, Renate became concerned. She decided to go look for them."

"Don't tell me *she* found them?" Kolb let out a gasp.

"I don't know if she found them or they were discovered by someone else, but an officer at the police station told me that she saw the corpses. It must have been terrible, especially because the little boy was there with her."

"Oh *Gott,* that is awful!"

"Just dreadful!"

Kolb said, "It would have been most useful to see the bodies as they were found."

"Usually, someone from the *Mordkommission* must sign off before the bodies can be removed. But because of the rally and subsequent rioting, the police had been diverted to Königsplatz and Gärtnerplatz."

Kolb said, "Once we visit the pathology lab, we will know more."

Berg said, "Afterward we can visit the crime spot. I'm certain that the police cordoned off the area with ropes."

"Yes, we can do that."

Berg heard the fatigue in the Professor's voice. "Or we can visit the scene in the morning. I don't want to subject you to such a long evening."

"I can manage a long evening." Kolb smiled. "Death, my friend, is even longer."

✠ ✠ ✠

SINCE THE PATHOLOGY LAB was located in the basement of the state hospital, most of the smell was confined to that area. Still, as soon as the two of them entered the stairwell, rank fumes rose up and Berg almost gagged. It was only the third time that he had ever been there and his two previous encounters had failed to prepare him for the third.

Kolb, on the other hand, seemed inured to the foul odor.

The autopsy assistant, the *Diener,* seemed amused by Berg's reaction. He was dense in build and stared out with sunken eyes, escorting them down the dark steps with the help of a gas lantern. Though the building had electrical lighting, the stairwells were not wired.

"We welcome the wintertime," the *Diener* said. "In summer the stench is much stronger. Then there are the insects. They are attracted to the stink of decomposing flesh. Specifically the black flies. And when the humidity increases . . ." He waved his hand in the air. "*Ach,* it is bad."

Berg continuously swallowed to keep the contents of his stomach down. He wrapped his scarf over his mouth and nose. As they reached the bottom, the stench became riper. He thought of the charnel of his own making. The smell of decay was stronger than the smell of murder.

"One accustoms to the rankness," the *Diener* went on. "On some days I even eat my lunch in the same room."

"That is repulsive!" Berg muttered.

"It is better than starving, Inspektor." They had reached the bottom step. The assistant opened the door to the lab. "This way, meine Herren."

Inside was a dungeon, a bone-chilling, dank concrete bunker with no visible windows, not even traditional basement dormers. No fresh air was to be had, and not a hint of natural light could come in, even in daytime. Electrical bulbs cast intermittent spots of urine-stained glow, along with old gaslight sconces mounted on the walls. Berg thought he had endured the worst of the odor when the *Diener* opened a hallway door. He was wrong.

"This way."

Inside the autopsy amphitheater, the fetid air was so intense that Berg nearly fainted. He felt ludicrous. In the Great War, he had breathed the malodor of death and disintegration as moribund bodies lay around him. In his job with the *Mordkommission,* he had examined many corpses in varying states of decomposition. But the rankness here was unparalleled.

Not only was the stench overpowering, the visual images suggested nightmares. Rows of steel autopsy tables, each one visited by a body, some fifteen to twenty in all. Some were decently covered, but at least half were naked cadavers staring upward with vacant eyes. Some of the corpses had been left in the elements too long, and the skin had withered and blackened like African shrunken heads. Others had grown mold like spoiled meat or moldy cheese. The bodies that hadn't made it to the tables were still wrapped in white sheets and placed on shelves. The carcasses were leaking body fluids as tissue broke down into watery components, dripping away corporeal existence one droplet at a time. Even the strong stench of antiseptic couldn't mask the stink of rot.

Several pathology doctors were conducting autopsies. One had just made the Y-incision from the shoulders to midchest down to the pubic region. Another had just removed the heart, his gloved hands filled with the bloody mass. Quickly, he placed the dripping organ on the scale to weigh it.

Palettes of red filled Berg's brain: red, ruby, crimson, scarlet, carmine, cerise, maroon, vermilion . . . so many variations of one wavelength . . . more reds than there were names.

At one of the tables, an elderly doctor looked up. He wore a blood-and-tissue–spattered white apron that protected a suit and tie. A paper cap sat on his scalp, rubber gloves obscured his hands, and a paper mask covered his mouth and nose. He sported a long white beard and wore rimless spectacles. He was quite paunchy. Had the apron been just a bit more vermilion, he could have passed for Saint Nicholas. He looked straight at Berg.

"You are *Polizei*."

"I am."

"Up so late?"

"Unusual circumstances." Berg pulled down the scarf to be understood. His nose was assaulted further, but the *Diener* had been correct. Slowly, slowly he became accustomed to the smell. He could breathe without choking. "Inspektor Axel Berg from Munich Police, from the

Mordkommission. I have been investigating the recent violent deaths in our city."

"Herr Doktor Jakob Gebhardt here." The man clicked his heels. "It is good to make your acquaintance, Inspektor."

"Same here, Herr Doktor," Berg answered, "although I would have preferred to meet you under less trying circumstances. This is the Polizei Daktyloskoper and foreign-material analyst Herr Professor—"

"No need for introductions, Inspektor, I've known the eminent Herr Professor Kolb for years." Gebhardt smiled. "All of us ghouls know each other. Give me a moment to close my charge up and I'll be right with you."

A moment was twenty minutes. Berg was fatigued, yet his nerves still shot poison through his system. He couldn't have slept even if he had chosen to try to do so. He couldn't bear to close his eyes for fear of what lurked behind them.

To Kolb, Gebhardt said, "You look tired, Josef."

"It is nearly one in the morning, Jakob. Some of us actually sleep at night."

"Night, day, it's all the same down here." Gebhardt addressed Berg. "Before electricity, we had our own building with windows and daylight and proper working conditions. But once the city wired the hospital and the surrounding buildings, it took away our lab and sent us down here. Of course, it's convenient—the hospital no longer has to transport the bodies—but the conditions are not good, especially in the summer."

"I was telling them that, Herr Doktor," the *Diener* piped in.

"I'm sure you were, Klaus." He sighed. "And look at this lighting . . . it is terrible. You can hardly see anything unless you supplement with kerosene lanterns. Sometimes, for a very bright light, I even use a torch! But then I worry about starting a fire."

Gebhardt threw up his hands.

"You know all those myths about creatures of the night that shrink in daylight? I think someone has seen one of our pathologists emerge from this cave, suddenly squinting from the brightness of the sun."

Kolb said, "I hope we're not disturbing you."

"Not at all." Gebhardt's expression turned grave. "What happened out there?"

"Hitler is what happened," Berg said.

"Will it ever stop?" Gebhardt shook his head. "Shall we take a look at the latest tragedies that have embraced our troubled city?"

"If you'd be so kind," Berg responded.

"I've got one of the bodies over here." Gebhardt stopped in front of a table where the body had been covered with a sheet. Even under the cloth, Berg knew it was the little girl. Such a compact little package. Berg thought of Monika's sweet face and instantly, beads of sweat gathered over his brow. The doctor did not appear to notice. He turned to his assistant. "Klaus, get down the mother. I believe she is resting in compartment five, letter G."

Once again, Berg regarded the shelves of bodies. A large brass plaque hung over the top rung of corpses. The engraved lettering was Roman print instead of the usual Gothic—logical because the words were in Latin instead of German.

Hic locus est ubi mors gaudet succurrere vitae.

"This is a place where death rejoices to teach those who live," Kolb translated.

"How true." Gebhardt pulled back the cloth, exposing the child's body. She was a pretty, little girl in death, no doubt even prettier in life: fair-complexioned with long golden hair. It was hard to tell the eye color because the pupils had reached maximal dilation, but Berg could make out the palest of blues that encircled her fixed stare.

"This little girl was an Aryan from top to bottom," Gebhardt said. "No doubt Hitler will drag this poor girl's death into his politics."

In the background, Berg could hear Klaus grunt as he worked to retrieve the body from the shelf. "How did she die?"

"See for yourself. . . ." Gebhardt gently rolled the little body onto its side. In this position, a substantial depression in the back of the skull was clearly exposed.

Kolb pulled out his own rubber gloves from his pocket and let his fingers gently caress the hollow.

"Any number of objects could have made that indentation," Gebhardt said.

"It is not a hammer," Kolb said. "The hollow is too broad. And such a delicate skull would have shattered under the blow of metal."

Gebhardt said, "And it is not a paddle, either. The hollow is too small. Nor does it look like a buckle from a belt. It is very regular in its circumference."

Berg interjected, "You think that a mother did this to her own child as overzealous punishment?"

"I've seen it before, Inspektor," Gebhardt answered. "Parents who don't realize how fragile a child is. Usually it's a father with the strap, and the victim is a boy. But I have seen mothers who have killed their small children . . . sometimes by accident, sometimes by temper. In those cases, though, I also see multiple welts on the legs, arms, stomach, and buttocks. Generally it is not a single whack to the head."

Berg said, "Since the mother was murdered, I think it is safe to assume that she was not responsible for her daughter's death."

"Exactly," Gebhardt said. "Then I thought about the woman's husband. Men can beat their wives quite harshly."

"She is a widow," Berg said.

"Yes, yes . . ." Gebhardt said. "That definitely rules out her husband."

Kolb said, "My guess is that it came from behind, someone smashing her with a walking stick."

Berg raised an eyebrow. "Was she also strangled?"

Gebhardt studied the body. "Her neck is intact. There are no ligature marks."

Kolb said, "Let's measure the size of the depression, shall we?"

Gebhardt took out a pair of calipers, measured the diameter, and gave him the exact figure in centimeters. Kolb pulled off his rubber gloves and stroked his beard.

"It's not the same size as the last one," Berg pointed out. "He used a different walking stick?"

"Not necessarily," Kolb answered. "A grown woman has harder bones. The stick would meet with more resistance. A child's skull is more delicate and thinner. In a child a dent made by the same instrument and with the same amount of force would be wider and deeper."

Berg looked pained. "Did she suffer?"

Kolb answered, "I would think that the whack would have put her out instantaneously."

Gebhardt concurred.

"Herr Doktor," Klaus, the *Diener,* said, "I have prepared the cadaver."

"Good, good!" Gebhardt exclaimed. "Let's have a look, shall we, gentlemen?"

At the sight of the naked woman, Berg involuntarily averted his eyes. When he brought them back to the corpse, he blinked several times before he could look at it objectively. Once this had been a living being named Edith Mayrhofer. Now she was a slab of dead tissue, the light gone from eyes that had been pale blue like those of her daughter. The skin had turned waxen and gray, the face creased by wrinkles even in death. Her hair was curly—tawny in color and streaked with white—except for the big, molasses-colored blotch on the right side of her forehead. The wound had oozed blood and brains.

Berg looked down at her neck. It was discolored, but it was hard to see if there were any signs of asphyxiation. "Was *she* strangled?"

Gebhardt peered through his spectacles and studied the skin of the neck. "As far as I can tell, there are no finger- or thumbprints, so nothing was done by hands. What do you think, Josef?"

Kolb examined the neck. "I concur. Nor do I see any ligature marks."

Berg sighed. This was not what he wanted to hear. The first woman had been slain by strangulation. Regina Gottlieb had been attacked, bashed over the head, *and* strangled. These latest victims had died from blunt-instrument wounds.

Did the murderer figure that it was easier to kill by

bashing his prey in the head with a walking stick? Had he changed his method, or was this a different killer?

Could it be possible that *none* of the murders were related?

"Was she raped?" Berg asked.

"At this moment, I'd say no. I swabbed her internally for semen and put the samples on several glass slides. I checked under a microscope, Inspektor, and there was no sign of spermatozoa. Of course, one has to consider that the fiend may have failed to complete the act. I haven't done an exam of her privates. I will check for bruising and tears, but short of that . . ."

Berg said, "The first woman had had sex, the second no . . . Regina Gottlieb yes, but these two no . . ."

"What are you thinking?" Gebhardt asked.

"I'm trying to establish a pattern where there is none," Berg thought out loud. "The first murder—the slaying of Anna Gross—appeared at the time to be a crime of passion. She did have semen inside of her."

"I thought her husband did it because she had made a cuckold out of him," Gebhardt said.

"That was one theory, yes. But her husband was lynched before all the facts came out." Berg didn't elaborate. "The second slaying was Marlena Druer . . . perhaps that was a crime of passion. We found something in her room that could have been a love letter. But she wasn't raped."

Berg stopped and collected his thoughts.

"The third murder was clearly a rape/murder. In these most recent slayings there was no rape." He paused. "Either we're dealing with different killers or . . . perhaps the thrill of murder has taken the place of the thrill of sex."

"Lustmord," Kolb said. "And in this crime, he has gone

even further to satisfy the urge: the killing of a child. Who knows what he'll do in the future to fulfill his desires?"

Berg shook his head in revulsion. "How can this be? The killing of a little child?"

"I suspect she wasn't the intended target," the pathologist suggested. "Perhaps the murderer didn't even notice her until he had captured her mother."

Kolb said, "Or perhaps she signifies a *potential* woman and that is what he detests. Kill it before it can kill. Freud has a theory that women secretly desire to destroy men because of penis envy. And they do this by sending them off to die in war. Men, on the other hand, are jealous of women because they are the ultimate creators of life. They get retribution by symbolically killing them over and over in the sex act."

"I have heard that before," Gebhardt said. "I don't know if I believe it."

"I agree with Herr Doktor Gebhardt," Berg stated. "There are many reasons to have sex other than to satisfy a lust for murder."

"But often the two are intertwined. Both acts involve an element of losing control."

Gebhardt said, "I lose control when I stub my toe, Josef. That doesn't mean I rape and murder."

"Of course not! Murderers don't materialize from the ether," Kolb said. "But you cannot deny, Jakob, that creation and destruction are the two primary driving forces in the world."

"No, I would not deny that."

Berg nodded as if Kolb had said something profound. He didn't understand all the excitement about Freud, how this Viennese Jew got so famous by stating the obvious.

FORTY-ONE

✠ At three in the morning, Berg fell into a nightmarish stupor and woke up with a start two hours later, finally crawling out of bed at six. Too tired to heat up water for a bath, he sponged off his body using a pail of icy water from the tap, washing his head and hair until his scalp was numb, rinsing away dirt and flecks of blood, watching it all swirl down the drain of the kitchen sink. He opened a new box of Sisu shaving blades and tore at his face with the razor, unmindful of the nicks, enjoying the bite of pain. He splashed his face with water, then slipped into long underwear, followed by long woolen pants and a thick cable-knit sweater. His feet were wrapped in double socks and stuffed into cracked leather boots.

Warm externally although his head and hands were still cold, his cheeks were still stinging from his careless shaving. Electricity provided a weak overhead light in the dining area, too dim to disturb Joachim as he lay on the sofa, legs dangling over the edge. Quietly and carefully, Berg opened the hatch of the stove, raked the coals, and adjusted the draft. Moments later, the radiator sputtered to life, bringing up a dull, wet heat that dissipated too quickly. With the stove tended, he started a pot of coffee. It took a few minutes before the water boiled and perco-lated through the grounds, but as soon as it did, the rich aroma filled the small room. Berg leaned over and breathed deeply, allowing the warm air to infuse his nose and lungs.

He took his steaming mug and peered out of the window, his eyes surveying a deserted street in a city still shrouded in darkness. There wasn't even a promise of light; the skies were overcast without a star in sight. He sipped the hot coffee until his mouth burned. His second cup was for taste rather than heat. He had just finished his breakfast of a roll, butter, and marmalade when he heard Joachim stirring. He glanced up to see his son nearly fall off the couch before his feet caught up with his body. He rubbed his eyes. "What time is it?"

"Six-thirty. Go back to sleep."

"Why are you up so early, Papa?"

"It was a busy night. I think it's going to be a busier day."

Again Joachim rubbed his eyes as he tottered to the dining table. "I heard it was awful . . . the rioting. Mama was worried."

"I called her. She knew I was safe."

"Still, she worries. She said—" He stopped himself.

Berg offered Joachim a cup of coffee with milk and sugar. "What did she say?"

Joachim took the liquid and sipped greedily. "Thank you."

"What did your mother say?" Berg asked again.

"Nothing important. She just gets upset when the city is in a mess and she doesn't know what you're doing."

"The city is always in a mess."

"Last night was exceptional."

"That is true," Berg concurred. "And today we all suffer the aftermath of that hyena's actions."

"It isn't Hitler's fault that some of his followers are goons."

"The leader sets the tone," Berg said. "The Austrian is a thug and he attracts thugs. You should have seen what his Brownshirts did to Gärtnerplatz. It was beyond shameful!"

The boy nodded solemnly. "What were you doing there?"

"Protecting our citizens . . . *all* of our citizens, and that includes the poor, the Gypsies, and the Jews." Joachim made a face that Berg ignored. "I'm sure they will be talking about the riots in school. Don't let those crazy-headed teachers of yours convince you that it wasn't Hitler's fault. It was!"

"I am glad you're fine, that's all." Joachim looked down. "What about the two new murders, Papa? I heard the little girl was around Monika's age."

Berg winced. "We're making progress. We might have made more progress if the Nazis hadn't torn up the city." He poured himself the last dregs of coffee. Tossing the grounds in the garbage bin, he rinsed the pot and made a fresh brew, the new aroma giving Britta a reason to wake up. "I promise we'll get him."

"Get who?"

His wife's voice. She wore a faded pink robe with old slippers on her feet, her big toe poking through the leather of the fleece. Her strawberry-blond hair was tousled and tangled. She raked the cowlicks down with her fingers. Berg poured her a fresh cup of coffee.

"The monster," Berg answered.

"Which monster? Hitler or the murderer?"

"I was referring to the murderer," Berg said. "I cannot single-handedly get rid of the Austrian scourge. We need to be unified for that."

"Then you might as well just hand him the chancellor-ship. We can't even unify our own city, let alone the country. We are not a people! We are a series of nomadic tribes constantly at war with one another."

"It's not like that, Mama," Joachim spoke up. "Look . . . I know you don't like Herr Hitler, but he knows the problems that face us. And he's working hard to bring the German race back to glory—"

"Oh, stop, Joachim! You're too intelligent for that nonsense." Britta took out a blue-and-white Watto cigarette tin, lit up two smokes, and gave one to her husband. "Besides, it's too early in the morning for propaganda."

"Thank you." Berg inhaled the smoke and looked at his wife. "Since when have you become such a detractor of the Austrian?"

"I'm sick of his tactics. If the ass can't control his thugs, how can he control a nation?"

"Sometimes you need to get the people's attention first," Joachim blurted out.

"Who have you been talking to?" Britta rolled her eyes. "Don't bother answering that—I know. Uwe Kanstinger, right?"

"I'm old enough to form my own opinions, Mother," Joachim huffed.

"If it's not Uwe, it's his older sister, right?" Britta sniffed. "Don't deny it. I've seen you two talking."

"I talk to lots of people." Joachim snorted.

To Berg, Britta said, "That girl's crazy. She's in love with the Austrian. She has his picture on the wall."

"Then she's not only crazy, she's an idiot," Berg said.

"Now who is being intolerant!" Joachim protested. "How would you know without talking to her? She happens to be very intelligent."

"She's a whore, Joachim."

The boy slammed his coffee cup onto the table. "That's not true! You shouldn't say things like that! It's wrong, Mother! *You're* wrong!" He got up and marched into his bedroom, slamming the door and waking his sister. Monika, still half-asleep, moaned in protest. Joachim snapped at his sister. Then the two of them began to fight.

"Quiet!" Berg shouted. "You'll wake the neighbors."

The arguing quieted to hostile whispers, eventually stopping altogether.

"Now I finally know what I suspected." Britta bit her lip. "That disgusting little bitch!"

"He's *banging* her?"

"You heard how he defends her! What do *you* think?"

"She's what . . . nineteen . . . twenty? Is she crazy? He's just a boy!"

"Obviously not to her." Britta stared at her husband. "And since when has a difference in age prevented a man and a woman from banging?"

Berg didn't answer. Not that it mattered anymore. It was over, as permanent as only death can be.

"You have to talk to him," Britta said. "He needs to know how to prevent an accident. Thank God the boy was baptized Lutheran and can do something about it."

"I don't believe we're having this conversation." Berg shook his head in dismay. "He just turned fifteen."

"Maybe if you spent more time at home and less time on the streets, you'd be aware of what's happening in the lives of your children!" She turned her back to him and marched into the bedroom, the slammed door signaling that the discussion was over.

Left alone at the table, Berg again peered out the window, noting that the sky had lightened from charcoal to pewter.

A new day had dawned.

✠   ✠   ✠

THE MORNING PAPERS—all except the *Völkischer Beobachter*—had printed the requisite host of columns and opinions, everything from finger-pointing, blaming, and recriminations to hand-wringing, self-flagellation, and a call for self-examination. How did this happen? Why did this happen? Hadn't the city learned a lesson from the first putsch (that answer was self-evident), and what was to be done with Hitler now?

This time the Austrian had been wilier, absenting himself from the public as soon as the rioting and mayhem broke out. He had learned from the mistakes of '23 and mastered the art of delegation, transmitting his wishes to subordinates who carried out the orders. Thus, the blame rested not on the bastard's shoulders directly, but on his minions, on the thugs and hooligans who Hitler claimed had "misinterpreted" his words. As the arrested and detained goons were paraded through the jails and holding pens on their way to the courthouses, the young Brownshirts remained defiant, laughing and joking, each one eagerly awaiting his turn to fart in the face of authority.

Any newspaper space not dedicated to the riots was taken up by the murders of Edith Mayrhofer and her little daughter, Johanna. The *Völkischer Beobachter* ran screaming headlines on the front page, hoping that a new phoenix of protests would rise from the ashes of yesterday's riots. Normally Berg wouldn't be interested in reading the trashy tabloid, but this morning he was looking at the front page simply because the paper had been foisted on him by the Kommissar.

Volker looked tired and dyspeptic. Although impeccably dressed, he was disheveled, his face needing one more go with a razor. He paced back and forth as he ranted.

"The paper has a lot of public support for its position."

"That's very bad."

"We can't control Hitler right now."

"That's very bad as well—"

"But what we *can* do is stop giving him ammunition to rile up his audience. I want a head on a plate and I want it now! Arrest someone!"

"We tried that with Anton Gross, Herr Kommissar. It didn't work. We need to get the real culprit."

"So do it!"

"I'm trying. I keep running into distractions. And now Müller and Storf are out of commission."

"So pull in Kalmer and Messersmit."

"If I need to do so, I will. Sir, there are things I could do that might help the case . . . if I were allowed to do them."

Volker stopped pacing. "Tell me!"

"I'm trying to verify information—"

"Berg, what do you *have*?" Volker fired at him.

"Not much individually, sir, but when these little facts are strung together, patterns start to emerge."

Finally, Volker sat at his desk and clasped his hands in his lap. "Go on."

Berg remained standing because he hadn't been invited to sit down. "So far I'm tracking down a calling card given to Anna Gross. The name on the card is Robert Schick. Anna's chambermaid believed that this man had visited Anna Gross several times when her husband wasn't around. She also thinks that Schick is a Russian Kommunist. So I started looking for him.

"A day later Marlena Druer was found dead. Looking through her belongings, we found a letter signed by a man named Robert. We went to the address written on the stationery. A Robert Schick had once lived there, but no one was in the unit when we came."

"He had moved out."

"Yes. And he left no forwarding address."

"Continue."

"As we were leaving, an American journalist living across from Schick poked his head out of his room. He told us that the apartment we thought belonged to Schick was rented to a so-called English aristocrat named Robert Hurlbutt. The building wasn't a tenement, sir, but no real aristocrat would ever live in such a flat."

"Obviously, we have a *Hochstapler*."

"Yes, but not completely. Ulrich was looking up citizens' records before the riots broke out. He found a promising family. The man was an antique dealer by trade but was also a minor attaché for the Russian diplomatic corps. His name was Dirk Schick, and he was married to a woman named Della Weiss who was born in Boston. They had one son named Rupert—"

"Aha!" Volker interrupted. "This is the man. Bring him in!"

Berg stared at him in disbelief. "I would bring him in, Kommissar, if I could find him. It would help if I could sift through the records without being pestered by civil servants. It might give me a clue to his current place of residence."

"They wouldn't be civil servants if they didn't pester you. Sit down, Berg. You're making me strain my neck to look up."

Berg sat.

Volker said, "How is Rupert Schick tied in to the Mayrhofer mother and daughter?"

Here Berg paused. "I don't know if he is. I haven't spoken to the family yet." He checked his pocket watch. It was close to eight. "I have several things I need to investigate. I'd like to go over to the crime scene and look for any leftover evidence before the ground is completely destroyed by pedestrians. Afterward, I could go over and talk to the victim's sister. It would be nice to find out if there is a connection between her and Schick."

"All right." Volker started patting his coat pocket. "Look over the crime scene, then speak with the family. I want you to find out as much as you can about the victims, especially the mother. I want to know the woman's friends, her enemies, her habits . . . everything about her. See if you can find a connection between the latest murders and the earlier ones."

"I will do my best."

"I don't care about your *best*! I want results! These

latest ones may be chance murders, you know, not at all connected to the earlier ones. The victims were murdered in daylight and were slain by bludgeoning, not by strangulation. It doesn't appear that Frau Mayrhofer was a woman of means, and this time the fiend attacked and killed a child."

"Regina Gottlieb wasn't a woman of means, either."

"But she was dressed in finery. Did you see Edith's frock?"

"Yes, sir."

"Rather plain in comparison."

"The sensible brown wool dress."

"Exactly my point, Axel. It was hardly silk and lace."

"One of her boots was gone. A missing article of apparel is consistent with the other murdered victims."

"Yes, but some other lunatic could be copying the first murders."

"How would he know about the missing shoe?"

"Because there are always idiots in the department who talk too much. How many confessions have we gotten so far for these crimes?"

"Four."

"Who investigated the claims?"

"I believe Kalmer and Messersmit. The claims were investigated and proved to be false."

"What did I tell you? The world is filled with lunatics. Somehow they all end up in Munich." Volker took out a tin of Grathmohl cigarettes, lit two, and offered one to his Inspektor. Berg wondered what had happened to the Kommissar's custom-made sterling silver cigarette case with the hand-rolled smokes. Perhaps Volker was annoyed with him and felt that he didn't merit such a luxury.

"Danke." Berg inhaled deeply.

"Bitte." Volker coughed. "While you're looking over the crime scene and talking to the family, I will try to clear you with Records. Although the clerks won't take kindly to your prying. So be it. We need to find this *bastard*!"

"Thank you, sir."

"You damn well should thank me." Volker exhaled a plume of smoke and rolled his eyes. "Working around the German bureaucracy is worse than the trenches."

Berg smiled.

"I'm serious!" Volker stated. "Now leave before my overwhelming desire to shoot someone is taken out on you."

Berg dropped the grin. Volker was serious about that as well.

FORTY-TWO

✠ The patch of death looked as ordinary as its surroundings, bare and stark and covered with the brown detritus of wet, decomposed leaves. The sycamores were beginning to green, and the tender shoots of crocuses poked through the ground. Officially, spring was still several weeks away, but nature ran on its own calendar.

This particular copse was off the footpath that hugged the Kleinhesseloher See at the northern end of the Englischer Garten. The wide and beautiful lake, constructed more than a century ago, was calm and majestic, filled with squawking ducks and honking geese. When the Great Inflation hit and food was scarce, poaching was common. Additional security was introduced to protect the ducks. That was years ago and since food was obtainable now, the police had been scaled back. This was a good reflection on Munich—honesty had been restored to the city— but unfortunate for Edith and little Johanna. More policemen in the park might have saved their lives.

"We found them here, Inspektor." Berg turned to the spot. The voice belonged to Leopold Hoss, a short and slight man who had served in Munich's police department for nearly twenty years. His face was round, as were his brown eyes. His upper lip, though very thin, was visible because his mustache wasn't much thicker than a line of charcoal. His unprepossessing stature had probably held him back from advancement. "The little girl was buried under leaves, but there was no attempt to hide the mother."

Maybe it was as Gebhardt suggested, that the little girl wasn't the target, and the burial was an attempt to rectify the horrendous act. Though far from consoling, it was better than thinking that the murderer had taken pleasure in shedding the blood of a child. Berg stared at the spot, at the impression left by the mother's body. "Was the woman faceup or facedown?"

"Faceup with her hair fanned about her." Berg's eyes looked up from the crime scene and focused in on Hoss. The policeman added, "It seemed odd to me . . . that someone would fan her hair like that . . . especially in daylight. Smoothing it out like that had to have taken time."

In his head Berg heard Herr Professor Kolb's voice: *An act of boldness and arrogance as well as an act of Freudian compulsion. The murderer had to create his artwork even if it was extremely dangerous for him to do so.*

Out loud Berg said, "As if her face was being framed for a picture?"

"Exactly." The policeman's upper lip twitched, sending the mustache into an undulating motion. "As if she was positioned to look like she was . . . sunbathing almost. Not in this weather of course . . . and not where she was." He fidgeted nervously. "The bash on her skull wasn't noticeable."

Hair flowing around the face . . . just as it had been in the cases of Anna Gross and Marlena Druer. But not like Regina Gottlieb. Or maybe Regina's hair had indeed been fanned around her face but Messersmit and Kalmer had failed to note it in the case file. Berg thought a moment. In the postmortem pictures, Regina was facedown. "Was her head resting in a pool of blood?"

Hoss shuddered, still clearly disturbed by the images. He wasn't the only one with nightmares. "Yes, there was blood . . . quite a bit of it. Though much had seeped into the ground, I think."

"She was clothed?"

"Yes. Both of them were clothed. I don't know what the pathology doctor has revealed, but there was nothing to suggest that the woman had been violated. She seemed to blend in with the ground."

"Maybe that's why it took some time for anyone to notice her. You say that she was fully clothed?"

"Yes, sir."

"And does that include shoes as well?"

Hoss fidgeted again, rubbing the palms of his gloved hands against each other. "Boots, actually. There was only one boot. The other foot was bare. We looked for the missing boot, but we couldn't find it anywhere in the vicinity. And we raked up quite a bit of ground searching for it . . . as you can tell." Berg regarded the nearby thickets filled with piles of dead leaves. The exposed ground was bare, hard, and cold. Hoss cleared his throat. "I was told that with the others, footwear was missing—a stocking or a shoe. This seems to indicate the same man, I think."

"Who told you about the missing shoe?"

Hoss averted his gaze in response to Berg's harsh tone. "I don't remember, Herr Inspektor. Only that it is a common rumor that is circulating."

This valuable information was supposed to have been kept quiet. Volker had been correct in his assessment of the department. It was a small, provincial town, filled with gossip, innuendos, and rumors. Berg cleared his throat, trying to dislodge aggravation from his voice. "What about the little girl? Was her shoe missing as well?"

The policeman checked his notes. "I do not have any remarks concerning the little girl's shoes. I think that means that she was found with both shoes."

"But you are not certain?" Berg emphasized.

"No, Herr Inspektor, I am not certain."

Berg made a note in his pad to recheck the victims' articles of clothing. He also jotted down a reminder to look at the crime-scene photographs in detail. The pictures should be developed later this afternoon—if he was lucky. Most likely, they'd be done by tomorrow. "Underneath the piles of leaves, the area was checked for any articles left behind?"

"Several times."

"And you found nothing other than the bodies?"

"No . . . yes . . . I mean we didn't find anything, Herr Inspektor. Nothing that . . ." He swallowed hard. "When she was removed . . . where her head was . . . there was lots of blood. Also, there were bits . . . chunks of tissue."

The poor policeman looked ill. Berg said, "It was probably brain tissue."

"I think so, Herr Inspektor. The poor woman was hit very hard."

✠ ✠ ✠

"COMPLETELY NONPRODUCTIVE, the interview was," Berg said to Müller. "According to Edith Mayrhofer's relatives, the poor woman didn't have an enemy in the world."

"Dead people are all saints, don't you know?" Müller answered.

"Edith was different from the other victims, Georg. She was a solid workingwoman—pure Bavarian from both sets of grandparents. She was not violated, nor was she strangled. She wasn't Jewish, she wasn't a Kommunist, nor had she ever flirted with Kommunismus. She wasn't bohemian or a Kosmopolit. According to her family, she wasn't even political."

"That is the first lie, Axel. No one in Munich is apolitical."

"She didn't seem to have any strong political ties, Georg, which makes her very different from Anna or Marlena. And she was murdered in full daylight, unlike the others. She and her poor little girl!"

"Dreadful. Our murderer has become emboldened because he keeps getting away with more and more outrageous behavior."

Again Berg heard his thought recited in Kolb's voice: *Killing has taken the place of sex. He will need more and more excitement to become stimulated.* "*If* the slayings were all done by the same hand."

"The shoe, Axel."

"Ah, yes, the shoe." Berg shrugged. "While it is true that we haven't made that information public, there are lots of people who know about the shoe."

"Who, for instance?"

"Just about everyone in the police department."

"That's not lots of people."

"It is if they talk to their wives and girlfriends who are, without a doubt, pressing them for all the information they have." Berg stared at the ceiling. "You know, Georg, we haven't even considered another distasteful possibility."

"What do you mean?"

"It could be one of us, you know—someone in the department."

Abruptly, Müller tried to sit up, then grimaced in pain. His left leg was still elevated, though he was no longer in traction. "*Bist du verrückt?* Who said that?"

"No one." Berg regarded his friend. Müller's face was more swollen and purple than it had been yesterday, a sign that the healing had begun, although he looked far worse because of it. "Just a thought."

"Axel, you can't seriously think it's one of our own."

"A crime done in daylight, Georg. An ordinary person might be noticed rummaging around in the bushes. But a policeman? When people see a uniform, they look away."

"I can't believe that. I *refuse* to believe that."

"Georg, this was done by someone very powerful and very arrogant. Who is more powerful and arrogant than someone in the department, someone who is used to controlling people, someone who has had experience with firearms, someone who has *access* to firearms, which are still illegal for the private citizen to own."

"We fought a war, Axel. Do you know how many men have a Luger or a bayonet hidden in their closet?"

"Lots."

"Yes, lots," Müller said. "Anyway, I can think of ten

people who have that kind of arrogance and who aren't policeman. Adolf Hitler for starters."

"So maybe it's Hitler," Berg suggested.

Müller laughed. "Axel, even a radical Kommunist like Gerhart Leit would have no problem identifying Hitler."

Berg frowned at Müller's logic. The man who had gone to the theater with Anna Gross clearly wasn't Hitler.

"The sacrificial lamb," Berg said.

"What?"

"Never mind." Berg ran his hands down his face as if he were washing it.

Müller said, "Axel, we have a picture from Leit, and we have an identification of that picture—a Russian named Rom or Roman, as in Romanov. Furthermore, we have the name Robert Schick, who was a Kommunist, from one of Anna Gross's calling cards. We have the name Robert on a letter that was in Druer's possession— also a Kommunist—"

"*Supposedly* a Kommunist," Berg broke in. "Supposedly he was also an aristocrat. What he is, though, is a *Hochstapler,* a fake."

"Even so, Axel, he exists. Rupert Schick comes from a family where the father was an attaché to Russia. My good friend, *if* you find a Russian in the police department named Robert or Roman or Rupert who matches Leit's sketch and who speaks English fluently, then you can start making accusations."

Berg rolled his eyes. "I'm not saying it is one of our own, just that it was done by someone with arrogance and power. Someone like Volker."

"*Herrjemine,* Axel, here you go again."

"Georg, we're not looking at this the correct way. We're missing something."

"I agree with that, but throwing out preposterous suggestions about Hitler or Volker isn't going to get us closer to the culprit."

"We need to think in a different direction, Georg."

"I disagree, *Kamerad*. Don't get distracted. Work with what we have. Find Rupert Schick."

Berg contained his irritation. "Any suggestion on how to do that?"

Müller closed his eyes. "I have no suggestions. My mind is blank, Herr Inspektor. Even laid up as I am, I think I have it easier than you do right now."

Berg chastised himself. He was taxing Georg's strength. "You must rest, my friend. You look very pale."

"I am tired," he admitted. "Where are you going after you leave here?"

"I'm going to try to visit Ulrich."

"I've heard he's improving, thanks be to God."

"Thanks be to God. Afterward, if Volker cleared me with the bureaucrats in Records, I will try to find out more about the family Schick."

"Good luck."

"*Danke.*" Berg patted his friend on the shoulder. "I will see you tonight, if time permits."

"More like if *Karen* permits."

"Ah." Berg smiled. "Your wife doesn't like my presence?"

"Right now, my wife is not fond of anyone in a uniform—policemen, doctors, nurses, bureaucrats, streetcar conductors, *U-Bahn* workers, bakery ladies wearing cotton aprons, butchers wearing leather aprons, waiters in restaurants, and, finally, anyone associated with an army or a political party."

Berg laughed. "That's all of Munich."

"Indeed. Karen is quite the misanthrope these days."

✠ ✠ ✠

FROM BEHIND THE WINDOW, Berg peered inside the isolation chamber at Ulrich resting inside an iron lung, his body wrapped in bandages that seemed to run head to toe. The surgeon had said that he was making remarkable strides—much better than expected. His other lung was beginning to pick up the slack for the injured one, and his breathing had improved. With time, luck, and God's help, the injured lung would inflate within a week.

Berg would just have to take the doctor's word because from his perspective, things didn't look good.

He thought for a moment, musings rather than ideas. Perspective was a mutable thing. Perspective changed radically when viewed from different angles. Looking at his injured friend, Berg decided that that was what he needed.

He needed perspective.

He needed a different angle.

FORTY-THREE

✠ Walking down the long hospital corridors, Berg considered Georg's simple words: Find Rupert Schick.

Whoever he was, Schick was *not* going to be found in this current incarnation. The name hadn't appeared on any of the city registries or in the registries of neighboring Bavarian towns. The only things Berg was going on were the name and the sketch. He kept thinking, What if Leit hadn't gotten it quite right? The sketch was vague enough to resemble a multitude of people: What if Berg was looking for the wrong man?

He hobbled down three flights of stairs, his hip improving with every day that passed. Outside it was a brisk but pleasant spring afternoon; the azure heavens mixed with fluffy cotton clouds, the sky paying respects to the state colors of Bavaria. He could have taken the streetcar, but the Hall of Records was just a ten-minute walk from the hospital. The stroll would give him time to think.

Who was masquerading as Rupert Schick and why?

Berg started from the beginning: Gerhart Leit.

Leit had given him the description of the man whom Anna Gross had been with. Maybe he had murdered Anna and was misleading Berg on purpose. Although Leit was thin and slight, certainly his hands were strong enough to tighten a stocking around Anna's neck. But why would he murder Anna? In all his inquiries, Berg had learned nothing to suggest that Leit had been involved. Although Leit was not completely dismissed as a suspect, Berg placed him near the bottom of his list.

He assumed Leit had been truthful, that the man with Anna Gross had been tall, had been dressed up to look like an aristocrat with a monocle and top hat, and had looked something like Putzi Hanfstaengl.

Berg considered Putzi Hanfstaengl.

The art dealer was certainly arrogant enough to have a mistress and boldly parade her around the theaters. He spoke English fluently. The American reporter Green had identified the man in the sketch as Lord Robert Hurlbutt and said that Hurlbutt was a well-known name at Harvard. Putzi went to Harvard and, like the elusive Schick, had an American mother. What if Putzi had met real aristocrats at Harvard? What if the piano player had decided to lead a secret life as a lord, sneaking out with mistresses, then murdering them when they caught on to his imposture?

But Hanfstaengl was more than just plain tall. He was very, *very* tall—and very, very recognizable. Even in disguise, he would have been noticed by *someone*. Berg conceded that Putzi wasn't a strong possibility, definitely not at the top of the list.

Anders Johannsen.

He had found not just one but *two* of the victims. He was tall and blond, and from a certain perspective could have resembled the man in the sketch. His little lapdog wore a gold necklace as a collar, and both Marlena Druer and Regina Gottlieb had been strangled with a chain. Moreover, there was something implausible about his life story: the absent father who hated him, the bohemian mother who died when he was very young, his independence at fourteen.

Berg took off his gloves and looked up at the sky. The sun was dancing through the clouds, and he walked in nature's spotlight, snagging the occasional bit of warmth on his face. Ideas were coming, faster and faster now.

In every lie there was usually a kernel of truth. What if Johannsen had been abandoned by his bohemian mother? Abandonment was certainly a reason to harbor resentment. Kolb was convinced that the fiendish murderer loathed his mother. Perhaps Johannsen also detested his mother. But was his hatred strong enough to propel him to murder *innocent* women?

Johannsen, like Putzi, was involved in the art world. The victims, except for the little girl, had been found in posed positions. Since Johannsen said that he had discovered his mother's body, Berg began to wonder how she was positioned at the time of her demise. Was her hair framing her face? Did she have on only one shoe? Was this Johannsen's deviant way of re-creating his mother's death?

By his own admission, Johannsen's English was serviceable. Did he also speak Russian? Could he have been the suave, sophisticated (albeit phony) aristocrat that the reporter Green had described?

Berg moved the Dane toward the top of his list.

Last was Berg's favorite suspect, Rolf Schoennacht.

The most recent murders had been the height of arrogance, and Schoennacht was as arrogant as they come. Schoennacht seemed brutal enough to be a killer. He was also tall and sophisticated and, under the right conditions, could have passed as the man in the sketch. His baldness meant nothing; toupees were readily available. Anyway, hadn't Leit said that the man had worn a top hat? Plus Schoennacht's initials were RS, the same as Rupert Schick's, and their ages roughly matched. Lastly, Schoennacht had a direct connection to Regina Gottlieb.

Ro as in *Rolf*.

But Schoennacht had been out of town when the last homicides occurred; Berg's men had watched him go into the train station. Still, it was possible that Schoennacht then changed his mind, deciding at the last minute to attend Hitler's rally.

Berg stopped walking. His brain was working faster than he could process the ideas. Hadn't there been a member of Hitler's Elite walking toward the stage who looked like Rolf Schoennacht?

Yes, Schoennacht definitely belonged at the top of Berg's list.

Johannsen, Schoennacht, and Hanfstaengl: all of them about the same age, all of them tall, and all of them art dealers. Berg thought about the framing of the victims by their hair: a perfect background for the portrait. Actually, corpses would be ideal models for any painter because once positioned, they never moved.

Maybe those hapless slain women were some kind of perverse collective art project. The killings had similarities but were not identical because there were multiple slayers . . . each *artist* had created his own interpretation of the same subject. God only knew how many secret societies Germany had birthed.

A cabal of *Lustmord*. Born in the trenches of the Great War, at a time when murder and duty were intertwined, when rape of the vanquished was common and blood flowed copiously in the Marne, *Lustmord* took that jump from the battlefield to civilian life, nourished by the avant-garde. How chic and current it was to express sexual murder as an artistic theme in paintings, literature, the stage, film, and photography.

Johannsen, Schoennacht, and Hanfstaengl.

They were a perfectly matched trio in a way—tall, urbane, sophisticated in the latest trends, dealers in modern art. The big difference was in their politics. Schoennacht and Hanfstaengl were ardent supporters of the NSDAP, whereas Johannsen scorned the Austrian.

And what about the Austrian?

If Berg was looking for an arrogant man, Hitler and his putsch embodied haughtiness. Because of his hubris, he had landed in jail. Though the Austrian had been temporarily constrained, he was hardly broken. Even locked up in jail, Hitler had flourished, aided by a cadre of constant supporters. Berg had to think back no further than a few days ago. The lunatic's rally drew in one hundred thousand cheering Germans. The Austrian had more than enough dedicated acolytes for an entire army.

There were also rumors that Hitler was a bastard, that his father had not died but had deserted his mother at the time of Adolf's birth. Even though the Austrian's stepfather had adopted him and given him his name, there was an underlying stigma associated with Hitler's origins. Such gossip was bound to scar a child, was bound to cause resentment between his mother and him.

But would such a stigma have fostered murderous hatred? And *why* would the Austrian ruin everything he had worked so hard to rebuild by murdering innocent women . . . and a *child* as well?

Johannsen, Schoennacht, and Hanfstaengl—all of them dedicated to *art*.

Hitler, too, because the Austrian had once had hopes of becoming a professional artist. He had even applied to the Academy. His dream was quickly squashed when he was denied entrance to the school. The professors said his work was trite and dull, unoriginal and uninteresting. He was simply *not good enough*.

All of this was true, in Berg's opinion. The Austrian's art was sophomoric and overly sentimental and didn't have an interesting thing to say about the human condition. Berg's own art wasn't much better, but he knew his limitations so he never had the aspirations.

But Hitler was different. He had had expectations—but surely such disappointment would not lead a sane man to murder.

Was Hitler sane?

A bastard child, a man of arrogance, a man who thought he had been given a special gift, only to be judged mediocre or worse. Perhaps the Austrian was out to prove the critics wrong in a very dramatic way.

✠   ✠   ✠

STATE REGISTRIES were housed in a three-story stone structure adorned by a set of Doric columns that flanked a dozen steps leading to carved walnut double doors. Inside, Berg rang the bell. A moment later, a desk clerk appeared—a round, red-faced Bavarian *Beamter*. After a brief exchange of words and a bit of paper shuffling, Berg passed official clearance in a remarkably short time. Finally, Volker had made good on his promise.

Escorted up to the fourth floor, Berg climbed the central staircase fashioned from black walnut, the railing glossy and smooth underneath his hand. The worn jade-colored marble tiles echoed under his footsteps as he walked down a white hallway, passing doors on either side of the foyer. The clerk opened one of the portals and motioned Berg inside. Then he excused himself and shut the door.

Berg took off his police cap, held it to his chest, and looked around. The room was impressive with its vaulted ceilings and big picture windows. It was also crypt cold and drafty. Despite the hiss of hot steam from a clanging radiator, he shivered. The furniture had been kept to a minimum: a long wooden table surrounded by ten wooden chairs. Electric bulbs on wires hung from above, casting amber light. Bookshelves lined one side of the room; the wall opposite the bookshelves held portraits of nameless politicians wearing expressions as stiff as the white collars encircling their necks. Two flagpoles held dual identities: the yellow, black, and red banner of Deutschland, and the blue and white flag of Bavaria. Despite the talk of a united Germany, allegiances changed as often as the direction of the wind.

The door opened, and an attractive, curvaceous redhead laid a stack of folders on the table. Her emerald eyes took in Berg's face; she was clearly displeased by what she saw. "Where's the other one?"

"Inspektor Storf?" Her response to his question was a shrug. "He's in the hospital."

The emeralds widened. She brought her hand to her mouth. "Is he all right?"

"He was beaten up in the riots."

She blinked several times. "That's terrible!"

"Terrible things happen when thugs take over."

"Where were the police to protect him?"

"Fighting for their own lives. Unfortunately there were more thugs than there were policemen."

Her hand still covered her mouth. "Can I visit him?"

Berg nodded. "It can be arranged." She was still staring at him. "When he is able to receive company, I will tell him that I saw you, that you were most helpful with the records regarding the Schick family." He pointed to the papers on the table. "Those are the records, yes?"

She nodded as her eyes started to moisten. "It isn't bad enough that we lose our men to foreigners on foreign soil? Now our own are fighting one another? It is insane."

"You have summed up the situation very succinctly." He took out his pencil and a notepad. "Again, thank you for your help."

"Is there anything else you require?"

"An ashtray perhaps."

"There's no smoking in here."

Berg stowed his cigarette tin back in his jacket. "Then I suppose I'm fine."

Without another word, she turned and slowly walked away, giving him a full view of her swinging hips and tight derriere. For a moment he contemplated calling aloud and asking for tea, a distraction to keep her in his presence. But then the urge along with the moment passed, evaporating like so many of his other missed opportunities.

✠ ✠ ✠

THREE HOURS OF READING brought more disappointment than revelation, but the registries did provide Berg with a timetable for Dirk Schick's ten-year sojourn in Munich. Schick appeared to have arrived in the midnineties. A year later, he met and married an American woman named Della Weiss. Eight months passed, and they were blessed with a son whom they christened Rupert.

The family was called back to Russia in 1905, a month after Bloody Sunday, the fateful clash between the Czar's army and the demonstrators at Saint Petersburg. Bloody Sunday was always touted by politicians as the reason why police should refrain from discharging firearms unless absolutely necessary. Hitler's thuggery two days ago was apparently not sufficient to warrant "absolutely necessary." If Ulrich had used a gun, he would have been cited and stripped of his duties.

As far as Berg could tell, the Schick family had never returned to Munich again. From all indications, Rupert had grown up in Soviet Russia as a Soviet citizen. While it was clear that the child spoke Russian, he'd also had the opportunity to learn German while living in Munich. Since the Schick name indicated German ancestry, father and son might have communicated in German, a paternal hope to keep the mother tongue alive. It was equally logical that the American woman, Della Weiss, taught her son some English.

Who was Rupert Schick, and where was he now?

Nothing in the records disclosed those crucial bits of information, but time spent going through Schick's official papers offered some reward. The registries produced three addresses. Two appeared to be business addresses in business districts, but one was an apartment number bordering the Schwabinger Bach—a small brook of runoff water from the Isar that cut through the Englischer Garten and ran along its western edge. This particular address was at the northern end of the park past the Kleinhesseloher See.

Maybe Rupert Schick was coming home to roost, taking care of some demented unfinished business by murdering women in the park. Just as important, maybe someone remembered Dirk and Della Schick from nearly a quarter century ago, before the family had disappeared from archival records.

FORTY-FOUR

✠ The area along the Schwabinger Bach had always been the Venice of Berg's imagination. The canal was bordered by the park on the east while graceful homes and apartment buildings lined the western side. All it lacked was a gondolier pushing a boat with a pole. Berg had been to Italy twice, but had never made it to the city. Life was long, he told himself. One day . . .

The water level was high from the recent rains, with only about two meters of concrete embankment exposed. The address he had written down corresponded to a yellow four-story structure covered by spiderwebs of leafless vines. Sprouting from the red tiled roof were a pair of symmetrically placed gables and chimneys. Inside the lobby Berg regarded a bank of mailboxes on his left; the stairs were directly in front of him.

According to the registry, the Schicks had sojourned in Apartment 7. Now the apartment belonged to the Beckmanns. When Berg knocked on the door, a little girl of six or seven answered, staring at him with bright brown eyes while fingering two straw-colored braids. She was attired in the traditional dirndl. Frau Beckmann followed seconds later—an older, less attractive version of the child—and yanked the girl back into the safety of her domicile.

"How many times do I have to tell you not to answer

the door?" The little girl's face scrunched as tears streamed down her cheeks. "No tears, Birgitta. If you are a good girl and wait quietly for Mama inside your room, I will give you a cookie."

"Chocolate?" Birgitta wiped her tears.

"Almond. But only if you go now."

The child disappeared. The woman looked at Berg, her eyes moving up and down his uniform. *"Grüss Gott."*

"Guten Tag. Inspektor Axel Berg of the Munich Police Department. I am looking for Frau Beckmann."

"You are an Inspektor?" Suddenly the woman turned white. *"Mein Gott!* What has happened now?"

"Nothing at all, Frau Beckmann, I assure you that all is in order." He waited for the woman to catch her breath. On a second look, she was actually quite pretty even with the wrinkles. "You are Frau Beckmann?"

"Yes." A deep exhalation. "What can I do for you, Inspektor?"

"Actually, I am interested in a family that lived here about twenty-five years ago—"

"We've only been living here three years," she interrupted. "I'm sorry but I can't help you."

She started to close the door in his face, but Berg was quick with his foot.

"On the contrary, I'm sure you can help me."

"I don't see how!" Her daughter cried out. "I must go—"

"I am looking for someone who might remember them." Berg had wedged his body across the threshold. "The name was Schick."

The woman looked blank. "I tell you I've only lived

here for three years. Why are you bothering me? Go bother the Nazis who throw eggs at the building."

"I will make a note to have a policeman check out the vandalism."

The woman's face was skeptical. "May I go now?"

"It would be cumbersome for me to knock on everyone's door, Frau Beckmann. Perhaps you know who has lived in the building longest?"

"Try Apartment 11." Her mouth turned down as she sneered. "Oskar Krieger. That lecherous old coot has been here forever."

✠ ✠ ✠

THE MAN APPEARED to be in his seventies, as thin as a spire with a shock of white hair that fell over his forehead. His complexion showed his age: a mottled palette of liver spots and orange freckles. But his eyes were as clear and lucid as any that Berg had ever seen. They were deep brown with a hint of a twinkle.

Berg introduced himself officially. "I am looking for Herr Krieger."

"Then you have found him. Are you going to arrest me?"

"Arrest you?" Berg held back a smile. "But what have you done?"

"Nothing at all, but that has never stopped the police before." He laughed loudly, then opened the door with a dramatic flourish. "Come in, come in. No sense talking out here for all the neighbors to see. That just invites gossip. Not that these old hags need a reason to gossip."

Berg went inside. The apartment reeked of cigarette ash, not surprising since piles of butts littered the room. In a single moment, Berg counted seven ashtrays. Despite the odor of stale smoke, the room was comfortable. A large plate-glass window provided a lovely view of the park, giving the place an expansive feel despite its cozy size. The walls were hidden by paintings hung wherever there was space, and by shelves holding hundreds of books. There seemed to be no unifying theme in the collection, just book after book spilling out of the units, heaped up on the sofa, and stacked on the floor. The artwork was varied as well, from classical portraits to multi-colored Cubist and Expressionist canvases. If Berg looked hard enough, he could discern representational objects, however abstract: a green face, a purple dog, a deconstructed orange and blue cello.

"Yours?" Berg asked.

"That so-called Cubist one, yes."

"It's very good."

"Actually it's dreadful," the old man said. "I did it twenty years ago and keep it up to remind me of my limitations. Humility is good. The traditional art is my father's work."

Berg's brain suddenly sparked. "Lukas Krieger?"

The old man shrugged.

"Ah, Oskar Krieger." Berg hit his forehead. "The poet."

"Poet, playwright, author . . . I am called all three and still cannot pay my bills. I sell off my father's paintings one by one. Thank God he was prolific; otherwise I would be languishing in debtors' jail."

"Your father and Lenbach . . . they were in competition for the longest time, no?"

" 'Competition' isn't quite the right word."

"Rivalry?"

"More like utter hatred." Krieger laughed and took out a cigarette from a case. "How does a policeman know so much about art and poetry?"

"It is a personal interest of mine."

"You are in the wrong job, my man."

"As you said, it pays the bills."

"Right you are." He offered Berg a lit cigarette. "Sit down. I will boil water for tea."

"You needn't go to any trouble."

"Nonsense, I was about to take tea myself." He disappeared into the kitchen and came back several minutes later. He had smoked his cigarette down to the butt and was in the process of lighting up another one. "My father . . ." Krieger began as he blew out smoke. "He abhorred the way the Academy was going—or not going—and of course, blamed it all on Lenbach. Papa was a Frenchman at heart. He was great friends with all the painters of light—Renoir, Monet, Degas, Seurat, Pissarro."

"Did you grow up in France?"

"No, not at all. Papa's behavior was incompatible with marriage, you see, too much interest in too many women. Mama and I were left to fester with resentment in Berlin. Then the Franco-Prussian war broke out. The Prussians considered my father French, and the French considered him German. He fled to Switzerland where he alternated between being French and being German, depending on what was expedient."

Krieger broke into unrestrained laughter.

"I was drafted and fought for Prussia. The ignominy of it all . . . I was captured by the French . . . probably one of the only prisoners they got. They left me to rot in one of their miserable dungeons in the Bastille. My diet consisted of rotten turnips and infected water. I contracted cholera and almost died on two separate occasions. Somehow I survived. My father got word of my incarceration and managed to fabricate some official French seals and forge some papers. It was easy enough for him to do: He was a masterful artist, after all."

More laughter.

"Good old Papa. He rescued me under false pretenses hidden by the cloak of night. Of course, by that time the Prussians had thoroughly annihilated Louis-Napoléon's army. I was liberated and whisked back to Prussia."

"So what brought you to Munich?" Berg asked.

The teakettle whistled.

"One moment and I will tell you." He left and returned with a tray holding two glasses of bronze-colored tea, lemon slices, and sugar cubes. He placed the tray on the couch, then propped one of the sugar cubes between his teeth as he sipped tea through it. "Ah . . . the only thing that interrupts my smoking. Please sit."

Berg looked at the chair, the mountain of books that covered the seat.

"Just put them anywhere," Krieger said.

Berg put the tomes on the floor, picked up the glass of tea, and sipped the steaming liquid. Then he sat down. "Thank you. It feels good."

"Yes, it is chilly in here. I can't get the blasted radiator to work . . . it's either too hot or too cold. I think it's the draft that comes up from the Bach."

"It's a nice view."

"The view is lovely. The smell in the summertime is not. Ah well, Venice in the summer stinks as well." He took another healthy swig of tea. "What brought me to Munich? Well, my friend, that is a long and twisted tale with many stops along the way: Paris, Rome, Venice, Salzburg, Prague . . . oh, those Bohemian women. At the turn of the century, Munich was a vibrant and cultural city, at the forefront of art and literature, liberal in spirit and in population. In my mind, I came to Munich strictly as a stopover, but secretly I confess that I felt homesick. I missed my language and my culture. That stopover has lasted thirty-five years."

"What convinced you to stay here?"

"Circumstances. When the Great War broke out, I couldn't exactly go back to France. They did not look fondly on Germans." He grinned. "I didn't mind. All those poor young men being shipped off to Belgium. As an older gent, I was only too happy to offer solace and comfort to the hapless women left behind." He winked. "I was very discreet and very good, which made me popular among those who desired my company." He lit up a cigarette. "Ah, isn't it nice to be freed from tobacco rations."

Berg nodded. "You've been in Munich for thirty-five years?"

"I am ashamed to admit it, Herr Inspektor, but yes, I have been here for thirty-five years." Another sip of tea, another puff on the cigarette. "My father is, no doubt, turning over in his grave. He was most certain that I would wind up in Paris as he did. Of course, Paris is glorious, beautiful, a city beyond compare. I love Paris!" He leaned forward and whispered conspiratorially. "It's just the French I detest. Of course, one can hardly blame the French for hating the Germans . . . all the havoc we wreaked on their soil."

"Blame Schlieffen for that."

"Schlieffen created the plan, yes, but it took the German government to put it into action . . . thanks to those miserable Austrians for inveigling us into their domestic troubles. These times are especially disconcerting, since it appears that yet another Austrian is going to lead us into a big, black hole."

"I certainly hope not."

Krieger sighed, shaking his head. "I've lived a long time. I have a feeling about that man. Austria has always been the bane of our existence. Either their royalty is getting assassinated or they are exporting their maniacs to us. That's why the Austrian Freud invented the inferiority complex—he was speaking from direct experience." He regarded Berg. "You never did state why you are here."

"Have you lived in this apartment building for the last thirty-five years?"

"I have."

"Then perhaps you remember a family—their surname was Schick. They lived in 3B." When Krieger's eyes remained flat, Berg said, "I realize that this was a long time ago. They had a little boy named Rupert—"

"Ah, yes, yes, of course! Della, yes?"

Berg could barely hide his excitement. "Yes, Della . . ."

"A lovely woman."

When he turned silent, Berg said, "What else can you tell me about her?"

Krieger appeared deep in thought. "A very sad woman, Inspektor. Like a caged bird, not at all fit for the confines of hearth and home."

"In what way?"

The old man grew quiet, his eyes focusing on pictures taken long ago. "Well . . . I remember the little boy, yes? She'd often take him for a stroll in the buggy. Several times I would run into her at the park. There she was . . . sitting on a bench, weeping, her small shoulders heaving up and down. Of course, her crying caused the baby to cry. Often, she was so upset that she wouldn't even pick up the infant to comfort him. The poor woman had no one to talk to. Every once in a while, I'd invite her in for tea, but she wouldn't stay long. Her presence in my apartment would garner too much gossip. Not that the neighbors needed an excuse to dish out the dirt. They would never dare to confront her face-to-face with their accusations, but how they chirped behind her back."

"What did they say?"

He waved his hand in the air. "That she was American and had loose morals."

"Was it true?"

Krieger laughed. "Maybe yes, maybe no. It didn't really matter. The women were very provincial. They thought that all American girls were schemers, with their short hair and their flapper skirts and their moonshine. Their purpose in life was to attract a rich man to marry them so they could push around servants and smoke their cigarettes."

"Libertine."

"Exactly the way I like them!" Again the old man let go with riotous laughter. "And Josephine Baker dancing around in banana skins didn't dispel the image either. I saw her once . . . not here, of course. I went to Berlin. She had such lovely dark skin and such a beautiful big rear end. I do believe the German women were frightened of the *Niggerlippen*—as if a dusky complexion were catching. I wish it were so."

"Was Della a libertine?"

"I wouldn't know from direct experience. I was always the gentleman with her—no sense fouling your own nest. I will tell you this, Inspektor. She adored that little boy. He was very cute and very smart . . . with a head of tousled straw and quite tall." Krieger cleared his throat. "His appearance was . . . at odds with his father, who was dark and short. Which caused tongues to wag even more than when she first moved in."

"I see," Berg said.

Krieger smiled impishly. "I must say Della kept those hens cackling. They used to whisper the word because they were too embarrassed to say it out loud."

"What word was that? That the child was a bastard?"

"Worse than a bastard," Krieger said. "Della was *divorced*."

Berg licked his lips, feeling his heart pound against his chest. "Della Weiss had been married before?"

Another puff on the cigarette. Another smile. "Yes, she was a fallen woman."

"Do you know to whom?"

"Some prig that looked like he had a walking stick jammed up his arse! Nobody liked him. The neighbors would clack . . . you know, say things like 'Who could blame her for not wanting to live with him as husband and wife! But she didn't have to go to such extremes and get *divorced*!' And of course, when she remarried so quickly, it really started the rumors flying. Especially because the child was born only eight months after she married."

"Babies don't always come out according to plan. It happens."

"Yes, but then the baby is usually not four kilograms."

"So . . . she was carrying on before she married a second time."

"It appeared that way. And then when the child looked neither like her first husband nor like the second one, it was very, very scandalous. You must remember the times weren't quite so forgiving as they are now."

"I see."

"Despite it all, Herr Schick appeared to be very good to her—as best I can recall—and she was good to him. I think they had a good marriage. Rupert was a very cute little boy. I think he helped ease the pain of her first marriage. It was a terrible thing . . . what her ex-husband did."

"What did he do?"

"He bribed the doctor to testify that she was an unfit mother. Which she wasn't."

"Why would he care? Especially if the child wasn't his?"

"Oh, it wasn't Rupert he cared about. It was her other boy, her other son."

Berg felt his heartbeat quicken. "She had a son by her first husband?"

"Yes . . . I believe he was around ten when she remarried. I saw him only once, when a nanny brought him to visit her. I'm sure her husband wasn't aware of it. The child, like his mother, was such a sad little boy: a sad boy and a sad mother. What a pity."

"Do you remember the name of Della's first husband?"

The old man thought a moment. "No. Sorry."

Berg started with the least likely suspect. "Was it Leit? Or maybe Johannsen?"

A shrug. "I don't know if I ever knew her first husband's name. But I do remember the name of the little boy. Della introduced us. He was such a serious little gentleman. He's probably a stiff by now—like his father."

Berg tried to hide his nervousness. "What was his name, Herr Krieger?"

"Ah, yes. His name, he announced to me, was Rolf."

"Rolf Schoennacht?"

"Rolf Schoennacht? The *art* dealer?" Krieger appeared stunned. "*Herrjemine,* are you saying that the child was Rolf Schoennacht?"

It was Berg's turn to shrug.

"That would be amazing. Schoennacht specializes in modern art, does he not?"

"Yes, that is his concentration."

Krieger's eyes were filled with amazement. "Who would have thought such a stiff and sad little boy would turn out to be so progressive in his tastes?"

Berg smiled thinly. "His tastes may be progressive, Herr Krieger, but his thoughts are anything but. He's a fan of the Austrian."

"That's too bad, but not unexpected."

"What do you mean?"

Krieger shrugged. "That's what happens when one's denied maternal love. All of us men need that motherly tit. And when we don't get it, woe to the world. Lack of tit, my friend, is what turns men into monsters."

FORTY-FIVE

✠ Birth certificates were more easily accessible than address registries. Still, the wheels of bureaucracy ground slowly, requiring Berg to fill out another set of forms and wait for approval. It wasn't until the following morning that the curvaceous redhead located the requested birth certificate.

"How is your colleague?"

"I haven't stopped by the hospital this morning."

She studied his face. "Rough night?"

Berg's smile told her nothing. Sleep was a series of nightmares. After several hours of dealing with the devil, he finally gave up. Right now, coffee was stoking the engine. How long that would last was anyone's guess. He put a thermos down on the wood-scarred table. "I have my tea. I'm fine."

"It is verboten to drink in here, Herr Inspektor. You might spill on the documents."

Berg held back a sigh. "All right."

"I'll turn my back, Herr Inspektor." The redhead raised an eyebrow. "Just make sure I don't see anything."

After she left, Berg opened the folder. A single document stared back at his bleary eyes. Rolf Josef Schoennacht was born in March 1885, making him forty-five, consistent with the valet's assessment. His father was listed as

Gunnar Schoennacht; his mother was Della Weiss. Rolf was a full-term baby weighing just under four kilos and stretching over fifty centimeters. He came into existence at three-thirty in the afternoon.

Gunnar was fifty-two at the time of his son's entrance into the world; Della's date of birth put her at eighteen.

Berg stopped to reflect: fifty-two and eighteen.

Naughty, naughty.

Then he thought of Margot. Her death had been investigated and closed, the murder reported as a whore stealing from her pimp (the desk clerk) after stealing and murdering two of her customers (Hitler's thugs). It was easy enough to snow officials because nobody gave a damn about the victims. He rarely thought about Margot when he was awake, but obviously he was thinking of her now: He knew because he had broken out in a ripe, cold sweat.

If Della had been eighteen when the child was born, she was only seventeen when the boy was conceived. Oskar Krieger had described Gunnar Schoennacht as a stiff prig. Krieger had stated that even gossiping hens understood why Della Weiss couldn't live with that man as husband and wife. How could any eighteen-year-old be attracted to a stuffed shirt old enough to be her grandfather?

It was likely that the marriage had been arranged. Older men made good catches for young girls because they had prestige and money. Often the men were less demanding sexually. Sometimes they were widowers with children from a previous marriage. . . .

Had there been another wife before Della?

It took Berg a few minutes to locate the redhead. Her desk was at the end of the hallway. Her nameplate stated that she was Ilse Reinholt. She looked up, half-glasses sliding down her sharp-edged nose. "Finished?"

"I need more information, Fräulein Reinholt. Everything you have on a man named Gunnar Schoennacht, his birth certificate, marriage certificate or certificates—I think there may be more than one—and finally, his death certificate, if there is one."

She stood up. "I'll get you the necessary papers to fill out for the request." She started to leave but Berg held her arm.

"Is there any way that we could . . ."—he cleared his throat—"just . . . disregard this little bit of bureaucracy . . . just this once?"

Ilse was aghast. "That is impossible! The clerk will not give me what you ask for unless I have the proper forms."

Berg made a face. "Um . . . perhaps the clerk will go to lunch and you will have an opportunity to borrow the files?"

"He eats at his desk. We all do. It's very efficient."

"It is good to be efficient." Berg was still holding her arm. Lightly, though. She could have broken away if she had so desired. He smiled, boyishly. "He must use the toilet, Fräulein Reinholt."

Again she stared at him.

"This one time only, I swear. I can't afford to lose another day waiting for some clerk to rubber-stamp the endless forms that we must fill out before we blow our noses."

"You weren't born here, were you?"

"I'm from Westphalia."

"I don't mean Munich, I mean Germany. You weren't born in Germany."

Berg smiled. "I was born in Denmark, but my family moved to Münster when I was three."

"Doesn't matter," she said dismissively. "You are still a Dane."

"Some would consider that a compliment."

"And some do not." Her smile was slow. "You know, Herr Inspektor . . ." She rubbed her stomach. "I eat the same lunch day in and day out: sausage with mustard. Sometimes I eat it with potato salad, sometimes cabbage salad." She sighed. "I wonder what it's like eating lunch in one of those fancy restaurants in the old city."

As much as Berg wanted the information right away, he wasn't going to bankrupt himself to get it. Restaurants were for special occasions, not for some woman attempting to freeload a meal. "I wouldn't know, Fräulein Reinholt. Those establishments are way beyond a policeman's budget."

Ilse quickly reassessed her options. "Yes, I'm sure they are overpriced for what they serve. I'd be just as happy with a quick lunch at Das Kochelhaus."

"Well, you are in luck, Fräulein Reinholt. I am hungry myself. Perhaps you'd like to join me for lunch?"

"What a nice invitation, Inspektor." Her smile glowed like a gaslight. "Wait here. I'll get my coat and hat."

✠   ✠   ✠

SHE WAS HIS AGE, although she looked younger. Like scores of women in their thirties, she had had a fiancé, but he had come back from the war without a set of legs. A year later, he died of influenza. After that, she had lost her taste for love.

Certainly not her taste for food, Berg thought. She wolfed down a plate of schnitzel served with potato salad, beet salad, and two slices of rye bread. She washed her meal down with two pints of beer, then ordered some apple compote for dessert. By the time she had finished her meal and tale of woe, an hour had passed and it was time to get back to work. On the walk back to the *Stadthaus,* she asked about Storf. Berg's response was one of guarded optimism.

"I'd still like to visit him. When I was eighteen, I took special training and volunteered to go into the fields. But then my brother was lost in the first battle at Ypres and my family said no. I suppose the thought of their young daughter tramping up the Marne was too much for them to bear. There was enough work for me to do behind the lines."

Absently, Berg nodded.

"Your mind is elsewhere, Inspektor."

The sharpness of her tone made him focus. "I suspect it is, Fräulein Reinholt, and I apologize."

"What are you thinking about?"

"Work."

"And that is usually what you think about?"

"Thinking about work is preferable to thinking about the war."

✠　✠　✠

GUNNAR SCHOENNACHT had first married at forty-four. His bride, Lily, was twenty-five at the time of her nuptials. Ten months later, she pushed out what was to be the first of four children before her demise six years later. She had succumbed to puerperal fever—childbed fever—making Gunnar a widower with four small children at the age of fifty. Two years later, Della Weiss took over the role of wife and mother, bearing her own child eight months after the wedding.

How difficult that must have been! An eighteen-year-old American girl in a foreign land, trying to settle into a life of hearth and home with an old, no-nonsense Bavarian, saddled with the responsibilities of five children.

How had this happened to her?

Then, ten years later, she took the almost unheard-of action of divorcing, losing her son in the process. How desperate she must have been to break free of Gunnar's bonds.

Or maybe it had been Gunnar who had initiated the legal action.

Berg thought about Rolf Schoennacht, and about Julia, who was at least twenty years younger than he was.

Like father, like son.

Berg skimmed through Gunnar Schoennacht's divorce papers, through the court documents that gave him sole custody of Rolf, ten years old at the time of the divorce, twenty by the time Della left for Russia. At that age, he was old enough to make his own decisions. Berg wondered if he had tried to contact his mother before she left Munich. And what did any of this have to do with Rupert Schick and the murders?

Was Rolf assuming the identity of his younger half brother, the product of an adulterous union between his mother and Dirk Schick . . . or possibly even another man? Oskar Krieger had said that the boy didn't look at all like his father. Was Rolf acting out his fury at women because his own mother had been branded a fallen woman with loose morals?

Berg flipped through the last of the documents, then

stopped short. Staring back at him was a third marriage certificate.

Two years after divorcing Della Weiss, Gunnar Schoennacht had remarried. So Rolf had not only a mother considered a fallen woman to contend with, but also a stepmother. And unlike Gunnar's first set of children, he had no full-blooded brothers and sisters with whom to share his misery.

That could make a man very angry.

Gunnar, at the age of sixty-four, walking down the aisle a third time. There weren't any other marriage or divorce certificates after number three. Apparently, Gunnar stayed married to his bride until he died at the age of seventy-seven in 1910. No records of children from the final union; Gunnar either couldn't reproduce or had no desire to.

The third wife's name was Hannah. At the time of her marriage, she was thirty-two years old, probably a widow herself or an old maid. Suddenly, Berg gasped out loud, clutching the paper as he read the name over and over and over.

Hannah Schoennacht.

Hannah Schoennacht née Hannah *Weiss*.

Way too much a coincidence.

Della, Dirk, and Rupert Schick were long gone and buried in that vast ice cap known as the Soviet Union. A death certificate had been filed for Gunnar Schoennacht, but none was there for Hannah.

Hannah Weiss Schoennacht.

She'd be about sixty-five *if* Berg could find her.

That turned out to be the easy part. Her address was listed in the current city registry.

FORTY-SIX

The address was located just a few short blocks from Der Blumengarten rooming house, the last known living quarters of Marlena Druer. It was an area of old, shuttered tenements, of rutted streets and backwater. Hannah Schoennacht's building was the exception. Recently constructed of flat gray stone, the apartment complex had four stories with a peaked red roof and an arched entrance. Basic in design but the structure had indoor plumbing, gas lines for the kitchen, glass windows, and electricity.

The woman lived on the third floor. Her white hair was tied into a bun, and her cheeks were smooth and plump. She was compact, thick in the arms and neck. A short-sleeved plum wool dress curved around a generous bosom, a dense middle, and wide hips. Short legs were covered by black stockings, and on her feet were black rubber-soled walking shoes. With a forest-green shawl draped over her shoulders, she looked like an eggplant.

After Berg identified himself as a police Inspektor, she invited him inside. Her smile was wide, revealing tea-stained teeth. They may have been discolored, but they were all her own. The one feature that showed life's vicissitudes was milky eyes—hooded, red-rimmed, and tired. They said that her sixty-five years on earth had been long and hard.

The flat was warm, the windows revealing the city's steely sky. The furniture had seen better times. The sofa and chairs were faded and lumpy, but cheered by the multicolored crocheted afghans thrown over their backs. Doilies in all shapes and sizes abounded, concealing the torn upholstery and covering scarred tabletops. Mounted on the walls on either side of the couch was a set of double-decker light fixtures in which round white glass balls holding electric lightbulbs were on top, and candle-shaped gaslights ringed the bottom. Both were shining equally bright, indicating that the woman had converted the bottom set over to electricity. Hanging between the sconces was a sepia-tinted portrait—an old man in military dress standing next to a zaftig young bride with big eyes. It could have been father and daughter, but Berg knew better. A radio was perched in the corner of the room, leaking out snippets of static-laced polkas.

Without asking, Hannah had put on the kettle. It whistled almost immediately, and she brought in tea and cookies. Berg sat on the edge of a chair.

"Sugar? Milk?"

"A little milk if you have it."

"I do, and it's fresh."

Berg smiled. "I'm sure it is."

She poured him a glass and added a spot of milk. "I just went to the Viktualienmarkt this morning. I go every morning. It's not that I don't trust the icebox, but there's just no substitute for fresh. My husband, Herr Schoennacht, used to say that."

"He did, did he?"

"Every day. He loved his fresh seed roll and coffee." She paused a moment, then handed him the glass of hot tea. "He's passed on . . . my husband . . . but I still hear him talking to me. Sometimes it's as though he is right next to me."

"How long were you married?" Although he knew the answer, he had to make conversation.

"Thirteen years."

Berg had been married longer than that. "A long time. When did he pass on?"

"Almost twenty years ago."

"Your husband was Gunnar Schoennacht, correct?"

She regarded him with faraway eyes. "You knew him?"

"No, Frau Schoennacht, I didn't have the pleasure. But I have met your son, Rolf Schoennacht."

"Ah." A pause. "Rolf."

"Actually, he is your stepson, is he not?"

"No, he is my son. I legally adopted all of Herr Schoennacht's children."

She smiled at him, and he smiled back.

"Are there grandchildren?"

"Fourteen." Her eyes darkened. "I don't see the grandchildren that often. I saw them more when Herr Schoennacht was still with us. They loved to visit Opa. He loved them, too." Her voice became disapproving. "He used to spoil them rotten. Whenever the parents weren't looking, he would give the little ones candy. It was very surprising to me because he was a strict father."

"I suppose spoiling is the prerogative of a grandparent."

"Of a grandfather, at least." Said with a tinge of resentment. "I am and always will be the sensible and moderate one. I was less strict as a mother, but I wasn't nearly so indulgent as a grandmother. Of course, one must be flexible when raising adopted children."

Stronger resentment had crept into her voice. Berg said, "Do you see your children often?"

"As often as I can." Her smile was sad. "They are very busy these days."

"With the care of their children?"

"With everything, it seems."

"Rolf doesn't have children."

"Not yet. But his wife is young."

"Ah, that's true." Berg waited a moment. "Rolf travels a great deal, doesn't he?"

Hannah nodded.

"To The States."

Another nod.

"You were born in The States, were you not?"

"An odd question." This time she directed her eyes on Berg. "I suspect that you already know the answer."

He smiled broadly. "You caught me."

"I'm sharper than I look." She wagged a finger at him. "You are here for a certain purpose. What would you like to know, Inspektor?" She sipped tea and waited. As self-described, she was a sensible and moderate woman.

"I've actually come here to find out information about your sister, Della."

Hannah stared at him for what seemed to be a very long time. "I'm sorry, but I can't help you. I haven't spoken to my sister in twenty-two years."

"I see." Berg's head was spinning. What to do? "Were you close as children?"

"Not really, no."

Neither of them spoke. The silence lingered until Berg

broke it. "How long have you been out of contact with her?"

"Twenty-two years. I believe I'm repeating myself."

Think of something to say! "I know it must be difficult to talk about her."

She sipped tea, regarding him over the rim of her glass. "Why are you so interested in Della, Inspektor? The past is over and forgotten."

"Not for me, Frau Schoennacht, because I believe it has bearing on the present. How did you come to raise your sister's child as your own?"

"Rolf was not my sister's child, he was my husband's child. And someone had to step in after she abandoned him."

"But he would not allow her to see him."

"She abandoned Rolf a long time ago, Inspektor, when she wasn't true to her loving husband. Herr Schoennacht was devastated when he found out. He had been madly in love with her. He had tried so hard to please her. My sister was the beautiful one—beautiful on the outside, at least. She threw everything away."

"She was seventeen when she married. Raising four stepchildren when she was just a child herself must have been very hard."

"*Ach* . . ." Hannah waved her hand in the air. "She had servants, she had nannies, she had anything she wanted. Herr Schoennacht would have given her the world. He was madly in love with her."

Said a second time but without rancor. It was just a statement of fact. Berg repeated, "She was still very young."

"Young, yes. Also rash and stupid." Her voice lowered

until it was barely above a hush. "Herr Schoennacht saved my sister from a life of shame. Della was already in the family way when he married her."

"So he did the right thing and made an honest woman out of her."

"Did the right thing!" She practically spat. "You don't understand, Inspektor. Rolf wasn't even his child! Herr Schoennacht was an old friend of my father's and was visiting The States when it happened. Della had always looked up to him as a kindly uncle. When she found out about the baby, she was too scared to tell our parents, so she told him. He stepped in like a gallant knight . . . offered himself to her, sparing my sister wretched humiliation. They married just three weeks later. Herr Schoennacht moved her to Munich, hoping that a sensible life as a Bavarian wife and mother would change her ways. But it didn't."

"She continued to have a roving eye?"

"It was terrible." Hannah bit her lower lip. "Then . . . when it happened again, Herr Schoennacht was stunned."

"What happened?"

"What do you think?" Her hands patted her tummy.

"Ah . . . another child on the way."

"Another . . ." Again she started to whisper. "Another *bastard*!" Her eyes moistened. "Gunnar had wanted to have children with her, but she always claimed she had enough babies raising his children. Of course, he wouldn't argue with her. She was the pretty one!"

Berg recognized the family pattern. Hannah was the older, homelier, sensible sister; Della was the beautiful and wild young thing. He had some empathy for her, but more for Della. Berg had always been the favorite son.

"What happened when Herr Schoennacht found out she was pregnant?"

Tears rolled down her cheeks. "He was just devastated."

"How did he know it wasn't his child?"

"It happened when he was on a long business trip. Even so, he still took care of her."

"What do you mean?"

"He made arrangements for her to . . ." She lowered her gaze. "A righteous Catholic man . . . and still he made the arrangements for her! Because that's what she wanted. Do you know how *hard* that must have been for him?"

"Terrible—"

"Disgusting!" she broke in.

Berg nodded. "But she decided to have the baby anyway."

"No. In the end, she decided to get rid of it, even after Herr Schoennacht offered to raise it as his own!"

Now Berg was confused. "She got rid of it?"

"They claimed the child died at birth. I have my doubts."

"What do you mean?"

"I think she gave it up for adoption and told people it died." She wrinkled her nose. "Of course, I have no proof."

Berg scratched his head. "If that baby died or was given up, who was Rupert?"

Hannah let out a bitter laugh. "That was the second time, Inspector, after Della freed herself from the first. Herr Schoennacht was sure that such a trauma would have an impact on her, that she would change her ways. But she didn't. Even after all she went through, after all *Gunnar* went through to save her, she refused to give up her paramour. When my husband found out who it was, he had had enough. Immediately, he filed for divorce and sole custody of Rolf."

"Even though Rolf was not his child—"

"Nonsense," Hannah fired back. "Herr Schoennacht was the only father Rolf had ever known."

"Yes, of course." Berg picked up a poppy-seed cookie and bit into it. "Delicious."

"Thank you." She managed a stiff smile. "More tea?"

"Yes, please."

She poured him another glass, then refilled her own. Berg tried to approach the subject as delicately as possible. "So . . . when did Rupert come into the picture?"

"Rupert . . ." Hannah shook her head. "Just a few weeks after the divorce was final, Della found out she was with child . . . again . . . and by the same man . . . the same *married* man. My sister was in a terrible bind because it was well known that she hadn't been with Herr Schoennacht as husband and wife for months. She was no longer married; she couldn't pretend anymore. That's when she made history repeat itself."

"Meaning?"

"It was clear by now that her married man was never going to leave his wife. So Della found an older sap to marry her. Dirk Schick was not a handsome man. He was a confirmed bachelor and much older than she was. She must have seduced him and somehow managed to convince him that the child was his."

"Could it have been possible for the child to be his? After all, he arrived only a month early."

"You have really investigated this, haven't you?" Berg's expression was enigmatic. "The baby was two months 'early,' but weighed over three kilos. Dirk had to have known something was awry, but the fool had already married her."

Berg remembered what Krieger had told him, how Dirk had been very good to her. Della must have had something very special to make men love her so much. "So now you are saying that Rupert wasn't Dirk's son?"

"Exactly!"

"And are you also telling me that Rupert and Rolf had the same father—the anonymous married man?"

"Of course, I couldn't know that for certain. . . . May God forgive me if I'm wrong, but . . ." Her voice dropped to a whisper, her gaze on her lap. "I'm sure I know who he is . . . was. I knew long before my own husband knew. It was treacherous because the three of them were boyhood friends."

"The three of them?"

"My father, Herr Schoennacht, and . . . this person." She had tears in her eyes. "I can't mention his name because the family is well known in Munich. All I will tell you is that he was a wicked man, Inspektor. A very wicked man because we were just children! He, Herr Schoennacht, and my father were friends from way back in Germany. My father married an American woman and moved to Boston. This man . . . His wife was from a prominent Boston family. He and Herr Schoennacht used to come and visit my father. They used to play with Della and me, acting as the fun uncles. As a matter of fact, we called him Uncle Hansy. That was what particularly appalled Gunnar, that the man was so vile as to seduce Della under my father's nose. Of course, Herr Schoennacht didn't find out about it until much later. Then, when I told him what had happened to me . . ."

Berg waited.

This time, the tears gushed out, rolling down her cheeks and dripping off her chin. "He seduced me first, Inspektor! I thought he loved me! I thought . . ." She dabbed at her eyes with a napkin. "But as soon as Della was just a bit older, he moved on to her. I was so stupid! I just thank God that what happened to Della didn't happen to me." She sniffed hard and blew her nose. "I saw him kissing her. He kissed her right in front of me, then *winked* at me. I was sick for a week afterward. I couldn't get out of bed. I certainly never talked to him again."

"He fathered her sons. Maybe she loved him."

"Maybe she just married Herr Schoennacht so she could move to Munich to be with him."

"It would be very helpful if I knew his name."

Hannah shook her head. "What difference does it make?"

"It may be related to some very important police business." His eyes took in hers. "Very, very important business!"

She remained resolute. "I'm sorry, but I cannot tell you as long as Rolf is alive."

"Rolf has never been told that Herr Schoennacht was not his father?"

Hannah grew rigid with fright. "I shouldn't have told you anything. You must promise me never to repeat what I have told you!"

It was time to show sympathy for this old woman's troubles. "You have lived with this terrible burden for a long time, Frau Schoennacht. Too long! Please don't feel guilty about talking to me."

"Then promise you won't tell Rolf what I told you."

"I don't see why I would need to tell him anything about it. Still, it would be helpful if you told me who this treacherous man is."

"I cannot, Inspektor. I am sorry."

"Please, Frau Schoennacht. If you can't tell me now, maybe you can tell me later."

Hannah nodded. "All right, Inspektor. I will think about it."

"Consider what I ask of you, *bitte*. Lives may depend on it!"

The woman bristled. She did not like being pushed into a decision. Berg backed off. "It must have been very hard for you, Frau Schoennacht, raising five children, including your sister's child."

"Rolf was *never* her child. She was never around for him . . . too busy carrying on with her married man. No, Inspektor, the only real mother Rolf has ever known is me. As far as Rolf is concerned, Della is dead and gone."

Berg wasn't so sure of that. Surely Rolf had some curiosity about his mother. The sneak visit with the nanny . . . "Is Della—in actuality—dead and gone?"

"I wouldn't know. When my mother died, Della disappeared from my life for good. Mother used to talk to me about her, so I suppose I had . . . indirect contact with my sister. But now, as far as I'm concerned, Della died years ago."

"And you took over as the true Frau Schoennacht."

"Yes, I did. I raised those children the way a mother should raise her children. I was there for them. *Not*

Della—me. I was there!" She looked pointedly at him. "Do you have children, Inspektor?"

"Two, Frau Schoennacht."

"Then you should understand what I'm saying. Children need a real mother, not just a mother in name."

"I know that. Motherhood is often a thankless job. Still, it is the most important job in the world."

"Exactly." Hannah finished her tea and offered Berg another glass.

"No, *danke,* but maybe just another poppy-seed cookie."

"Take some for your children."

"I will, thank you."

"Let me wrap them up for you." She got up slowly and went to find some paper. Berg thought about what she had told him, how she refused to tell him the name of the paramour. But she had allowed it to slip out anyway.

Uncle Hansy.

Anders Jo*hann*sen? Except he wasn't old enough to be one of Hannah's father's friends. The man could have been Anders's father, the merchant seaman. *If* Hannah hadn't said something else revealing.

His wife was from a prominent Boston family.

Katherine Hanfstaengl was part of the Boston Sedgewick family. It was a point of pride with her.

In Berg's mind, Della's lover was probably Katherine's husband, and Putzi's father, Edgar, though he had no way to prove it. Berg longed to ask Hannah more, but he knew that she'd retreat into silence. It wasn't fair to heap her awful past on her in one visit. Hannah was a lonely woman. He'd come back, and she would welcome him like an old friend . . . and they'd talk again.

If he was correct about Hanfstaengl, it would mean that Schoennacht, Putzi, and Rupert Schick were all half brothers. If Schoennacht or Schick was the man who'd accompanied Anna Gross to the theater, he could very well have been the *Putzi Hanfstaengl* type.

All three men had reasons to hate Della: To Putzi, she was a home wrecker; Rolf had been abandoned by her; and Rupert hated her because she was a whore. Just maybe Rupert had come back to Germany to settle old scores.

Berg felt he had hit upon something, but at this point, his theories were all conjecture. He was thinking too hard. He needed another mind, a fresh injection of ideas. He needed to pay Georg a visit.

Hannah came back with newspaper and started to wrap up her cookies.

Berg said, "So you haven't heard from your sister since she moved to the Soviet Union?"

Hannah stopped wrapping. "No, I haven't. I've already told you that."

"I need to get hold of your sister, Frau Schoennacht."

"Why?"

"Police matters, Frau Schoennacht. I'm not at liberty to discuss the details. But I will tell you that I must talk to your nephew Rupert Schick right away."

"That's not possible, Inspektor."

"All I need is an address. I promise I will not tell anyone that it came from you."

"It is not possible for you to talk to Rupert because he died in 1915."

"In the Great War?"

"I suppose." Hannah shrugged. "My mother never went into details, and I didn't ask."

Then it dawned on Berg what she had just said. "Rupert is *dead*?"

"One might even say it was God's retribution." Hannah quickly gasped. "That was an evil thing to say. The Lord is merciful and forgiving."

Berg was too shocked to respond. All this time he had been looking for a dead man! A host of new questions came to mind: Who was the Robert Schick on Anna Gross's calling card? Who was the man in the sketch, the one identified by the lute player as a Russian? Who was the mysterious Robert Hurlbutt of Harvard? If it wasn't Rupert Schick, was it Schoennacht or Putzi? Or was Robert Schick another person altogether?

What was he missing?

And then it came to him. "Did . . ." He exhaled and started again. "Did Della ever have any more children?"

Hannah appeared pensive. "You know what?" She nodded slowly. "I think I remember my mother telling me that Della had adopted an orphan shortly after Rupert died . . . a teenage boy whose parents had died in the Bolshevik revolution."

"So there *was* another child."

"I reckon there was. I heard from Mother that Della was finally settling down and adjusting to married life. Maybe it was losing Rupert. Maybe it was the Soviet harshness. Maybe she thought about the child she had given up and decided to do something noble. Or . . . it may have been wishful conjecture on my mother's part."

"Would you happen to remember the adopted boy's name?"

"Yes, I do remember. It was Rodion. A nice Russian name—so I am told."

"Rodion," Berg repeated, more to himself than to her.

"I remember it because I thought it was a coincidence. All of my sister's sons had names beginning with the letter R, even the *adopted* one!"

FORTY-SEVEN

✠ Fluffing the pillow, Berg placed it behind Müller's back and helped him sit up in the hospital bed. Georg said, "If all goes right with the medical exam, I should be out of here tomorrow."

"I'm sure you'll be glad about that."

"It cuts both ways, Axel. The nuns here are tyrants, but so is Karen."

"I would think a known tyrant is better than unknown ones."

"I'm not so sure about that. You've seen Karen when she gets worked up."

Berg handed him a glass of water. "It's good you're on the mend. It'll be even better to see you up and about."

Georg laid his hand on his leg cast. "Leaving this place certainly will be a good start."

"Absolutely." Berg looked up at the ceiling. "I've come from visiting Ulrich—"

"He is having visitors?"

"For only a few minutes at a time. He is off the iron lung."

"What *wonderful* news!"

"Yes, the doctors say he's progressing." Berg smiled. "He recognized me today . . . actually mouthed 'Berg.' "

"Ah, but that is marvelous!" Georg handed Berg his

empty water glass, then drew the bedsheet over his stomach. "So he is able to talk?"

"In fits and starts." Berg licked his lips. "I'm sure it's just a matter of time." He looked at Müller, hoping his anxiety didn't show. "I am almost there, Georg. But I need *help*."

"What about Kalmer and Messersmit?"

"*Ach, bitte!* Those two are sufficient if someone is holding a bloody knife and standing over a dead body. Anything that requires thought . . ." Berg waved his hand in the air.

"We can't all be clever." Müller adjusted his position in the bed. "Besides, Axel, you've done quite nicely on your own. This Rodion . . . Della's adopted son. You are assuming he's the lute player's Ro."

Berg shrugged. "I didn't find any Rodion Schick in the registries, but this man has registered under so many aliases, he could be anyone. The only thing I'd say right now is that we are seeking a man who speaks fluent Russian."

Müller nodded, stroking his chin as if lost in thought.

"I also think we need to look at Rolf Schoennacht more carefully," Berg stated. "This Rodion Schick and Schoennacht have the same mother, and Rolf has a direct connection to Regina Gottlieb."

"Schoennacht wasn't even in the city when Edith Mayrhofer was slain."

"Maybe he sneaked back into town."

"Axel, according to Hannah, Rolf Schoennacht hadn't seen his mother since she left for Russia. Rolf probably didn't even know that his blood brother Rupert died in 1915. Why on earth would he be aware of a boy his mother adopted years later? They weren't even blood relatives."

Berg bit his lip. "Don't scoff at this, Georg, but is it possible that Della adopted back her own son after Rupert died?"

"As possible as a man on the moon." Müller wrinkled his nose. "Berg, how would she even know where to find her lost son?"

"Maybe she kept track of the boy. Maybe she knew he was languishing in an orphanage—"

"Bitte!" Müller shook his head. "Go back to Rolf Schoennacht, Axel. At least he lives in Munich."

"All right." Berg smiled. "Let's look at Schoennacht. He was an illegitimate child whose mother abandoned him. He is angry with her, but he cannot murder her because she is no longer accessible to him. So he does the next best thing in his warped mind. He murders women and blames his acts on his phantom brothers, Rodion and Rupert Schick."

"Robert Schick."

"Close enough. The point is, he is exacting revenge on his mother and her bastard children by killing under their names. Schoennacht's hatred runs very deep. It is a vile hatred that will never be resolved. No matter how many lives he takes, he will kill again until he is stopped. *And* he must know English. He had an American mother and stepmother."

"First of all, why would Schoennacht start murdering now after living in Munich as a solid citizen for all his life? Second, in the case of Regina Gottlieb, why would he kill a woman whose death would cast suspicion on him? Third, although I concede it is likely that Rolf probably knows English, you have no proof that he knows Russian. Fourth, Schoennacht wasn't in town when Edith and little Johanna died. And last, the sketch you have shown around does not look like Rolf Schoennacht."

"The sketch is general enough to be anyone. If you changed a few features, it could be Rolf."

"If you changed the features, it could be *me*."

Berg wasn't ready to concede that just yet, but it made no sense to belabor the obvious. He moved on to another avenue of investigation. "What about Putzi Hanfstaengl masquerading as Rodion Schick?"

Müller pondered the idea for a moment. "Hanfstaengl is American, so he would speak English, as well as German. But as far as I know, Hanfstaengl does not frequent bars in Soviet Munich, nor does he speak Russian. Also, Hanfstaengl is decidedly *not* the man in the sketch."

"What do you think about Putzi's father as the sire of Della's children?"

"If you were a magician, Axel, it would be good to pull rabbits out of hats. But it is very bad for an Inspektor with the *Mordkommission*. You have no reason whatever to suspect that Hanfstaengl or any of his relatives are involved."

"Gerhart Leit said the man with Anna Gross was the Putzi Hanfstaengl type."

"Correct me if I'm mistaken, but Gerhart Leit also made a point of saying the man *wasn't* Putzi Hanfstaengl. If I were you, I wouldn't start any gossip. Hanfstaengl has connections."

"Hitler?" Berg laughed. "I'm not worried about a thug, a felon, and a foreigner."

"That's not what I meant. Hanfstaengl has enough

money to hire a top barrister. The family will not tolerate the police circulating unfounded rumors about him."

"Hannah Weiss Schoennacht referred to the man who tried to seduce her as Uncle Hansy."

"Interesting, except that Putzi's father is named Edgar."

"*Hanf*staengl!" Berg pointed out. "What about the last name?"

"Then it would be Uncle Hanfy." Georg sighed with impatience. "Axel, I will give you credit for creativity, but you have nothing to back up these claims. You don't like Hanfstaengl because he is rich, he is a snob, his mother is from a rich, blue-blooded American family, and he is a staunch supporter of the Austrian."

Berg started to speak up in his own defense, but then *thought* about what Georg was saying. "Actually, you're correct. I don't like him for all of those reasons."

"And you don't like Schoennacht, either, which is why you keep bringing him up as a suspect."

"That's not true . . . well, I don't like him. But I would have my suspicions whether I liked Schoennacht or not."

"But we're not looking for a *Bavarian* who speaks English. We're looking for a *Russian* who speaks fluent German and English. You have a name, my friend. Go back to Soviet Munich and pass the sketch around." Müller was emphatic. *"Look for Rodion Schick!"*

Berg threw back his head. "Okay. I'll go to Soviet Munich and pass around the sketch once again. And I will look for Rodion Schick."

"Finally!" Müller sunk back into his pillow. "Good man!"

Berg was worried. While he spent hours or days

passing around a sketch, the murderer would be plotting his next move.

Who was this fiend?

Berg was not ready to give up on Schoennacht, not after he had seen the *Lustmord* painting in a prominent place on his walls. The lute player hadn't said the man's name was definitely Rodion. He had said the name was Ro, and Ro could be Rolf. Still, it was useless to watch the art dealer's house since he was out of town. Moreover, there was nothing to suggest that Rolf Schoennacht spoke Russian.

Whoever the mysterious assassin was, he probably wasn't German-born. Even the American Green mentioned that he spoke German with a slight accent. Yet the murderer came to Munich and must have integrated into Bavarian society sufficiently to woo and capture the hearts of Anna Gross and Marlena Druer—two women who had flirted with Kommunismus. Rodion Schick was definitely Russian. He had been raised under Kommunist rule.

Rodion Schick.

Anders Johannsen came to mind.

Ro as in Jo? Anders wasn't born in Munich. By his own admission, he had traveled extensively. Could his travels have taken him to Russia for an extended stay? And what about that gold collar around his little dog's neck? That could have been the murder weapon. Also, it was bizarre that Anders Johanssen had found not just one but *two* of the bodies. Berg knew that repeat murderers, like Haarmann and the Düsseldorf killer, enjoyed playing a cat-and-mouse game with the police.

On the other hand, Johannsen's distress after finding

Regina Gottlieb had seemed genuine. He also was too old to be Rodion and did not look like the man in the sketch.

Rodion Schick: a murderer so bold as to kill in daylight.

He had to be someone with authority, someone used to wielding power. Anders Johannsen was not a bold person—quite the contrary: He was a disillusioned homosexual. It was known that homosexual murderers usually killed other homosexuals.

Rodion Schick.

Someone who was very sure of himself, very sure of his position in life.

Rodion Schick.

Rolf and Anders were tall. Putzi was a giant.

Rodion Schick.

Ro for Rodion. Ro for Rolf. Ro for Jo. Ro for Roderick . . . except that Schlussel was a born and bred Bavarian and way too old to be Della's son. Ro for Vo, for that matter, except that Volker also was too old.

Rodion Schick.

Schick Rodion.

Suddenly, Berg's eyes widened.

Georg had disparaged Berg's creativity. But creativity sprang from musings deep in the subconscious. It was from that very place that the idea came to him.

FORTY-EIGHT

✠ It all pieced together, the odd mixes of color and form assembling into an eerie portrait of hatred and revenge. Berg spoke softly but clearly, leaning close to Müller as if he were wooing a lover.

He whispered a name.

Müller's eyes widened in disbelief and distrust. He turned ashen, then broke into a sweat. "You can't be serious!" Berg wiped his colleague's face with a tissue. "You shouldn't even suggest things like that in a public place!"

"That's why I whispered the name."

"Don't even do that!" A spot of color crept back into Müller's cheeks. "Axel, I keep telling you he's not one of ours. Yet you persist. It's going to get you into serious trouble, my friend."

"At this point I realize it's conjecture—"

"Damn right! You don't have anything by way of proof!"

"Would you like to protest his innocence, or would you at least like to hear me out?"

Müller shook his head. "I think you're daft. But have a go at it. I'll try to listen with an open mind."

That was the Georg Berg knew. "Thank you."

"Proceed."

Berg began his tale.

Della and Dirk Schick adopted a teenager named Rodion. Maybe the boy had been a true orphan in Russia, or maybe he was the biological son Della reclaimed after losing Rupert. The only thing known was that Della took on Rodion sometime after Rupert died in 1915.

Müller held up a finger. "We can't even ascertain if that's true."

"That's what I was told, Georg, so that's why I assume it's true. Otherwise the Robert Schick connection goes nowhere and we have nothing on this monster. The alias fits, the approximate age fits. And even you must admit that . . ." *No names,* Berg reminded himself. ". . . that he looks somewhat like the man in the sketch."

"So do a thousand other men."

"Yes, you have said that before."

"And I will continue to repeat it if for no other reason than to slow you down. Assuming there is a real Rodion Schick could be our first big mistake."

Berg kept his patience. "May I please continue?"

Müller smiled. "Yes, sorry. Go on."

Della adopted Rodion after Rupert's death. That meant that the teenager had been brought up in the Soviet Union by a Russian father with German ancestry and a German-American mother. Hence, he could speak all three languages. That took care of one problem: how to integrate Kommunist Ro with the German Robert Schick on Anna Gross's calling card and with the English-speaking Lord Robert Hurlbutt.

Rodion wasn't happy living in the Soviet Union. Who would be happy living under Stalin? But there were additional subconscious reasons for his melancholy. He had lost his childhood, and even though he had been lucky enough to be adopted, he knew he wasn't the *wanted* son. Instead, Rodion was a weak substitute, a replacement for the two sons Della had lost. Rodion nursed his resentments: against his dead brother, against his living German brother, but most of all against the mother who had cast him in this predetermined role. Teenagers are angry anyway; this one had a reason. His fury began to grow wildly like weeds. His wrath was soon out of control. He began to harbor unnatural thoughts of revenge.

Müller was listening with interest. Berg continued with newfound confidence.

When Rodion reached manhood, he made his way across borders, passing himself off as a German and eventually settling in Munich. Maybe he had some familiarity with the city from his parents' recollections. It was also the city where both of his hated brothers had been born. He was charming like his mother, and certainly without scruples like his mother. He remained unmarried, for two reasons: First, a wife and children might accidentally expose his true identity. Second, lacking the tethers of family, he was able to work and work until he rose to a position of power.

The man had a distinct nose for who could do him the most good politically. He was always a political animal: as political as he was secretive. Only a secretive man could have successfully passed for all these years as a native German police official. Only a very secretive man could reinvent himself as a Russian count or an Englishman when it was expedient for him to do so.

"But why would he assume so many false personae and risk exposing his true identity?"

"A very good question."

"So let's hear an answer!"

"A moment, please! I haven't entirely thought it out."

Again Müller smiled. "Take your time. I'm just being difficult. It's been a long week."

"Indeed. If I were you, I'd be going out of my mind by now." Berg collected his thoughts. "I think that after play-acting all these years as Della's son, assuming other personae must have been easy for him. I'm sure he enjoyed the subterfuge. Also, there was money to be made by posing as a Russian count. Marlena Druer was a rich, unattached bohemian enthralled with the idea of revolution. Rodion pretended to share her enthusiasm for Kommunist insurrection. He told her he was going to put into practice what they had fantasized in words; she gave him money for his plans."

"Wouldn't she have known who he really was?"

"She was not from Munich, precisely the reason he had chosen her. She certainly wasn't familiar with the upper echelons of the police department. To Marlena, the Russian count who signed his name 'Ro' was set upon bringing Kommunismus to Munich as Kurt Eisner had done nearly a dozen years ago."

"All right," Müller said. "That makes some kind of sense. Now, how does Anna Gross fit in?"

"Ro could never marry because his identity was too much at risk. He needed a woman."

"That's why there are whores, Axel."

"I'm sure he went to whores. But a man such as he would also court risk because it gave him a thrill. What is more exciting than taking another man's wife? Impostors play roles because they *enjoy* doing so. In his role as Russian count, he was a thrill seeker: the rebellious

Kommunist and a bohemian. What a contrast this must have been to his mundane daily life as a proper German public servant."

"But surely Anna, who lived in Munich, would know who he was."

"Not necessarily. Mostly, he is out of the public eye, operating behind the scenes. And what if he took great pains to go out only in disguise? When you are seeing a Russian count, you don't see a Munich policeman, eh? Whether Anna knew his true identity or not, we will never know. But we do know that Anna was pregnant at the time of her demise. And we do know from Anna's maid that Anna and her husband had been trying unsuccessfully to conceive a child."

"The baby wasn't the Jew's."

"Exactly. And perhaps all would have been well if Anna had pretended that the child was her husband's. But let us suppose that she didn't want to pretend anymore. Let us suppose that Anna had fallen in love with her glamorous Russian count and wanted to marry him. That would never do. First of all, she had already been married to a Jew, which would have made her a very undesirable wife for someone in politics. Second, Rodion knew that if he married her, eventually his facade would be discovered. He had to get rid of her."

"But Druer was murdered first. How does that figure into your tale?"

"I've given that some thought," Berg said. "I think that Marlena found out about his affair with Anna and threatened to expose him and cut off his funds. So he wrote Marlena a letter promising a romantic relationship with her once he settled his affairs. The letter mollified Druer, enough for her to bring a large sum of money to Munich for him. Once Rodion had the money in his pocket, he took care of Marlena first . . . then Anna."

Müller said, "But it doesn't make sense, Axel, when you consider how much money we found in Marlena's strongbox."

Berg considered Müller's objection. He lowered his voice again. "When we took out the cash, I made sure to leave some bills there because an empty strongbox would look suspicious. Maybe that's what he did, Georg. Suppose that originally there was even *more* money than we found? He knew that we would go through Marlena's room, so he left cash inside the box so *we* wouldn't get suspicious."

Müller was quiet. Then he said, "Even if I believed such a tale, it still doesn't explain why he continued to murder after Anna Gross."

"Because he developed a *Lustmord*—"

"That's ridiculous!"

"The two murders emboldened him," Berg said. "Feeling a new surge of power, he was ready to enact his revenge, and who better than Regina Gottlieb? The third murder was a truly diabolical deed because Regina was not a threat to him. He killed Regina only because he wanted to lead us to Rolf Schoennacht, his mother's true son, a man he utterly despised."

Müller laughed. "But how would he know about Schoennacht's alleged lecherous desires for Regina?"

"We know that he and Rolf are members of the same political circles. He belongs to many *Vereine,* and so does Rolf Schoennacht. He could have befriended Rolf. It's possible that Schoennacht confessed his unhealthy desire for Regina Gottlieb."

"Axel, you have no proof the two men ever met, let alone that they are confidants."

"It's not so hard to find out which clubs they belong to," Berg countered. "And even if Rolf had never been told about his adopted brother Rodion, Rodion would know about his lost brother Rolf. At last, Ro had discovered a way to set up his brother—by blaming him for the murder of Regina Gottlieb."

"All right," Müller said. "I suppose if we stretch things considerably, I can accept that theory. Now, Axel, you must explain how the last two victims fit in—a solid German workingwoman and her little daughter? Rolf Schoennacht was out of town, so he couldn't possibly be blamed for them. And those two murders inflamed the people and incited riots in which people died! It made the police look very bad. Why would he want to foul his own nest?"

"To stir up the department. Max Brummer is in deep trouble. Our man is now in a position to seize more power for himself."

Müller responded with a shrug. "Interesting, Axel. You have created a saga of mythical dimensions: the seduction of a young girl and forbidden love."

"That was told to me by Della's sister—I did not make it up."

"But this invention of a quest for revenge, brother against brother."

"It is as old as the Bible."

"Yes, that is certainly true." Müller let out a small laugh. "All right. I like the story. I admit you may be on to something. But before you make any accusations, you need verification. You mustn't repeat any of this to *anyone* until you have more proof. Loose lips could make you deadly enemies!"

Berg took a deep breath and let it out. "That's precisely why I'm only telling you my theories . . . to give you a chance to mull over what I've said. Even if you can't actively work, you can certainly think."

Müller laughed. "I suppose sometimes that's true."

Berg said, "My first objective must be to watch his movements in case he strikes again. When I know positively that he is at work, I will quietly look into his false registration papers. Also, I must investigate Schoennacht's clubs and see if I can find people who can attest to a friendship between Rolf and him."

"Quite a substantial load for one man, Axel. How do you propose to be in two places at one time?"

"I can't. That's why I need *you*. You've got to get better, man! I need *help*."

✠ ✠ ✠

AS BERG WAS LEAVING, at the main door of the hospital, he met up with Volker, who regarded him with keen eyes. "Inspektor."

"Kommissar." Berg felt his heart pound against his chest. The last person he wanted to talk to right now: someone high in the department.

"How are they doing—Müller and Storf?"

"Actually, they are much better, sir. Storf is responding to simple commands." Berg looked at the ceiling, trying to calm his breathing. It wasn't just Volker who was setting him on edge, it was everything he had talked about with Müller. "Georg is doing very well, I think. I believe he said something about being discharged tomorrow."

"Good news."

"Yes, it is."

The silence that followed seemed to linger past what was acceptable.

"How did the research at the registry go?"

"Good, sir. Very good."

"Then you are close to finding out Schick's identity?"

He hoped he wasn't stuttering out loud as badly as he was stuttering mentally. "Not as close as I had hoped. But tomorrow is a new day."

A good, neutral answer.

"Really, Axel, I don't know how much more advantageous it would be for you to pursue such an avenue."

Berg said, "I was thinking the same thing . . . that perhaps it would be best if I went back to basic police work." Volker waited for him to go on. "You know, talk to more people who knew Edith Mayrhofer. Maybe there was a mystery man in her life."

"The same mystery man involved with the others?"

"Maybe yes, maybe no." Berg worried that he was being too obvious, too ready to drop his first line of investigation. "I would like to show her friends the sketch I made from Gerhart Leit's description—the man who was with Anna Gross. I'm still not ready to give up on Rupert Schick. Still, if he turns out to be a dead end, I must have another plan of inquiry."

"I agree," Volker said. "And if you find a different mystery man in Edith's life, one who appears to be a good suspect, then you will assume that Edith's and her daughter's deaths were not related to the others."

"Possibly." Berg managed a smile. "Right now, I'm not sure what to think. That's why I'm a good Inspektor. I take in all the facts before I come to a conclusion."

Volker's thin lips moved upward, the expression halfway between a smile and a sneer. "I don't know if that's entirely true, Inspektor. I seem to recall your making many wild assertions in the past."

"Assertions possibly, but not conclusions."

"I believe you are nitpicking, Axel."

This time Berg's smile was real. "But, sir, if you don't nitpick, how do you get rid of lice?"

FORTY-NINE

✠ As he boarded the Triebwagen, Berg's head was spinning with newfound suppositions and what-ifs, backed up so far by nothing but zeal and verve. The short encounter with Volker had left him reeling. He knew he had to go through Records and Registration to give his theories some credence, but in order to do that, he needed a signed request from Volker.

That would be impossible, considering whom he was investigating.

He'd have to do it surreptitiously. He was now alone, without recourse, because aside from Georg, whom could he trust?

As the streetcar pulled away, he realized he was still standing. He grabbed a strap, deciding he was too nervous to sit. His mind was running lap after lap of futility: a circular, endless conundrum.

There was always Ilse Reinholt. Berg knew that the redheaded clerk could be bribed, although this time it would take a lot more than a lunch at a beer hall to get what he needed. He still had almost all the stolen money from Marlena Druer's strongbox, not to mention the bills that Gottlieb had shoved into his hands before he left. What better use of pilfered lucre than to solve murders?

He checked his watch.

Records had closed hours ago. He would go tomorrow morning. . . .

Someone jostled him, bumping him hard on the shoulder. Berg spun around only to face a group of seated passengers with disinterested eyes.

Was he imagining things?

Easy, Axel, easy. Take a deep breath.

He knew he shouldn't go home, that he should be spying on Rodion. It was monstrous to leave him running loose in the city. But logistically, how could he do that? Should he walk ten paces behind him, waiting for him to go in or out of a theater or restaurant? Was he to prowl around Soviet Munich, where surely he would stand out as a foreigner? Must he keep an all-night vigil at the man's apartment? Just a half-hour ago, he had been inspired by his vivid play of ideas. In the reality of afterthought, he wasn't so sure of himself. He had too few facts embellished by much too much speculation.

Abruptly the streetcar stopped and Berg lurched forward.

He was only a man—a simple, frail human being who needed basic things: food, water, sleep . . . love. His body ached with pangs of hunger and loneliness. He needed to go home and nourish himself physically and emotionally. He needed to kiss his wife's forehead and hug his children. He needed to rid himself of thoughts of blood and lust and murder because something inside his brain kept reminding him that he also had played God and snuffed out life. Had he endured the same upbringing as Rodion, he might have become a madman as well.

So immersed was he in his own waking nightmare, he almost missed his stop. He jumped out of the car just as it was pulling away from the stop, the conductor's scolding voice ringing in his ears.

Calm down, Berg. Breathe slowly.

Cutting through the chilly, dark veil of a foggy evening, he walked the several blocks to his apartment. It had been an exhausting day: Mental gymnastics were often more tiring than physical labor. The streets were forlorn except for a single motorcar parked across from his building.

He opened the door to the foyer, collected the mail from his box, then slowly trudged up four flights in a stairwell made warm by dinnertime cooking. The welcome aroma of food wafted into his nostrils, making his stomach growl. He suddenly realized that he had barely eaten all day. Even during lunch with Ilse, he had eaten very little. His fatigue was undoubtedly brought on by his hunger. He was not simply hungry; he was famished.

Down the hall to his apartment.

Still plagued by his guilt over Margot's death, he scarcely noticed that his front door was unlocked. That wasn't really unusual. They knew all their neighbors. Doors were often left open, especially at suppertime . . . someone always borrowing something—an onion or a turnip or a teaspoon of salt. Delicious smells came from inside. Britta was a fantastic cook.

It wasn't until he was inside that he noticed something was very wrong. His wife and children sitting on the edge of the couch, terrified looks on their faces. Britta in the middle, hugging Monika and Joachim with tears escaping from her eyes.

Berg looked up from his family.

Behind them stood the man who had occupied his

every thought for the past hour. Images raced through his brain like a child's animated flip book. Taken singly, the pages held static drawings. But when the edges were flipped quickly, a scene was played out.

He was holding two guns, one in each hand: a Luger P.08 and a Mauser C96.

"Hello, Inspektor."

"Kommandant . . ." he whispered.

"Come in and close the door. You don't want to catch a draft."

Berg did as he was told. Then he took a step forward, but stopped as soon as he heard the hammer draw back and the pin click.

The Mauser was pressed against his son's temple. He was as clever as he was evil. A son was what a man treasured most in his life. The Kommandant had already killed a helpless little girl; certainly an older boy wouldn't trouble him.

"Do not move unless I tell you to do so."

"Yes, sir," Berg answered.

"Ah, a good policeman you are." Stefan Roddewig waved the gun in the air. "Take a seat, why don't you."

Berg moved toward the couch.

"No . . . not there."

Berg stopped.

"In your chair, Inspektor. Across from your wife, your son, and your daughter. That way I can see you . . . face-to-face."

Berg sat on his chair.

"Put your hands in your lap so I can see them."

Berg complied.

"I received a visitor today," Roddewig said. "A fine

citizen of Munich who was very perturbed. It seems you've upset his mother by poking into private matters."

Berg didn't say anything.

"Old family matters."

Berg remained silent.

"You do know who I'm talking about."

Berg was still quiet.

"Answer me!" Roddewig shot the ceiling with the Luger, and plaster rained down. Monika let go with a piercing scream, but Britta wisely clamped her hand over her daughter's mouth. "The next time I shoot, it will be the lad. I don't like to be ignored."

"I apologize for my impudence, Herr Kommandant." Berg's voice was surprisingly strong. A quick glance at his family to make sure they were still whole. They were suffused with dread but otherwise all right. He focused his eyes on the Mauser. Roddewig's hand was sure and steady. "I believe you are referring to Rolf Schoennacht. I certainly didn't mean to upset him or anyone else, especially you."

"Oh, is that so?" The Kommandant appeared calm and in control. Only a slight tic in his eye gave any hint of a crack in the steel demeanor. "Then you have failed miserably."

"Again I apologize."

Roddewig exhaled angrily. "If the problem had only been that idiot Rolf, we could have handled this in office. Just you and me, Berg, and that would have been that. But you got his mother involved!"

Rolf wasn't the idiot. I was an idiot. Of course, Hannah would tell her son about the visit.

"What were you thinking?"

What had *I been thinking?* But then Berg realized something. How could Hannah have talked to her son when he was supposedly in Paris or America? Either Rolf had cut his trip short or he had never left Munich. That meant he could have been in the city when Edith and her little girl were murdered. Maybe Roddewig and Schoennacht were perpetrating the murders in tandem.

"I'm . . ." Berg forced himself to remain calm, even managing a quick smile for Joachim. The boy was too paralyzed to respond. "I'm very sorry. Deal with me however you want, Herr Kommandant, but please leave my family alone."

The wrong thing to say. A smile played on Roddewig's lips. "Ah, so now you are a good family man, settling for your wife now that your mistress is dead."

Berg closed his eyes, not daring to look at his family. Then, he snapped them open.

Don't take your eyes off the gun, you idiot.

Berg jumped as he heard a soft click, as if a gun with an empty chamber were being fired.

"Something the matter, Inspektor?"

Berg looked at Roddewig's Mauser, which was still aimed at his son's temple. Now he was hearing things. The brain playing tricks on him.

"Nothing."

"You jumped."

"A chill in the room."

"Sit still. You make me nervous when you jump. You don't want me nervous, do you?"

"No, sir, not at all."

"Good." Roddewig smiled. "Now I understand why Martin insisted that you lead the *Mordkommission*. You are exacting. You make his command look sharp. Your meticulous and dogged pursuit of the killer has been impressive. But not as impressive as all the details that you have miraculously unearthed, constructing a plausible story from nothing but fragments."

Berg's natural instinct was not to answer, but he knew he had to say something. "Thank you, sir."

"You were so close, my good man, so very *close*."

Berg licked his lips. "You give me too much credit—"

A shot rang past his shoulder. The Luger pointed in his direction, a bullet discharged before he could finish his sentence. Berg was startled, but somehow managed not to move.

"You're not a fool, so don't act like one. While you may know some things, Berg, you don't know everything. Shall I fill you in?"

There was the eye tic. Not as pronounced this time. He was becoming calmer as time passed.

"I'd like to hear whatever you'd like to tell me," Berg said.

Roddewig nodded. "Good answer. You may not report directly to me, Inspektor, but I know what's going on. Records do tell an interesting story, don't they?"

Only two people knew he had been to Records this morning. One of them was in the hospital. The other was Volker. How stupid and naive he was to trust the Kommissar with his game plan.

"If you had kept your sights on Rolf, if you had investigated him, you would have realized that he *was* in town at the time of Edith's murder. His alibi about going to America would have made him look very, very guilty."

"I'm sure I would have found that out, sir. And I would have charged him—"

"*No, no, no!*" Roddewig's tongue clucked. "Don't insult my intelligence! As soon as you spoke with my dotty aunt, I knew it was only a matter of time before you discovered my identity."

There it was again. That distinct click. It *wasn't* imaginary! Berg tried to keep his face expressionless and his brain focused. The sound was coming from behind him. Someone else in the room? He dared not turn to look over his shoulder. Instead, he gazed past his wife's head at Joachim's charcoal drawing on the wall, the one that he had framed himself and covered with glass. In the reflection, he failed to see anyone in back of him.

But the click was *real!* If it wasn't from someone in the room, it had to be coming from the other side of his front door.

The *unlocked* front door.

Someone was trying to come inside but being very quiet about it. With any luck at all, he would live long enough to find out who it was.

Stall the bastard!

And remember to duck!

Berg cleared his throat. "We still can blame all the murders on Schoennacht, sir. He was the one who knew Regina Gottlieb. Regina worked for his wife. Schoennacht hated Jews. It would make perfect sense for him to murder her."

"He *did* murder her, you dunce!" Again, Roddewig's mouth turned upward into a sickly grin. With the eye tic, it would have been comical if the man hadn't been armed. "Rolf Schoennacht . . . my favored older brother . . . the one my mother held up as an example of sophistication and taste. The one for whom my mother ached even though it was she who had deserted him . . . though to hear Mother explain it, nothing was ever her fault, the gutless harlot."

The gun was still in Roddewig's right hand, but it had slid from Joachim's temple, the barrel now pointing at his jawbone. If it were to drop just a tiny bit more, Berg would have a chance, providing he was fast enough.

". . . the great Rolf Schoennacht crying like a baby." The smile grew wider. "He came to me in a panic, hoping I could extricate him from the situation. But even his panic and fear didn't stop him from having the Jew bitch . . . *twice*."

Berg swallowed. "He took advantage of her *after* she was . . ."

"When the urge hits"—a wide smile—"but of course, you know that very well, Inspektor. Margot was quite lovely."

This time Berg didn't dare close his eyes, although the temptation was very strong. The unadulterated look of hatred in Britta's eyes was a knife through his heart. He deserved bitter condemnation. His stupidity had put his family in mortal danger. He couldn't live with such guilt—he was better off dead. Most likely that was going to be the outcome anyway, but why did he have to take down his family as well?

Roddewig was talking.

". . . out of our deep friendship, I told Rolf that I'd take care of it. Obviously I knew how the others had been slain. . . ."

Because you had murdered them.

". . . replicated the exact marks on Gottlieb with the same necklace as on Marlena. I knew that the hook-nosed Jew Kolb would be shrewd enough to pick it up."

There it was. That click from behind again.

Stall him.

Berg had to make his plea. "The police and the public have already decided that Anton Gross was responsible for Anna's death. All we have to do is make Schoennacht responsible for the others, Herr Kommandant. That will not be difficult at all."

"And that's exactly what I plan to happen, Inspektor. Rolf will take the blame. Unfortunately, that will not help you at all. You know too much about the murders, and more important, you know too much about me. It is too dangerous to keep you alive. But I am a man of mercy, my friend. I'll kill you before I kill your family, so you won't have to watch. And as far as my aunt goes, she will meet with a very gentle death." A grin. "Gentle because she is family."

The noise coming from behind had stopped.

Keep stalling.

"Just between us, sir. How did you intend to blame Schoennacht for the murders of Edith and little Johanna Mayrhofer?"

"Rolf was supposed to leave for Paris. He didn't. His change of itinerary makes him look utterly guilty."

"Why didn't he leave?"

"Hitler asked him to attend the rally. Schoennacht was honored. The man is a dupe for anyone of prominence. That is why we got on so well. He felt he had the police in his pocket, idiot that he is."

The gun fell off Joachim's jawbone and was now

pointed across his chest at Monika's head. Berg could possibly save his son, but it would most likely kill his daughter. He'd have to be patient. "I see."

"Rolf Schoennacht is a bully, Inspektor . . . a very disturbed man. Once I bring official charges against him for the murders of Marlena and Regina, the public will have no problem believing the two other murders were from his hand as well. They will *want* to believe it, I think."

Roddewig was right about that. The citizens of Munich demanded answers. The problem was that any answer would suffice. If the police blamed Anton Gross for the murder of his wife, then Anton Gross was the murderer. If the politicians claimed the monster was Rolf Schoennacht, then it was Rolf Schoennacht. Honesty was a virtue, but if the truth was not easily found, a scapegoat would do. Such was the national mentality: a people too proud to admit defeat, too haughty to assign rightful blame.

It was always someone else's fault.

Roddewig was talking. ". . . be regarded as a hero, as the one who has solved these terrible crimes and restored order to our city. I will be the one who has brought a murderer to justice. The politicians will flock to kiss my feet, the selfsame politicians who have lost regard for Herr Direktor Brummer because he failed to keep order at Hitler's latest rally. Did you know that he is being asked to resign?"

"And you will be the logical one to take his place."

"Just as you predicted this afternoon. I must admit, Berg, that you are a very clever man."

Predicted this afternoon?

How could Roddewig know what I said this afternoon . . . to Georg?

Unless . . . ?

How could he?

Seeing the utter dismay on Berg's face, Roddewig laughed out loud. "It's a very sad state when strong alliances just can't be trusted."

The betrayal was too much to fathom. Berg had worked with Müller for almost two years. They ate together, they drank together, they had even *stolen* money together. Their wives knew each other. Their children played together. Berg even knew the whores Georg frequented. How could Müller have perpetrated such an act of disloyalty . . . such *treason*?

Roddewig smiled. "Müller has always had ambitious designs, but unfortunately he is very lazy. Did you know that he was quite put out when Volker assigned you to head the *Mordkommission*? Of course, it was the proper choice, but that doesn't mean he accepted it. After all, he is five years your senior, and he is Bavarian and you are not. He came to me in secret, asking me how he could get promoted. I told him what he had to do for me, and we struck a deal. He was getting impatient, but then these murders came up. This entire episode was very fortuitous. With you gone and Storf incapacitated, he will be first in line for promotion."

Berg was numbed by Roddewig's words.

How could this be true?

But of course, Roddewig's invasion into Berg's home bespoke the absolute truth. Again Berg heard a single click of the doorknob, followed by the very soft creak of the door opening. It snapped him back to the present, to how stupid and foolish he was for nursing betrayal when the lives of his family were at stake.

Keep talking. Don't let him hear what I hear.

"So . . ." Berg cleared his throat. "Georg told you everything."

"He phoned the station-house emergency line the moment you were out the door. It was fortunate that it took you some time to come to the truth. If he had still been in traction, he would not have been able to get to the telephone so easily. Now he can sit up in a wheelchair."

Keep him talking.

"So tell me, Kommandant, exactly how close was I to the actual truth?"

"You were wrong about the murder of Regina Gottlieb."

"I know that now, but what about the others? What about Anna Gross? The child was yours, of course."

"I don't know if it was mine, but it certainly wasn't from the Jew." Another smile. No more tic. He was perfectly comfortable. "The odd thing is, Berg, murder was not originally on my mind. Marlena had always given me money. She thought I was a good Schwabing Soviet who was using it to promote Kommunismus in Munich. I had intended to use some of it to provide Anna with an abortion."

"But Anna refused."

"Yes."

"She threatened to tell Marlena."

"She did tell Marlena, the bitch."

"So there went your money."

"The bitch!" Roddewig repeated. "It was only after I proposed marriage that Marlena calmed down."

"But you couldn't marry her."

"I couldn't marry anyone. I was playing the role of

Kommunist count to several ladies. If Marlena or Anna had found out about my position in the police department, all my funds would have been cut off."

"So you had to murder her."

"I didn't want to, but . . ." Roddewig blinked several times. "I told Marlena I was planning a major Kommunist rally in Munich and needed a lot of money to finance it properly. I told her that if all went as planned, Munich would be in revolt, and then we'd be married."

"She believed you."

"I am from the Soviet Union. I can recite the *Kommunist Manifesto* verbatim. Why shouldn't she believe me?"

"You met her at her boardinghouse. You took most of the money but left some behind for the police to find. Then you killed her."

Roddewig's eyes glazed over. "I was not assigned to battle during the Great War, Berg."

"You didn't miss anything."

"On the contrary, I felt like an outsider. My idiot father used his considerable sway and money to ensure me a desk job. So unlike most of my *Kameraden,* I had never killed anyone before. I was surprised by how easily it can be done." Roddewig paused. "I have this rare gift, Berg, to kill and not to feel. Keeping the money and murdering Anna seemed like a much smarter thing to do than giving this stupid girl an abortion. And things would have died down if Rolf hadn't mucked it up by murdering that Jew bitch."

"And that's when you decided to blame both Regina and Marlena on Rolf."

"Precisely."

"Then why go after Edith Mayrhofer and her innocent daughter?"

Roddewig's eyes narrowed. "The appetite for *Lustmord* is very strong, Berg. You don't know until you've tasted it."

"I think I would find it repellent, sir."

"Thanks to God, most of your fellow beings feel as you do. Otherwise the women of the world would all end up dead."

"But why the *child*?"

"Because she was there." Roddewig stared at Berg with dead eyes. "No, Edith wasn't my first *Lustmord*." The barrel of the Mauser was now aimed under Britta's chin. "Nor will she be the last." A hand on her face. "But this one won't be blamed on Schoennacht." He started drooling with anticipation. "I've got it precisely planned, Berg."

Again Berg heard the door creak. "Tell me how, sir."

"Do you *really* want to know?"

"I am a curious fellow."

"That is true." Again his eyes narrowed. "Müller has been telling me how obsessed you've been with the murders. With your mistress dead, you had no place to go for relief. You had to depend on your wife. When she refused your advances . . . well, that was too much."

Berg nodded. "Ah . . . I see."

"No, you *don't* see everything. So I will tell you. First, you had your way with her. . . ." Roddewig began to stroke Britta's face. She was so quiet, so brave.

Berg's eyes dared to engage hers.

I'm so sorry, darling, so very sorry.

Tears rolled down her cheeks.

Roddewig went on. "The police will find proof that you forced yourself on her."

Another creak.

"You forced yourself on her with your children watching. They begged you to stop."

Now there was silence.

"Then . . . under the strain of what you had done to your own wife . . . you couldn't face her . . . you couldn't face your children. You simply snapped."

The door flew open with a gust of wind.

Instantly, Berg sprang up and slammed his family to the ground, shielding them with his body as the cross fire of bullets hummed over their heads. Instincts from his soldier days had taken over.

He remembered to duck.

FIFTY

✠ Roddewig had fallen backward, two holes in his chest, one in his face.

Martin Volker was unscathed. "That's the problem with those who have no combat experience." He picked up the Kommandant's guns and stowed them in his coat. "They don't know how to cover themselves, and they shoot like girls."

One by one, Berg brought his family to their feet. He hugged his children. To Britta he said, "Take them in the bedroom and shut the door." He kissed her cheek, hugging her while whispering, "Hide under the bed. Don't come out for anything." Aloud he said, "Go."

"I want to stay with you, Papa," Joachim said.

"You *can't* stay with him," Britta answered angrily.

Berg took his son's face and looked into his eyes. "It won't be more than a few minutes. Besides, you have to take care of your mother and sister." He kissed his forehead. "Always take care of your mother and sister."

"Why?" Tears were trailing down the boy's cheeks. "What are you going to do?"

"I'm losing patience," Volker told him.

Britta grabbed the children and disappeared into the bedroom. Several seconds passed, then Berg heard furniture being moved. They were barricading themselves in.

Berg regarded the Kommissar. "How did you know the Kommandant was here?"

"No great deductive feat." Volker held Roddewig's Mauser in his hand. "I overheard Müller talking on the telephone, actually shouting into the mouthpiece. The static on the line must have been terrible. I'm surprised at you, Axel. You didn't notice the motorcar parked across the street?"

"I did."

"How many people in your neighborhood own a motorcar?"

Again Berg cursed his stupidity. "How long have you known about Müller?"

"I suspected it for a while. Several times in the past year, I've seen him leaving Roddewig's office when the hour was very late. The man is a jellyfish—absolutely no spine. With the tiniest bit of provocation, he told me everything."

"Did Müller know that Roddewig was the murderer before this afternoon?"

"I don't know, Berg. He's not a very truthful man, so any of his disclaimers would be suspect. Why you wanted to work with him has always eluded me."

"I considered him a friend." He steadied his shaking hands by slipping them in his pants pockets. "I was wrong."

"Wrong about Müller, but right about Roddewig, the arrogant little worm. This is going to be the death of Max Brummer." A hint of a smile. "It will not sit well with the politicians that Brummer appointed a mass killer to the position of Kommandant."

"One would assume that you'll be next in line."

"One would assume . . . except that there are going to be those who question my wisdom in shooting a superior."

"But he was a mass killer!"

"Yes, yes, of course. Still, someone's going to think I did it for my own purposes."

Berg met Volker's eyes: They told him that his days were numbered.

Volker shook his head. "I have a very messy problem . . . explaining everything. And even though you would back me up, it would be wholly inconvenient. You'd always know the truth, just as you know the truth about Margot. Unfortunately for you, you simply know too much."

Berg heard the click of a hammer being drawn back, the barrel of the Mauser on his forehead. "I saved your family, Axel. I saved you from being recorded in history as a mad killer, another German monster afflicted with *Lustmord*. I saved your wife, I saved your little daughter, and I saved your only son. It's a pity that I can't save you."

Berg didn't answer.

"One shot to the head from Roddewig's gun. All your police work was not in vain. You shall die a hero."

Berg was surprised by his steady heartbeat, his acceptance of the inevitable. Even if he could fight off Volker, he was living on borrowed time. With the death of two superiors in his living room and no support at all in the department, Müller would fabricate a story against him. He would be arrested, he would be tried, he would be condemned. He would die in jail or at the hands of an executioner. His family would be ostracized and excommunicated.

Right now, he was more dead than alive. It was time to write his will, assigning Volker the position of executor. "And my family?"

"I'll take care of them."

"How will you get them to trust you after you've murdered me?"

"Because I will tell them that I did not murder you . . . you did that yourself."

Berg smiled. "Suicide?"

"Because of the guilt and shame you carried inside regarding Margot. You could no longer face your wife and children. You accomplished this one final act of bravery so your family would be spared humiliation."

"Britta won't believe you."

"The shot will be at close range, Berg. Surely you would not allow me to kill you without a fight. Besides, Britta won't care. She detests you."

"She detests you as well."

"But not as much as she despises you right now. You are responsible for putting her and the children in peril. I will tell her that *you*, Axel, invented a cover story to hide your shame and suicide. That, for your family, you bravely managed to wrest a gun away from Roddewig, but it was too late. Though you shot him in the breast and head, he wounded you mortally in the head."

"I see."

"I came in as you lay dying."

"Yes, I think she'll agree to that." Berg rubbed his hands together. "Promise me you'll get them out of the country."

Volker raised an eyebrow.

"Roddewig was a good friend of Hitler's," Berg said.

"The Austrian has lost a valued contact in the police department. When he comes to power, he will not deal kindly with my family."

"Hitler has no power."

It was Berg's turn to smile. "Once I also was the optimist." He shook his head. "Thugs beating me up . . . I still had hope. Not after that last rally, Kommissar, after I saw what his men are capable of. Not after I saw one hundred thousand cheering Germans supporting him. Surely you see it as well. The Austrian is as ruthless as he is relentless. It's only a matter of time, Kommissar . . . or should I say Direktor."

Again Volker lifted his brow.

"Eventually you'll have to join him, sir. If you're not actively with him, he'll consider you against him. That's the way it is with savages." Berg shrugged. "I'll not be around to see it. I need you to promise me that you'll obtain visas for my entire family and spirit them out of the country. Then I'll do what you ask."

Volker kept the gun steady against Berg's temple. "You have family in Denmark, don't you?"

"I don't want them in Denmark, sir. Get them visas for England or, even better, get them visas for The States."

Volker was taken aback. "Do you have relatives in The States?"

"A distant cousin. Everyone has some distant relative in The States. But I have another idea. Contact a reporter named Michael Green. He works for a paper in London . . . the *London Eagle* or something like that. He's originally from Boston. Tell him that you will give him the English exclusive on this mass-murder story in exchange for his support in securing United States visas for my family. Tell him that I wanted them to be far, far away from the dreadful memory. Leaving Germany is the only option. Have Green write it up and pull out all the stops. After all, the government would have to be heartless to deny the deathbed request of a hero. That's what you must do. You must tell Green that it was my last wish . . . as I lay dying . . . in your arms."

Volker shrugged. "I suppose that can be arranged."

"No, you must *promise* me. You must swear to it."

Volker shrugged. "I swear."

"*Vielen Dank.*" Berg straightened his shoulders. "Where should I stand?"

"Well, I suppose that if you wrested the gun from Roddewig, you'd have to be close to where he went down."

"Tell me where."

"Right in front of the couch, I think." Volker walked around to where Roddewig was standing before he fell backward, then looked Berg in the eye. "Stand still."

"I'm not going anywhere."

Volker pointed the gun at Berg's head. "Why The States, Berg? Why send them so far away from their native land?"

"My son always wanted to see Josephine Baker dance."

"He could go to Berlin for that."

Berg stopped to formulate his words. "How many times have you heard Hitler say that there has to be a reason why two million Germans died on foreign soil?"

"Go on."

"Of course, there was a reason, Volker. A very simple reason. We waged a war of territory and we *lost*. We pride ourselves on a brilliant history of conquests: Our shame of defeat is still too great to utter aloud. So we deny that we ever really lost the war. There are no physical reminders of combat, because no battles were fought here. The only remnants of the Great War are the lame and the wounded soldiers who are slowly dying off. Hitler doesn't accept defeat. Neither does half the population of our country. There are many who demand revenge and who seek vengeance.

"In 1917, we were winning the Great War, Volker. We were *so close*. The Entente was in dire straits: Belgium was decimated; France was torn and tattered; England was straining at the seams, exhausted and overworked."

Berg smiled wryly.

"Then the Yanks entered the war. Millions of fresh-faced soldiers shipped over with guns and ammunition and modern airplanes and bombs."

He shook his head.

"The Entente didn't win the war, Volker. *America* did. The people in The States returned home with the thrill of victory in their hearts, leaving us ignominy and embarrassment that have plagued this land for over a decade. I would like to think that if there ever was another war— in which millions of men died in open fields—at the very least, my son would die wearing the uniform of the victorious."

"Dead is dead."

"Ah, but one can be alive in body but dead in soul. Just look at Hitler. That man is the future of Germany. If you prove to be honest, Volker, at least he won't be the future of my children. And that is why I will take your bullet with a smile on my face."

EPILOGUE

New York, 2005

✠ I did not die in an open field, although I was in the fields. True to my father's dying wish, I was wearing American green. You see, I know all about my father's final wishes because while my sister and mother acted as good Germans, obeying Father's orders, I was rebellious and hotheaded. I insisted on listening through the keyhole. Mother did not protest. By that time, Mother had given up on all the males in her family.

I never did tell my mother or my sister what had transpired in the living room of our tiny apartment. But I confronted Martin about it soon after the Münchener Post ran the headlines. He kept his word, something I will never quite fathom. Maybe it was because my father had died honorably, fending off a fiend. Stefan Roddewig was declared the Munich Murderer, posthumously charged with the slayings of Anna Gross, Marlena Druer, and Edith and Johanna Mayrhofer. Anton Gross was posthumously declared innocent of the murder of his wife. The case of Regina Gottlieb remains officially unsolved. I suppose Martin needed Schoennacht for other purposes. The last I heard of Rolf, he had been convicted of war crimes and was murdered right before sentencing. Murdered most horribly, I heard.

By the time the Yanks entered the war, I had garnered a small reputation as an artist and photographer.

I was drafted and sent overseas to record both in ink and in silver nitrate what went on during the bloodiest battles. I also witnessed death countless times on the beaches of Utah and Omaha, where the deceased lay honestly in a profusion of mangled bodies, gutted carcasses, and detached limbs—the result of guns, grenades, and combat.

I also witnessed the walking dead. Sent in with the Seventh Army—the Twentieth Armored Division to be exact—I recorded the skeletons, their skin infested with maggots, rotting in chunks from gangrene and infection. Their brains were feverish from typhoid and other horrible diseases. Hundreds of them—men, women, children—crammed into small spaces, peeking out from corners and crevices, staring at us, some daring to touch us with their bony hands and knobby fingers.

The prisoners in Dachau were emaciated from starvation. The Americans didn't know better and tossed them canned goods and chocolate bars. Many of the inmates survived the treachery of the Nazis only to die from eating rich food that their stomachs couldn't digest. "Canned-good" deaths, they were called. I photographed all of this along with the four charred ovens. The land of Bavaria was heavy with the stink of burning bodies, eyes burning from the smoke of the crematorium. The town claimed to know nothing.

We know only what we want to know.

It was 1945, and for the first time in almost a decade I dared to use my German. After Mother died of pleurisy in 1936, I had had no use for the language. Only my sister and I were left and, since we loathed being labeled greenhorns, we always spoke to each other in English. It was easy to forget my native language: The only time I heard it coming out of my mouth was in my nightmares.

When I began to dream in English, the nightmares ceased.

So I was shocked by my fluency when those first Teutonic words escaped easily from my lips. The camp inmates wept when I spoke to them. My Bavarian accent pronounced and correct. They did not cry because I spoke to them in German. They cried because I told them I was a Jew. With Berg as my surname, I could pass for a Jew, although if the inmates had been healthier, surely they would have found my Semitic origins lacking in credibility. With my blond curly hair and my blue eyes, tall and muscular from lifting barbells, I was a poster boy for Hitler's Aryan race.

My captain was stunned. Where had I learned such flawless German? You see, I had reinvented myself as an orphan—which I was—but an _American_ orphan— which I was not. I was immediately put to use as a translator, even though many of the prisoners weren't German Jews, but Polish. Still, after a bit, I could easily understand their Yiddish as they recounted horror story after horror story. There were many in the United States who refused to acknowledge the veracity of such tales. What kind of human beings could have perpetrated such cruelty?

I, on the other hand, had no trouble believing them. Although we emigrated to the United States long before the extermination camps were built, there were those who were farsighted enough to have seen what was coming. Others, such as Martin, needed a direct threat. He emigrated to The States as soon as Heinrich Himmler became Kommissarischer Polizeipräsident of the Munich Police Department in 1933. It wasn't because Martin was rabidly anti-Nazi. It was only because he and

Himmler had hated each other ever since that fateful rally.

My mother signed papers for him, pretending to be a close relative, something I will never quite understand. Martin was responsible for my father's death, but I suppose my father would have died a horrible death anyway. He would never have left Munich, and he certainly would not have allowed his only son to be drafted into the German army to fight for Hitler. So I think that even the terror that must have gone through his mind as Martin pulled the trigger was preferable to the torture and eventual murder he would have faced as a political dissenter in Dachau.

I paint in reds because red is the color of blood. The critics tell me that my paintings are saturated with war and death. This is partly true, but not exclusively. Blood represents death, but blood is life as well. Sometimes it is both simultaneously. Because my father chose death, he gave my sister and me a better chance at life without the guilt and shame and abasement that saddle and burden many of my boyhood friends. They have to face their children and explain what they and their nation did under the guise of being civilized. They have to explain why they stood by or even cheered while a segment of their indigenous population was beaten, gassed, burned in ovens, and shot without mercy—men, women, children . . . babies with their tiny bones melting into blood-soaked ground.

Although I do not condone my old mates, I do pity them. How could I not when so easily I could have become one of them?

I paint in red to honor both life and death.

I paint in red to honor my father.

PETER DECKER AND RINA LAZARUS
RETURN IN

The Garden of Eden
and Other Criminal Delights

a thrilling collection of short works by

Faye Kellerman, the master of the criminal mind.

Coming soon from Warner Books.

Please turn this page for a preview of the short story
"The Garden of Eden."

It began as something recreational, a way to pass the time pleasantly, but then as insidious as a burrowing maggot, it turned into an addiction. By six months, every room in the house was a biological testament to Rina Decker's hobby; from the bedrooms and bathrooms, to living rooms and the laundry room, plants, sprouts, shoots, and cultivars crowded space once reserved for human inhabitants. Given the dire circumstances, she knew she'd have to act, but the decision was tortuous. Which ones merited the honor of being houseplants, and which ones had to be sacrificed for the good of the family?

"I feel like I'm living in the Congo," Peter Decker complained as he sipped coffee at the breakfast table. He was about to tackle the Sunday paper though he harbored little hope of finishing it. Something always came up.

"What's wrong with the Congo?" Rina countered. "It's foreign, it's exotic . . . where's your sense of adventure?"

"Sucked out by the miscreants in the streets of Los Angeles, thank you very much. God and Koolaire have given us creature comforts for a reason, Rina. If I wanted to live in a tropical rainforest, I'd pick a more idyllic spot than the San Fernando Valley. The house has become unbearable— way too hot, dripping wet, and teeming with bugs."

"That's because you leave the back door open."

"I leave the back door open because I'm a big guy and I need circulation. Otherwise I drown in my own sweat."

That was true. Peter was six-four, two-thirty, and in great shape. The bulge of his winter gut usually melted away in the more active summer months. The only hint of his life in the fifth decade was the increasing streaks of white coursing through his mustache and ginger-colored hair. Rina's husband still cut a handsome figure. She said, "I know you need circulation. That's why the ceiling fans are on all the time."

"All they do is blow around the hot air. We need air conditioning, darlin'."

"Orchids are sensitive."

"So are husbands." The ribbing was good-natured, but there was a lot of truth in it. "Look. I can tolerate the bathrooms. Bathrooms are usually wet and hot. And so are kitchens and laundry rooms. I'll even acquiesce to the living room and den. But I put my foot down with the bedrooms. Even Hannah's complaining. She feels that you've expropriated her space."

"That's ridiculous. There's nothing in her room except a few African violets."

"Fifteen at last count."

"They barely fill up her windowsill."

Decker took a deep breath in an attempt to harness patience. "Rina, both your daughter and I are glad you found something that taps into your instinct to nurture and that pleases your aesthetic eye."

"It's my calling, Peter." Rina stifled a smile.

"Fantastic!" Decker said wryly. "Everyone should have a passion. Unfortunately instead of a passion, I have a job . . . a demanding job. I've got to work, which means I've got to sleep. It's either your Bletilla striata or me."

Rina saw the desperate look on her husband's face. He had reached his limit. "I'll clear the bedrooms. I think I have a millimeter's worth of space on a shelf in the laundry area."

Inwardly, Decker chided himself for his laziness. "I know I've been promising to frame the prefab greenhouse." He wanted to add, *the one that's taking up most of the room in the garage so that my vintage Porsche has been relegated to the driveway under a measly cover.* But years of being married had taught him a little tact. He didn't know why he kept putting off the construction of the greenhouse. It wouldn't take more than a half a day to build it. Maybe, psychologically, he was afraid of what would happen if she had even *more* room for plants. "And I appreciate that you haven't nagged me to build it even though we bought it months ago."

"You work hard and put up with long, long hours. Your time should be your own." Rina was using her best self-sacrificing voice. "That's precisely why I took up gardening. To occupy my time during those long, long hours—"

"All right, all right!" Decker broke in. He covered his face with his hands, then looked up. "Just promise me you won't turn into a dotty old lady like whatsername."

"Cecily Eden."

Decker smiled. "Yeah, dotty old Cecily with the eponymous garden. Is Eden really her last name or did she change it to match her obsession?"

"As far as I know, it's her given last name and she's not dotty. She's very sharp—a retired microbiologist. She always jokes that she went from growing aerobes to growing aerides." Rina laughed out loud. When Decker didn't respond, she gently nudged his shoulder and said, "A little inside gardening joke."

Decker tried to remain serious, but finally gave in and laughed. She was so cheerful this morning. Rina was still his twenty-six-year-old bride though she had climbed over the forty mark a few years ago. In the past, they had been mistaken for father and daughter even though he was only twelve years older than she was. Rina had a beautiful complexion and her hair was still black, although he rarely saw it in its full glory. Ultra Orthodox Jewish convention dictated that married women cover their locks whenever they went in public. Lately, she'd taken to wearing big, straw sun hats and goofy sunglasses.

"You really should see Cecily's garden, Peter. It's magnificent. She has the most unusual plants. The crowning jewel in her back yard is an imported Chinese Sacred Tree. It's like a magnolia but has these smaller white blossoms with an intoxicating citrus aroma. It's so green and gorgeous. And being that it's from China, it blooms in the fall, just when most plants in the Northern hemisphere are fading away."

"I'm sure it's a sight to behold."

Rina clicked her tongue. "How ironic that you're being sarcastic. When we first married, you were the one who convened daily with nature—Mr. 'I can-build-it-myself-Cowboy.'"

"Yeah, but I never brought the horses into the house. Do you need help with the plants, darlin'?"

Rina stared at him, then broke into a grin. "You want to *garden* with me? That would be great!"

Decker backtracked. "Uh, I meant do you need help

taking the plants out of the bedrooms and into the laundry room?"

Rina smiled to hide her disappointment. "No, I'm fine. It's not exactly strenuous work."

Now she looked dejected. To Decker, gardening meant chopping down trees or hacking away brush, not transplanting cultivars. He took her hand and spoke in earnest. "You know, Rina, it's a beautiful day. How about if you clear the bedrooms of the foliage and bring all the plants outside while I finally build the prefab greenhouse. We can christen it together."

Rina managed a weak smile. He was trying. "You don't have to build it today, Peter. I can cram the plants in the laundry room."

"No, no, no. I'm determined." Decker stood up, a small physical step that signified the morphing of a theoretical idea into action. "C'mon. Hannah's at Julie's. Let's spend some time together outdoors. You garden and I'll build. Afterward, I'll pick some lemons and you'll make lemonade. Then I'll go get some sandwiches from the deli and we'll watch the Dodgers game together. How does that sound?"

This time, Rina's smile was genuine. "Actually, it sounds wonderful."

"Great! Let's get to it!" Decker picked up the paper and headed for the compost pile. One Sunday *Times* would make a week's worth of excellent mulch.

Tuesday, from twelve to two, had been earmarked as Rina's weekly get-together with Cecily Eden, and she couldn't wait to tell her elderly friend about the newly built greenhouse. To celebrate the construction, Rina was pretty sure that Cecily would insist on giving her all sorts of plants and would spurn any proffered payments. In order to offset this inequity, Rina had come to her friend's house armed with a plate of chocolate chip cookies fresh from the oven.

As usual, she walked up the driveway to the backyard gate and automatically turned the knob. She found it locked. Usually Cecily left it open when she knew Rina was coming. It was good that the old woman was finally taking precautions. Rina would often scold her.

You shouldn't be so trusting, Cecily.

The old woman would laugh. *At my age, what does it matter? If anyone breaks in, he can take whatever he wants.*

Backtracking over the driveway, Rina went around to the front door. Cecily lived in a ranch house built in the fifties, what realtors called mid-century style. Her kitchen and bathroom still had original tile from the era and her furniture had lived through enough years to be considered retro. The old woman kept the place spotless. Having worked with germs all her life, she was a stickler for cleanliness.

The structure wasn't much bigger than a bungalow, but the property was over a half acre. Rina rang the bell, and when no one answered, she rang it again. Then she knocked and still got no response.

Strange, Rina thought, because she knew that Cecily was expecting her. She was about to walk away, and almost as an afterthought, gave a quick jiggle to the knob. She was shocked that the door yielded with the turn of her wrist.

The gate was lock . . . but the door was open.

Instinctively Rina knew that something was wrong. She should have called Peter, but what was the sense of disturbing him at work before she had proof that things were amiss? As a lieutenant, Peter had his hands full of mishap and mayhem. She didn't want to add to the mix unless necessary.

"Cecily?" she called out. "It's Rina. Are you home?"

She stepped inside a tidy living room abloom with spring flowers—roses, lilies, irises, daffodils, tulips, and Cecily's prized orchids. The couch had been upholstered in old floral fabric that looked something like wisteria vines through trellises. Two wicker chairs sat opposite the sofa. The carpet was green; the walls were peach-colored and plastered with botanical artwork—plants and flowers rendered in oil paintings, watercolors, crayon, pencil, charcoal, pastels—every possible drawing media. Some were good, some were bad, and lots were mediocre. It was hard to enjoy any individual work because there were so many of them hung chockablock. Still, Rina was always effusive when Cecily presented her latest acquisition picked up at a junk shop or flea market.

I've been collecting them for years.

Again, Rina called out the old woman's name. When she didn't get a response, she began to worry although nothing seemed out of place. She walked through the dining room, placing the cookies on the table, and into the kitchen. Maybe Cecily had been called away suddenly. Rina knew that the old woman had two grown daughters and several grandchildren. Cecily had mentioned them in passing, nothing extensive, but nothing to indicate that the relationships were strained.

"Cecily?" She walked through the kitchen and laundry room, then out the back door. "Cecily, are you home?"

It was mid-May and the garden was in full bloom, a riot of colors, heavy with fragrance. Cecily had divided and subdivided her lot, creating ecosystems and micro-climates connected seamlessly by pathways and lanes. She had placed her rose gardens, bulb gardens, and cutting gardens where there was an abundance of sun and some partial shade. Tucked in a back corner lot was the Zen garden with a pavilion and a small fish pond covered by barely visible netting that kept out the predators— stray cats, squirrels, raccoons, and herons. The other corner was her greenhouse. The orchard took up the rest of the space—giant avocados providing shade for aromatic citrus trees. In the center was her rare Chinese Sacred tree. A year ago, Cecily and her gardener had built a bench around its trunk. It was one of her favorite spots for reading and relaxing.

It was there that Rina discovered the body.

Gasping, she rushed over and felt for a pulse—for any signs of life—but she knew it was hopeless. There was no heartbeat and no breathing. Cecily's pupils were dilated and fixed, empty eyes brazenly staring into the sun. Still, Rina called 911. Then she called her husband.

The investigator from the Coroner's office was named Gloria, a woman in her mid-thirties who had recently come to the profession. Wearing traditional dark scrubs emblazoned with CORONER INVESTIGATOR in yellow, she got up from her kneeling position and snapped off her latex gloves. She looked at Rina. "Do you know if she had any health problems?"

Rina shook her head.

Decker said, "Find anything sinister other than the bruise on her left temple?"

"Nope, and the bruise was probably caused by her falling and hitting her head on the ground. Nothing to indicate blunt force trauma. She was an old woman. She must have had a doctor."

"Henry Goldberg," Decker said. "He's a cardiologist. I found out his name from one of Cecily's daughters. He's on his way."

"Great." Gloria said, "I think I'm done here. You can go over the body if you want, but I'm feeling that she died of natural causes. If Doctor Goldberg feels comfortable signing off on the death certificate, that's fine with me. That way the next of kin can call up the funeral home and they can come pick up the body. If not, have the guys bring her to the morgue and one of our doctors will sign her off."

"No autopsy?" Rina asked.

"Not unless her physician or her children demand it."

"Thanks," Decker said.

"You're welcome, Lieutenant."

After Gloria left, Decker turned to his wife. "What have you been waiting to tell me?"

Rina bit her thumbnail. "It's probably stupid."

"It probably isn't. What's bothering you?"

"Cecily usually unlocks the back gate for me when she knows I'm coming. I tell her not to, but she does it anyway. *This* time, she locked the gate . . . but the front door was *unlocked*. I find that odd."

Decker agreed. "What do you know about her family?"

Rina shook her head. "Two daughters. The elder one is married with the children."

"Edwina Roland."

"Yes, Edwina, that's the one. I didn't know her last name. Cecily would mention her occasionally, usually in connection with her grandchildren. The younger daughter is Meredith. I don't know a thing about her other than her name."

"Did she ever talk about tension between her daughters and her?"

"No. Why?"

"Between you and me, I looked around the house. Everything's neat and in place."

"Cecily was tidy. She used to say it came from years of working in a lab."

"Except one of her bedroom dresser drawers wasn't shut tight. A piece of a sweater was wedged between the drawer and the framework. It was a heavy sweater. You know how warm the days have been. Why would she be looking in her sweater drawer?"

"Maybe it's been wedged that way for a long time."

"All the other drawers were shut tight. This one drawer doesn't fit with her image as being tidy, does it?"

"Maybe she just never noticed it. You probably wouldn't have noticed it if you hadn't been looking."

"Of course."

Again, Rina bit her nail. "What is it, Peter? Do you think I might have interrupted a robbery?"

"Possibly. Someone heard you yelling over the gate. Someone bolted out of the front door and didn't lock it."

"I didn't see anyone."

"That doesn't mean there wasn't anyone. Did you happen to hear a car take off?"

"Honestly I don't remember. Was the door jimmied open?"

"I didn't find any obvious pry marks and the lock was a deadbolt. I think if someone was inside the house, he or she got in with a key."

"Or Cecily could have let them in."

"Of course. Maybe I'm on the wrong track totally. Still, I'd like to find out who had a key to her house."

"I'm sure her daughters do." Rina made a face. "I can't believe they'd hurt her. And didn't the Coroner's Investigator say it looked like natural causes?"

"Sure, it could have been a heart attack. But what if the heart attack was brought on by a bad argument? What if she didn't fall to the ground but was pushed? We have an unlocked door, a locked gate, and a drawer that's askew in an otherwise compulsively neat bedroom. I've been a cop too long not to ask certain questions and my first one is who has a key to her house." Decker looked at the garden gate. Two distraught women had corralled Gloria, the Coroner's Investigator. They spoke to her while waving their arms frantically. Decker put his arm around his wife. "Go on home, honey. We'll talk later. Right now, it's time to meet the next of kin."

"This is dreadful!" Meredith sniffed back tears. "Just terrible."

"I'm so sorry for your loss," Dr Goldberg, the cardiologist, told Cecily's daughters. He had shown up five minutes after the daughters had come. He was in his sixties, a short, slight man with long, tapered fingers. "I handled many patients in my years. Your mother had a wonderful spirit. I think it was her attitude that helped her last this long." He turned to Decker. "She had had two prior heart attacks."

Edwina blotted her wet eyes with a tissue. The gaze went from the doctor to Decker. "She gardened because she could no longer rock climb or go white water rafting."

"Ah," Decker said. He observed the sisters, noting that although there was a strong familial resemblance, they were nothing alike. Edwina, who drove a new 450 SL Mercedes, was precise and meticulous in her appearance: dark business suit and heels, clipped and styled blond hair, long manicured nails. Meredith wore a T-shirt, jeans, and sneakers. Her hair was shoulder length, brunette streaked with gray. She drove a twenty-year-old Dodge Dart. Both women had oval faces and hazel eyes. They were in their forties, no more than a couple of years apart. "Your mother was very active in the past?"

"Until her first heart attack," Edwina said.

Goldberg said, "The second one came a year later. That was ten years ago. We stabilized her, but at her age . . . "

Everyone nodded solemnly.

"Mom was one of a kind. She did exactly what she wanted to do and always encouraged us to do the same."

"She certainly had a love of beauty," Decker answered. "This place is paradise."

"Mom's version of paradise." Edwina smiled. "I live in a townhouse overlooking the ocean. No grass, no yard . . . just a terrace with a couple of potted cacti and a stunning view of the waves. That's my version of paradise."

"That's pretty great also," Decker said.

"If there's anything else I can do for anyone, don't hesitate to call me," Dr. Goldberg said. "I must be getting back. I have patients waiting for me."

Edwina's smile was brief. "She spoke very fondly of you, Doctor. Thank you for everything."

"It was a pleasure being her doctor. Again, my condolences."

"Thank you," Edwina answered.

A forlorn Meredith watched as the men from the funeral home loaded her mother into a van. She shook her head as tears leaked out from her eyes. "I can't believe she's gone!"

"She was old, Merry," Edwina said. "It wasn't unexpected."

"It's still a shock, Ed! She wasn't hospitalized or anything like that."

"I should start making arrangements."

"What do you mean by *I*, Sis?"

"*We*, then. *We* need to start making arrangements. I suppose the smartest thing to do would be to contact Mom's lawyer."

Meredith said, "Mr. Mortimer?"

"Yes, Mr. Mortimer. I'm sure Mom had specific instructions. I know she had a will." Edwina handed Decker a business card. "My phone number if you should need to reach me."

"Why would he need to reach you?" Meredith asked.

"It's a formality, Merry."

"Actually, I do have a few questions if you don't mind," Decker said. "For both of you."

"What kind of questions?" Meredith asked.

Edwina checked her watch. "How long?"

"Not too long," Decker said. "Who, besides your-selves, has a key to the house?"

"What do you mean?" asked Meredith.

Edwina glanced at her sister. "Why do you ask?"

"Just trying to button down a few details. Anyone else other than you two have a key to the house?"

"No." Meredith looked at her sister. "Right?"

"The gardener," Edwina answered.

"He *does*?" Meredith's eyes went wide. "Thanks for clueing me in."

"Mom gave it to him, Merry. I wasn't consulted."

"You didn't approve?" Decker asked.

"I just thought it was weird, but Mom was insistent. She claimed he was here more than either of us." Edwina turned to Decker. "Why are you so interested in keys?"

"The front door was unlocked when my wife came over. Do you know if your mother had anything valuable stashed— "

"Oh dear!" Meredith shrieked. She bolted toward the house; Decker ran after her. "Hold on, hold on!" He caught up with her when they reached the bedroom. "Don't touch anything! This could be a crime scene!"

Meredith folded her arms across her chest. "Mom kept cash in one of her dresser drawers. I want to see if it's still there!"

Edwina caught up with them. Anxiously, she asked, "Is it there?"

"I don't know. He stopped me from checking."

"Okay . . ." Decker took out several pairs of latex gloves and handed them to the ladies. "Carefully show me where your mother kept the cash. Please be neat about it."

Edwina slipped on the gloves and went right to the

sweater drawer. She opened it with a tug. Meticulously she rooted through the contents, carefully picking up a stack of folded sweaters and sliding her hand to the back. Her face paled as she shook her head. "It's not here!"

"What do you mean, it's not here? Where else could it be?" Meredith bent down, about to check the drawer herself, but Decker stopped her.

"Can I look for the both of you? If a burglary took place, I'd like to prevent any kind of contamination of evidence."

"Yes, yes! Hurry up!" Meredith scolded.

"You two watch me." Carefully, he went through the sweater drawer. There was nothing inside it but clothing. "Is there any other place she could have put the money?"

"She's always kept money there!" Meredith said. "That was her hiding place!"

Edwina chimed in. "Damn it, I kept telling her to put it in investments! Something that would grow. Mom could be so stubborn sometimes."

"All the time!" Meredith was crying now. "I was *counting* on that money to pay off some loans!" She quickly gasped. "Not that I was thinking about my mother's death to get money!"

Decker nodded but filed her words in his memory bank.

"I know what you're saying," Edwina said. "Losing all that cash is a complete and utter waste!"

"Exactly!" Meredith blew her nose. "Exactly."

"I'm going to check the other drawers now," Decker said. "Watch me, all right?" Twenty minutes of careful searching proved fruitless. He stood up, rolled his shoulders, and shook his head. "How much cash are we talking about?"

"Twenty thousand dollars," Edwina answered.

Decker had to refrain from choking. "Twenty thousand *dollars*? *Cash*?"

"Can you believe that!" Edwina snarled. "It is infuriating! I should have known something like this was going to happen!"

Decker looked around. The room overflowed with flowers and plants: dozens of botanical drawings and paintings plastered all over the walls. It made Rina's obsession look moderate.

"Tell me about this gardener," Decker said.

Meredith was sobbing too hard to talk. Edwina bit her lip. "His name is Lee Kwan. He's about seventy years old. He's small and slight and Mom has known him for over twenty years. I can't believe he'd ever rob her, let alone hurt her."

"What about the lawyer you mentioned?" Decker asked. "Mr Mortimer. Could he have a key?"

"It's possible," Edwina said.

"What's the name of the firm?" Decker asked.

"Mortimer, Dratsky, and Farrington."

Decker wrote it down. "Anyone else who might have a key? Think hard!" After both women pleaded ignorance, Decker said, "I'll need to speak with Mr. Kwan. Would either of you have a phone number or address for him?"

Edwina went over to the window and drew back the curtains. "Today's your lucky day, Lieutenant Decker. Kwan's truck just pulled up to the curb."